DARKENED SKIES BOOK FOUR

BEYOND VEILED DESTINIES

H.E. BAUMAN

First paperback edition June 2024

Cover design by MiblArt

Map by Cartographybird Maps

Jeanine Harrell of Indie Edits with Jeanine

ISBN 979-8-9888024-6-4 (paperback)

ISBN 979-8-9888024-7-1 (hardcover)

ISBN 979-8-9888024-5-7 (ebook)

www.hebauman.com

Content Warnings

Thank you for picking up *Beyond Veiled Destinies*, the fourth book in the Darkened Skies series. If you have not read the first three books yet, you will need to do that before you read this book.

This story includes themes and events that may not be suitable for some readers:

- Fantasy and magical violence, including artillery and other "modern" weaponry, used both in war scenarios and against civilians

- On- and off-screen character deaths, blood, and injuries

- Alcohol consumption

- Nightmares, panic attacks, anxiety, and PTSD

- Stalking and threats

- Reference to sexual assault (does not happen, discussion of hypotheticals), torture, parental death, current war, historical wars, & rebellion

Please take care of yourself as you read.

THE NORTH SEA
TALMARIS
GRAND DUCHY OF NOVARIA
ZINDIR
THE ZAIKUD EMPIRE
MACADIAN MOUNTAINS
POSAN
FORT AVALON
NARIZON
FORT BLACKROCK
CORSYCA
FORT IRONWING
KINGDOM OF DELIA
SAPOI
THE WESTERN SEA
CAPITAL CITIES
CITIES
NOTABLE TOWNS
FORTS
MEMATOS
ILESOURIA

IRVINA
THE LOST ISLES
THE HELOSIAN EMPIRE
MOUNTAINS
THE BADLANDS
RING OF FIRE
KALAMA
SEZIA
LE BAY
REPUBLIC OF TORNAMA
THASIA
KATAVENA
TAIPOLI ISLANDS
THE EASTERN SEA
THE SOUTHERN OCEAN

To those who are grieving

Chapter 1

Grand Duchess Ysabel's office was just a blur of color and energy: orange anxiety, gray hate, white panic, deep blue grief. They pushed against Astrea, overwhelming her every sense, as her friends listened to Ysabel make the same arguments she'd been making for days.

Prince Kaius Auris of Helosia had Jin's team and Adi's sister in custody. And though he was somewhere over the border, preparing for a meeting with Jin and Eliana, there would be no meeting. At least not if Jin had his way.

"We're going to have to talk to him eventually," Grand Duchess Ysabel said, resting her forearms on the edge of her desk. It was the third time in less than a day that she'd tried to have this conversation with both Jin and Eliana. "You cannot ignore your brother or your father."

"I don't plan on ignoring them," Jin said. "I plan on stopping them. Are you with me or not, Ysabel? There's time for you to back out. We'll find another way."

Ysabel huffed. "That's not what I want, Varojin."

"Then allow me to make this very clear." Jin crossed his arms tightly over his chest, wrinkling his black shirt. "There is no negotiating with my father and brother, not when it comes to this. Give them an inch and they'll take ten miles. Surely you recognize that from the times you've dealt with my father over the years."

"Yes, but there are lives directly on the line now, not hypotheticals." The grand duchess looked at Eliana. "Talk some sense into your brother."

"He's right, though." Eliana held Ysabel's gaze, unyielding as faint sheens of red anger and gray distrust bled into her aura. "Kaius is going to do whatever it takes to get whatever it is he wants. Have we received word from him yet? Caliban should've been back to him by now."

"No word," Crown Prince Veiko said. He stood behind his aunt's desk, as always, the picture of a casual royal with his plain white shirt and black slacks. His chestnut brown hair was slightly mussed, no doubt due to the way he'd stayed up all night planning with Lucian and Zephyrine. "They can't be far over the Helosian border, though. Logistically, it wouldn't make sense."

Astrea leaned against the wall near Ysabel's office door. She wasn't sure why, exactly, she'd been called into this meeting. But Ysabel had asked to see her, too. She was supposed to be on her way to see Ivy, the head palace healer, but it would have to wait a little while longer.

"Then we head down to Fort Silverpine as planned, and we move forward with the mission," Jin said. "Simple as that. I'm getting my people back in the next forty-eight hours."

"Impossible," Ysabel muttered, pinching the bridge of her nose. "Fine. Go." The corners of her mouth twitched. "Miss Sovna. Commander Lucian tells me you've found a particular way to attack the void mages?"

So that's what this is about. "Yes, Your Highness." She'd had a long conversation with Lucian about that just the morning before, about the way she'd been able to reach through that impossible cold and find Solana and The One's energy beyond the shroud that seemed to cover them. "I've told the commander as much as I can. I've only done it twice."

"Twice is good enough," Ysabel said. "When you get to Fort Silverpine, I'd like you to share this information with the Lightbringers stationed there."

"Of course, Your Highness." Were those Lightbringers Souleaters, then? When Ysabel didn't elaborate, Astrea kept her mouth shut. She'd just ask Lucian when she had a chance.

"Veiko, see to it that Varojin has whatever he needs," Ysabel said. "I believe Commander Lucian is preparing the airship now."

"Of course," Veiko said with the smallest of nods.

"I need a few minutes to speak with you," Jin said to Ysabel. "Just the two of us."

Orange anxiety wavered around Eliana, but Ysabel replied with a simple "Alright." With a wave of her hand and a few falsely kind words, the rest of them were dismissed.

Astrea led the way into the hallway beyond the grand duchess's office, Eliana on her heels and Veiko not far behind. When the door closed behind him, he sighed.

"I apologize for my aunt," he said, running his hand through his tousled hair and just making it more of a mess. "I know she's worried about Varojin going on this mission—"

"From what I've gathered about my brother's experiences in the Helosian army, Veiko," Eliana said, "this mission isn't going to be a problem. I am, however, worried about what he's going to say to Ysabel." She glanced at the door.

"Hopefully nothing to put her in a worse mood," Veiko murmured. "I'll smooth things over as much as I can. Go, make sure you have what you need. I'll check in with Commander Lucian."

Veiko strode down the hall, not giving either of them a chance to argue. Not that Astrea would; she needed to finish her other task before leaving for southern Novaria.

"You coming, Az?" Eliana asked.

"I promised Cress I'd go see Ivy before we leave."

Eliana half smiled. "Well, when you're done, come back upstairs. We should be ready to leave within the hour."

"I'll be as quick as I can."

As Eliana headed down the corridor in the same direction as Veiko, Astrea let her shoulders drop. Beyond the door, she heard nothing. No murmurs. No shouts. And there wasn't even a shred of emotion coming from the office to give her any clue as to what Jin was saying to Ysabel.

Later. She could figure it out later.

As Astrea approached the infirmary, the guards and soldiers she passed made little eye contact with her—not that Astrea minded. Besides, the emotion around her said everything. They were upset, worried, nervous, no doubt because of the second void mage attack and Prince Kaius's looming presence.

The infirmary, at least, was quiet as Astrea stepped inside. Just one other patient was in, someone Astrea hadn't expected to see: the Stargazer Mariya. She had just pushed herself up to a sitting position, and Ivy was walking away from her cot.

"Oh, good!" Ivy called in her light, soothing voice. "Take a seat, Astrea."

Astrea wove her way through several rows of cots until she got to the back of the room where Mariya sat. The Stargazer offered Astrea a tight-lipped smile.

"Good to see you up and about, Miss Sovna. That was quite the fight a few days ago, at least according to the commander."

"Yeah," Astrea replied, not really sure what else to say. What *was* there to say?

"You're in good hands," Mariya continued as she smoothed back some of her tight curls. "Ivy's one of the best healers we've ever had here at the palace."

"Are you feeling alright?" Astrea asked.

"Oh, fine, fine." Mariya waved her hand dismissively. "I've had problems with my joints ever since I was a little girl. Weekly healing treatments stave off the worst of it."

"I'm glad Ivy's able to help."

"Me too." Grabbing her cane, Mariya pushed up onto her feet. "Back to work for me. Safe travels."

Astrea settled down onto her cot and folded her hands in her lap, feeling entirely awkward. She'd never really had to see other healers before, although once, when she was twelve, she'd scraped her knees so badly while playing a game with Eliana that Jin had taken her to the palace healers back home. Astrea had always eased her own bumps, bruises, and ailments as long as the royal siblings hadn't seen them first.

"I'm very glad to see you back here," Ivy said. She circled Astrea's cot, hands resting on her wide hips. "Have you taken my advice and been resting?"

"I have," Astrea said. "Though it's only been a day."

"Indeed." Ivy gestured to the cot. "Lie down for a quick exam."

"I feel fine," Astrea said as she settled back against the flat pillow. It was a half-truth at best; she was so tired. But she'd extended her magic far beyond what she knew was possible, not just for herself but others, too. Of course she was tired. "Just fatigued, but I thought we expected that."

"We did." Ivy said nothing else as she worked, drawing a small stream of water from a nearby bowl. It circled her hands, then Ivy began pressing down on different parts of Astrea's body. Her forehead, her abdomen, her sternum. "This all feels okay?"

"Fine." And it did, except for the cool dampness of the water.

"Good." Ivy sent the water back to the bowl, then helped Astrea sit up. "I've heard through the grapevine that you're heading out again already."

"We are, yes."

"And what happened to my prescription to rest?"

Astrea almost shrank back under Ivy's scrutiny, but the Purifier's blue eyes were gentle and her tone kind. Her demeanor reminded Astrea of Sarsali, actually. She perked up a bit. "My team needs me. There's a lot we need to do."

"And yet, if you burn yourself out, you can't help them at all." Ivy smiled. "Rest while you can. You're leaving . . . ?"

"Shortly," Astrea said. "Though I don't think we'll be heading out into the field immediately." She actually wasn't sure what Jin's full plan was, just that they needed to get down to Fort Silverpine and Irvina as soon as possible. "And Commander Lucian's joining us, so I won't be the only Lightbringer."

"Good. Try to take another day at least, if you're able. The exhaustion should feel better by then. It'll help if Lucian takes a bit of it on if he can, too. Could speed the process up for you."

"I'll talk to him," Astrea said.

"Good." Ivy smiled again. "Then you are clear for restricted duties, Miss Sovna. Be safe."

By the time Astrea made it back upstairs in the far wing of the palace, she'd expected to find Jin waiting for her in their shared room. She'd hoped to go straight to him, find out what he'd spoken about with Ysabel. Apparently the stars had other plans.

"Az!" Cressida called from her open bedroom door. "Can you come here?"

It wasn't just Cressida's interruption that prevented Astrea from going to find Jin. He wasn't in their room, at least not according to her magic. Was he still with Ysabel?

Astrea headed for Cressida's room, following her best friend inside and shutting the door behind her. A tight knot of anxiety bloomed around Cressida, a mirror to the one strangulating Adi's aura. He stood at the far end of the sitting room, Marko not far away. But Marko was unreadable, as he often was. The only thing giving away his worries was the crease on his forehead.

"What's wrong?" Astrea asked.

"Ellie and Jin aren't back," Cressida said. "Where'd they go? Aren't we leaving soon?"

"Ellie said she was coming up here before I went to see Ivy. If she's not here, I don't know where she is. And last I knew, Jin was having a private conversation with Ysabel."

"About?" Marko asked.

Astrea shrugged. "I'm not sure. He asked for the meeting, though Ysabel doesn't seem thrilled with his plan. I think she's frustrated with him."

"Hm." Marko's attention slid to Adi. "You did warn me."

"I want to go on this mission as much as anyone," Adi said, that orange flaring brighter in his aura, "but I'm not sure he's thought it through. We don't even have intel on where Kaius is, do we?"

"Not that Jin seems to be aware of," Astrea said. "But we'll find him, right?"

Adi's tight expression gave her no confidence.

Marko patted him on the shoulder. "We'll find Prince Kaius, your friends, and your sister. I'll make sure of it."

Adi tried to muster a smile. He'd been a ghost in the last day, never around when Astrea was. And quieter than his usual self since they'd fled Kalama, too. She hated seeing him like that. Adi was sweet and kind and smart, and his little sister certainly didn't deserve to be in Kaius's custody.

"We'll be at the fort tonight," Cressida said, "and then you and Jin can head out first thing in the morning."

Adi shrugged. "Yeah, I guess."

"Maybe we could finish packing?" Astrea asked. "I need to, anyway. Then we can get on the airship as soon as Jin's ready. We won't waste a moment."

Adi nodded. "Sure."

"I'll be ready in ten," Cressida said. "Meet you outside?"

As Marko, Adi, and Astrea agreed, they shuffled out of Cressida's room and into the guard-filled hallway beyond. Marko headed down the corridor, but as Adi turned to go to his room, Astrea reached out and touched his forearm. He turned toward her, eyebrows drawn together over his usually happy dual-colored eyes.

"Jin's going to do what he must," Astrea said. "I know he will."

"I know," he said.

"We'll figure it out as a team."

"I know."

Astrea hesitated, then pulled him into a quick hug. Laughter bubbled out of Adi as he patted her on the back.

"What's that for?" he asked.

"You looked like you could use it."

"Yeah, I suppose I could."

"Tell Marko to hug you, then," Astrea said. "I'm sure he wouldn't mind."

"Oh, I think—" It was his turn to hesitate. But then he smiled just enough for the dimple under his green eye to appear. "Maybe."

They parted ways after another quick hug, and Astrea hurried into her room across the hall. Just as before, Jin wasn't there. He'd have to show up soon, right?

Astrea tried not to pay any more attention to it. Instead, she changed into a loose black training shirt and the thick cotton pants that went along with it. She didn't love it, but it seemed more appropriate than showing up to the fort in a dress. She'd just pulled on her boots and finished packing her knapsack when the bedroom door opened. Jin strode in, his features tight.

"I'll be ready in just a few minutes," he said, barely even looking in Astrea's direction. "Ellie said the airship's waiting." He went straight for the wardrobe and yanked out his knapsack.

Astrea watched as he tossed his bag onto his side of the bed and began rifling through the contents. "Jin?"

He grabbed a few extra things from the wardrobe and shoved them into his pack. "Yeah?"

"What did you talk to Ysabel about?"

"Just making sure she and I are on the same page."

"And what page is that?"

"That I'm not going to sit around and wait for her approval to do what I need to do."

"And?"

"And she's not going to get in my way."

But did that mean Ysabel had agreed or that Jin was simply going to do what he wanted regardless? Astrea supposed that if the grand duchess were trying to limit his actions, he wouldn't be finishing packing. One of the palace guards would be trying to wrangle him away from the airship.

Jin shouldered his bag. As Astrea met him near the door, he took her bag, too.

"I'll help however I can," she said, taking his hand.

Jin paused at the threshold, then leaned down and kissed her gently. "I know," he said. "Let's just get out of here, then we'll figure out the plan."

Chapter 2

As Astrea, Jin, Cressida, Adi, and Marko approached the airship waiting just outside the palace's thick compound walls, Astrea had expected two things. First, she'd expected to see Eliana. She'd also expected to see the Nikaphoroses and Saros. And while both those expectations were met, something about the scene was off.

Saros held a suitcase in one hand.

Gray confusion flared around Cressida. "Did you know—"

"No," Astrea murmured.

Why was Saros there with a suitcase? This wasn't part of their vague plan.

Crown Prince Veiko, Commander Lucian, and Zephyrine were also there, all in a loose semicircle around Eliana and deep in conversation. Orange anxiety snapped through Eliana's aura, quick but biting.

"You should go see what's wrong with Ellie," Astrea said to Jin. "She's upset."

Though she'd tried to take her knapsack from Jin before they left the palace, he'd insisted on carrying it for her, especially once she'd told him Ivy's orders to continue resting. Astrea didn't think that carrying her own pack was going to burn her out, but Jin was obviously upset about both the recent fight with Nazarov and losing his team. Maybe letting him take her bag would help him feel like he was doing something; Astrea understood that. She often felt like she needed to be doing something, *anything* to help. Still, as Jin walked toward his sister with both knap-sacks hanging from his shoulders, she wondered if she should have taken it back from him.

Doesn't matter. What she really needed to do was figure out why Saros was there with luggage.

Astrea and Cressida both headed for their family, whose auras radiated anxiety.

"You girls have everything you need?" Balthazar asked.

"Got it, Dad," Cressida said. "Don't worry."

"I thought we'd have more time." He set one large hand on Cressida's shoulder.

"Skies, you act like this is goodbye forever," Cressida quipped. "We'll be gone for a week, maybe less. Jin's not going to let it go on for much longer."

"Uncle," Astrea said. Saros shifted his weight to his left leg. "You're joining us?"

"If it's alright with you," he said. "I thought I might go to Irvina and start looking for information about your father."

"Oh." Astrea hadn't considered that, not really. Fort Silverpine was a short distance away from Irvina, where she'd been born and lived until Saros took her to Kalama. "Well, sure. If you're allowed to join us?"

"Eliana's already spoken to Prince Veiko on my behalf," Saros said.

When did that happen? Still, Astrea nodded. "Alright." She glanced at the Nikaphoroses. "You're staying here?"

"Thought we'd settle in and try to help the librarian . . . what was his name?" Sarsali asked. "Tim?"

"Tomas," Cressida corrected.

"That's right, Tomas," Sarsali said with a little sigh. "Any way we might be useful."

"I'm sure Tomas will appreciate it," Astrea said.

After a few hugs, the Nikaphoroses headed back into the palace compound, flanked by two of Lucian's guards. Saros excused himself to get settled in the airship, and Marko and Adi weren't far behind. Even Cressida headed inside, but Astrea stopped short when she saw Eliana hug Jin.

That wasn't right. Eliana was supposed to come with them.

Hesitation scraped Astrea's skin as she approached. Nicos stood just behind Eliana, his lips pressed into a thin line.

"Ellie?" Astrea asked. Jin stepped to one side to make room for her, his hand finding the spot between her shoulder blades.

"I'll join you in a few days," Eliana said.

"Why?" Astrea asked. "At our meeting earlier—"

"Jin, why don't you go see if the commander is ready to leave?" Eliana asked. He hesitated, then pivoted and called out for Lucian. As he left, Eliana leaned in closer to Astrea. "Jin has some concerns."

"What?" Astrea asked. Jin hadn't really mentioned any concerns. He'd said Ysabel was going to stay out of his way.

"He just needs me to keep the peace here for a few days so he can . . . do whatever it is he does."

"Oh." Keep Ysabel distracted, then. "Well, alright," Astrea said. "If you're sure. I hate not seeing you."

"I'll be here, waiting for the official word from my brother and Caliban," Eliana said as she looped her arm through Astrea's. "And as soon as we receive that word, I'll head down to you. Make sure Jin's nice to you."

"Jin's always nice to me."

"Good. And listen to Ivy, alright? Jin said you were told to rest?"

"Skies, not this again . . ." Astrea sighed. "Yes, I'll rest."

"Good." Eliana gave Astrea a quick hug at the bottom of the airship ramp. "See you soon."

Fort Silverpine was little more than a smudge of darkness in the Novarian forest and looming twilight. Astrea pressed herself to the window as the airship descended closer and closer to the base. Weak lights lit up the fort, revealing damaged sections of its outer walls and myriad vehicles in an expansive courtyard. There was even machinery—large guns?—mounted to the outer walls.

"It looks . . ." Cressida trailed off.

"Heavily fortified?" Astrea offered.

"Rustic."

"That's your concern?"

"Rustic isn't exactly my taste. Hopefully it's better than Rami's hotel back in Thasia."

"That wasn't that bad."

"I'm surprised you'd disagree," Cressida quipped. "Cramped up in that tiny, tiny bed with Jin's giant—"

Footsteps made Cressida cut herself off. In the reflection of the window, Astrea found Saros approaching.

"This is the place?" he asked as he, too, peered out the window. "This didn't use to be here when we lived in Irvina."

"Really?" Astrea asked. She didn't remember that much of her childhood, mostly just flashes of the town, of long days spent with her mother and Saros, laughing and playing outside with both of them. She certainly couldn't remember Fort Silverpine either way.

"No," Saros said. "Though I'm surprised, given how close we are to the Helosian border. Seems like a previous ruler would've installed something here. Ysabel was smart to do so."

Astrea nodded.

"At least they seem prepared," Saros said as the airship drew closer to the ground. Now, soldiers were easier to pick out among the camp's low light, a flurry of activity as their airship landed with a soft *thunk*. "Although I don't love that we're staying right where this Victor Nazarov attacked."

"Doubt he'll hit the same spot twice," Cressida said. "And those launchers on the armaments? Should be able to take out anything, whether an aircraft or a bunch of void mages."

"Oh?" Saros asked.

"They look like the ones we were building at Lodestar last year," Cressida said. "I mean, probably not *ours*, but we're not the only ones working on that kind of tech."

Astrea hoped that Nazarov hadn't found a way to get any of "that kind of tech" for himself. Would he have tried to take it during the attack? Could he have possibly raided some Helosian base if he had some of their airships? What other weapons or information would he have that could ultimately be to his advantage? Astrea made a note to ask Lucian and Zephyrine about it.

Once the airship had landed and the engines cut off, everyone congregated in the main cabin, belongings in hand. Commander Lucian led them out into the cool night air; Novaria had turned even cooler in the weeks they'd been gone. The weather would only get colder as autumn settled over the land and winter approached.

Around them, blue-uniformed soldiers darted around, taking care of the airship and following orders barked by one short, stout man dressed in a black uniform trimmed with silver. Little badges, like those Lucian wore on his formal uniform, were pinned over the man's heart.

"Well, well, well," the man said. "If it isn't Commander Lucian Astor."

"Commander Alekzi Tarkun," Lucian said, no sharpness in his tone. "Good to see you're in one piece."

"Hardly." The man barked a laugh before surveying their group. The flickering gas lamps cast long shadows over his face, so Astrea could only make out his wide nose, cool brown skin, and bald head. "This everyone?"

"For the time being."

"Cryptic," Commander Tarkun muttered.

"We'll talk once everyone else is settled in."

Tarkun nodded. "I'll show you to your rooms."

Astrea felt entirely out of place as they maneuvered through camp. Every soldier they passed was a different story: steel pain, gray confusion, orange fear, and even solid walls. Some Earthmovers were busy repairing pieces of the damaged fort walls, while other mages were busy smoothing out the brick paths that had been marred, no doubt during Nazarov's attack. Jin, at least, had finally given Astrea's bag back to her, so she fiddled with the straps as she walked.

After a few minutes and passing several nondescript buildings, they arrived at a taller, wider one. It was three stories tall—as high as the fort's walls—and was alight inside. The two guards flanking the double doors saluted Tarkun and Lucian as they led the rest of the group inside.

It had to be the officers' quarters or something like that, at least based on the quality of the furnishings. It was no barracks, that was for sure. The smooth wood floors, blue wallpaper, and expensive gramophone in the corner guaranteed that.

Commander Tarkun led them up to the third floor, where several doors off one hallway stood wide open. "It's no palace," the man said to Lucian, "but it'll have to do while you're here."

"It's fine, thank you," Lucian said. "Shall we go and talk? I'd like you to meet General Zephyrine Kanakos. We have much to discuss."

Wariness rolled off Commander Tarkun in slow, steady waves that weighed heavily on Astrea's body. His gaze—small, dark brown eyes, Astrea could now tell—flicked over to Zephyrine and Jin. "May I speak freely?"

"Of course," Lucian said.

"I don't love having Helosian royalty and military in my fort."

"Well, there's another Helosian royal on the way, so you'd best adjust," Lucian said.

"Would a conversation help, Commander Tarkun?" Jin asked. "I don't want to make you uncomfortable. I know my sister won't, either."

Tarkun grunted, a whisper of rusty annoyance leaking into the air around him. "No need. I'll speak with you in the morning, Your Imperial Highness." He turned back to Lucian. "Let's go talk, Lucian."

Jin's shoulders deflated as soon as both commanders had walked away, Zephyrine on their heels. She shot Jin a look over her shoulder, and although Astrea picked up nothing behind Zephyrine's wall, her expression seemed to say "Just let me handle it."

"Well . . ." Cressida drew out the word, as if waiting for someone else to pipe up. When no one did, she said, "Are we just going to stand here all night?"

"No," Jin said with a heavy sigh. "Let's just go to bed. I don't want to upset Commander Tarkun."

"But you'll push the grand duchess?" Cressida said.

"I know how to push her. And she knows me, my intentions. Tarkun doesn't."

"Fair enough, I suppose," Cressida said.

Though there were plenty of rooms for them all to have their own, Astrea didn't miss the fact that Marko slipped into a room behind Adi, then closed the door. Cressida disappeared into the one next to them. Saros, though, loitered in the hallway with Jin and Astrea.

"Is this . . ." Saros frowned, his forehead wrinkling. "Is this safe for us, Varojin? If the base commander doesn't appreciate your presence . . ."

"Plenty of people haven't approved of me being around for my entire twenty-six years, Saros," Jin said, voice rough but not sharp. "Commander Tarkun's just going to have to get over it. We have a mission. I don't leave my people behind, least of all with my brother."

Saros looked between Jin and Astrea, though Astrea couldn't quite discern what the look was. Approval? Relief? Relief that it was surely safe, or perhaps relief that Jin was sticking to his convictions? *Maybe he'll see that Jin really isn't like his father.*

"Alright," Saros said. "Good night."

Her uncle had barely started for his own room when Astrea went into the one behind her and Jin. It was small but tidy, with a decent-sized wood-frame bed, small writing desk, and just one bedside table. A small lamp sat on the desk, too. No bathroom. *Great.*

As soon as the door clicked shut behind Jin, Astrea's shoulders sagged. She let her pack drop down to the floor. Jin picked it up for her and set it on top of the desk. He set his there, too, then closed the few steps separating them. His arms wrapped around her, strong and steady.

"I'm fine," Astrea said as Jin's worry scraped over her skin. "I know we have a mission—"

"Lucian will go with us," Jin said. "Stay here and talk to some of the other Lightbringers, like Ysabel said. Help Saros look into The One."

Astrea leaned into his embrace, breathing in the faint smell of eucalyptus. "I want to help you find them."

Jin slowly pulled away from her, but only so he could look down at her. Skies, that gentleness in his eyes. That sheen of pink. Astrea's breath hitched.

"I know, Az. But I really think you should stay here, even if you hadn't used too much magic."

"Why?" Some small part of her was hurt, but a larger part was curious.

"Because it's Kaius," Jin said. "He knows how to get under my skin. If you're here, he can't use you against me. Adi, Zephyrine, and I will be able to do this a lot faster if I stay focused."

"We'll have to work on that, you know," she said. "Your focus when I'm around. I don't think we can stay away from Kaius forever."

"I know. But for this mission? At least until I know exactly what we're dealing with."

"You *are* the expert, I suppose."

He laughed, a tired sound. "You suppose?"

"Remains to be seen," Astrea teased.

Jin pulled her close again, the sunshine warmth radiating off him. He sighed into her hair. "Thank you for understanding."

"I may want to help, but I won't be that stubborn." And besides, if Astrea was honest with herself, she was beyond tired. She didn't think she'd be useful to anyone if she had to ship out the next morning. So she'd listen to Ivy. Recovering was the best way to help her team for now. She'd get back out in the field eventually.

Chapter 3

Though she'd known Jin had become a leader on his team in Helosia's military, and though she knew about some of his old missions, Astrea still found watching him step into that role foreign.

After a night of restless sleep, they'd been ushered into another building at the base, a low bunker that was all bare bones inside. The domed metal roof and walls, long wooden table, and maps hanging around the space revealed it to be some kind of command center. And for the last ten minutes, Jin had been grilling Commander Tarkun on questions Astrea hadn't even thought of.

"You're sure this is Kaius's last known location?" Jin asked from the head of the table, arms crossed over his chest. In his fatigues and body armor and in the glow of the low overhead lights, he looked more like a shadow than a person. Add his mask and hood, and Astrea was sure he'd be an intimidating sight.

"It was our last best guess," Tarkun corrected. "My scouts haven't been able to get too close. Intelligence suggests your brother has scouts of his own crawling through the northern foothills."

"No doubt waiting for Novarians," Lucian said from farther down the table.

"Or waiting for us," Adi said. He stood to Jin's right, his pose identical. Marko stood on Adi's other side. In that moment, Astrea was especially glad the three men were her friends, not enemies. "You think he's expecting us?"

"Probably," Jin muttered. Though Saros had opted not to attend this meeting, everyone else from their group was there. "What do you think, Zephyrine?"

"I'm sure he's just waiting for you to show up," Zephyrine said. "How prepared he'll actually be is another story. Do we have any idea how large of a force he's traveling with, Commander Tarkun?"

"It's unclear," Tarkun said. "With this Paragon group using Helosian ships, my scouts aren't exactly sure what it is they're looking at."

Reasonable, at least in Astrea's opinion.

"Any idea where the Paragon are?" Jin asked. "Any word from other bases?"

"None, on both counts," Tarkun said. "Nobody's seen them."

"Well, shit," Cressida whispered, barely loud enough for Astrea to hear.

It was shit, yes, but they'd barely had time to look for Nazarov. Grand Duchess Ysabel had mobilized all the troops she could spare to find him. Both of his attacks on Novaria couldn't go unanswered.

"What would you like to do, Your Imperial Highness?" Tarkun asked.

Jin remained motionless as he stared down at the map spread out on the table. Except for his occasional blink, he may as well have been a statue. Finally, he nodded. "Adi, Marko, Zephyrine, Lucian, and I will go look for Kaius," Jin said. "If we can engage, we'll engage. If we can't, we'll come back and gather more people. We'll need ground transport to the border, then we'll go the rest of the way on foot."

Astrea swallowed hard. She didn't like the idea of Jin—of any of them—going out there, but it had to be done. He'd survived far worse than Kaius over the years.

"Very well," Commander Tarkun said. "I'll make arrangements. Can you be ready in an hour?"

"We can be ready in twenty minutes," Jin said. "The sooner, the better."

"I'll see to it," Tarkun said, already heading for the low door on the opposite end of the bunker. "Meet me by the garage when you're ready."

Lucian followed him out, leaving the door open behind him. Cool air wafted inside, making a few of the maps on the walls rustle. Astrea breathed it in, trying to steady herself.

"What do you need me to do, Jin?" Zephyrine asked.

"Can you find the kitchens and get us some rations?" Jin asked. "And check that the med kits are all stocked?"

She nodded.

"I'll make sure the commander and I both have what we need," Marko said.

"Thank you," Jin said, both to Marko and Zephyrine as they headed out into the clear morning.

"And us?" Cressida asked, motioning between herself and Astrea. "I know we aren't going, but what can we do to help from here?"

Jin pressed his lips together, then said, "Bring Commander Tarkun up to speed on the aetherium weapons, and talk to him more about the void mages and their capabilities. He's been briefed, but it's not the same as hearing it from someone who's been on the ground and dealing with it themselves."

Cressida nodded. "Sure."

"And definitely talk to his Lightbringers, Az," Jin said.

"I planned to after you left."

Astrea still wasn't entirely clear on how many Lightbringers could gain that same mastery over emotional energy. How many were actually Souleaters. Surely some of the ones at Fort Silverpine would be powerful enough to learn. There'd be no void mages to practice on, but Astrea would try to impart what she'd learned the last couple of months. Anything was better than nothing.

"I'm going to go to the garage," Adi said. "Make sure Tarkun's giving us what we need. Grab my pack for me, Jin? It's in my room."

The four of them headed out, with Cressida offering to go with Adi to check on the state of the vehicle they'd be traveling in and Astrea heading with Jin back toward the officers' house. Heavy silence floated between them, even with the sounds of the base echoing through the air. Engines, shouts, wariness, and even a few laughs.

They entered the building and headed back for their rooms in silence. Jin grabbed Adi and Marko's packs, rifling through them both. Checking for what, Astrea wasn't sure. Then they went to their room, and Jin rifled through his own knapsack, too.

"You have everything you need?" Astrea asked.

"Yeah." Jin closed up his bag, double-checked the straps and buckles were secure, and slung it over his back. "Everything."

"Okay . . . good."

Astrea took Marko's bag while Jin carried Adi's. What was this strange silence? Jin hadn't been so quiet going to Kalama. He hadn't been this quiet in months, not even when she'd come back from the Paragon's meteorite tunnels. Not even when he'd been trying to make amends when they were first forced to work together.

The ground under their boots was solid pavement, no crunchy gravel like back at the palace. Astrea kept pace with him as he headed for the garage, weaving around and past Novarian soldiers dressed in varying shades of blue. Repairs on the battlements and the fort's exterior wall were nearly complete. A few of the Novarians glanced their way, echoes of rough annoyance floating toward Astrea on the breeze.

The garage wasn't as busy as the rest of the base. Just a few soldiers loitered inside while Commander Tarkun, Adi, Lucian, and Zephyrine all circled around a large, boxy forest green truck. Cressida had its hood popped open and kept examining the same spot on the engine. Its two doors were closed, and its tires were thicker than any Astrea had seen before. A large, round-topped canvas covered what she assumed was the flatbed of the truck.

"My people keep these in constant maintenance, Miss Nikaphoros," Commander Tarkun said. "Was this all necessary?"

"Just making sure," Cressida said. "Can never be too careful."

The commander's gaze flicked to Jin and Astrea, then past them. Astrea peeked over her shoulder only to find Marko not far behind.

"We're all good?" Jin asked Cressida.

"All good." Cressida closed the hood with a loud, metallic thunk.

"I'll drive," Marko offered as he passed an unmarked tan bag to Adi. "Shouldn't take us more than a couple hours to get to the border. I know these roads well."

Everyone shuffled about, passing knapsacks around and discussing who was sitting where. It seemed Lucian was going to ride in the passenger seat while the three Helosians sat in the back. As Cressida spoke with Marko about the engine checks she'd done, Astrea followed Jin around to the back of the truck. Zephyrine and Adi had already climbed inside.

Jin shoved his bag through the canvas flap, and Adi's brown, sun-spotted hand reached out to grab it. Orange anxiety and yellow worry flared around Jin, bright against the dark vehicle.

"Jin?" Astrea asked.

He turned around, shoulders and expression tight. And while Astrea thought he might finally say something, he didn't. Jin dipped his head toward hers and snaked his arms around her waist. Their bodies pressed flush together as he kissed her. Astrea stiffened for just a moment, all thoughts of their team and friends disappearing as she relaxed and threaded her arms around his neck. That worry swirled around her, joined by Jin's sunshine warmth and tart desire and cold anxiety. His mouth moved against hers slowly. It was a painfully sweet, burning kiss, one that made her ache for more.

"I'm sorry," he whispered as he pulled away, the words so low Astrea barely heard him over the roar of the truck's engine starting.

"Why?" Astrea asked.

"Because I've been shutting you out for the last couple days when I shouldn't have."

"You're worried about your team. I understand."

"Still." He kissed her again, chaste and gentle. "That's not fair to you. Or myself. I'll see you in a couple days."

"Please be careful." The words nearly lodged in Astrea's throat. "Please."

He half smiled. "I will."

"No getting shot or stabbed."

"I'll do my best."

Astrea pushed up on her toes even as Adi called for Jin to "get going." She pulled his face to hers, kissing him one more time. But when Adi called for Jin again, Astrea forced herself to pull away.

"I love you," she whispered.

"I love you, too." Jin kissed the top of her head. "We'll be back soon."

He turned around and climbed into the bed of the truck, those colors still circling him in a tight knot. Orange, yellow, pink. She tried to imprint those same colors in her mind, and she really, really hoped Lucian would be able to steer them away from too much danger.

Cressida circled the truck, joining Astrea at the back. It rolled forward, engine rumbling as it started through the camp. Astrea swallowed hard.

Jin would be alright. Adi would be alright, too. And they'd find the others. They'd figure out a way to bring the team back together.

Commander Tarkun shouted orders to a nearby soldier, then turned to the women. Even he looked worried, though Astrea couldn't read him past his wall. "So," he said as he approached them, "you're supposed to talk to my Lightbringers, right, Miss Sovna?"

"Yes, Commander," Astrea said. "If you can gather them up, I'll meet them in an hour."

He nodded, the top of his bald head catching the sun. "They'll be waiting right outside the officers' house. Please, teach them whatever it is the grand duchess wants you to teach them. They are yours to command."

Before Astrea could even think of a reply, the commander stalked off and was lost among the crowd. Despite the cold worry drifting off her, peach amusement flashed around Cressida.

"What could you possibly find funny right now?" Astrea asked.

"Lightbringers, *yours to command*." Cressida snaked an arm around Astrea's shoulders. "To think that a few months ago, nobody even knew about your magic, and now you've got Lightbringers to *command*."

"I'm hardly their commander."

"Whatever you say, Az. Whatever you say."

It took everything Astrea had to not think about the fact that Jin and the others were on their way to the Helosian border. Their small room at the base was suddenly too empty; she'd only returned to put on her body armor and fix her hair into two braids instead of one.

She didn't know who these Lightbringers were. She'd meant to talk to Lucian before he left, but in their rush to get started on their quest,

Astrea just hadn't had the opportunity. Tying off her second braid, Astrea shook out her arms. She'd just have to figure it out.

Stepping out into the hall, Astrea found Cressida leaning against the wall opposite her door. She was dressed identically to Astrea, though instead of braids, her short, tight curls were pulled up into two buns.

"Ready?" Cressida asked as she pushed off the wall.

"Oh, yes, I'm *so* ready for my first day as a Lightbringer trainer."

Cressida laughed, a tight, almost uneasy sound. "It'll be fine."

They still had a bit of time before they were supposed to meet the other Lightbringers, but Astrea wanted to be early. The officers' building was quiet aside from a handful of guards they passed on their way downstairs.

"Have you talked to Saros yet?" Cressida asked as they began descending the staircase that would take them to the ground floor.

"No," Astrea said. "I'm surprised he came."

"Maybe he wants to help," Cressida said. "You know, after being so obtuse for so long."

"That's one way to describe him."

As they entered the foyer, someone clad in midnight blue stepped into their path, startling Astrea. They were just a fraction taller than either Astrea or Cressida, and their build was boxy, all sharp lines and no curves.

"Apologies," the stranger said. "Miss Sovna, Miss Nikaphoros." They extended their hand for a shake. "I'm Captain Vernie Dragmir."

"Oh, Vernie." Astrea forced herself to smile past the unnecessary anxiety swirling in her belly.

She'd never actually met Vernie, but she knew they were one of Lucian's most trusted guards back at the palace. Their dark, silky hair fell to their broad shoulders, and their light tawny skin and small, round eyes were similar to that of the Zaikudi people who lived on the other side of the Macadian Mountains. And those eyes, they were the prettiest of blues, like the early morning sky.

"I know we haven't met yet," Astrea said, "and please don't take this the wrong way, but I assumed Commander Lucian would've had you stay at the palace." How had she not known they'd have another person joining them? Was she that distracted? *Or maybe just that tired,* some small part of her mind whispered.

Vernie nodded. "Indeed, but the grand duchess asked that I help keep Silverpine safe for the time being, especially with Lucian being away."

"Well, that's much appreciated," Cressida said.

"Commander Lucian asked me to assist with the Lightbringer training," Vernie explained. "While you were recently on your mission in Kalama, we began testing some of the palace Lightbringers for this Souleater ability."

"Lucian wasn't doing that before?" Cressida asked.

Vernie shook their head. "He's always kept that secret close to his chest."

"Are you a Souleater?" Astrea asked.

"It appears I am," Vernie said.

Now Astrea just felt even more awkward about being asked to act as instructor to these other Lightbringers. She'd always been a student—and a good one at that. But if Vernie was one of Lucian's trusted people and a Souleater, too, shouldn't they be leading this exercise? Surely they were more experienced in all necessary areas.

"Commander Lucian tells me you've figured out a way to attack void mages in our *particular* way," Vernie said. "Is this true?"

"Yes, though I've only done it twice," Astrea said.

"Would you be willing to teach me?"

"Of course." Astrea would teach any Lightbringer—Souleater—Lucian trusted if it meant having help with the void mages.

Vernie's thin lips pulled into a smile. "Thank you. Shall we go see if the students are ready?"

Astrea gestured for Vernie to go first. "Lead the way."

Exiting the building and stepping into the late morning sun, Astrea found five Lightbringers, all dressed in midnight blue fatigues, waiting for her. She swallowed hard. Vernie led the way over to them, stopping at the edge of the semicircle they'd formed.

"Good morning!" Vernie called out, a mix of friendly and commanding. Everyone straightened. "I'm Captain Dragmir, and this is Miss Sovna. We're here to test your lightbringing abilities, specifically with Miss Sovna teaching you a new ability."

"Hi, everyone," Astrea said. They studied her, hesitation written all over their expressions. Three of them were easy to read, gray uncertainty wavering in their auras. "It's my understanding that only some Lightbringers may be able to do this, so please, don't be frustrated if you can't. But first, can you please introduce yourselves?"

The five Lightbringers introduced themselves one by one. There was Nadia, who had umber skin and light purple irises; she was younger than Astrea by a couple years. Milos introduced himself next; his blond hair and narrow nose reminded Astrea of Marko, but Milos had a much paler complexion and had to be close to Saros's age.

Next was Lilia, a young woman with short black hair and tawny skin similar to Vernie's. Kostya and Daria were siblings from the southeastern part of Novaria, right where Helosia, Novaria, and Tornama met. The siblings shared the same lightly tanned skin and deep brown hair.

"It's nice to meet all of you." Astrea glanced at the courtyard right outside the officers' building. "Vernie, is there someplace we can go to practice? This . . . probably isn't ideal."

Milos raised his hand. "I know where we can go, Captain Dragmir."

"Lead the way," Vernie said.

Milos moved to the head of the group, and the other Lightbringers fell in line behind him. It was only then that Astrea realized he was nearly as tall as Jin, though not nearly as broad. Milos was leaner, more gangly. After a few minutes, they stopped near a wide area separated from the rest of the fort's courtyard by thick wood fencing. A sparring ring of some kind, though it wasn't circular in shape.

"Will this be alright?" he asked Astrea.

"It's great, thanks," she said.

As everyone moved inside the ring and got situated again, Astrea moved to the head of the group. Vernie stood next to her. She waited for Vernie to say something, but they remained quiet.

"So, uhm, I'm not sure how much you know about the current state of affairs," Astrea started, her face burning. "But, well . . ." She cleared her throat. "We've recently discovered there's a sort of *subtype* of Lightbringers who have additional abilities."

"What?" asked Daria, orange anxiety and green curiosity tangling around her. "What do you mean?"

"In Talmaris, Commander Lucian Astor and I have begun testing Lightbringers such as yourselves for this ability," Vernie said. "At the grand duchess's order. You've all been briefed on the existence of void mages and how they feel to your magic, yes?" When Vernie received an affirmative response, they said, "Some Lightbringers, called Souleaters, have the ability to damage others with the emotional energy they feel around them. We can control it."

"We?" called out Lilia. "I thought you said it was rare."

"We as in Souleaters," Vernie said. "I am one. So is Miss Sovna."

The five Lightbringers shifted uneasily.

"I've dealt with these void mages personally," Astrea said. "To make a long story very short, it was only after I attacked one of their allies this way that they began calling me a Souleater, and I recently found references to this in very old, obscure texts as well. It seems the ability was mostly lost to time and secrecy, but we're going to need it in this war."

The group murmured their discomfort at both the name and the ability. Astrea understood. Skies, she understood. She hated the name, and she hated the ability. But it had saved her and her friends several times already. It would save countless others, no doubt, as the Novarians prepared for a war they never should've been roped into in the first place.

"We'll begin by going through this one by one to see if any of you are Souleaters," Vernie said. "We won't waste your time or ours if you're not." They turned to Astrea. "Miss Sovna, if you'd demonstrate on me?"

Astrea hesitated. Skies, she hated doing this. But the class—if five people could be called that—would certainly need a demonstration.

"Alright," Astrea said, following Vernie's lead and moving several feet away from the group and each other. Cressida waited nearby, ever watchful. "Whenever you're ready."

Hints of color bled into Vernie's aura—anxiety and pain, orange and steel gray. Astrea's fingers twitched. Oh, she hated this so much.

"I'm ready," Vernie said, widening their stance and bracing themselves.

Flinging her hands out in front of her, Astrea let her anxiety and worry flow freely toward Vernie. The colors mingled in the air like paints on a canvas. Astrea squeezed her hands into fists, Vernie's anxiety like electricity in her palms.

She pulled back. Vernie stumbled. Pain pinged and pinged in Astrea's chest, echoing between her and Vernie in what felt like an endless loop. It was almost as if she could sense the other Lightbringers feeling the ghost pain, too. Every nerve in her body tingled. Some of the students gasped.

Astrea squeezed her fists tighter, her nails digging into her palms. Vernie stumbled again, then raised their hand in a silent gesture to stop.

Astrea cut the connection immediately, sucking in a deep breath as her muscles went slack.

Vernie rubbed at their sternum. They shook their head violently, then straightened. "So you see," they said, voice slightly strained, "in a real fight, with far more for you to control and manipulate, that could be a powerful tool if you're able to do so. It's effective. Painful."

Whispers of distrust and disbelief filtered through the group, cold against Astrea's burning face.

"We'll test you one by one," Vernie continued.

"But how do we actually do that?" asked Nadia. Her arms were folded tightly over her chest, almost like she was trying to protect herself.

"Remain open," Vernie said. "Let your emotions bleed into mine. And pull back, quite literally, just as Miss Sovna did, once you have that energy in your hands."

Astrea pressed a hand to her sternum, letting a faint light build on her palm before pushing it into her skin. That burning pain in her heart stopped, but she was still nearly out of breath. Ivy had been right about getting more rest. That was not normal.

She moved back as the first volunteer, Milos, stepped forward to try the move on Vernie. Astrea corrected movements as each Lightbringer tried their hand at the ability, and she answered questions about it, too. It took some time, but after going through the ability over and over again, only one of the five seemed to be a Souleater. Nadia, the youngest of the bunch.

"I'm kind of glad we can't do that," Daria whispered to her brother as they headed back to their regular duties with the others.

"Nadia, please stay here for a moment," Vernie said.

Nadia stood at attention, the perfect picture of a soldier except for the bright orange anxiety spiking around her in time with her pulse. Cressida wandered over and bumped Astrea's shoulder in silent greeting.

"This doesn't change your current station as a healer," Vernie said to Nadia. "But I'd like to work with you, time permitting, on this ability. As Miss Sovna explained earlier, it will be useful going into war."

Nadia swallowed hard. "I understand."

"I know it's kind of awful," Astrea said, "but it's saved my life on several occasions now. It's worth practicing just in case you need it."

"Of course." Nadia ducked her head.

"We'll begin lessons later this week," Vernie said. "Go ahead back to your assigned duties; I'm sure Commander Tarkun will be expecting you."

Nadia gave a quick salute, then hurried off in the direction of the other Lightbringers. The anxiety dancing around her never faded, even as she retreated farther and farther into the distance.

Astrea shifted her weight from foot to foot as she watched the Lightbringers leave. "Is that normal?" she asked Vernie. "To find so few in a group."

"I'm actually surprised we found one in five," Vernie said. "In the testing Commander Lucian and I were able to complete the last few weeks, it seemed to be only one in ten, and that's being generous."

"It's that rare?" Cressida asked.

Vernie shrugged. "It appears to be."

"So . . ." Astrea folded her arms across her chest. "What does this mean for us? As Souleaters, I mean."

"Honestly? I'm not entirely sure. We'll just have to keep testing and training anyone we find." Pressing their lips together, Vernie asked, "You're truly able to attack void mages with this?"

She nodded. "That cold that surrounds them is almost like a veil rather than a wall. Black, like shadows, sometimes leaks past. Lucian's seen it, too. I was able to grab hold of that and reach past the veil. Whatever it is, it just shrouds their energy."

"And when we reach past it, we can attack them as Souleaters?"

"I could," Astrea said. "I don't think it should be different for you."

Vernie's eyebrows rose. "Commander Lucian said you're very strong. I would think it would be easier for you than others."

"He did?" Astrea asked, her whole body heating. She hadn't realized Lucian saw her that way. Only a couple months ago, he'd been calling her coddled and weak.

"He did." Vernie gave her a small smile. "I'll try to keep this shadowy aura in mind should the time ever come that I'm face-to-face with one of these Paragon."

"If you can make them mad, that seems to help," Astrea said. "I've only done it to two. I'm not sure what the full extent of the power is."

"Two times is good enough for me," they said. "Thank you for the lesson, even if it was brief. It's much appreciated."

"I'm glad I was able to teach you anything," Astrea said. "If you have questions about it, please let me know. I'll do what I can."

Vernie nodded, then said their goodbyes and headed back toward the officers' house.

Astrea's shoulders slumped forward. The sun hadn't quite reached its zenith yet, but she was exhausted. Where were Jin and the others? It had only been a few hours since they left, but dread had been steadily building in Astrea's bones.

Cressida's hand on her shoulder made Astrea jump. "I was going to talk to Commander Tarkun about the aetherium," she said. "Want to join me?"

"I should actually probably go find Saros." Skies only knew what he was doing or where he'd gone off to. Hopefully he'd just be in his room.

"And take it easy?" Cressida asked as they headed away from the training ring.

"You're worse than Jin," Astrea said. "And worse than Ivy."

Cressida grinned. "Yes, well, I know you. I doubt you want to just sit around."

"Like you do?" Astrea shot back. "If I remember correctly, you had a metal rod jammed halfway into your abdomen not that long ago."

"That you expertly healed," Cressida said, half whining. "Ivy cleared me!"

Astrea rolled her eyes. "Bed early tonight, alright? For both of us."

"Yes, Mother." Cressida slung her arm around Astrea's shoulders. "I think we're both going to need it."

Chapter 4

Saros was, at least, back where Astrea hoped to find him: in his room. He answered the door with prickling unease, but when he saw Astrea, his shoulders loosened. His dark hair was damp and tied back into a loose bun.

"There you are," he said, opening the door wider and stepping aside so she could enter.

"I went to see the team off, then was talking to the other Lightbringers." Astrea took a few tentative steps into his room. It was much the same as her and Jin's, sparsely decorated but comfortable enough. "Are you settling in alright?"

"Just fine, my dear." Saros returned to his open suitcase on the bed and pulled out a notebook. "I have everything I need."

Astrea nodded. The last few days between them had been awkward at best. But Astrea didn't want to push Saros away. He'd made plenty of mistakes, but he was here now. He was trying. That counted for something, right?

Besides, Jin's words echoed in her head. *I'd hate for you to not give him a chance. Most people deserve a second one.* Astrea didn't want to stay upset with Saros, nor was that what she needed. She needed Saros's help and support, perhaps now more than ever.

"I don't know if we'll be able to go to Irvina," Astrea said. "I haven't spoken with Commander Tarkun about it yet."

"Shall we go find him, then?"

"Cress actually went to speak with him about the aetherium."

"Perfect, then we'll go find both of them. I'd like Cressida to join us when we go. I'll feel better if we don't split up."

Astrea wouldn't mind Cressida joining them at all. In fact, maybe it would alleviate some of that awkwardness. Or at least bring in someone else to stew in it with Astrea.

They made their way down a few corridors, descended a set of stairs, and were back in the fort's courtyard. Saros headed toward that bunker without so much as a comment. With a sigh, Astrea hurried after him. With his loose-fitting slacks, white button-down shirt, and wingtip shoes, he looked so out of place here. Even the notebook tucked under his arm seemed wrong. He looked exactly as he always did back home, certainly more fit for an afternoon in his office than weaving among the ranks of soldiers.

A group of Novarians walked past, pulling a large machine gun—similar to the ones on the battlements—and one soldier with a thick auburn braid cast Astrea a strange look, perhaps not one of curiosity but uncertainty. Astrea could only shake her head. Definitely not the place for Saros. Or herself, really.

"Did Varojin say when he'd return?" Saros asked as he slowed down so Astrea could catch up with him.

"No, he didn't." All Jin had said was that they'd be back "soon," which could've meant anything, really. A few days, maybe? Astrea doubted they'd be back that same night.

"Hm."

"What?"

"Nothing."

"Uncle . . ."

"Nothing, I promise," he said. "I was just hoping we'd know more about Kaius soon. He bothers me. I don't like waiting to see what he'll do."

That certainly made two of them. "He never mentioned plans to come north?" she asked.

"No, and he became more and more secluded the last month or so in Kalama," Saros said with a sigh. He switched his notebook from one hand to the other. "I'm curious to know what Varojin finds."

Astrea hoped that Jin and the others would be able to locate Kaius, free the twins and Adi's sister, and get out of there quickly. And maybe they would. If anyone would be able to, it was Jin and the others, right? This wasn't unlike some of Jin's old assignments he'd told her about.

The bunker door was closed, and a guard with skin as pale as Astrea's stood outside. His dark blue uniform was neatly pressed, and even the beret on his head was perfectly angled. One gun with a large barrel hung from his shoulder, and a smaller pistol was strapped to his hip. On the other side was a sheath with a long knife. She swallowed hard.

"Hello there," Saros said as they approached. "We're looking for Commander Tarkun."

The soldier raised an eyebrow, but his amber eyes revealed nothing. Was he a Metalli? Jin had mentioned Metalli sharpshooters in the Helosian military. This man certainly seemed like he might be one, given all of his weapons.

"We're Astrea and Saros Sovna, here at the request of Grand Duchess Ysabel," Astrea tried. "We need to speak with Commander Tarkun. Please."

"The commander isn't here."

"And where might we find him?" Astrea asked, forcing herself to smile even as the guard shifted the machine gun hanging from his shoulder.

"In the commander's office."

"And where is that?" Astrea asked.

The soldier grunted as prickly annoyance scraped over Astrea's skin. She may as well have been running a cactus over her arms. "Go across to that building." He pointed at a two-story brick building set up against the fort's tall outer wall. "His office is in there."

"Thank you," Saros said before ushering Astrea away.

It took asking two more soldiers within the building to actually find Tarkun's office. The place was a labyrinth of doors, many of them unmarked. But at last, they approached the commander's door, set on the top floor and nestled right in the middle of the building.

Astrea knocked. Confusion danced over her skin, delicate like butterfly wings, before Tarkun called out, "Come in."

She cracked the door open. Sure enough, Commander Tarkun sat behind his large desk opposite the door. And there was Cressida, seated in front of it. She turned over her shoulder, brows furrowing when she caught Astrea's eye.

"Apologies for the intrusion, Commander," Astrea said as she stepped inside. Saros followed. "We—"

"Commander Tarkun," Saros said quickly, "I asked my niece to come with me to speak with you. I was wondering when we might be able to go to Irvina to begin our search for information? I believe Commander Lucian was supposed to speak with you about that."

That was . . . bold. So unlike Saros, at least around strangers and authority figures. He usually saved his more straightforward moments for family dinners with the Nikaphoroses.

Tarkun's thick eyebrows drew together. "Yes, Lucian mentioned it to me."

"I'd like to begin as soon as possible," Saros said.

"As soon as possible." Tarkun nodded, but it was a stiff, slow motion. "Traveling into Irvina when there's still the unknown threat of this

Victor Nazarov, plus the fort rebuilding efforts, *and* Commander Lucian isn't even here to escort you."

"We don't need Lucian's escort," Astrea said. She swore warm pride radiated out from Saros and Cressida both, but it was gone before she could be sure.

"I certainly can't spare anyone to escort you, Miss Sovna."

"We could take . . . Vernie." Astrea nodded, mostly to herself.

"Vernie, as in Commander Lucian's Vernie?" Tarkun asked.

"Yes."

"I was going to have them—"

"I thought the Lightbringers were mine to command." It sounded lame as it left Astrea, but hadn't Tarkun said that just a few hours before? She pushed her shoulders back.

"I meant for a lesson," he replied. "Not forever."

"Well, this is another lesson. They won't get much practice sensing void mages if we can't be out in the field . . . unless you'd rather wait for the void mages to return to your base."

Lavender surprise sparkled around both Cressida and the commander. Tarkun glanced from Astrea to Cressida, then back again.

"I'll go with them, Commander," Cressida said. "One less guard you've got to assign. The four of us are capable of handling ourselves."

"Very well," Tarkun said with a sigh. "I'll arrange for transportation in the morning."

"We can't go now?" Saros asked.

"Unlike Kalama, Mister Sovna," Tarkun said, "things close early in this part of the world. Irvina's town hall closes in"—he looked above the doorway for a moment—"under an hour. You won't be able to get there in time, and it's the best place to begin looking for whatever records you need."

"First thing in the morning, then?"

"Of course, Mister Sovna." Tarkun's attention fixed on Cressida again. "Shall we continue?"

Astrea grabbed her uncle by his forearm and tugged him toward the door. She was proud of herself for standing her ground, but if Cressida was making headway with the snappish commander, Astrea needed to make sure neither she nor Saros did anything to mess that up.

Tossing and turning on the hard bed was doing Astrea no good.

She flopped onto her right side and peered at the clock on the narrow nightstand. The two hands suggested it was just after the tenth evening bell. Astrea wasn't sure it was accurate; it felt like it had to be closer to two in the morning.

The last time she'd slept by herself was when she'd been with the Paragon. And before that? Some time much closer to the summer solstice. Ever since that palace dinner party back in Kalama, she'd been sharing a bed with Jin. And now, one night without him had her feeling all out of sorts.

Being with him just felt natural. Right. Like the easiest thing in the world. She didn't have to pretend around him, nor did he have to pretend around her. They could just *be*.

She'd even flipped on the small lamp in the corner of the room. She'd curled up with a pillow and put on one of his extra shirts to sleep in. Neither had helped.

Like a lovesick teenager, she chided herself.

But really, what was wrong with finding peace with one's partner? Because that was what Jin brought. He brought Astrea peace. He always had.

Astrea rolled onto her back and stared up at the plain wood ceiling. Where were Jin and the rest of the team now? Taking care of themselves, she hoped.

Lying there and ruminating wasn't helping her. Astrea pushed herself up and out of bed. Exhausted as she still was after everything, Astrea needed to do something.

After dressing, she slipped into the hallway beyond her room. One of the fort's soldiers stood guard outside her door, as did several others in the hallway.

"May I help you, Miss Sovna?" the young woman asked. She had tawny skin a few shades darker than Eliana's, and her eyes were a beautiful dark brown. An Earthmover or Fireweaver, perhaps?

"I was just hoping to go for a walk," Astrea said. "I can't sleep."

"Do you need me to accompany you?"

"Uhm." Astrea fidgeted. Across the hallway, a tall, lanky man with pale skin stood guard outside Cressida's door. "I was actually hoping to wake my friend. We'll be fine by ourselves."

Before Astrea could even take a step toward Cressida's room, the door opened. Like Astrea, Cressida was dressed in day clothes.

"Thought I heard you," Cressida said with a sheepish grin. "Let's get out of here."

They made their way through the quiet halls in silence. Outside, the air was cold. Astrea shivered. It may as well have been a Kalamian winter, which, sure, were mild. But her sweater did little to ward off the chill in the air.

"Skies damn this place," Cressida said, laughing as she wrapped her arms around herself. "I miss home."

"Me too."

They started down one of the paved paths running through the court-yard. The gas lamps positioned every hundred feet flickered dimly in the night. High above, only a sliver of stars were visible when the clouds parted. Somewhere nearby, a radio broadcast was recapping a sports match.

How many nights had Astrea spent in the Nikaphoroses' back garden, listening to the sports matches on the radio in Cressida and Balthazar's workshop? This wasn't exactly the same, but still, it was familiar. A comfort somehow.

Was this how Jin's life had been the last eight years? He'd once told her that he spent a lot of nights alone, drinking whiskey and reading. But did he also pace the confines of his fort, looking for some peace when he couldn't sleep?

"So," Cressida said, "Tarkun says we should go into Irvina by the ninth morning bell tomorrow."

"Sure," Astrea said. After leaving the commander's office, Astrea had returned to her room to eat dinner by herself and try to get some rest, as prescribed by Ivy. Her efforts hadn't yielded much, nor had the food been very good. "Whatever we need to do. Do you think Saros is actually going to be helpful?"

"He was down in the Islands."

"Yes, for the first time in what seems like years."

"Damn, Sovna," Cressida said with a chuckle.

"What?"

"Cut the man a little slack."

"Cut him some slack? Cress . . ." Astrea huffed, familiar frustration curling in the pit of her stomach. "He kept so much from me. From me and from Jin. He tried to convince the emperor to send Jin away from Kalama, all to protect me." When Cressida said nothing, Astrea continued, "He apparently had visions of me and Jin both, together, years ago. He saw us surrounded by red eyes, Cress."

"Like Caliban and some of the Paragon."

"Yes."

"Damn."

"I know."

With all that had happened, Astrea hadn't really had a chance to talk about any of that with Cressida. Astrea and Jin had barely even gotten to talk about it.

"Jin thinks I should give Saros a second chance, and I know Saros is trying to be helpful now, but it just feels like so much could have been avoided if he'd been honest."

"Oh, Az." Cressida's voice was gentle. "I don't think that's true. Knowing about those visions wouldn't have stopped the Paragon from coming out of hiding. I thought they told you they'd been setting these plans in motion for decades."

"They did."

"I'd be so angry with Saros, too, if I were you," Cressida said, "but I don't think him being honest would've really changed any of this. Maybe given us some more clues, but not . . ." Cressida gestured vaguely.

Astrea scrubbed at her face. "Skies, I'm tired."

"Do you want to go inside?"

They'd made nearly a full loop around the central courtyard. Back near the garage, a few lights were on in the open bays, and the silhouettes of soldiers moved about.

"Not really."

"Then let's talk about something other than Saros," Cressida said. "What do you want to do when we're done with all this?"

A tight laugh left Astrea as they continued walking. "Jin asked me the same thing recently, when we were in the Islands."

"And?" Cressida pressed.

"I said I wanted to travel. And go back to work at the library."

"Of all the things you could name, you're thinking about *work*?"

"Not just work, but I can't just putz around Kalama when this is all over."

"Do you actually want to go back to the library?"

Astrea shrugged. She'd always enjoyed her job. But what else might be waiting on the other side of this war, if she made it to the other side? What possibilities could there be? "Do you think Raela's alright?"

"I don't know. Maybe Kaius has her wherever he's got the others."

"Maybe." Astrea pulled the sleeves of her sweater over her hands. She definitely needed to ask someone about securing warmer clothes. "Do you want to go back to Lodestar when this is all over?"

"Maybe," Cressida echoed. "Or maybe I'll actually start that bakery."

"You should. I know it'd be the best one in Kalama."

Cressida nudged Astrea's shoulders with hers. "I think you're right."

"I'd certainly be there every day."

"I'll make you whatever you want if you come spend money at my bakery every day."

"Spend money?" Astrea asked. "No free pastries for your best friend in the whole world?"

"Everyone's got to make a living."

Despite the heaviness in her heart, Astrea smiled. "I'll always pay for your baked goods, don't worry."

"At least I know I'll have one customer."

"Oh, I'm sure your parents will be there. So will Ellie."

"Ah, up to four, then. Business will be booming."

"Let's get you back to bed before you catch a cold and your bright business future is ruined."

"I'm not that cold," Cressida muttered as a gust of wind blew through the fort. "Fine. Let's go back in."

They made their way inside, and the warmth of the building stung Astrea's skin. She did her best to ignore it, though, just as she tried her best to ignore the questioning looks of the guards in the hallway outside their rooms. The two of them parted ways, leaving Astrea alone in her room once again.

And so, after changing back into Jin's extra shirt, Astrea climbed into bed. It wasn't the same, but Astrea settled in as best she could and hoped with every fiber of her being that their friends—that Jin—were being safe.

CHAPTER 5

The truck rumbled up the road at a steady pace, Vernie at the wheel. Like Lucian, they weren't very chatty, but Astrea didn't blame them. It was hardly the ninth morning bell, and now they were on their way to Irvina. Vernie probably didn't appreciate being a glorified nanny for the day.

It was strange sitting in the back of the military truck with Saros. Cressida had joined Vernie up front. Where was the rest of the team? Situated just like this, maybe? Scouting the Novarian and Helosian border for signs of Prince Kaius?

Astrea wanted them to find Kaius quickly, not just to get the twins back, but selfishly, she hated waking up without Jin. She never used to mind, but these last months with Jin had been such a comfort. She wanted him back by her side.

"Az, look," Cressida said from the front seat.

Outside the window, a town came into view. Buildings not more than a few stories tall peeked out from behind the leafy trees, and to their left, a lake sparkled in the distance.

Irvina.

Astrea hadn't been there since she was just ten years old. Saros had whisked her away to Kalama right after her mother's funeral, and they'd never returned. Well, Astrea *had* been at the edge of town a few days earlier when she'd fought Victor Nazarov, but she didn't think that really counted.

Vernie navigated them through the quiet streets, passing by cars with simple paint jobs. There were plenty of those in Kalama, but there were also many flashy vehicles in the Helosian capital. And unlike Kalama, which was home to several million, the sign marking the town's entrance listed a population of just under ten thousand.

Irvina wasn't completely different from Kalama; its buildings were painted a mix of pastels and deeper hues, and there was plenty of green space, too.

After parking the car along a quiet street, Vernie said, "We'll walk to the town hall from here. It's not far."

"Yes, I remember," Saros said. "Just up this street, then we take a right and continue for two blocks."

As they climbed out of the truck, Astrea shook out her skirt and adjusted her satchel. Being able to wear her favorite things again was nice. Cressida, too, looked like her old self. She'd even put her hair back with a silk scarf Sarsali had picked up for her when they were all down in the Taipoli Islands.

Saros breathed in deep, then murmured, "It's good to be home."

Vernie led the way, their emotions a mix of focus, curiosity, and anxiety. No doubt they, too, were searching for voids or anything suspicious the way Astrea was. But Irvina, true to its quiet image, had quiet citizens. A smattering of people walked down both sides of the street, dressed not unlike Astrea in their dark hues. Some of them nodded to her group, while others offered tight-lipped smiles, and some of them even grinned.

"Anything?" Cressida murmured as she and Astrea fell in step behind Vernie and Saros.

"Seems fine."

After passing several storefronts, restaurants, and offices, Vernie stopped at the steps of a narrow building. Its faded bricks had surely once been white, but its sweeping arched windows and pediment above the door were still in pristine condition. Gold letters on the front double doors read Town Hall.

Vernie ushered everyone inside. The town hall's interior had clearly once been much more grand. The dark wood floors, though freshly polished, showed signs of their age and creaked with each step Astrea took. The windows let in plenty of light, which was useful, considering the chandelier hanging above the lobby seemed to need some of its light bulbs replaced.

"May I help you?" A woman standing behind the counter on the far wall peered over the tops of her spectacles. Her graying hair was pulled up into a bun, and her simple blue dress contrasted prettily with her pale skin. A thick wall surrounded her energy.

"Yes, actually," Vernie said as they strode forward. "We need access to your town records dating back to the years 995 through 1006."

The woman raised one unruly eyebrow. "A decade's worth of records? Why?"

"The crown's order." Vernie pulled a letter from their pocket and set it on the counter.

Frowning, the woman picked up the envelope and turned it over. She ran her fingers across the seal on the back, then opened it. Only after reading the letter did she say, "Well, alright. Follow me."

Could it really be that easy? Cressida shot Astrea a satisfied smile as they sauntered after the woman.

"My name's Eka." She started up a set of stairs near the front doors, holding onto the railing on the right side of the stairwell. "I'm the clerk here. What brings you all to Irvina? We rarely get visitors on government business."

"We're looking for information about a man who was in town in the year 995 and possibly after that as well." Vernie's boots clacked heavily with each step they ascended. "We think he may be connected to a few crimes we're investigating."

A few crimes? That hardly even covered the scope of the Paragon's activities. But Astrea just adjusted her satchel on her shoulder and hurried up the last few stairs.

"A criminal?" Eka scoffed. "Is this connected to what happened at Fort Silverpine? Or that scuffle on the edge of town a few days ago?"

Astrea hesitated, and orange anxiety flared around Saros. Vernie and Eka paid them no mind as they headed deeper into the building's second floor. Row after row of narrow aisles stretched out before them, and just two tables were placed near the stairs.

"Why would you think that?" Vernie asked.

"Timing's strange is all, I mean no disrespect." Eka stopped and turned on her heel to face the group. "Irvina's quiet. The worst we get are some rowdy folks at the bars after the work day's done, sometimes a few soldiers from Silverpine looking for an outlet for their energy."

"Well, rest assured, Miss Eka, there's no connection between the two," Vernie said. "My associates and I just need to do some research, then we'll be out of your hair."

"Hmph." Eka gestured to the aisles. "Be my guest. Do you know who it is you're trying to find? A name would help you."

"Unfortunately, we have no name," Vernie replied.

The woman snorted. "Good luck."

"Actually," Saros said, "records on the Sovna family might be useful."

"Sovna? Haven't heard that name in years." Eka's attention lingered on Astrea and Saros for a beat too long. And then her face lit up with disbelief and curiosity. Recognition. "Wait. Are you—You're Roxana's brother, aren't you?"

Saros hesitated, then said, "That would be me."

"Where'd you run off to after she died? The whole town talked about it for weeks."

"I had a job waiting for me in Kalama."

"Kalama?" The wall surrounding Eka cracked, letting a whisper of confusion escape. "Why'd you go that far south?"

"Fresh start."

"Hm." Eka pressed her lips together. "And you must be her girl."

"Yes, ma'am." Astrea fiddled with the strap of her satchel.

"She was a good one, your mother. Always went out of her way to heal all the patients on her rounds, no matter how late in the day it was or how tired she got. She helped me once when I fell and broke my shin at the end of a very long day."

"We really need to be getting to work," Vernie said. "The aisle with Sovna?"

With a sigh, Eka gestured toward the far end of the room. "That way. It's marked alphabetically." After one last pointed look at Astrea and Saros, Eka added, "I'll be downstairs if you need assistance."

As Eka disappeared down the stairwell, Vernie turned toward Saros. Their jaw tightened. "Was that necessary?"

"If she'd had another few minutes, she would've recognized me anyway," he said.

"We're here to find information, Mister Sovna."

"And I'm working on finding it, Captain Dragmir," Saros drawled.

Cressida's eyes widened. Astrea bit the inside of her cheek. Saros rarely took that tone with anyone, let alone someone who was, in a way, in charge of the situation.

"Vernie—" Astrea started.

"I'm sorry." Saros ran a hand through his dark hair. "Apologies, Captain Dragmir. I'm just trying to get to the bottom of this. That doesn't mean I need to snap at you."

What is with him? Saros's emotions were a tangle of colors: orange anxiety, red determination, green curiosity, deep blue sadness. Astrea hadn't expected a return to Irvina to come without complicated feelings, but switching so quickly between behaviors wasn't like Saros at all. He usually got stuck in his moods.

"Indeed," Vernie said after a long moment. "No apologies necessary. Let's just get started, shall we?"

Irvina's town hall had all sorts of documents: birth records, death records, marriage certificates, land deeds, census records. It had taken them a little while to find records on Astrea, Saros, and Roxana; the place wasn't *exactly* alphabetical like Eka had promised. Such disorganization was disappointing to Astrea on a professional level.

Her record had been just two sheets of paper, detailing her birth in the spring of year 996 and then the census records from the years she'd lived in town. Saros's folder hadn't had much more information than that, either, just his own birth record, census records, and a copy of the paperwork completed when he'd sold Roxana's house before they moved to Kalama.

Roxana's file had been the most complete, though it still hadn't offered much. No marriage certificate. No father named on Astrea's birth certificate—not on the original copy or the one made to put in Roxana's file. Information about when she'd purchased the house Astrea had grown up in; Roxana had bought it from an elderly woman, Saros confirmed. And her death certificate, of course.

"What about a census from 995 and 996?" Astrea asked as Saros stacked up their family files on the worn table. "Maybe he was living in town at the time."

"Maybe," Saros said. "Narrow it down by comparing it to the records from the years before and after, then start pulling files on those who might be candidates."

Astrea glanced out at the aisles as Cressida muttered, "Well, that'll take forever."

"Perhaps we should get something to eat first," Saros said.

"We're supposed to be looking for records, Mister Sovna." Vernie gestured to the clock on the wall behind Cressida. "It's too early for lunch."

"Ah, but that doesn't mean someplace doesn't still have food," Saros replied. "Let's just take a short break, then get back to it."

Saros, suggesting a break? Saros, suggesting not just a break but a break to eat? Who was this man, and what had he done with her uncle? He was starting to sound a little more like his old self from before the emperor's special projects. It almost made Astrea feel hopeful, even if it *was* strange. Maybe getting away from Kalama would help him.

"I could use a break," Astrea said, mostly to Vernie. "I haven't felt a single thing out of place since we got here."

"Yeah, and I could really use some coffee, especially if we're going to be stuck up here"—Cressida gestured to the room—"for the rest of the day."

"I suppose some coffee would help," Vernie said grudgingly. "Alright. We'll go someplace close by in case we need to leave quickly."

Saros smiled. "I know just the place."

They put away the Sovna family files, then traipsed downstairs. Eka told them to come back if they needed more information, to which Vernie said they would *definitely* be back. Saros led them outside and down the street, farther past town hall and farther away from where Vernie had parked the truck.

"Where are we going?" Vernie asked.

"I told you I know just the place," Saros said over his shoulder. "Come along."

They crossed the road, then turned right. After passing a few quiet stores, Saros paused in front of a café with tables spilling out onto the sidewalk. A few patrons occupied seats outside while a few more were inside, too, but it was hardly busy.

A bell above the door tinkled happily as they entered. Astrea's light-bringing swept through the place again and again, but all she found were relaxed, happy folks. No voids. No hatred or anger or anything malicious. Her shoulders relaxed, as did Vernie's.

A waitress circled the counter and called, "Table for four?" Her accent was distinctly Tornamian.

"Yes, please," Saros said.

As she led them toward a table in the middle of the café, her long green skirt swished around her ankles. Her dark hair was styled into several long braids, and her sea green eyes were bright.

"I'll bring coffee for the table," the waitress said as everyone sat down. She hurried back toward the counter. A moment later, she returned and set down four coffee cups. With a twitch of her fingers, coffee flowed from the pot behind the counter and into each cup. Astrea had never seen a Tidebacker use their magic for that before. "What would you like to eat?" the woman asked.

Astrea opted for pancakes while Cressida chose eggy bread. Saros ordered sausage and toast, but Vernie ordered just a single jam-filled pastry. As the waitress wandered off to get their food, uncomfortable silence settled on Astrea's skin despite the upbeat song playing on the radio behind the counter.

"I think we should split up the work as much as possible when we go back to town hall," Saros said before sipping on his coffee. He grimaced and set the cup back down on the glossy wood tabletop. "Finding someone out of place in the census should be doable. Irvina's always been a small town. Most families have lived here for several generations, and the population was smaller back when Astrea was born."

"I can work with Az." Cressida took a sip of her coffee, then scowled. "Skies, that's weak. I don't know how you survive up here, Vernie."

"It's not *that* bad," Vernie said.

"Would the clerk at town hall be willing to help us?" Astrea asked. "It might go even faster. I mean, she did know Mom."

"We need to keep a low profile," Vernie said.

"We need to figure this out," Saros corrected. "All due respect, Captain Dragmir, but playing it safe and quietly searching won't do us any good."

Saros, *not* wanting to play it safe or lay low?

"In fact, I wonder . . . Miss!" Saros called to the waitress.

Rusty annoyance snapped out toward Astrea as the waitress looked up from where she was counting money behind the counter. "Your food will be out soon."

"I actually have a question, if you have a moment."

The register closed with a loud thunk before the waitress returned. A few wrinkles formed on her forehead as she focused on Saros. "What do you want to know?"

"How long have you lived in Irvina?"

Her eyes narrowed even more. "Why?"

"I'm looking for someone."

"Mister Sovna . . ." Vernie sighed. "This is not the way to gather information."

Saros ignored them. "I'm hoping you might know an old friend of mine, one Kira Toreli. She's a Purifier who—"

"Kira?" The waitress's eyebrows furrowed. "What's an outsider doing asking after Kira?"

Saros scoffed. "Outsider? I lived in Irvina the first twenty-six years of my life!"

A bell behind the counter chimed. "I'll be right back," the waitress said, though that annoyance dancing around her calmed to curiosity. She returned with several plates, then set them out on the table. "How do you know Kira?"

"My older sister was friends with her, colleagues actually. She used to be a healer in town."

Astrea vaguely recalled her mother mentioning Kira, possibly seeing her, too. But her memory of her childhood was so fuzzy, like it was simultaneously there and missing completely. Much of her early life was just a few vague images and feelings: the lake near Irvina, getting treats in town, playing outside, Saros visiting on his breaks from university, sometimes going on house calls with Roxana to heal ailing townspeople. One thing Astrea knew for sure, though: her life with her mother had been quiet and happy.

The waitress searched Saros's face for a moment, then appraised the rest of them. Whatever she was looking for, she must've found it because she said, "Kira lives just north of town, in the large green house near the lake. Clinic's closed tomorrow, so you should be able to find her at home."

"Outstanding, thank you."

"Sure," she replied before walking away.

"Charming," Vernie muttered as they picked up their pastry. "You think this Kira will know more about Astrea's father?"

"She might," Saros said. "But Kira always got people talking. You say we need to keep a low profile, but Kira's our woman if we want to figure out who knew what about Astrea's father."

Something about going around town and shouting that they were looking for her father didn't sit well in Astrea's gut, but maybe Saros had a point. They needed an answer as soon as possible. If they paid this Kira a visit and she either had information or could point them in the right direction, maybe it was worth it.

"When did you get so bold, Saros?" Cressida teased. "You're not usually so direct."

"I've wasted enough time these last months." Saros looked at Astrea as he said, "We're going to solve this."

Saros had been evasive and vague for so long, always hiding things and giving her half-truths. But as he said those words, Astrea believed him.

They were going to figure it out, one way or another.

Chapter 6

Saros's plan to search through the census documents from the years 995 and 996 proved long, boring, and ultimately fruitless. There was not a single person out of place compared to the preceding and succeeding years. Nothing that would clue them in to who Astrea's father was.

Now that it was officially Kira's day off, Astrea, Cressida, Saros, and Vernie were all back in the truck and headed up the road to Kira's house. Indeed, the large green house on the lake north of Irvina had been easy to find. It stood proud in the midmorning sun, its abundant garden bright with colorful flowers and fruit trees. It wasn't that far from where Astrea grew up, and some distant part of her memory recalled coming to this house once or twice before.

As soon as they got out of the car, a head popped up from behind the white fence. Tight black ringlets complemented the woman's dark brown skin and blue-gray eyes. The sleeves of her yellow shirt were pushed up to her elbows, and judging by the dirt on her gloves, she must have been gardening.

"Is that . . ." The woman's soft voice trailed off, like a whisper on the wind, as their group stopped on the other side of her fence. "Saros Sovna?"

"Hello, Kira," Saros said.

Kira Toreli had to be close to Saros's age, if only because of the fact that she'd been old enough to work with Astrea's mother all those years ago.

Kira's brilliant smile and the warm enthusiasm gliding along Astrea's skin said everything. *At least she's happy to see us.*

"Where the skies have you been?" Kira said as she shucked off her gloves and reached to unlatch the gate. "Fourteen years with just one call to let me know you'd arrived at your destination?"

He ducked his head. "It's a bit of a long story . . ."

Kira opened the gate and stepped through, first smacking Saros on the arm with one of her well-worn gardening gloves and then pulling him into an embrace. Her gaze flicked to Astrea, and that smile returned as she wriggled away from Saros. "And this must be Astrea. A silly thing to say, but my, you've grown so much!"

"Hi," Astrea said, feeling entirely out of place. She still couldn't place Kira in any specific memories, though the woman's warmth was so familiar.

"Let me look at you." Kira took a step closer, matching Astrea's height. As she searched Astrea's face, her smile softened. "You look so much like Roxana."

"Doesn't she?" Saros asked.

Astrea did her best not to squirm under their observation.

Kira patted Astrea's arm, then appraised Cressida and Vernie, lingering on the other Lightbringer. Though the rest of them had worn street clothes, Vernie had opted for their Novarian uniform. "You said it's a long story, Saros. I'm assuming you aren't just here to tell me that."

"No, I can't say I am."

"Then why don't you come inside? I'll put on some tea."

Astrea followed them through Kira's front gate. Cressida lingered at the back of the line with her. "What do you think?" she whispered. "Can Kira help?"

"Honestly? I have no idea."

The inside of Kira's home was full of warm-tone wood furniture, pastel accents, and plenty of fresh flowers. Kira led them into the kitchen and gestured for them to sit at her small kitchen table as she prepared the tea. As she did, Saros made introductions for Vernie and Cressida.

"Now then," Kira said as she set a tea pot and five cups down on the table, "what's this long story, Saros?"

"Well . . ." He looked at Vernie.

"To make a long story short, we're investigating the recent attack on Fort Silverpine for the grand duchess," they said. "Mister and Miss Sovna believe her father may be connected somehow."

Vague but true.

Gray confusion bubbled up around Kira as her eyebrows furrowed. "Your father?"

"I was hoping Roxana may have told you his identity," Saros said. "She never told me, nor did she tell Astrea. We don't even have a first name."

"Your father . . ." Kira poured steaming tea into each cup, then brought over a basket of sugar. Saros plunked several cubes too many into his cup. "Roxana never told me a name, but I remember her saying he'd traveled to town from Helosia."

"He was Helosian?" Astrea asked.

"Well, I assume that was him. It was right around the time she got pregnant, and your mother was always very picky about who she let into her life." Kira chuckled. "Always said it was easy to weed out the bad apples, so to speak. With her lightbringing."

Helosian? Astrea slumped back in her chair. She didn't care what her father's ancestry was; lots of people on the continent were from mixed backgrounds. Cressida's family was from Tornama, Helosia, and the Taipoli Islands. Nicos's family was Helosian and Delian, while Adi's was Helosian and Taipoli. And Jin . . . Well, he was Helosian and Novarian, too. Could that have something to do with why the Paragon placed the prophecy on their shoulders? She didn't see how it would be relevant, but the more they both uncovered about their families, the more similarities there seemed to be.

Besides, this might slow them down. Would they have to try to figure out where in Helosia he was from? How the skies would they do that? It was a very, very big place.

"Did she ever tell you why he was in Irvina?" Saros asked.

"No, she never said." Kira frowned. "You know how private Roxana was. Never wanted to talk about such things, no matter how hard I pushed. Pushing just made it worse."

Just like Saros, Astrea thought as Cressida glanced her way. They both knew Saros's tendency to shut down and ignore the hard and uncomfortable questions.

"It's very important we figure out who he is," Saros said. "Anything you can remember from that time might be helpful."

"Let's see . . ."

"A date, a time, someplace they may have gone together in town?"

"I can't remember a thing about it, Saros. She was so young, though. I worried about her raising Astrea by herself."

"How old was she?" Cressida asked.

"Twenty-four."

Astrea couldn't imagine having a child at just twenty-four—her current age—let alone doing it all by herself.

Vernie said, "That's not *that* young. My sister had her first at twenty-three."

"No, but to raise a child on her own? While she worked long hours at the clinic?" Kira shook her head. "It was a lot for one young woman, but she always managed."

"Is there anyone still working at the clinic who knew my sister?" Saros asked.

"A few of the healers, yes. Do you want me to ask around?"

"Could you?" Saros asked.

"Of course. Consider it done."

"When you speak to your colleagues, please don't mention the connection to the attack on the fort," Vernie said. "That's where we're staying, though, if you need to reach us."

"Indeed," Kira said.

Silence blanketed the table until the tinny sound of a phone ringing in another room made Kira jump to her feet. She excused herself and left the kitchen in a hurry.

"Well . . . now what?" Cressida asked.

"Knowing he was Helosian might help," Saros said. "Does the government keep track of who enters and exits the country?" he asked Vernie.

"Not consistently back then. Most of the southern border was open at that time, especially for those traveling on foot or horseback. Papers were always checked on trains and airship depots, but there are none close by."

"We don't know he came up from the southern border," Saros said.

"No, but it seems likely considering how close we are," Astrea said.

"Perhaps."

"That was one of my patients," Kira said as she strolled back into the kitchen. "I need to go into town. House call. I'm so sorry to cut our visit short. Will you be staying in the area long?"

"Hard to say," Saros said. "If we're not here, we'll be in Talmaris, though."

"Do you need a ride?" Vernie asked. "I'd be happy to give you one. It's not far out of our way."

"Oh, no, but thank you, Captain Dragmir," Kira said with a smile. "I prefer to take my own car."

After helping Kira tidy up the tea cups and kettle, they made their way back out into the fresh morning air. She walked them to their truck.

"As I said, I'll reach out if I learn anything," Kira said. "Please don't hesitate to stop by the clinic if you need something."

"We will, thank you," said Saros.

With another goodbye, Kira disappeared around the side of her house. A few moments later, an engine roared to life, and she was soon passing by them in a small red car. She honked and waved, then continued down the road toward town.

"Let's get back to Silverpine," Vernie said as they climbed into the driver's seat. "Unless there's anything you three need to do in town?"

"Not me," Cressida said.

Astrea shook her head and settled into her seat in back. "Me either."

"I'd best give Kira some time," Saros said. "I'll check in with her in a few days."

The engine rumbled loudly as Vernie turned the key in the ignition. "Silverpine it is, then."

Silverpine was nothing but routine after routine, at least for the soldiers stationed there. Astrea was a bit jealous of them, actually. Anything normal and routine sounded nice.

She'd just finished up a lightbringing session with Vernie, or perhaps more appropriately, souleating session. They'd been practicing that ability on each other and Cressida for the last hour, trying to devise some way to give Vernie practice on grabbing a void mage's emotions. They hadn't come up with anything, and ghostly discomfort pulsed through Astrea's body again and again even though they were done for the day.

"That's certainly effective," Cressida said as she sat down under the tall, leafy tree at the edge of the training grounds. She rubbed her sternum with one hand. "I didn't realize it'd hurt *so* much. Damn."

"That's why I don't like doing it to people," Astrea muttered, plopping down next to Vernie. She picked at a few blades of grass. "It hurts me, too."

"Effective but maybe not efficient," Vernie mused.

Astrea couldn't help but wonder if Nazarov would've gotten away that day if she'd been operating at her best, not weakened by lack of sleep and taking on some of Adi's fatigue. Could she have controlled him for long enough for Jin to show up? Or . . .

"Do you think that could kill someone?" Astrea asked Vernie.

"Kill them?" Shrugging, Vernie stared out at the soldiers taking their places in one of the sparring rings. "It seems painful rather than deadly. I can't imagine using it to that extent. You haven't asked Commander Lucian?"

"It never crossed my mind before, not really," Astrea said.

"Seems like it'd be hard to kill someone like that," Cressida said. "Maybe weaken them?"

"Yeah, probably." Astrea sighed. Nazarov's death would ultimately make the world safer, but part of it still felt wrong to her, unnatural. "Vernie, can I ask you something?"

"Of course."

"Have you ever taken a life?"

They grimaced. "That's an unexpected question."

Astrea ducked her head. "Sorry."

"No, don't be. I have . . ." Their mouth set in a hard line, and the sheerest layer of steel pain settled on their skin. "Why do you ask?"

"How did it feel to you as a Lightbringer?"

"I take it this isn't something you've discussed with the commander either."

"No, but he doesn't seem like he'd have any qualms about it."

Vernie raised an eyebrow. "And you do."

Astrea shrugged.

"Honestly, I can't compare it to how others might feel, but you know of mirrored pain and healing. Imagine feeling an echo of death. It's not pleasant."

"That's an understatement," Cressida murmured.

"I've felt it before around people dying," Astrea said, "but I've never been the one to kill. I mean, not really." There had only been that fight not long ago, in which she accidentally pushed The One onto Nazarov's blade. Her throat tightened.

"Take all those complicated feelings," Vernie said, "and then add in the echo of death."

"Does it feel unnatural?" Astrea asked. "We're healers. We don't take lives."

"Maybe not, but I think our magic can be used in other ways for a reason," they said. "Anything can heal or hurt. I certainly prefer to heal."

Balance. Even Lifestealers, void mages who could steal life energy, were balanced in a way. Hurting others to heal themselves.

"Our roles are not a pleasant one, not now that we're at war," said Vernie. "Situations may arise where you must make tough decisions, not just about who to attack but who not to help. You must prioritize if the whole team is hurt."

"That's not a responsibility I want," Cressida said.

"Always go from most injured to least," Vernie replied. "It doesn't feel good, but it's the most efficient."

What might life be like for Astrea if she didn't have to hurt others to protect herself? If she could go back to just lightbringing? Astrea still didn't know much about Kira, nor did she remember much about her mother, but knowing there were other healers out there working to help people? Living quiet lives of service, not in wartime but just helping everyday people? That sounded nice. A future Astrea could imagine for herself.

Maybe her and Jin at a house not unlike Kira's, something by the water and mountains. Jin did say he loved the mountains and that he wanted to be normal. Maybe when all this was over, they could have that life. She could work as a healer, and he could be a fireweaving teacher. How nice that would be . . .

"Captain Dragmir," said an unfamiliar voice. Astrea snapped back to reality only to find a soldier with blond hair and sunburned pale skin towering above them. "Commander Tarkun wanted me to deliver a message."

"And that is?" Vernie asked.

"Commander Lucian has made contact to let you know he'll be returning with the search party by midnight tonight."

Relief flooded Astrea's veins, and mint coated her tongue as Cressida let out a happy sigh. Jin, Adi, and the others would all be back in just a matter of hours.

"Do you know if they found the targets?" Vernie asked.

"He didn't say."

"Wouldn't he have said if they'd found something?" Cressida asked.

"Not necessarily," Vernie replied. "Thank you, soldier. Back to your post."

The soldier saluted, then headed off toward the main part of the fort.

Cressida pressed her lips together. "So, now what?"

"Now," Vernie said, "we wait."

Astrea hated waiting.

Intense thunderstorms had begun right after dinner. For hours, they'd been battering Fort Silverpine. Torrential rain, endless lightning, and thunder so loud it shook Astrea to her very core.

It was already past midnight, but no trucks had rolled in through the gates. Nobody new had arrived at the base.

Jin and the others were late.

"Do you think something happened?" she asked, mostly directing the question at Cressida even though Saros and Vernie were nearby. They were in the officers' dining room, just downstairs from where they were lodging. With the late hour, few people were around.

"It's probably just the weather," Vernie said.

"Probably," Cressida agreed despite the tight knot of orange anxiety twisting around her body. "It's bad out there."

As if on cue, thunder rumbled overhead, so loud that Astrea's seat shook.

She pushed out of her chair and strode to the window on the far wall. Pulling the drapes to one side, she peered out. Little was visible in the dark night, but as lightning streaked across the sky, it illuminated the thick blanket of rain pouring down. Water was building up in dense puddles, and just before the light faded, a couple of Tidebackers came into view, their emotions frantic as they began redirecting the water.

"I don't like this," she whispered.

"They're not that late," Saros said.

Astrea glared at her uncle. According to the clock on the wall, it was nearly half past two in the morning. Two and a half hours late. That was *very* late.

"Perhaps try focusing on something else," he said. "Or go up to bed."

She was already having a hard time sleeping without Jin around. But now, knowing this storm was raging on and there was no way to check if he was alright? She doubted she'd sleep at all.

Astrea had half a mind to go out there and look for them, but she didn't know their last location. Where would they search in the dark, storm-battered Novarian forest? Maybe they could put together a team, mages to help stave off the worst of the weather if they were powerful enough. Would Tarkun have anyone like that stationed at his base? Perhaps—

"Commander Tarkun," Vernie said, tone flat. "Any news?"

Letting the drapes fall back to their resting position, Astrea turned to find Commander Tarkun loitering in the doorway. His uniform was dry, though his boots were wet. Nothing escaped his wall, no hint of what news he might have.

"We've not heard from Lucian or anyone else on the team," he said. "We'll keep watch tonight and let them in should they arrive."

"What if they need help?" Astrea asked.

His expression pinched, dark eyebrows drawing together. "*If* they need help and manage to get word to us, of course we'll help them, Miss Sovna."

"Send someone out to look for them," she said. "This can't be normal."

"I will not send my people out in this—"

"Why?" Astrea pressed. "Too dangerous for them but fine for everyone else?"

"Az, come on," Cressida said gently. "They can take care of themselves."

Tarkun huffed. "I understand your concern, Miss Sovna, but it's no use going out in conditions like this. The trucks will get stuck in all the mud. It's best we wait until the rain ceases."

"So we just have to sit here and do nothing?"

"Yes," he said. "I suggest you go to bed and stop worrying over this."

Astrea rolled her eyes so hard it hurt. As if it were that easy, to simply *stop worrying*. Maybe some people could do that, but she couldn't. Her life would be far easier if she could react exactly how she wanted, whatever way was easiest and least consuming.

"If you hear from them, please come get me," she said to Tarkun. "I don't care what time it is or what the weather is."

"You will be among the first to know."

"*The* first."

He arched an eyebrow. Astrea didn't know if he'd actually tell her first, but "among the first" didn't sound all that promising.

"Very well," he said. "Good night."

As Tarkun's loud steps faded down the hallway, Astrea sighed. She really didn't want to go to bed. But what else was there to do? Stare out at the storm all night long? With another heavy sigh, she bid good night to Saros and Vernie, and she was about to say something to Cressida, but her best friend was already following her out the door.

"Obtuse man," Astrea muttered as they started upstairs.

"Tarkun?" Cressida asked. "I think he means well . . ."

Astrea understood why going out to search would be difficult, maybe even dangerous. The mud, the rain, the storm. Flash flooding. But if it was dangerous for Tarkun's soldiers, it was dangerous for Jin and the others, too. They didn't even have a Tidebacker with them.

"I'm worried, too," Cressida said, "but we have to trust them to find their way back."

Of course, Astrea trusted Jin and the others. It was the weather she didn't trust. Prince Kaius. The Helosian army. Any number of situations might arise for Jin and the rest of the team.

"Will you stay with me tonight?" Astrea asked as they neared their bedroom doors.

"Why, to keep you from running off into the forest in the middle of the night to look for Jin?" Cressida teased. "Of course I'll stay. Let me grab my things."

"Thank you," Astrea called over her shoulder as they went into their separate rooms.

And in just a few minutes, Astrea had changed into her nightgown, and Cressida had returned in a set of silk pajamas and her hair in a matching bonnet. They climbed into Astrea's bed. Her worries hadn't settled at all, but having Cressida nearby and seeing that tight knot of orange anxiety still twining around her at least made Astrea feel a little less alone.

"Oh, we forgot the light," Cressida said, already starting to get up.

"Wait," Astrea said. "I left it on purposefully." When Cressida's eyebrows furrowed, Astrea added, "After the Paragon, the dark . . ."

"Oh." The corners of Cressida's lips quirked up. "Right, sorry. I wasn't even thinking—"

"That's alright."

Cressida adjusted her pillows, then flopped back into them. "Is this usually Jin's side?"

"Yeah, why?" Astrea lay back, too.

"Just feels a little strange, that's all."

"Why?"

Cressida swallowed hard. "It's silly . . ."

"It's not," Astrea whispered, watching as deep blue regret tangled around Cressida's body, too. "Whatever it is, I promise it's not."

"It's the side Len slept on when we had to share in Thasia."

"You really care about her, don't you?"

"Is *that* silly?" Cressida rolled over to face Astrea. "It's not like I even really know her. I'd only been joking about it the first night I saw her, but . . . I don't know. I like her a lot. She's . . . she's brave and kind and funny, and I haven't felt anything about someone in a *long* time."

"I don't think it's silly," Astrea said, squeezing Cressida's hand. "I mean, skies, I hadn't seen Jin in eight years, and after a month, we practically started living together. And Ellie's been shacked up with her *guard*—"

Cressida snorted. "Well, when you put it like that . . ."

"Talk to her when you see her again," Astrea said.

"I suppose I will."

"You have to if you want the possibility of moving forward with her."

"So wise now that you're a committed woman," Cressida said with a yawn.

"Just be quiet and go to sleep," Astrea said, teasing. "The sooner we do, the sooner morning comes."

"And the sooner we might find the team." Cressida yawned again, then rolled over onto her other side. "Night, Az."

"Good night, Cress."

Astrea rolled over, too, but she didn't close her eyes. She stared at the small clock on her bedside table, watching the hands slowly move. Wherever Jin and the team were, and wherever Lennor, Civan, and Noemi were, Astrea just hoped they were all safe.

Chapter 7

Sunlight danced through the trees. Behind her, Jin laughed and Eliana squealed with joy. Ahead, Cressida turned a sharp corner and called out, "You won't catch me!"

Astrea pumped her legs faster and faster, but as she tried to turn the corner, she slipped on the loose gravel. Tumbling to the ground, she scraped her knees and palms on the small, rough stones.

"Az!" Jin's worry pressed painfully into Astrea's skin, as painfully as the rocks. He stopped beside her and dropped to his knees. "Are you alright? Here, let me help you up."

She looked up at his face, expecting to see thirteen-year-old Jin. But he was grown. And as she looked down, Astrea realized she was, too.

She faced him again. Shadows circled around him, and his golden eyes morphed into bronze, then red, as darkness took over the whole sky. Some invisible force sucked Astrea forward, away from the darkening gardens and into nothing but void.

"Hello, little Lightbringer," Nazarov said. He stood before her, wearing a perfectly pressed pinstripe suit. "Miss me?"

"No."

"How rude."

"You were going to kill me the last time I saw you," she snapped at him.

"Was I?" he asked, tone laced with false hurt as he placed a hand over his heart. "Doesn't sound like me."

"*What do you want?*"

"*To talk.*"

"*What could you possibly have to say to me?*"

"*I heard The One's little confession before we killed him.*"

"*Before* you *killed him, you mean.*"

"*Oh, come now, Astrea.*" Nazarov clicked his tongue and took a tentative step forward. "*You're the one who pushed him into the dagger. It was a team effort.*"

A team effort. She hadn't meant to kill The One. She hadn't even known Nazarov's blade had been there. In fact, he hadn't been there. He'd jumped in at the very last moment.

"*What do you want to say to me?*" Astrea tried again.

"*We may have let things get out of hand the other day. I have some things I need your help with, so I don't plan on killing you . . . though I can't say the same for your friends.*"

"*What?*"

"*If you agree to bring me the book and talk in person, I won't have to kill you, Miss Sovna. There's much we need to discuss. You are, after all, touched by the void.*" *When Astrea stayed quiet, Nazarov took another step forward.* "*Or should that base's commander have a little scuffle with my airships again?*"

"*I don't have the book in my possession.*"

"*Maybe not, but I'm sure you know what happened to it. Get it, then bring it to me near the Path of Ruin. I'll be waiting for you, but remember, I'm not a patient man.*"

The darkness suffocating Astrea pushed in closer, and Nazarov's image dissolved into mist.

She jolted upright, chest heaving. She dug her fingers into her hair and squeezed her eyes shut.

Nazarov was back already. She'd hoped to have a little more time. Just another week or two before she had to deal with him, so she could figure out what to do with the book and who her father was. Maybe make another aetherium weapon, like the one Cressida had, to understand all of it better.

But here she was, barely the sixth morning bell. No more thunder rumbled, not like it had all night.

"Cress," she said, leaning over and shaking Cressida's shoulders. "Cress, wake up."

"Huh?" Gray confusion spiked around Cressida as she squinted against the morning. "What's going on?"

"Nazarov just dreamwalked to me."

"Oh, shit." Cressida pushed up on her elbows. Yellow worry took over her aura. "Like, just now?"

"*Just* now. I need to find the commander."

Throwing back the covers, Astrea scrambled out of bed and into one of her dresses. Cressida stumbled to the door and across the hall to get dressed, too. Astrea ran a brush through her hair, then grabbed some extra ribbon and tied it off into a braid before heading out into the hallway.

"Where can I find Commander Tarkun at this hour?" she asked the older guard standing outside her door.

"He should be in the bunker, Miss Sovna. He's still waiting for word from Commander Lucian."

"Thank you."

Astrea reunited with Cressida. Neither said much as they passed Saros's door and headed downstairs. Outside, rain still poured down from the sky in heavy sheets, but no lightning crackled. They ran across the courtyard, Cressida cursing the weather every step of the way.

Guards stood on either side of the bunker door as usual, watery shields hanging over their heads and the entrance. As Astrea and Cressida stopped underneath, Astrea wiped rain from her face.

"Can we help you?" one of the guards, a man with dark brown skin and a shaved head, drawled. His blue eyes flicked over them, then out to the rain.

"We need to speak with the commander," Astrea said. "It's about the void mages."

The blue-eyed guard raised his eyebrow, but his companion, a woman with skin so pale she looked almost translucent, said, "Just let them in, Darie."

With a sigh, Darie pushed the bunker door open. Astrea slipped into the dim interior, Cressida not far behind.

"Miss Sovna? Miss Nikaphoros?" Tarkun pushed out of his chair, palms pressed flat against the table. The only other person with him was a woman in a wheelchair, who didn't even look up from her paperwork. "I'm in a meeting." He turned to the woman. "Apologies, Captain Sarafova."

The woman—Captain Sarafova—waved a dismissive hand. "Take your time, Commander."

Pressing his full lips together, Tarkun moved around the table and joined Astrea and Cressida near the door. "What is it?" he asked, almost annoyed.

"Nazarov dreamwalked to me," Astrea said, keeping her voice low as she glanced toward this Captain Sarafova. The woman didn't seem to be paying attention to them at all.

"When?" Tarkun asked.

"Ten minutes ago or so. I just woke up from it."

"What did he say?"

"He made vague threats against my friends and family—and this fort—if I don't bring something to him in the Antare Mountains." She kept the part about being "touched by the void" to herself; surely that was some reference to her being The One's niece, and Tarkun didn't need to know about that.

"You interrupt my meeting for vague threats?" Tarkun asked.

"I mean vague in that he wasn't specific about what he'd do," Astrea said. "The threat is very real, I'm sure."

"He's never specific," Cressida added. "It's the most irritating thing, really."

"What if he's not in the mountains?" Astrea asked. "What if he's the reason Jin and everyone else are late? What if he has them already?"

Nothing seemed impossible to Astrea, and with Nazarov, it was hard to predict what his next move would be. Helosian airships? That hadn't even been a thought to cross Astrea's mind. Attacking a Novarian base? What was next, the Novarian palace again? Maybe striking Tornama? Or, quite possibly, abducting Jin and the rest of the team?

"I hardly doubt he's taken Prince Varojin and the others," Tarkun said. "Though I don't appreciate any threats being made against my fort, vague or not."

"Well, even if he hasn't taken them, I think we should go look for them," Astrea said. "They need to know Nazarov's made contact with us again. It never leads to anything good."

Folding his arms over his wide chest, Tarkun huffed. "Miss Sovna, we're not going out to look for your friends. Last night's storms did a lot of damage to the roads, including downed trees and washed-out areas."

Couldn't a handful of mages clear that up? Astrea held her tongue.

"And if this Nazarov is really threatening the base again, it makes more sense for everyone to stay here," Tarkun said. "Strength in numbers. We will more easily be able to defend ourselves if everyone is here."

We could more easily defend ourselves if Jin and Adi were here. Astrea had no doubt about that, nor that Zephyrine, Marko, and Lucian would be crucial in a fight against the Paragon. But again, she said nothing. The set in Tarkun's jaw told her it was pointless.

"The roads are that bad?" Cressida asked.

"They are," called Captain Sarafova from across the room. She ran a bronzed hand over her thick black braid before finally glancing up from her work. "That's what we were just discussing, that and how to keep supply lines open if we can't get out there to clear it up quickly."

Tarkun mumbled something under his breath, then said, "I suggest you two return to your quarters and be patient. I'll let my Lightbringers know about the void threat, but we're staying put until we know more. Is that understood?"

Astrea clenched her teeth. But Cressida set a gentle hand on her forearm and said, "Sure thing, Commander. You know where to find us if you need us."

Tarkun nodded as Cressida half dragged Astrea back toward the door. The rain had slowed to a steady drizzle, and despite it, they took their time walking across the courtyard.

Only when Astrea was sure they were out of earshot of anyone did she whisper, "We can't just leave them out there, Cress. What if Nazarov's on his way here?"

"You want to go out there by ourselves?" Cressida asked. "It's not smart, Az. I know you're worried. I am, too." Astrea could see that clearly; orange and yellow tangled around Cressida in tight knots. "But I think the commander's right, at least about Nazarov possibly coming here. And besides, what if it's a trap? What if he's just somehow trying to lure you out of the base?"

"But why would he need to if he has this army and these airships?" Astrea asked. "He implied he could just attack us here."

"With that man, I honestly never know what to think."

"And that just proves my point about him possibly targeting Jin . . . if he somehow knows Jin isn't here." Astrea paused a few dozen feet from the officers' building doors and turned her face up to the dark clouds. "I'm just supposed to sit here?"

"We'll find something to do today," Cressida said. "Watch, I bet by lunch time, we hear from Lucian again."

Astrea sighed. "If you say so."

Finding a way to pass the time at a military base on a rainy day proved to be difficult, just as Cressida's prediction proved to be wrong. Lucian and the team *hadn't* contacted the base again, and it was already approaching the ninth evening bell.

Astrea stared out over the gloomy fort courtyard from the safety of the garage. The pouring rain hadn't let up at all. And now, the anxiety that had threatened to consume her all day kept pushing against her skin, painful and unwelcome.

No distraction seemed like enough. They hadn't even been able to go back to Irvina thanks to the weather, so Saros hadn't had anything to do all day either. Vernie had suggested Astrea not practice her lightbringing—souleating—either, not with the way fatigue still clung to her like a wet blanket. Vernie's words, not Astrea's, though she had to admit she was exhausted.

"Az?" Cressida asked from where she sat nearby.

"Yeah?"

"Can you hand me that wrench?"

Astrea looked to where Cressida was pointing at a set of tools scattered on the garage floor. It had been Cressida's attempt at distracting both of them and trying to earn them a little goodwill with Commander Tarkun—fixing up a truck that had been damaged in the attack but nobody had spent time to repair yet. With her magic, Cressida had reshaped the bent metal frame, and she'd been working on engine repairs for the last hour.

Stooping, Astrea picked up the wrench and brought it to Cressida. The Metalli took it and crawled back under the vehicle.

"You don't have to do this for the commander, you know," Astrea said.

"Yeah, well, I like having something to work on." Cressida's voice was muffled. Metal thumped against metal. "Makes me less anxious. It's not truly for him, though I guess it's good that it helps him out, too."

How many times over the years had Astrea and Cressida been in similar positions, not in some foreign military base but Astrea handing Cressida tools as she worked on something? At least, whenever Cressida worked on the family vehicles. Astrea still didn't like her workshop, but garages weren't so bad.

Cressida scooted back out from under the truck, then heaved herself up to a stand. She brushed off her dark pants and readjusted the colorful floral bandanna holding her curls back. "I think that'll do it. Shall we try it?"

"Sure, if you think it's fixed."

"I'm . . . mostly sure it's fixed. This thing is older than what I'm used to."

The wrench in Cressida's hand drifted into the air toward a nearby work bench. As it landed with a gentle thunk, a set of keys next to it flew across the room. Catching them, Cressida climbed into the truck's front cab, eyebrows furrowing. Astrea took a few steps back. The engine turned over twice, then roared to life, echoing through the large garage.

Cressida whooped from inside the cab, then leaned out the open window and called, "It's perfect!"

"Sounds great, Cress!" Astrea yelled back, adding a thumbs-up for effect. But really, it sounded far too loud. "Can you turn it off?"

"What? Can't hear you!"

"Turn it off!"

Astrea took another step back, and Cressida finally cut the engine. Her laugh poured out the truck's windows. "Sorry about that."

As Astrea started to reply, disbelief and confusion slammed into her from her right. She'd been keeping her senses pushed out wide all day, and whoever felt that wasn't exactly close. She took half a step back, but more of the same slid over her skin, followed by cool relief and blistering anger. A few soldiers shouted incoherently outside, and some took off toward the gate Astrea knew was to the right of the garage.

"What's all the fuss about?" Cressida asked as she joined Astrea near the open bay door. She wiped her hands on a rag and frowned, then scrubbed harder at them.

A truck rolled through the courtyard, covered in mud and looking worse for the wear. Astrea's stomach dropped. Several Novarian soldiers followed the vehicle.

"Is that . . . ?" Cressida asked.

"I don't know."

The truck stopped, then the driver maneuvered so they could back into the empty garage bay next to the one Cressida and Astrea were in. But they stopped again about twenty feet from the door.

Astrea's pulse doubled. The truck's back tent flap opened, and out popped familiar chestnut curls.

She bolted forward. Rain pummeled her skin and soaked her dress. She didn't care. Jin had barely hopped to the ground when she threw herself into his arms.

"Whoa." He steadied both of them, mint relief coating Astrea's tongue and sunshine warming her aching bones.

"What happened?" Astrea asked, her words muffled by Jin's arms circling tightly around her. "You were supposed to be back yesterday."

"Weather turned bad."

"Well, I know *that*." Astrea pulled away, looking him over even with her senses pushed out. Fatigue laid heavy on her skin—far more than what she'd been feeling on her own—but otherwise, everything seemed alright. Even behind Jin, the others—still in the truck—seemed fine. Just five people, though. Not eight. She had a dozen questions and desperately wanted to throw herself back into his arms, but Astrea forced herself to only ask, "Any luck finding them?"

"Some." Jin sighed, a heavy sound. "I'll tell you more in a bit."

Right. They'd need to debrief with Commander Tarkun and Vernie. They'd need to come up with some kind of plan, whatever it was they'd found that was "some" luck.

"Glad you're back in one piece, Auris," Cressida said as she approached behind Astrea.

"Glad to be back, Cress," Jin said, his tone lacking all the teasing Cressida's held.

When Adi hopped out of the truck next, Astrea hugged him, too. He squeezed her shoulders, and though Astrea wasn't certain, it seemed the anxiety he'd been feeling days before had lessened just a fraction. Was she imagining it?

"You're back, Your Imperial Highness," Commander Tarkun said as he approached the back of the truck. A soldier was hot on his heels, a wide shield protecting them from the rain. Lucian and Zephyrine weren't far behind. Marko, instead of driving, climbed out behind Adi. "How was it?"

"If you insist on using titles, Commander, then at least call me Captain," Jin said.

Tarkun nodded. "Captain Auris, what did you find?"

"Can we go sit down to debrief?" Jin asked. "I'd like to look at a map."

As they walked through the darkness and headed for the low dome-roofed building on the other side of the fort, Jin fell in step with Astrea. His hand found hers.

She laced their fingers together even as she asked, "Is it really appropriate for Captain Auris to be holding hands on his way to a meeting?"

He laughed quietly. Lucian and Zephyrine were at the front of the pack, while Cressida, Marko, and Adi trailed the rear. "Probably not, but I don't really care." He brought their joined hands to his mouth, then pressed a rough kiss to the back of Astrea's hand. Her belly flipped. "Everything was alright while we were gone?"

"It was quiet," Astrea said. There had been, of course, some things going on that they needed to talk about, but most of that could wait. "Quiet until Nazarov dreamwalked to me this morning. Tarkun knows. We can talk after."

Hesitation whispered over her skin. "Nazarov's back already?"

"Unfortunately."

"Alright," he said. "We'll talk later."

They followed the others into the bunker Commander Tarkun seemed to prefer. Nobody had even sat down before he asked, "Report?"

"Weather delayed our return," Lucian said as he dropped his knapsack onto the floor with a thunk. "Roads are half-flooded out there. Is that normal?"

"Unfortunately," Tarkun said. "Infrastructure down here needs repairs that just seem to always be put off in favor of other projects. What else?"

"Do you have a map?" Jin asked, dropping Astrea's hand. "Of this part of Novaria and about twenty miles into Helosian territory?"

"Somewhere over on that table." Tarkun gestured to a long, narrow table tucked in one corner.

As Jin and Adi set the bags down and sifted through the papers, Lucian said, "We were able to find a way across the border, but there are patrols stationed as far as we could tell."

"By Emperor Aelius?" Tarkun asked, red anger spiking above his head before his wall shifted back into place.

"Him or Kaius," Zephyrine said.

"Once we crossed the border, we were able to locate an old Helosian base by following some of those Helosian scouts," Lucian said. "Prince Kaius must be there; the military presence was heavy, and Varojin said the airships looked like royal ones."

"They were my father's airships alright," Jin said as he carried a map back to the central table. Astrea tried to get a good look at it, but upside down, she couldn't make sense of it. Jin pointed to the map. "The base is about fifteen miles across the border, here. I'd guess he has at least two platoons with him but no more than three."

"Any artillery?" Tarkun asked.

"Not that we could see, but possibly," Zephyrine said. "That base wasn't decommissioned that long ago. Could be some leftover equipment there."

"Why was it decommissioned?" Cressida asked.

"It's older," Zephyrine said. "Emperor Aelius was building a new one to replace it before his focus shifted to the Badlands. I don't know if the new fort was ever completed."

"Do you know if that's where he's keeping your missing people?" Tarkun asked.

"No way to confirm, but I'd bet money on it," Jin said. "We need to go back with support. I want to break them out."

"What about Kaius contacting us?" Lucian asked. "Do you think he'd hurt your people if he realized we didn't follow instructions?"

The suggestion made Adi flinch.

"And your sister told that Caliban fellow to tell Kaius she was coming, too." Lucian raised an eyebrow. "Do you think she'll insist on coming on this mission?"

"She won't be joining us in Helosia," Jin said. "It's not safe."

"Like it is for you?" Lucian challenged. "I don't mean to be harsh, Varojin, but you're still the emperor's son. There will be severe repercussions if you get caught."

"Then why not force me to stay behind already?" Jin's jaw muscle flexed. "You think I don't know what's at stake?"

So much for Jin and Lucian getting along. Astrea glanced at Cressida, who merely shrugged. Had the rest of their mission been like this, the frustration from both men?

"I think we should wait to see what Prince Kaius says before we make a move," Lucian said. "Try to gauge his strength and motives better before we barge in."

"I don't want my people with him for one more day," Jin said.

"I think we could all use a short break before we get into any plans." Zephyrine looked pointedly at Lucian, then Jin, as she added, "Clean ourselves up and get a hot meal before we get back to work. We're all tired."

Jin huffed. "Fine."

"I'll have the kitchen prepare you something," Tarkun said. "I'll be here when you're ready to talk."

The group filed out the bunker door one by one. They'd only been inside for a few minutes, and the rain hadn't let up at all. That Tidebacker soldier was also nowhere to be found. Rain pelted Astrea's skin.

"Let's all meet back here in an hour," Lucian said, then he turned and stalked off toward the main officers' house.

Zephyrine ushered the rest of them back across the courtyard to the garage. When a few of the Novarian soldiers saw them approaching,

Marko waved them off. They dispersed, leaving two of the garage bays clear for Astrea and her friends.

"What's with Lucian?" Cressida asked once they were back under cover.

"The usual stick up his ass," Jin muttered.

"Jin." Zephyrine sighed. "You and I are normally in agreement, but surely you understand why Lucian is trying to be cautious here. It's a delicate situation."

"What's delicate about it?" Jin asked. "Kaius sent Caliban to the palace with threats and has kidnapped our people."

"The Novarian government—"

"I don't give a damn about them," Jin snapped. "Lucian doesn't have to come. Besides, where was that concern when we were breaking into Kalama?"

"You know as well as I do that with Kaius so close to the border, it's different than the last mission. We can't just do whatever we please right now. Lucian understands you want to get your people back."

"Does he?" Jin asked. "Do *you*?"

Zephyrine's white eyebrows furrowed. "Are you really asking me that?"

Annoyance scraped over Astrea's skin. She frowned, unable to believe that Jin would ask Zephyrine, his mentor, that question.

"Maybe we all need a break," Marko said. "The last few days haven't been easy."

"I'll, uh, go check that food's being made for you all," Cressida said. She shot Astrea a concerned but confused look, then headed back out into the rain.

Astrea stayed rooted to her spot. Part of her wanted to follow Cressida and let Jin and Zephyrine argue about this, but something was holding her in place.

"I think I'll go check on the commander," Marko said before he, too, headed out.

"Jin, you know Zephyrine has a point," Adi said. "I mean, I want to get Noemi out of there more than anything, but Kaius doesn't seem stable. We don't even know if he's acting alone or doing this on your father's order. What if we make a wrong move and he hurts them?"

Jin scrubbed at his face and let out a loud groan. "Fuck," he muttered. "Fuck, I can't stand Kaius."

Zephyrine set a hand on Jin's shoulder, then one on Adi's. "I really want to get them back too, Jin, but constantly pushing back against Lucian isn't going to get us what we need or want. Take a shower. Eat. You aren't thinking straight right now."

"But—"

"A couple hours won't change anything at this point," Zephyrine said. "Go. Take care of yourself."

Adi put an arm around Jin's shoulders and steered him out of the garage. Astrea followed them, peeking over her shoulder just in time to see Zephyrine head for the bunker. She slipped inside, closing the door behind her. Was she going to talk to Tarkun alone? Maybe about getting things moving in the right direction?

"Lucian was that annoying on the mission?" Astrea asked once they stepped into the empty foyer of the officers' quarters, drawing tight laughs out of both men.

"I wanted to knock some sense into him a few times," Adi said.

"You're usually so patient," Astrea said, meaning it. Adi was one of the most patient people she knew. Jin was the one who'd always had the most issue with the commander.

"Yeah, well, Jin's not wrong," Adi said. "Lucian's being too cautious. We can go in alone if he doesn't want to risk Novaria being *technically* involved."

"What does Marko think?"

"He's willing to go in with us," Jin said.

"Zephyrine stayed behind to talk to Tarkun," Astrea said. "Maybe if all of us are against Lucian, he'll cave."

"Doubtful," Jin muttered. "But worth a try, I guess." He slung his arm around Adi's shoulders and said, "We're getting them out of there."

"I know." Adi smiled, though it was tired and sad. "We don't leave anyone behind. Except maybe Commander Lucian."

At that, Jin laughed. "Alright. You heard Zephyrine. Shower. Eat. Debrief."

"Yes, Captain," Adi said, voice laced with sarcasm.

He headed for the stairs, and as Jin made a move to follow, Astrea tugged at his hand.

"Are you alright?" she asked, voice low.

Jin wrapped an arm around her and tugged her into his side. "Yeah. You know how Lucian gets under my skin."

"I know."

"I'll try to be more patient. We'll get this done."

"I know."

And Astrea did know. The conviction in Jin's tired voice was clear and strong. They left no one behind.

Chapter 8

Astrea rolled her opal necklace between her fingers, following the rust red annoyance and dark green concern pulsing through the bunker in unpredictable waves.

Jin had barely eaten a thing before heading back out for their full debrief. Astrea very much wanted to climb into bed with him and call it a night. That seemed irresponsible at best, but listening to Lucian and Tarkun drone on and on with their updates did little to hold her attention.

"And that was when the storms rolled in and set us back," Lucian continued. "It was a flash flood. We should've brought a Tidebacker with us."

Jin sucked in a breath as if preparing to say something. She could almost see it in his tired eyes. *Civan is a Tidebacker.*

"That's not all that far from base," Tarkun murmured as he followed Lucian's finger to the map on the long table.

"Between that, damage to the truck, and trying to get it unstuck, well . . ." Lucian shrugged. "We considered walking back, but that didn't seem wise, nor did abandoning a Novarian military vehicle so close to the border. Not with all those patrols. Speaking of which." He withdrew his hand from the map. "We need to send more of our people down there, Tarkun."

"Would the grand duchess agree?" Tarkun asked. "It may be seen as a move of aggression."

Pushing his shoulders back, Lucian said, "As much as Varojin and I may disagree about exact timelines for getting his team back, Prince Kaius's *aggression* cannot go unanswered. We need to bulk up security at the border. Groups of four, stationed at every quarter mile."

"That will require thousands of soldiers if you want to cover the entire border."

"Then we start with twenty miles in either direction from Kaius's base of operations until we can shuffle enough people around and get them down here. That's just a few hundred people to start. Surely nearby bases can help out in the short term."

With a heavy sigh, Tarkun rubbed his eyes. His annoyance scraped over Astrea's skin as he muttered, "Very well."

"We still don't know if Kaius is doing this on his own or if your father's involved," Adi said.

"I think we can safely assume my father knows," Jin said, "but what I can't figure out is why he would let Kaius do this. Did he give any indication of his plans when he met with Ysabel and my sister?"

"No, but that was before he knew you were in Kalama," Lucian said.

"And Kaius would have had to capture the twins and Noemi before your father returned," Adi said. "Or sometime around then. Wouldn't he have contacted Ysabel if he was using this as leverage of some kind? Wouldn't he at least have tried to negotiate?"

"I agree with Jin that it's safe to assume Emperor Aelius knows something about it," Zephyrine said. "The real question is what is he going to do about it? Send reinforcements? Set a trap since Jin's obviously pissed them both off?"

Astrea didn't like the sound of that at all.

"You couldn't tell from what you saw of the base?" Tarkun asked.

"No," Jin, Zephyrine, Adi, and Lucian answered in unison.

"I still think our best course of action is to set up the border guard, then call Talmaris and see if Eliana's heard from Kaius or if she plans on joining us," Lucian said.

"You would let her come?" Jin asked. "I don't want her near Kaius. Skies knows what he'd do to her."

Astrea twisted her necklace again. Jin certainly had a point. Last time Kaius had seen Eliana in Kalama, he'd threatened to kill her, and that was *before* they'd returned to the country and stolen the book.

"I think that if Kaius wants to speak with his siblings, Eliana may be a good distraction for you to accomplish the mission," Lucian said.

Lucian had a point, too. Kaius would undoubtedly want to meet Eliana face-to-face if he could. He always liked to talk. Constantly talked too much, in fact.

Jin pinched the bridge of his nose. Exhaustion poured off him in waves. Had he slept at all while they were gone? If he had, it couldn't have been much. Astrea placed her hand on top of his knee under the table. His hand enveloped hers, and he stroked the top a few times with his thumb.

"Adi," Jin said. "What do you think?"

"I think we don't have much of a choice," Adi said. "Based on what I know about Kaius, he might do something drastic if we break in. We should probably meet on his terms and then see what we can accomplish."

"Alright, yeah," Jin said. "Yeah, I'll call Eliana first thing in the morning and see what she wants to do. Then we can make a plan."

Returning to their shared bedroom had taken longer than Astrea anticipated. Not because of her fatigue but Jin's. He was moving slowly, a testament to the exhaustion that pulsed out from him in a slow, steady rhythm.

But finally, they returned. And as soon as the door closed behind them, Jin was on Astrea, pulling her into a hug so tight she almost couldn't breathe. He buried his face in the crook of her neck and pressed a gentle kiss to the delicate skin there.

"Skies, I missed you," he whispered before kissing the same spot.

"I missed you, too." Astrea's fingers tangled in his hair, still slightly damp from his shower earlier in the night. They'd hardly gotten a private moment since he'd returned, and now, Astrea soaked it all in.

He claimed her mouth with his. His kiss was desperate yet soft, chaste but hungry. As Astrea pulled away, his hand drifted to the back of her neck, holding her head in place as he kissed her again. Competing lust and fatigue rolled through Astrea, a heady mix.

"Sorry." He let her go. "Alone for all of one minute and I can't keep my hands off you."

"I don't mind."

"Hm." He smiled—barely. "We still haven't talked about this dreamwalking."

Astrea had shared the vision with everyone at the beginning of the debrief, but they'd gotten so caught up in everything Jin's team had learned that they hadn't had a chance to discuss what Nazarov might have planned or be trying to do.

"Can we at least get ready for bed first?" she asked.

"Of course. I wanted to go check in with Adi anyway."

"About?"

"To make sure he wasn't just saying that at the meeting to assuage Lucian."

"You think he would?" Astrea asked.

"Not fully, but he hasn't been very vocal about his sister since we left Talmaris. Or the twins. I don't know what he's thinking."

"I know he's worried; I can see that much."

"I won't be gone long. I don't think he's going to want to talk."

"Well, if he does, take your time."

Jin kissed the top of her head, then slipped back out into the hallway. As soon as the door closed behind him, Astrea sighed. She didn't love hearing that Adi was closing himself off, at least from Jin. They were best friends, brothers. Astrea could understand Adi not wanting to voice all his worries to people he didn't know well, like Commander Tarkun, but to not tell Jin? To not tell Zephyrine?

Astrea made quick work of cleaning herself up in the bathroom down the hall, then returned to their quiet little room. She changed into a pinstripe nightgown, its narrow straps and thin fabric useless against the chilly night air, then wrapped one of the blankets around herself.

A few minutes later, the bedroom door opened. Jin said something in a low voice, then the heavy wall that always seemed to be outside the bedroom moved a little ways away. Jin stepped into the room, shut the door, and shoved a towel into the crack between the door and the floor. Then he crawled into bed, sighing as he flipped onto his back.

"How's Adi?" Astrea asked.

"He stands by what he said at the meeting, but I don't think he'll be in the mood to talk until Noemi's back with us."

"Would he talk to Marko?" Astrea asked. When Jin raised an eyebrow, she said, "I know you see it between them, too."

"Yeah, I do." He sighed again. "Honestly, I don't know. I feel like I don't know anything anymore. This thing with Kaius is really messing with my head."

"You're exhausted," Astrea said.

"I am."

"We can talk in the morning."

"I want to hear more about this dreamwalking." He rolled toward her, then pushed up on one elbow. His gaze roamed her exposed clavicles, arms, and thighs, appreciative but not entirely distracted. "And whatever it is you and Saros learned about your father."

Astrea shrugged. "Not much so far. We tracked down one of my mother's old colleagues, a Purifier who still lives near Irvina. She said my father was Helosian."

"Helosian?" Jin asked, almost like he didn't quite believe it. "Wouldn't there be some record of his immigration?"

"Apparently back then, the borders were easier to cross without anything getting written down. A lot of people would travel between Irvina and Helosian border towns. We read through as many records as we could at Irvina's town hall."

"I see."

"Kira—that's my mother's old friend—didn't know my father's name or anything else about him. She said she was going to ask around to some of the other healers and people in town to see if anyone knew anything."

"That's good, right?"

Astrea stared down at where her hands rested in her lap. "We'll see if it turns anything up." She wasn't so sure it would, but they were out of options.

"And this dreamwalking?" Jin asked.

"Nazarov just . . ." Astrea blew out a harsh breath. "He wants me to get the book and meet him at the Path of Ruin. He said we have 'much to discuss.'"

"Isn't that where The One asked you to meet?"

"Yes."

"I don't like that."

"Neither do I. And you already know he's threatened to attack us and the base again if I don't go to meet him."

"Did he give you a deadline?"

"No, he just said he's 'not patient.'"

"Fuck," Jin muttered.

She shrugged. "He said I was 'touched by the void,' too. The One said something similar back when we were in the Islands. I think that was some reference to me being his niece."

"Seems so," Jin said.

"I'd rather focus on getting Lennor, Civan, and Noemi back for now," Astrea said. "Giving in to his demands doesn't seem like the right thing to do."

"I agree, but if we tell Ysabel about the dreamwalking and this location, she can build up her forces and head that way. It might be where the rest of the Paragon went."

"Tell her on your call to Ellie in the morning?" Astrea asked.

"Sure. Tarkun may have already called Ysabel . . . or Lucian might be doing that now." With a groan, Jin tugged Astrea down so her head rested on the pillow next to him. "And your lightbringing lessons with those at the base?"

"Vernie's a Souleater, too," Astrea said. "One of the others could do it. Vernie's going to work with them more. Apparently Lucian started testing Lightbringers while we were in Kalama, but there aren't many able to do what we can."

"Wonderful." Yawning, Jin wrapped his arm around Astrea's waist.

"You should sleep," she whispered. There was so much they needed to figure out and accomplish, but Jin would be of no use if he didn't get some rest.

"So should you."

"I will."

Jin smiled sleepily and kissed her forehead. "I'm glad to be back. Trying to sleep in the back of a truck with Lucian loitering nearby isn't easy."

Astrea laughed. "Well, you're here now."

"And I wouldn't have it any other way."

CHAPTER 9

Jin and the rest of the team may have been back, but there was a lot they needed to do. Astrea swirled sugar into her coffee, grimacing as she took a sip of the weak liquid. Where was Zephyrine's supply of the good stuff?

Astrea had tried to get Cressida and Saros to both join her, but neither had wanted to get out of bed after late nights full of worry. So, Astrea had left Jin to call his sister and gone in search of coffee for herself.

Tight anxiety pulled at Astrea's muscles, and a moment later, Adi walked into the dining room. Marko was right behind him, voice low as he murmured something in Adi's ear. Adi didn't even crack a smile. Marko frowned.

"Hey," Astrea said as Adi pulled out the chair next to her. "You sleep alright?"

"Fine," he mumbled.

Astrea glanced at Marko, who shrugged. This wasn't the Adi who'd returned the night before. Jin was right; Adi wasn't dealing well with any of this. Not that Astrea blamed him. Who would?

She poured coffee into two spare cups on the table, passing them to both men. Adi took his but didn't drink. Astrea tapped her fingers on the table.

"Where's Jin?" Marko asked Astrea.

"He went to call Ellie. Should know more soon."

"So early?" Marko looked down at the small watch on his wrist. The leather straps were worn in, and the gold timepiece winked at Astrea as it caught the ceiling lights. "It's barely the seventh hour."

"He wanted to call even earlier but didn't know if he'd be able to reach her."

Marko flicked his gaze to Adi, then back to Astrea. She barely shrugged at him. Other than the anxiety twisting around Adi in steady orange, Astrea couldn't glean a thing off him.

"We're going to get them all back, Adi," Marko said gently. "I promise."

"I know." Adi sighed, his green and brown eyes both markedly dull. "I just hate to think what Kaius might be doing to them."

Astrea hoped Kaius was just holding them prisoner but otherwise leaving them be. Would he be as awful as Nazarov had been to Astrea? Would he use Caliban or another void mage to send awful visions to the three of them, try to force them to talk? Kaius had always been an ass, but what lines would he cross to get what he wanted?

"Wondering that will do you no good." Marko's pale, scarred fingers twitched. "We talked about that."

"I know," Adi said again, voice tight. "It's bad enough that he has Lennor and Civan, but Noemi . . . She's not even a mage." Adi sucked in one deep breath. "I'm sorry."

"Don't be sorry, Adi," Astrea said. "You have every right to be upset."

"I need to stay focused. Losing it won't help Noemi or the twins."

Astrea's heart ached. How many times had she felt that way these last few months? Trying so hard to stuff away her feelings for fear they'd cloud her judgment? And maybe there was a time and place for that, but Astrea didn't think it was now, in this empty dining room.

"Do you want to go back upstairs?" Astrea asked. "I could get the kitchen to send some breakfast up to you if you want time alone."

"No, that's okay, Az," Adi said, trying but failing to force a smile. "I'll spiral if I'm alone. Breakfast would probably be good, though."

Astrea patted his shoulder. "Let me go get you something, then."

Winding her way through the empty dining room, Astrea slipped through the back door that led to the kitchen. Cressida had found it on their second day at Silverpine and made friends with the staff back there—or as much as one might call quick, friendly conversation with strangers friendship. Astrea didn't recognize anyone working there that morning, but when she asked about breakfast, a tall, burly man with a thick red beard said they'd start serving in a few minutes.

As Astrea made her way back toward their table, only one thing had changed. Marko and Adi's fingers were twined together. The moment they saw her, they began to pull away from each other. She couldn't help the small laugh that escaped her.

"You two don't have to hide anything from me," she said as she sat down.

Marko rolled his shoulders. "I don't know what you're talking about."

"I've sensed it since the first night at the ruins, Marko."

"But that was—"

"Months ago? I know." Astrea sipped her coffee, grimacing again at the weak drink.

Some of the knotted anxiety around Adi loosened as he relaxed into his chair. "Guess we can't hide things from a Lightbringer."

Astrea smiled. "Nope."

Marko's cheeks flushed pink, which only made Adi laugh. A full, hearty laugh, too, like he really meant it. Even Marko smiled a bit at that, though the blush returned when Adi twined their fingers together again.

"Hey," Jin called as he pushed the dining room door open. "There you are."

"Did you get in touch with Ellie?" Astrea asked.

Marko and Adi pulled away from each other again. Jin didn't seem to notice; his attention was fixed on Astrea. "Well, I spoke with Ysabel. Kaius reached out to them just before sunrise. Ellie's already on her way."

"To Silverpine?" Marko asked.

"Yes, and she'll be here in a couple hours." Jin tilted his head toward the door. "We should get ready. I want to make a plan as soon as she arrives."

Fort Silverpine was just a blur of activity as everyone prepared for Eliana's arrival. Astrea didn't think most of the preparations were necessary, nor did she appreciate that Eliana's arrival was being treated obviously differently than Jin's had been.

Not that Jin seemed to care at all. But it still felt wrong to prioritize one sibling over the other.

Everyone gathered in the main courtyard. The rain had stopped, though the water-logged ground had only dried thanks to the combined work of several Tidebackers and Fireweavers. The sun had returned and was crawling its way through the midmorning sky. Astrea tried to focus on anything but the anxiety threading in and around her friends.

"When Princess Eliana gets here," Lucian said to Tarkun, "I want to make sure she has a full security detail. She'll be arriving with her own personal guard, but even he'll need to rest. I want your best people on this."

"I already assumed as much," Tarkun grumbled. "She'll be well pro-tected."

Astrea wasn't so sure. Yes, they'd been safe at Silverpine so far, but the damage from Nazarov's attack had only just been repaired, and besides, he'd threatened to return. But what choice did they have with Kaius demanding a meeting?

There really wasn't a choice. They had to go.

"To warn you, though, I don't think Eliana will be receptive to it," Lucian said to Tarkun.

"No, she won't be," Jin said as he joined them. He'd been running around the base all morning since news of Eliana's arrival had spread, trying his best to help prepare everything. "But I agree with you. Kaius is going to target her, I'm sure of it."

"Then why is she joining us, Captain Auris?" Tarkun asked, an unexpected edge in his voice. "I'm no diplomat, but it seems to me that she'd be better off staying put in Talmaris if the dangers are that serious."

Astrea pressed her lips together. Of course Eliana would be better off staying in Talmaris. But Eliana also wouldn't miss out on an opportunity to confront Kaius and try to stop him, whatever that looked like.

"Did Ellie think this through?" Cressida whispered as she leaned over to Astrea.

"Nicos would try to stop her if he thought it was too dangerous."

"So . . . what you're saying is that she probably hasn't thought this through and got into a fight with Nicos about it."

"I'm saying . . . she's probably hoping to get a head start on her plans. Capturing Kaius or something would definitely help her do that."

"You think that's her plan? To capture Kaius?"

"Oh, I don't know." Astrea fiddled with the end of her braid. "But knowing Ellie, she's thinking about something like that. Like the targeted strikes she's mentioned before."

"Ship should be here in a couple more minutes," Jin said as he came up behind Astrea. "Does anything feel amiss?"

"Not that I can tell," Astrea said. The fort was just a heavy tangle of anxiety, anticipation, and warring curiosity and disinterest. Nothing to suggest Nazarov or Kaius was lurking around.

"Good."

"Why does this feel like the time your father came all the way out to Fort Avalon?" Adi murmured to Jin. He gestured to the growing crowd. "Only maybe not as vaguely threatening."

Jin smirked, his attention fixed on where a tiny airship cleared the trees. "Oh, Ellie could make this threatening if she wanted to."

The craft descended slowly as it finally neared the courtyard. It landed with little more than a heavy thunk on the ground, and as the engines shut off and the wind died down, Astrea could only pick out two additional sources of energy. Bright yellow worry flickered in the airship's windows.

Jin stepped forward, cutting ahead of both Lucian and Commander Tarkun. Only as the airship door unsealed did Astrea finally catch a glimpse of Zephyrine's white hair emerging from the crowd. The door opened, and Eliana stepped out of the ship.

Despite leaving Talmaris before sunrise, not a hair was out of place on Eliana's head. And she'd certainly taken dressing the part seriously. She was in her armor and black training gear, but the polished knee-high black boots and braid crown wrapped around her head somehow made her look incredibly elegant. Even a hint of red lipstick colored her mouth.

"Your Imperial Highness," Commander Tarkun said from behind Jin. "Welcome to Fort Silverpine."

"Commander Tarkun," Eliana said, smiling as she descended the couple of steps to the ground. "I'd say it's a pleasure to be here, but I don't think it is, given the circumstances." She surveyed the crowd of soldiers. "I hope this isn't all on my account."

Nice, Ellie, Astrea thought as Tarkun's approval and embarrassment swept over Astrea's skin.

"I believe everyone just wanted to see if the reports were true, that you were really coming, Your Imperial Highness," Tarkun said. "I'm sorry to welcome you under most unfortunate circumstances."

Tarkun hadn't been nearly so accommodating for them the last couple of days. If anything, he'd been prickly. Astrea had to stop herself from shaking her head. Was this just for the optics of it all?

"Then let's get straight to business, shall we?" Eliana suggested. Behind her, Nicos climbed out of the ship. Even he was the picture of perfection, his auburn hair slicked back in a neat bun. "I want to know everything about what our brother is doing just across the border."

"Let's go someplace private to discuss," Lucian said. "Tarkun?"

"This way, Your Imperial Highness," Tarkun said, ushering Eliana through the crowd.

As Eliana passed, she smiled tightly at Astrea and Cressida. She was unreadable now, but that control felt desperate, unstable, like she might be trying to hold back a flood.

The crowd began clearing out as Tarkun barked orders at them. Eliana, Nicos, and the rest of them followed him. Astrea fidgeted with her dress as they walked, all too aware that she stuck out next to everyone in their gear. At least Cressida did, too. They were both in civilian clothes, Astrea in a black and white gingham dress and Cressida in wide-legged black trousers and a jade blouse.

As soon as Marko closed the bunker door, before anyone had even made it to the table, Tarkun said, "Though we sent a team to scout out your brother's movements, Your Imperial Highness, it's a bit unclear what he's doing. It seems he's holed up in a decommissioned base."

"Fort Nightshade," Eliana said. "Our father decommissioned it a few years back."

"We've been over that already," Jin said.

"Right, well, Kaius says we are to meet him there tomorrow morning to discuss . . ." Eliana sighed. "We're to discuss 'returning what belongs' to you, Jin. His words."

"Shall we sit and call for some coffee, Your Imperial Highnesses?" Tarkun asked, motioning to the table. "It seems there's much to discuss."

"I already told you yesterday there's nothing to discuss, Commander," Jin said. "All due respect, but there's only one option. We go to Fort Nightshade."

"What else did Kaius say?" Zephyrine circled the table and took a seat at the far end. Lucian followed suit. "What does he want to talk to you about, Eliana?"

"All he mentioned was what 'belongs' to Jin. The Rusas twins and Noemi Kuwat, I assume." Eliana flashed Adi a small smile. "We're to meet him by the tenth morning bell. We'll get our people back, I promise."

"We'll need to leave early," Lucian said. "Fourth morning bell, perhaps."

Jin nodded. "We'll make it work."

"Excuse me." Tarkun's sharp words cut off whatever Marko was about to say. "You're really going to go there without any other intelligence on the situation? We know nothing of his capabilities or movements. What if he's going to use his airships to attack Silverpine while you're gone? Or worse, what if he's got the base fully armed and operational?"

"I don't like going in with so little information, Commander, but what choice do we have?" Jin asked. "Unless you can get scouts there right this moment and see something we couldn't."

Astrea hated to admit it, but it'd be nice to have a void mage with them, someone who could jump locations like Caliban and Nazarov. That might make it easier to sneak into the base.

"We'll just have to evaluate the situation as we go," Zephyrine said. "Revisit what we know, not just from the last hike out there but my own knowledge, too. The emperor decommissioned the base while I was on the council. I remember the talks."

"Good," Jin said as Tarkun let out a resolute sigh. "That'll help."

"But before we get into that . . ." Eliana nodded at Nicos.

He shifted a bag on his shoulder; Astrea hadn't even noticed it. Unbuckling the top flap of the knapsack, Nicos reached in and pulled out a large chunk of dull metal.

"Ellie, is that—" Cressida started.

"Aetherium." Eliana took the metal from Nicos and set it on the table, where still only Zephyrine, Lucian, and Tarkun sat. "With what Tomas and your parents have found in that book you all brought back from Kalama, I think it's important we begin making weapons like this for ourselves. If they truly hold the power of these Lifestealers, then we must have them at our disposal. They could make all the difference."

"Ellie . . ." Cressida swallowed hard. Cold, heavy fear pressed into Astrea's entire being.

"Commander Tarkun, maybe you can go ensure we have some vehicles ready for tomorrow," Jin said. "Zephyrine, maybe you can assist?"

"Yes, let's go look at what you've got, Commander," Zephyrine said. "I don't think the last truck will cut it if we're taking a larger team. We need something . . . sturdier."

Anxiety and curiosity leaked into Tarkun's aura, but he slowly stood, murmuring something about "Your Imperial Highnesses" before following Zephyrine out of the bunker.

"What did Tomas find in that book, exactly?" Jin asked once the door was closed.

"Mostly what the Nikaphoroses already told him was in there," Eliana said. "But he started comparing some of the story in it to history from the

Great Wars, and, well, he thinks these Paragonian weapons were causes of mass destruction. The level of death in some of the battles around the Novarian borders . . . The connection made sense to him."

"And you want to bring weapons like that into our war?" Jin asked, voice tight.

"I don't *want* to, Jin, but Father already has the information. He might even have weapons just like it. We need to at least be prepared to balance the fight."

Huffing, Jin half turned away from his sister and crossed his arms over his chest. "Unbelievable."

Rusty annoyance arced out from Eliana. "Oh, don't be naive, Jin."

"I'm not being naive," he snapped. "The power that metal has, the things Adi and I have already seen in Corsyca—" Pain bled into his aura, gray and cold. "The things I've seen in the last eight years . . . I don't like it."

"I don't either," Cressida said. "That dagger in Kalama . . ."

Astrea didn't like it, either. What that metal would do, the pain it would cause . . . It was far beyond anything a normal knife or bullet might do. It would suck the life energy right out of its victim, causing untold pain in the process. Just the memory of the ghost pain—not even what the victims fully felt—made Astrea's skin prickle with unease.

Lucian cleared his throat. "You have a point, Princess Eliana. I don't relish the thought, but we should be prepared, as you said."

"Lucian—" Cressida started.

"It doesn't mean we use them, Cressida," he said. "It just means we have the option ready. It means we bring them tomorrow."

Astrea didn't like the thought of bringing weapons like that into war, but she also didn't like the thought of war at all. Maybe Eliana and Lucian were right. No, not maybe. They *were* right. They had no choice. Why take the chance of Emperor Aelius and Kaius getting ahead and overpowering them with aetherium weapons? The Helosian Empire already had far more resources, more artillery, more soldiers.

"You haven't seen what those weapons do, Ellie," Cressida said. "It's not normal."

"I know it's not normal." Eliana scoffed. "Of course it's not normal. But I don't think that means we take the option off the table."

"And let me guess," Cressida said. "You want *me* to make these weapons for you?"

"I trust no one in the world more than you or your father. He's agreed to make some more in Talmaris. I just thought it'd be good to have you make a couple more before we go back into Helosia tomorrow."

"Fuck." The swear was barely more than a whisper as it left Cressida's mouth. "Fuck, Ellie, come on. Don't ask me to do this."

"I don't want to take any chances with Kaius tomorrow. Please, Cress."

"It's just two or three more daggers," Nicos said.

Cressida glared at him.

With a huff, Jin said, "I think Ellie's right."

Cressida gaped at him. "But Jin, you *just* said—"

"I know what I just said." Jin shook his head. "I know. But Ellie's right. My moral objections can't stand in the way of protecting ourselves if and when the time comes. If you aren't comfortable with it, though, that's fine. You don't have to do it."

"You aren't the only person in the world who can make weapons," Eliana said. "Or the only person on this base. We'll find someone else if you won't help."

"It's not fair to force Cress to do that if she doesn't want to," Jin said.

"I won't *force* her. I'm not Father. I'm just saying there are other people who will help."

Anxiety and anger pulsed out around Cressida, bright orange and red against her green shirt. "Az?" she asked.

"I mean . . ." Astrea tapped her fingers against her thigh. "I don't like it either, Cress, but they're right."

"Skies damn it." The red spiked high above Cressida's head. "You know what it does to people, Az. You *know*!"

"Yes, and if having weapons like that protects us from Emperor Aelius using them on us, I'd rather his people feel that pain . . ." Saying that felt cruel, but if it was her or one of Emperor Aelius's supporters? Astrea would much rather not be on the sharp end of an aetherium dagger.

"Fine," Cressida muttered. "I'll make them."

"Your father's going to teach Ysabel's people to work with the material, so these can be the last ones you make if you want them to be," Eliana said.

Cressida's shoulders and jaw remained rigid as she said, "We'll see."

"Is there anything else we need to know about Kaius?" Jin asked.

"No." Eliana shook her head. "I just need to figure out what I'm going to say to him tomorrow when I see him."

"Maybe we should call for that coffee Tarkun offered," Lucian said. "It seems like we'll be here for a while."

Chapter 10

Going on missions was always going to be foreign to Astrea; she was sure of that. This was not the life she was meant to lead. Armor and daggers and ancient magic . . . it still somehow all seemed wrong.

She adjusted her armor one last time, then headed for the courtyard where Saros stood with Cressida, Vernie, and Zephyrine. Saros hadn't been involved in any of the planning for the mission. In fact, he hadn't been around much at all the last couple of days. Astrea wasn't sure why; everything had been going well between them while searching for information about her father. So what was bothering him now?

"There you are," Saros said as Astrea approached the group. His voice was all wrong, too tight. "I wasn't sure you'd wake up in time."

"I'm here." Astrea frowned. "Jin will be down shortly."

"Adi and Marko just went to check everything over with Lucian," Zephyrine said.

"And Eliana?" Saros asked Astrea.

The night before, Eliana and Nicos had been focused on the plans Jin and the others had drawn up, so much so that Jin practically had to force both of them to go to bed. Eliana wouldn't miss this.

"On her way," Astrea said, though she actually wasn't quite sure what Eliana was up to.

Saros pressed his lips together.

"Maybe Cressida, Vernie, and I should go help them," Zephyrine said. "Get the checks completed more quickly."

"Sure," Cressida said, shooting Astrea a quick glance over her shoulder as she walked away.

Saros shifted his weight from foot to foot. "Is this really necessary?" he asked.

"What?" Astrea looked down at herself. "The armor? I think so." She'd asked Jin the same question once, back on their first trip to the ruins.

"No, although that is a strange sight." Saros sighed. "I mean you going to this *meeting* with them. Surely Varojin and his team can handle it. I'd feel better if neither you nor Cressida went, and her parents would feel the same if they knew."

Irritation scraped over Astrea's skin, her own. It bubbled up within her, unwelcome after a peaceful week with Saros. She tried to even out her tone as she said, "I have to, Uncle."

"But why? Vernie and Lucian are both healers. They don't need you there."

Shoving her irritation—and offense—down deeper, Astrea said, "I'm done hiding."

"It's not about hiding, it's about—"

"No," Astrea said with more force than she meant. "No, Uncle. I know you mean well, but I hid myself away for fourteen years. I'm not going to sit back while people Jin and Adi care about—people I care about—are in danger."

Orange and yellow swirled around his body, his anxieties heavy in the air. "But—"

"Cress and I handled ourselves in Kalama and when our airship was shot out of the sky," Astrea said. "What more do we have to do to prove that we can handle a meeting with Kaius?"

"It's not about what you can handle," Saros said. "I don't want either of you two getting hurt. I'm worried."

"Then I suppose it's a good thing we'll have three healers on the team, isn't it?"

Saros half smiled. "You're just as stubborn as your mother once she'd set her mind to something."

"Thank you."

He laughed, a tight, uncomfortable sound. "Well, please watch out for each other. Balthazar and Sarsali will kill me if something happens to either of you."

"I promise we'll be careful."

"Good."

It wasn't the most productive conversation, but Astrea was just grateful that Saros seemed to accept what she wanted to do. That was a big change from how he'd been earlier that summer and earlier in her life. Still protective, of course, but perhaps not *quite* so rigid.

"Your Imperial Highness!" Tarkun's booming voice called from the other side of the courtyard. "Where is your sister? We need to leave."

Glancing back over her shoulder, Astrea found Jin striding toward her, all business and intense focus. He moved across the courtyard with determination, unreadable behind his wall. Even his eyes, usually soft, had hardened. She'd only seen that look a few times before. When they'd fought Nazarov and Kaius in the past.

"She's on her way," Jin said as he joined Astrea and Saros. Tarkun met them, too. "Are the trucks ready?"

"Trucks?" Saros asked. "You're not flying over?"

"If Kaius has artillery, being in the sky will just make us even easier targets," Jin said. Saros paled. "Trucks will at least give us a chance."

"Your people were just having a second look over them," Tarkun said, "but we're ready to go when you are."

"We're ready."

As Tarkun headed for the garage, Astrea expected Saros to get one more word in, something about being careful or staying safe. But he simply stuck his hand out to Jin for a shake and said, "Good luck."

Jin took his hand. "Thank you, Saros. We'll see you soon."

Saros smiled at Astrea, yellow worry vibrating around him. She smiled back, then hurried after Jin and Commander Tarkun toward the garage.

Three large trucks had been pulled out of the bays, each vehicle towering over even Jin's head. The dark green paint reminded Astrea of the forest. A group of Novarian soldiers were climbing into one of the trucks, their dark blue uniforms the only thing setting them apart from the Helosian team.

"Should we really be bringing so many people?" she asked Jin as the distance between them and the trucks shrank. "Will Kaius be offended we've brought the Novarians?"

"Kaius is going to be offended no matter what, Az," Jin said. "I'd rather have a little extra strength."

"You don't think it'll make your father do something drastic?"

"Honestly? I have no idea. But Ysabel's willing to send them, so we may as well take that risk."

"Right." Any extra force against Kaius would be worth it, Astrea supposed. It wasn't like Ysabel didn't understand the risks of this mission and sending her own people into Helosia.

Jin glanced down at Astrea, then over his shoulder. "Oh, finally, Ellie's here."

Saros was gone, but Eliana and Nicos were hurrying toward them. Eliana looked much the same as the day before, though now gold laurel leaf pins held her braided crown in place.

"Just in time," Jin said to his sister as she and Nicos caught up to them. "We need to leave."

Eliana murmured some excuse Astrea didn't pay much attention to. Up ahead, near the final truck, orange anxiety wavered around Cressida. She held her hands out, dark metal catching the sun.

"I don't have any preference on who carries them." Lucian's voice rang out clear above the sounds of the base. "Whoever's comfortable with them."

"Comfortable with what?" Eliana asked as they merged with the rest of the team.

"Your daggers," Cressida said, voice tight.

Astrea had tried talking with Cressida about it the night before as she worked in the base's forge, but Cressida had insisted it was fine. That the situation didn't bother her. It obviously did, but when Cressida didn't want to talk, she wouldn't. Astrea couldn't force her. But she was going to have to sort it out with Eliana at some point; the two couldn't be at odds now, not when things were escalating with Kaius.

"Adi?" Jin asked.

"Sure," was all the Earthmover said in response.

Jin turned toward his mentor. "Zephyrine?"

"If you think it's best." She flicked her long white braid over her shoulder. "Unless you or Lucian want it."

"As I said, I don't particularly care," Lucian replied.

"You take it; I'll just use my fire," Jin said to Zephyrine. "Do you want to keep the third?" he asked Cressida. "The original?"

Jaw tight, Cressida pressed her lips together and sighed. "Yeah."

Astrea's eyebrows rose a fraction. She'd expected Cressida to dump all the aetherium weapons as soon as she had the chance.

"Then we're set," Jin said as Cressida passed the two new daggers to Adi and Zephyrine. "Lucian, go with the Novarians in the front truck. Cress, Az, go with Ellie and Nicos in the middle. Adi, Zephyrine, Marko, Vernie, with me in the rear."

This, they hadn't discussed. Astrea's throat tightened. She kept her mouth shut. Jin surely had his reasons if he was splitting up.

The team murmured among themselves as they scattered to get into their respective vehicles. As they did, Lucian pulled Vernie and Marko to one side. Cressida spun on her heel and followed after Adi. Eliana's eyebrows furrowed as she watched Cressida stalk off, but Nicos ushered her toward the middle truck.

"Az," Jin said, voice low as he brushed her forearm.

"Yeah?" She turned to face him.

"Keep an eye on Ellie? There's a radio in the truck if you need to call either me or Lucian. If Nazarov or anyone shows up."

"I'll do what I can."

"Alright, good." Then he leaned down and, taking her face in his hands, kissed her gently. He kissed her again, his skin warm against hers. "I'll see you in a few hours, alright?"

With a tight smile, Jin finally moved his hands away from Astrea's face. He skirted past her, calling out to Adi. Astrea pushed her shoulders back, sucked in a deep breath, and headed for the middle truck. *You can do this, Az. We can all do this.*

Sitting in the back of a military truck thick with tension was hardly Astrea's idea of a good time. Eliana and Cressida, though sitting opposite each other, had barely spoken a word in the hour they'd already been on the road.

"So . . ." Nicos pursed his lips. "Did we tell you Prince Veiko departed for Thasia?"

"That's good," Astrea said.

"Yes, we're hoping it yields *something*," Eliana murmured. "It would be ideal if the Tornamians agreed to ally with us against my father, but we'll see. President Sikori's always been keen on staying out of Helosia's . . . political issues."

Cressida's features tightened as she folded her arms over her stomach.

"And your parents wanted me to tell you to be careful," Eliana said to Cressida. "Both of you."

"And they're settling in alright?" Astrea asked.

"Yes, they seem to like it in Talmaris, actually." Eliana smoothed a nonexistent wrinkle from her pants. "Your mother's won over the grand duchess by touring the gardens with her. Hardly the most pressing matter at hand, but I suppose spending time building goodwill never hurt anything, right?"

Cressida mumbled some kind of agreement.

Eliana huffed. "What, Cress? Are you mad at me?"

"No." Cressida's response was barely audible over the rumble of the engine.

"Is she mad?" Eliana asked Astrea.

"Don't drag me into this," Astrea muttered. "We have enough to worry about without the two of you fighting."

Eliana lifted her chin, rust red annoyance flaring bright around her. "We're not fighting."

"At least that's one thing we agree on," Cressida said.

"Oh, so we *are* fighting?" Eliana leaned forward, closing little of the gap between their opposing benches. "Is this about the daggers?"

Cressida turned away from her. "If you have to ask, you're denser than I thought."

"For fuck's sake . . ." Nicos ran a freckled hand over his face. "You two had better figure this out before we get to Helosia. Kaius is going to be all over it if he senses anything wrong between us."

"I don't understand why you're so upset," Eliana said. "You kept your dagger when Jin offered you the opportunity to hand it over to someone else."

"Just because I understand why we need to make weapons like this doesn't mean I like it or even agree with it," Cressida snapped. "Fuck, Ellie, you didn't see what this"—she pulled her dagger out of its sheath on her belt—"did to that Paragon guy in Kalama. You didn't see what the weapon *I* made did to him."

"He tortured Az and was going to do the same to Jin. He would've killed you both in Kalama. I'd hardly call his death a tragedy."

"Just because I hated him and he was dangerous doesn't mean . . ." Cressida huffed and shoved the dagger back in its case. "Never mind."

"Tell me."

"No."

"Where is this coming from?" Eliana asked, yellow worry and gray confusion pulsing around her. "I don't understand."

"I don't expect you to."

"What kind of friend am I if I don't at least try to understand?"

"You didn't seem to want to understand yesterday. You shot me down in front of *everyone*, like my concerns didn't even matter."

"That's what this is about?" Eliana asked.

"You just waltz in here at the last minute and start giving orders—"

"I hardly think asking you to make a couple of weapons is giving orders," Eliana said.

"In front of everyone? Saying you'll find someone else to do it?" Cressida scoffed. "At least own up to it."

"I don't feel as if I have anything to own up to!"

"What I think Cress is trying to say, Ellie, is that we haven't exactly been, well, *involved* in any of this like she and Az have," Nicos said.

"We've been involved," Eliana protested.

"I mean, sure, in Talmaris, but it's not like we went on that mission to Kalama," he said. "It's not the same. We've barely left Ysabel's palace for the last few months."

"Because nobody's let me," Eliana said. "Jin didn't even want me to go talk to Kaius, remember? And I'm here anyway. It's hardly my fault that Jin and Ysabel are trying to protect me."

"Nicos is right," Cressida said. "You don't *get* it, Ellie. You didn't see any of it. It's just frustrating to have you come in out of nowhere and start giving orders."

"I didn't order you—"

"It sure felt like it."

Red anger and steel pain spiked in both Eliana and Cressida's auras, the colors crossing the gap between their seats and braiding together.

"You know," Astrea said gently, "it seems like you two are feeling a lot of the same things."

"Really?" Cressida asked skeptically.

"Red anger," Astrea said. "Steel pain. You're both upset."

"What's it like?" Eliana asked. "Seeing that all the time, I mean."

"Overwhelming sometimes, but I'm used to it. And it's very useful when two stubborn friends don't want to find some common ground."

At that, Nicos actually smiled. "All the times over the years I could've used your insight, Az," he said.

"Yes, well, we're here now," she said. "And Nicos is right. If Kaius even suspects there's an issue, he'll try to find a way to exploit it. You know him, always trying to make every situation worse."

Eliana scoffed. "You can say that again."

As Cressida took a deep breath and blew it out slowly, the colors raging around her dimmed and wavered. They shrank back until they were just a sheer veil around her. "I just don't appreciate feeling like I'm not being heard, Ellie," she said. "And if you're going to really lead the rebellion, like *really* lead it, and take over Helosia, I think you need to listen more."

Hot anger burned Astrea's skin, followed by scorching embarrassment. "I'm sorry," Eliana said. "I didn't mean to make you feel that way. I just thought the weapons were important."

"They are," Cressida said. "Despite my discomfort with them, I understand. They level the playing field, so to speak. I'll make more if we need them. Just know that I really, really don't like them."

"Your objections are noted," Eliana said. "And thank you."

"You're welcome."

Tenuous silence settled over the truck, or as much silence as they could have with the terribly loud engine.

Until Nicos said, "That wasn't so hard, was it?"

"Skies, you're annoying," Cressida said with a laugh.

He smiled. "And you're laughing, so doesn't that make it all better?"

Eliana leaned back in her seat. "I won't feel better until we get what we've come for and are back in Talmaris."

"That we absolutely can agree on," Cressida said. "I hope Lennor's alright. And Civan and Noemi, too."

"You like Lennor?" Eliana asked.

"Skies, don't start."

"She does," Astrea said.

"Hey!" Cressida nudged Astrea's shoulder. "Don't rat me out."

"How is it ratting you out when obviously Ellie picked up on it?"

"I can't get out of this truck fast enough," Cressida mumbled.

As the rest of the tension between Cressida and Eliana bled away and was replaced by murmured worries and hypotheticals for their visit with Kaius, Astrea settled back into her bench as much as she could. She was with Eliana; they couldn't be done with this fast enough for her liking.

Chapter 11

It was official; Astrea hated sitting in trucks for so long. Her bottom hurt, and her back muscles were tight, and despite not actually *doing* anything, fatigue was seeping into her bones. Fresh air and a stretch would be nice.

"We should almost be at the border." Nicos leaned forward to look through the front of the truck. "And then it's not a far drive to the base from there."

"Thank the skies," Eliana muttered.

Astrea leaned forward, too, and followed Nicos's gaze. There wasn't much to see other than tall trees and the truck in front of them and . . . why was it stopping?

"What's going on?" she asked Nicos.

"I'm not sure," he said.

They all straightened in their seats. Astrea had kept her senses pushed out relatively wide for the duration of their trip, but she pushed them out wider and wider. Other than a whisper of confusion from the truck ahead of theirs, nothing seemed out of the ordinary. Nothing changed. No cold spike in energy. No anger or hatred.

Astrea scooted forward until she was on the edge of the hard bench. Outside, several soldiers in red uniforms approached their truck.

"Helosians," Nicos said. "Maybe Kaius's. Don't say anything."

The driver rolled down their window, and Astrea couldn't hear much of the conversation she had with the Helosian guard. She was one of Lucian's people; Astrea knew that much.

"What's going on?" Cressida whispered to her.

"I guess they're doing some kind of security check?" Astrea half asked, half stated. Yes, it seemed to be based on the conversation she could hear. But why would Kaius bother? Surely he'd alerted the guards on the border about the convoy coming in.

After another tortuous minute, the truck in front of theirs rolled forward. Then their driver put the vehicle back in gear. They started on again, passing by a few more Helosian soldiers on either side of the road.

"Was that it?" Cressida asked. "That easy to get back in?"

"I'm sure they're expecting us," Eliana said. "Still . . ."

Astrea leaned against the truck's wall, wincing as her lower back twinged. She wished she was with Jin, if only to ask him about what he expected from Kaius. When they'd talked about it the night before with the team, he hadn't really had any expectations for this mission. He'd said to be ready for anything. That felt impossible, though. *Maybe I'll have a better read on Kaius once we're face-to-face with him.* Kaius had always been open to her magic, but that hardly made his messy energy easier to interpret.

More than half an hour later, Nicos sat up straighter and peered out the front windows again. Orange anxiety and red determination surged forth in his aura. Astrea, Cressida, and Eliana all leaned forward, too.

"Is that it?" Cressida asked.

"That's Fort Nightshade," Nicos said.

"How can you be sure?" she asked.

"Besides the fact that it's where we directed the Novarians to go?" Nicos asked. Astrea couldn't see, but she was sure he rolled his eyes. "My parents were stationed at a base to the south for a few months when I was young. I visited here once when I was six."

"And you remember that?" Cressida asked.

"I remember enough. It seemed bigger when I was a child, though."

She frowned. "And you didn't think to mention this last night?"

"I did," he said. "You'd left the room for the night."

"Oh."

Astrea hadn't been in the room for that part of the conversation either, apparently. "Your parents were stationed nearby?"

"Yeah," Nicos said. "We left when I was seven. Haven't been back here in years. I don't think one visit as a young child makes me an expert on this place."

"At least we're here," Eliana said. "Now we can figure out how to deal with Kaius."

Uncertainty swept through Astrea like a storm, her palms growing clammy. She wiped them on her pants, but the thick fabric did nothing to dry them. She repeated the motion twice before giving up.

The truck slowed, nowhere near the entrance to the base. Nicos moved toward the rear and opened the doors. He jumped out. "Wait here," he said before disappearing around the corner.

Eliana had already pushed herself to a stand, not having to duck thanks to her short stature. Cressida, though, stooped a little as she also shoved to her feet. Astrea stayed on the edge of her seat.

All around her, more emotions and walls started flickering into her awareness. Many were far away, though some were the very people on her team. A familiar, heavy wall approached, then Jin poked his head into the back of the truck.

"You can come out. I don't think he's going to shoot us," Jin said.

"Oh, wonderful news," Eliana deadpanned as she headed out.

"Here we go," Cressida whispered to Astrea as they, too, exited the truck.

The landscape here in northern Helosia was similar to that near Fort Silverpine: tall trees as far as the eye could see, though the area around the base was mostly cleared out. It was remote, that was for sure. Astrea couldn't see anything besides the tan brick fort walls and the blue sky.

"Anything, Az?" Jin asked as they circled the middle truck.

"Just what I'd expect," she said. "No Caliban, though. At least not within my range."

"I'm not sure I like that. I'd like to know where he is."

There was really only one way for Astrea to figure that out. They had to get closer to Fort Nightshade.

They joined Lucian and a few of the others. The first truck in their convoy blocked out the sight of most of the base. Behind Astrea, Adi, Marko, and Vernie approached.

"We're ready to go?" Lucian asked none of them in particular.

"Let's get this started, Commander," Eliana said. "The sooner we're done with Kaius, the better."

"We leave if anything seems off," Jin said. "And I mean anything."

Lucian barked orders to some of the Novarians, commanding most of them to stay put and keep the trucks ready. Then he motioned for Jin to lead the way.

Was it wise to have Jin walk at the front of the pack? And was it foolish for Eliana to step up right alongside him? Probably, but Astrea hurried after them anyway.

Fort Nightshade rose up in front of them, its tan brick exterior walls clearly weathered over the years. No artillery lined the battlements like back at Silverpine, though several red airships sat quiet nearby.

The only thing that gave Astrea pause was where Kaius stood outside the fort's gates, dressed in Auris red and aura bursting with energy. Gray hate, rusty annoyance, even a tinge of orange fear. What could Kaius possibly have to be scared about? He was the one who had called the meeting, the one who had kidnapped Jin's team and Adi's sister. Did he fear the retribution Jin would surely rain down on him given the opportunity?

Giddy anticipation slithered up Astrea's limbs. The feeling made her want to pull her energy back until she felt nothing at all. Instead, she pushed it out as wide as it could go, reaching past Kaius in hopes of finding—there. That cold, somewhere deeper inside the fort.

"Caliban's here," Astrea said. "I assume it's him, anyway."

"Yes, I feel him," Lucian replied from behind her.

"Just him?" Jin asked. When Astrea and Lucian confirmed, he said, "At least it's just the one."

There might've been just one void mage, but Astrea still didn't like it. At least Lucian and Vernie could souleat like her. With any luck, they would be able to control him. Well, with any *real* luck, they wouldn't need to do that, and they could get Lennor, Civan, and Noemi back without any violence.

"Can you feel if anyone's hurt?" Jin asked.

Astrea didn't feel any kind of pain, but that didn't mean Lennor, Civan, and Noemi were fine. What if Kaius was drugging them like the Paragon had drugged Astrea? There would be nothing for her to feel if the twins and Adi's sister were unconscious.

"None that I can feel, but we'll stay on the lookout," Lucian said.

"Let's make this quick." Jin continued on, aiming straight for Kaius. Everything in his posture was aggressive, predatory, highly controlled. If his wall hadn't been up, surely the heat of his rage would've burned Astrea's skin.

"Varojin! Eliana!" Kaius called, raising his hand up in greeting as they got closer. The guards at his back remained stiff, unmoving. "So good to see you made it."

When they were about twenty feet away from Kaius, Jin and Eliana stopped. It was a strange sight, witnessing the Auris siblings literally at odds like this. Standing on opposite sides of a Helosian base, one backed by red-clad imperial guards and the others backed by black-and-blue-clad Novarians and Helosians.

Astrea pushed her shoulders back, watching bright, clear energy snap out around Kaius. Red anger. Green curiosity. White fear. Gray hate. Rust red annoyance. His anticipation still crawled up Astrea's limbs, making her nauseous.

Jin crossed his arms over his chest. "Where are my people?"

"Really?" Kaius drawled, his lips forming a perfect pout. "No greeting for your big brother?"

"My people?" Jin asked again.

"So self-righteous." Kaius huffed. "They're fine."

"That's not good enough."

"What I think Jin is trying to say"—Eliana took a step forward—"is that we're here, as you've asked us to be. What is it you wanted to see us for?"

"I wanted to see why the fuck you two are going against Father. I knew you were up to no good when you fled that day, but sneaking back into the capital? Stealing from us?" Kaius's cold golden gaze slid to where Astrea stood with Cressida. "Miss Sovna. Miss Nikaphoros. I'm offended you didn't say hello to me at the library."

Astrea blanched. Yes, they'd been there, but how did—

"Don't look so surprised. Miss Zornovski told me everything."

"Did you hurt her?" Jin asked.

Kaius sniffed. "She'll pay for her crimes."

What did that mean? Prison? Worse? Astrea's stomach dropped.

"As for you lot and *your* crimes," Kaius continued, "I know you've rejected Father's offer since you're obviously trying to interfere with his plans."

"And?" Eliana asked.

"I'm here with a new opportunity for you. Let's go inside and discuss."

"I'm not going anywhere until you tell me where my people are," Jin said. "This isn't just about your negotiations."

"I will show you your people if you would just follow me," Kaius barked. "I'll only offer it this once."

Grudgingly, Jin sighed and stalked forward. As Eliana rushed after him, Nicos pulled her back.

"Wait, Ellie," Nicos hissed under his breath. "Let Jin go first."

Adi, Zephyrine, and Marko were right behind Jin, flanking him in a way that made Astrea think it might be some practiced formation. Astrea, Cressida, and the rest followed.

Kaius paused at the base's gate and looked over his shoulder. "No Novarians," he said.

"You have your people, so we should have ours," Jin said.

Kaius surveyed the group, skipping from Marko to Vernie to Lucian, then back again. "You," he snapped at Lucian. "You can come."

"Why me?" Lucian asked.

"Because you're obviously their leader." Kaius stormed into the base.

Jin glanced at Vernie and Marko, then Eliana. She nodded. With a sigh, Jin said, "Vernie, Marko, stay here. If something happens, go back to Silverpine."

"You don't want us to come in after you?" Marko asked.

"No."

Lucian nodded at his people, some silent signal. Did he really think that was a good idea? Astrea fidgeted with the end of her braid. With Lucian's apparent approval, Jin continued on after his brother. The rest of them followed his lead.

The inside of Fort Nightshade was significantly smaller than Fort Silverpine. Its interior was sparse, save for the Helosian soldiers and a few trucks parked nearby. No artillery. No weapons Astrea could see. No sign of their missing team, either. The deeper they walked into the base, it was just more of the same. Nothing Astrea could feel signaled where Lennor, Civan, and Noemi might be.

Kaius led them across the courtyard, past the watchful Helosian soldiers, and toward a door leading into a tan brick building. A guard dressed in Auris red opened the door. Kaius waltzed through.

"Keep following, Varojin," he called over his shoulder.

Jin's back heaved as he crossed the threshold. Nicos went next, then Eliana followed him through into the waiting shadows. Although Astrea sensed nothing nefarious—besides Kaius's usual nonsense—unease prickled the back of her neck.

"Go, Az," Adi whispered as he nudged her forward. "We're right behind you."

She forced her feet forward.

Kaius led them down several dimly lit hallways; the candles in the wall sconces did little to help.

"Where could he possibly be taking us?" Cressida whispered, the words strained.

"I don't know," Astrea murmured. Something about it didn't feel right, even if Kaius had agreed to take them to Lennor, Civan, and Noemi. Could Jin sense it? Or Adi? Orange anxiety wavered around Cressida, but Astrea couldn't read the rest of them.

After what felt like forever traipsing through the bowels of the fort, Kaius stopped in front of another door. This one, solid dark wood, was guarded by four Helosians.

"Prince Kaius—" one with pale, freckled skin and red hair started.

"Stand aside," Kaius snapped.

The redheaded guard peered over Kaius's shoulder—surely looking at Eliana and Jin—and swallowed hard. Rough hesitation and cold fear warred on Astrea's skin. The four guards shuffled away, farther down the hall. With them gone, Kaius pulled a key from his pocket and unlocked the door. It opened with a heavy groan. More cold fear pushed against Astrea, coating her from the inside out.

Kaius stepped into the room. "Someone's here to see you."

Red rage flared around Jin as he followed his brother. "At least you weren't lying," he said to Kaius.

As Astrea peeked around Jin's broad frame, she caught sight of familiar small, round faces and a young woman who shared Adi's dark brown complexion. They were locked behind platinum bars at the far end of the room. No pain surged through Astrea. White fear and mint relief pulsed in the air erratically.

"They're uninjured, at least as far as I can tell," Astrea said to Jin.

"I've been a perfectly agreeable host considering the circumstances," Kaius said, mostly aimed at Jin. "Your people will tell you as much."

Lennor moved in front of Civan and Noemi. "We're fine, Captain," she said quietly. "I promise."

Motioning between the prison cell and the open door, Kaius said, "And now that you've seen your people, it's time we talk."

"So talk," Eliana said.

"Not here." When she huffed, Kaius added, "Patience never has been your strong suit, Eliana. And patience is a necessary trait in a leader. Just one more reason you're unfit for the throne."

As if Kaius himself were patient? The mere suggestion was laughable.

"Give me a minute with them," Jin said to Kaius. "Then we'll talk."

Astrea expected Kaius to refuse, to blow Jin off like he always did. But with a small nod, he said, "Fine. I'll be waiting."

As Kaius shoved past them and out the door again, Astrea set a hand on Eliana's shoulder. The electricity around her was palpable, making the hairs on Astrea's arms stand on end. "He's just trying to get to you," Astrea whispered.

"He always gets to me," Eliana said. "Just being in the same room as him gets to me. His *existence* gets to me."

Jin crossed to the other side of the room, then squatted down in front of the bars. "You're truly alright?" he asked Lennor.

"Fine," she said. "Not great but fine."

Adi joined them, squatting down next to Jin and reaching out toward his sister. "Noemi, I—"

Noemi moved around Lennor and grabbed Adi's hand. "I'm fine." Her voice was scratchy, like she hadn't had any water. Her black ringlet curls were pulled back into a low bun, and her eyes were red and tired, just like the twins'. "I'm fine, Adi."

Adi looked back at Astrea, as if to ask if his sister was telling the truth or not. She nodded at him. Mint relief coated her tongue.

"And Kaius hasn't touched any of you?" Jin asked.

Lennor shook her head. "There was a scuffle when he caught up to us, but he hasn't actually come near us otherwise."

Adi's shoulders rolled forward, and he leaned his head against the bars, squeezing his sister's hand again. Astrea wasn't sure if Kaius had left the twins and Noemi alone because he had some small shred of decency left in him, or if he feared what Jin would do had his team been hurt.

"Varojin! Eliana!" Kaius's voice boomed from in the hallway. "Time's up! Come chat."

"I'm sorry," Jin said to the three of them. Shoving to his feet, he added, "We'll be back, I promise."

Astrea knew they couldn't *do* anything in that moment, but it seemed wrong to just leave the room. She swallowed her reservations and followed everyone else out the door.

Kaius stood a few feet away from the entrance, hands tucked in his pockets. The guards near him shifted awkwardly as he said, "Took you long enough."

"I'd like to leave Commander Lucian, Adi, and Cressida here with them," Jin said.

Kaius raised an eyebrow. "Don't trust me?"

"I'd just feel better if someone else stays with them."

Kaius's lips pursed, as if he were considering what Jin had said. His focus slid to Eliana, then to where Astrea stood in the back. "I'll allow it."

Mint relief snapped out from Adi in sharp, quick beats. But that still begged the question of how they'd actually get the twins and Noemi out. The prison bars were platinum, which meant Cressida couldn't use her magic. And Astrea doubted Kaius would release them out of the kindness of his heart. He didn't have a kind heart.

Shouting orders at the guards standing nearby, Kaius turned and continued back down the hallway they'd come from. Astrea snuck a quick glance over her shoulder as she followed the others, watching as more of that minty relief spread around Adi and Cressida. They returned to the holding room with Lucian.

She pushed her shoulders back and tried to focus on Kaius. He was still a mix of emotions: annoyance, anger, pride, worry, anticipation. It suffocated Astrea, and for a moment, she considered just grabbing hold of all that energy and forcing Kaius to his knees so they could grab the team and run. But in a base full of Helosian soldiers? That wasn't wise.

Besides, the very loose plan Eliana and Jin had agreed upon was to see what information Kaius would hand over, then try to negotiate the release of the twins and Noemi. And if Kaius wouldn't negotiate, then the backup plan was to use "any means necessary." It wasn't a very solid plan, but going in with so little information, what else could they do?

They turned down one more hallway, this one brighter and wider than the others. Kaius led them into a large room filled with crates and sheet-covered furniture. It looked more like storage than someplace fit for anyone to work out of.

"You have some nerve, Varojin." As Kaius leaned back across the desk, its white cloth cover wrinkled. "I mean, defying Father's direct orders and coming back to Helosia, not to join us but to become little more than a thief and kidnapper."

"As if you aren't?" Jin challenged.

"Taking deserters into custody after *they* kidnapped an innocent civilian is hardly wrong."

"And putting that innocent civilian into prison?"

"Now suspected of treason." Kaius waved a hand. "Honestly, do I have to spell it out for you?"

Jin clenched his jaw as he said, "And what must I do to secure their release?"

"Give me the book your little girlfriend stole from me." Kaius smiled at Astrea. "Though I must admit, Miss Sovna, I didn't think you had it in you. But it's always the quiet ones we must watch out for, isn't it?"

"We don't have the book," Astrea lied.

"Oh?" Kaius cocked an eyebrow. "Then where is it?"

"It was destroyed when our airship was shot out of the sky by the Paragon," Jin said. Kaius didn't react to the name at all. "We lost everything when the ship crashed."

"How convenient," Kaius drawled.

"I'd hardly call nearly dying *convenient*," Eliana said. "What else can we do to secure their release since we cannot meet your terms?"

"Well, I'm afraid there's nothing else *to* do," Kaius said, "unless you both want to return to Kalama in handcuffs in their place. Bring the Lightbringer, too. Or you could actually come home and help Father, though it seems you've already decided not to do that."

"What does he need help with?" Eliana asked.

"Oh, you know exactly what he's doing, Eliana." Kaius scoffed. "The Badlands? He's getting closer to what he's been looking for, and then, he'll finally be able to put an end to things in Corsyca. He's going to finally be able to fulfill the Auris dynasty's destiny."

Eliana's voice didn't waver as she said, "And what is that?"

"What it's always been." Kaius sniffed, as if Eliana's question was entirely foolish and the answer completely obvious. "Expanding across the continent."

What Astrea didn't understand was why. Why build the Helosian Empire up across the entire continent? Didn't Emperor Aelius already have enough? Hadn't he and his ancestors conquered enough? Was it about pride rather than resources? Ego? Or just power?

"We don't need to make Helosia any bigger," Eliana said. "Kaius, come on. Surely you see how many people will be hurt if Father begins that kind of conquest."

"If people simply stand down and welcome him as their rightful leader, nobody has to get hurt."

Was Kaius that much of a fool? Astrea glanced up at Zephyrine, who stood next to her. The general's fingers twitched.

"Rightful leader? Kaius, our family has no *right* to anything just because we've ruled Helosia for generations," Eliana said. "We only came to power because of war and bloodshed."

"Spoken like a true rebel," Kaius mused. "Or like a true traitor."

"Not wanting innocent people to die makes me a traitor?" Eliana snapped. Lightning flickered around her fingertips. "Fine. Then declare me a traitor. Tell the Senate and aristocracy why I've run, that I'm not willing to let Father run amuck with these weapons he's trying to build."

"Oh, so you *did* read the book before it was lost." Kaius's lips curled into a mean smile.

"Ellie's right, Kaius," Jin said. "You don't understand the scale of destruction it will bring."

"I understand exactly what it will bring. You said we only came to power through bloodshed and war, Eliana. You were right. But what you don't seem to understand is that's the only way to maintain power. You think the Zaikudi and Delians will just let us exist?" Vermilion pride and crimson rage swirled around Kaius in a bloody wave. "No. The moment we stop pushing into their territory, that's when they'll move into ours. So what better way to stop them than just taking them over entirely?"

What was the point in trying to reason with Kaius? It was clear he'd never see the fault behind his words and logic.

Jin huffed. "If we can't give you the book to secure my people's release, then what do you want, Kaius?"

"I already told you. Return with me to Kalama, or I'll be taking your teammates and Miss Kuwat in your places."

"Absolutely not."

"Well," Kaius drawled as the temperature in the room dropped, "*that's* too bad."

"Jin—" Astrea started.

Shadows swirled up from the ground. Caliban blinked into existence. The void seemed to coat his skin, snaking up his arms and even tinging the ends of his snow white hair. Darkness swirled around his palms as the shadows at the edges of the room stretched and grew.

Astrea flung one hand out. The cold burned her fingers, crackling painfully along her skin, up her arms and into her chest. It suffocated her.

Caliban smiled. "Nice try, *Souleater*." The shadows crawling along his skin pulsed in time with Astrea's heart as he said, "Your Imperial Highness?"

Kaius nodded. "Do it."

Swirling darkness shot forward from Caliban and every corner of the room. Hot fire exploded around Jin, heating Astrea's freezing skin. It circled around the five of them—him, Eliana, Nicos, Zephyrine, Astrea. Outside the barrier, the shadows pressed in closer, like they were trying to find a way through.

Jin motioned for the door. "Go!"

Nicos shoved Eliana forward. She grabbed Astrea's arm. They passed through the door just as that cold spiked again.

Wrenching her arm free from Eliana's tight grasp, Astrea pivoted back toward the room. Black shadow and orange flames churned together behind Jin. He grabbed Astrea's shoulders, pushing her back as the floor trembled.

Rock and brick exploded out from the room. Astrea fell back as everything went dark.

Chapter 12

The boom of the explosion cut off abruptly, like someone had turned off a radio. Astrea's ears rang. Her vision spun. Jin lay on top of her, a heavy shield, for just a heartbeat.

He hauled her to her feet. Fire and shadow swirled together in the doorway. Caliban stepped forward. Blue lightning flickered behind him.

"Go help Adi and Cress," Jin said to Astrea, though his voice sounded like he was underwater. "Meet back at the front gate. Be quick."

He and Zephyrine stepped forward, a gust of wind pushing Caliban and the lightning—Kaius—back several feet. Lightning, fire, and shadow melded together as red anger and gray hate spiraled through the air.

Eliana grabbed Astrea's hand and tugged her away. Shoving her reservations down, Astrea sprinted back into the base with Eliana in front of her and Nicos behind them both. Astrea had to trust that Jin and Zephyrine could take care of themselves.

As they approached a corner, Astrea stopped. "Wait," she said. Light danced around her fingers as she placed her hands on either side of her head. The ringing in her ears subsided. "Ellie?"

When Eliana nodded, Astrea repeated the healing on her, then on Nicos, too. Her ears felt half full, almost like she had a head cold, but at least there was no ghostly ringing.

"Thanks, Az," Eliana said.

"Keep going." Nicos nudged them both forward. "Go, go."

They continued on, running down corridor after corridor. The walls and floor still shook occasionally, no doubt the effects of Jin and Kaius's fight. Astrea forced her legs to keep going no matter how badly she wanted to turn back to help.

As they neared another junction, confusion, fear, and anger singed Astrea's skin. "Guards up ahead," she said.

They rounded the bend. Four Helosian soldiers dressed in crimson uniforms stood in the hallway. Two stepped forward, their red anger swelling into hot, heavy rage as they stared at Eliana.

Fire burned over one man's palms. It shot forward. Nicos lunged between Astrea and Eliana, catching the flames with one large hand and sending it slamming back into the other Fireweaver. He tumbled to the ground, smashing his head against the ground and groaning.

Astrea bit her tongue as echoes of his pain flooded her senses.

Rage sparked around the second mage. The woman stretched her hands out. Astrea grabbed the soldier's anger, yanking it back and then pushing it forward again. Its heat burned Astrea's palms. Sweat beaded on her forehead. The woman screamed and dropped to her knees, whispers of her pain pinging in Astrea's chest.

"What . . . what is she doing?" one of the other two Helosians asked. Both of them stood to one side of the hall, looking between Eliana, Astrea, and the guards now on the floor.

Astrea's arms trembled, her breath coming in quick, sharp gasps as she twisted and twisted the soldier's rage. Red swirled in her vision. Bile crept up her throat.

Nicos stepped forward. "Do you two follow Prince Kaius?"

"We . . ."

"Do you follow my brother?" Eliana asked. "Do you know what he's doing here?"

"No, Your Imperial Highness," said one of the guards. She was a short, plump woman with red hair and a fair complexion, much like Nicos's. "I was conscripted last year for the war. I got reassigned to this unit a month ago."

"Then will you let us pass?"

The redhead looked at her companion, a man with sepia skin and close-cropped black hair. He nodded, and then the redhead nodded at Eliana. "Yes, Your Imperial Highness."

"Ellie—" Astrea couldn't get out any more than that. Her body strained as that hate threatened to bury her.

"Here." The man pulled something metallic off his belt. "To hold them."

Nicos knelt next to the Fireweaver first, then rolled his unconscious form over and secured his hands with the cuffs.

The woman trapped by Astrea's souleating let out a sputtering cough. Her hatred pushed and pushed into Astrea's bones, setting her whole body ablaze.

Nicos cracked a punch across the woman's temple, catching her body as she slumped to the floor. Astrea dropped her outstretched arms, sucking in a deep breath as she tried to think of everything good she could. But those thoughts of Jin, of her friends and family, weren't enough to stop the nausea and pain from overwhelming her. She turned and retched, little more than water and bile coming up.

Astrea squeezed her eyes shut and wiped the corners of her mouth. *Just focus.* She straightened and made herself step up next to Eliana.

"She'll know we let you go," the redhead whispered as Nicos handcuffed the unconscious Earthmover.

"Then come with us," Eliana said hurriedly. "We'll take you to Novaria."

"Novaria?" The redhead's eyebrows furrowed, and lavender surprise spiked around her. "The rumors are true?"

"Yes." Another explosion rocked the building; it sounded like it had come from where they left Jin and Zephyrine. "Come now or make it to the Novarian border on your own," Eliana said. "I'm sorry, I can't stay. You'll be welcome at Fort Silverpine if you decide to follow us."

Heavy regret pushed against Astrea's skin as Eliana rushed past the soldiers. Astrea forced her legs to carry her after the princess.

Recruitment. Eliana was recruiting people to follow her. While Kaius and Jin were fighting in another part of the building. While they were trying to escape.

How quickly now would confirmation of the rumors spread through the Helosian ranks? Even if those two soldiers deserted, the angry ones would surely talk about what happened.

They rounded another corner. Lavender surprise exploded around Eliana as she slammed into someone dressed in dark blue. Astrea barely skidded to a stop in time to avoid running into her.

"Your Imperial Highness." Lucian's hands rested on Eliana's shoulders as he steadied them both. "What's happening?"

"Kaius and Caliban attacked us. Jin and Zephyrine are holding them off," Eliana said. "The twins? Noemi?"

"Adi and Cressida are working on it."

"And the other soldiers?"

"More coming. We need to go back to the others."

Behind Astrea, worry and uncertainty reached out for her, faint as the energy moved farther and farther away. Wind howled somewhere down the corridor.

"Quickly, quickly." Lucian ushered them all past him. "Up ahead, turn right."

Nicos moved around Astrea, leading them through Lucian's directions. A few Helosian soldiers were unconscious on the floor, apparently unharmed. A small part of Astrea was surprised Lucian hadn't done more.

"On your left," Lucian said.

"I know!" Nicos called over his shoulder.

They veered left into a familiar room. Inside, Cressida and Adi were unlocking the cell with a small key. The cell door swung open with a screech. Adi lunged inside, pulling Noemi into a tight embrace. Relief pulsed through the room, minty cool and impossible to ignore.

"Make it a quick reunion, please." Lucian stalked back toward the doorway. "Nicos, with me. Five are coming this way."

"Stay with Cressida," Adi said to his sister as he pulled away. "I'll be right back. Check on them please, Az!" He bolted for the door.

Outside, shouts in Helosian were followed by a clash of metal on metal, the roar of fire, and bright light that cast strange shadows along the corridor walls. Every part of Astrea's mind screamed at her to go help, but that was not her fight. She needed to make sure everyone was alright. Astrea helped Noemi out of the cell; her limbs trembled, making it hard for her to walk.

"Can you take a deep breath?" Astrea asked her. She sucked in a deep breath herself, then pushed it out slowly. "Like that."

Noemi's shallow breaths evened out with each passing second until finally, she breathed in and held it for a few seconds.

"Keep doing that." Beyond the noise and panic building in the room, and beyond the echo of rage still causing pain in her own body, Astrea couldn't separate out how Noemi was feeling. "Is anything hurt? I'm a healer."

"Not hurt," Noemi whispered. White terror spiked around her as another explosion rocked the walls. A few pieces of the ceiling broke away and crumbled onto the floor. "What's happening?"

"My brothers are fighting," Eliana said. "Let's get you out of here, alright?"

Noemi nodded as Cressida put an arm around her shoulders and guided her toward the door.

"You two good?" Astrea asked the twins as they exited the cell.

"We're good." Lennor shook her arms out. Her black fatigues were rumpled, and her skin was a bit sallow. A bruise on her forehead had begun healing, now mostly yellow. "Kaius confiscated our armor and weapons."

"I'll make you new armor," Adi said, poking his head back in the room. "We gotta go."

Astrea followed them all into the hallway, where more Helosian soldiers lay unconscious on the ground. A few of them were bleeding. Cressida kept one arm around Noemi as Adi and Lucian led the way through the maze of corridors.

She couldn't help it; Astrea kept looking over her shoulder even though she sensed no one heading their way.

"Jin said to meet him by the front gate," Astrea called to Adi. "Are we going the right way?"

"I think so!"

"You *think* so?"

Stopping in the middle of the next hallway, Adi pointed to the floor. There was a small door there, likely leading to some kind of basement. "Here."

"That'll take us out?" Eliana asked.

"Leads to tunnels," Adi said. "You feel 'em too, Cress?"

"Yeah," she said. "Now let's go!"

Adi opened the door. There weren't even stairs; there was just a drop down into the dark tunnel waiting below. But nobody argued, instead dropping in one by one. It took every ounce of strength Astrea had left to shove her fear away and follow her friends. Her belly flipped as she descended into the darkness, but Civan helped steady her as she stumbled forward. Light exploded over Lucian's hand just as Adi jumped inside and yanked the door closed with him.

"We'll tunnel up into the courtyard to meet Jin," Adi said.

"Yeah, but we'll be going up blind," Nicos replied.

"Not if Az and Lucian can tell us where people are."

Astrea had no idea where they were in the fort, let alone how to tell when they'd reached the courtyard. She'd just have to try.

As they jogged after Adi, Lucian's light cast strange shadows along the floors and walls, revealing tan brick instead of the dark aetherium Astrea had been scared to see.

Chaotic energy pulsed high above them. Worry, pain, anger, anxiety, fear, terror, rage—it was all just out of reach, like Astrea's magic wanted to take hold of it but couldn't. They continued on like that, Astrea and Lucian's light and Nicos and Eliana's fire the only thing keeping the shadows at bay.

"Do we have an airship out of here?" Lennor asked.

"Trucks," Lucian said.

"Oh, *great.*"

"Do you think the Helosians attacked your people, Commander?" Nicos asked.

"If they did, so help them . . ."

Adi stopped short, his breath steady despite the run. "I think we can go up here," he said, and Cressida confirmed. "Lucian? Az?"

"Nobody in the immediate area," Lucian said. "Though I cannot guarantee they're far off."

"Good enough for me," Adi said. "This should be where Jin wants to meet. Len, Civ, take Noemi to the trucks. Marko should be around here somewhere to help. Cress, take out any weaponry you sense. Az, Lucian, with me. We need to find Jin. Ready?"

Astrea steeled herself as Adi and Cressida pulled the earthen ceiling apart, then formed stairs for them all to ascend. She followed Cressida up, squinting against the afternoon sun. All around them, Helosian soldiers scrambled around. They sprinted past, ignoring her group as they climbed out of the ground. That didn't seem right. But white terror trailed in their wake. The wind kicked up, whipping Astrea's braid around.

A swirling tornado ripped through the area. More Helosians sprinted past, away from the onslaught.

"That's Zephyrine!" Adi shouted over the noise.

How could he be so sure? Astrea didn't see the general or Jin anywhere.

Pointing to their left, Adi yelled to the twins, "Gate's that way! Three Novarian trucks waiting!"

Lennor took Noemi's hand, leading her in the direction of the terrified Helosians.

An explosion boomed near the rear wall of the courtyard. Astrea flinched. Red flame and black smoke rose into the air, unobscured by the dying tornado. The wind cut off as familiar white and chestnut brown hair came into view.

There.

Zephyrine and Jin sprinted away from the fire and toward the gate. And there . . . Jumping closer was Caliban, Kaius in tow. They landed, then disappeared again as ice chilled Astrea to her core.

"Go!" Jin shouted. "Adi, go!"

"You heard the man," Adi said over his shoulder. "To the trucks, now!"

Astrea stayed glued to her spot, watching as Kaius and Caliban appeared, then disappeared, again and again. Adi and Cressida ran forward, arms raising up over their heads. The ground behind Jin and Zephyrine rumbled. Massive earthen spikes littered the courtyard, barely any flat ground to land on except whatever was in front of Jin and Zephyrine.

The next time Kaius and Caliban appeared, they both shouted a curse before disappearing again. They didn't reappear, but Astrea was sure they wouldn't be far off. Caliban couldn't jump that far.

"Go, go, go!" Jin yelled as he got closer.

Lucian grabbed Astrea's forearm and dragged her forward. They cleared the fort's gate, aiming for the field surrounding the base. Helosians and Novarians fought each other, a cacophony of magic. Starlight sparked somewhere ahead, then an echo of pain surged in Astrea's sternum and back, right where it hurt whenever Lucian used the souleating ability on her. Wind gusted, blowing two angry Helosians flat on their backs. A mop of familiar blond hair appeared next to Astrea as Marko fell in line with her.

The fighting slowed as the Novarians retreated, their scarce numbers barely fending off the Helosian attacks.

How were they going to get out of this? Astrea didn't see an escape route.

"There's too many, Commander!" Marko shouted to Lucian.

"We can take them," Astrea said to Lucian between heavy breaths. "You, me, and Vernie."

Teal understanding blossomed around the commander. "Vernie!" he screamed. "Vernie!" Several hundred feet away, near the trucks, someone's attention shifted. Astrea didn't know how Vernie could possibly hear Lucian's shout, but that must have been them. "On my count," Lucian said to Astrea. "Take the right. Vernie and I will take the left."

The Helosians to Astrea's right were giving chase to the retreating Novarians, focused and angry. There had to be two dozen of them, all open and hers for the taking.

"One," Lucian said. "Two. Three."

Skidding to a stop, Astrea threw her hands out in front of her. She reached for all that energy, the anger and pain and fear and chaos surrounding the Helosians. She snapped up color after color, red and gray and white, until her palms burned. She pushed and pulled the energy, letting her own anger bleed into the connection. And when more terror popped up, she plucked those strings even harder.

Pain pulsed through her body again and again as the Helosians fell to their knees, then onto their sides. She lost the energy of several as they passed out, then more of them as wind gusted through the area, so strong it sent them sprawling.

"Go, Az." Jin pushed her forward. "That's good enough."

Her connection with the energy faltered as Jin nudged her forward again. Her muscles seized, then loosened, as the searing heat of it all rushed away. Her head pounded. Her mouth went dry. But she kept going, trailing behind Lucian, Eliana, Nicos, and Cressida.

Civan ran toward them with long, steady strides. Why was he back? He was supposed to be with his sister. He was supposed to be at the trucks.

"Need help?" he asked Jin as he reached them.

"No, let's get out of here."

The distance between them and the trucks continued to shrink. Engines rumbled. Marko sprinted ahead, shouting orders in Novarian.

They were almost there. The Helosians were still trying to recover from the souleating.

They could make it.

Astrea pushed her legs faster.

A metallic *ping, ping, ping* echoed through the open space. Sharp pain exploded in Astrea's abdomen, and she cried out as she stumbled. Civan shouted as he fell forward.

"Sharpshooter!" Adi yelled. An earthen wall shot up behind them, and Adi knelt down next to Civan. "Hey, Civ, hey. Come on."

Adi rolled him over. Blood leaked from Civan's gut, staining his already black fatigues even darker. A loud boom shook the air.

"Incoming!" Cressida shouted. The earthen wall shot higher, arcing over their heads. Something collided with it, and Cressida grunted as she stretched her arms out, holding it in place. "I thought they didn't have any artillery!"

"Doesn't matter," Jin said. "Adi, Az, get Civan out of here. Cress, Zephyrine, with me."

An earthen stretcher formed under Civan, lifting him into the air. Astrea pulled on as much light as she could muster, setting her hand on Civan's chest. Pain seared her stomach, burning a hole straight through her. Civan moaned.

Moaning was good. It meant he was still alive.

As Adi propelled the stretcher forward, Astrea ran to keep up with it. She didn't dare take her eyes off the Novarian trucks ahead of them or the way Marko was helping Noemi scramble into the back of one of the vehicles.

"There, Cress!" Jin yelled. "Right corner!"

The air sizzled. A thunderous boom pulsed in the air, making the ground tremble and shake. Pain shot through Astrea, a thousand times harder than anything she'd sensed from the team. Screams met her ears, distant but unignorable.

Astrea nearly tripped over herself, trying to keep up with Adi and the stretcher. Civan groaned even as Astrea kept her hand on his shoulder, light pulsing between their two bodies. Fully healing him would take so much more. So, so much more. She needed to stop, take a breath, focus. But he was holding on. If they could just get him to the trucks . . .

"Hold on, Civ!" Adi yelled over the sound of artillery firing.

The distance between them and the trucks was closing. A couple hundred feet, maybe less.

"Hold on, Civ!" Adi yelled again. "We're almost there!"

Another boom rippled through the sky, high above their heads. Astrea flinched. A warm, heavy, familiar hand found that small spot between Astrea's shoulders. Jin pushed her even faster, so fast she was sure her legs were going to give out.

Cold crackled across Astrea's skin, piercing the very core of her being. It jumped closer and closer behind them.

"Prince Varojin!" Caliban's voice echoed over the noise.

Skies damn it.

"Get him to Lucian," Astrea said to Adi as she pushed one last bright pulse of light into Civan's body. "Now." She spun out of Jin's way as he skidded to a stop, turning just in time to see Caliban blink into existence a dozen feet away.

Astrea grabbed for that agonizing cold, gritting her teeth as her insides twisted and tumbled at the wrongness of the feeling. That ice traveled through her fingers, her palms, up her arms, and into her chest, burying itself in her heart. She pulled and pulled, clawing it away until she found it.

Hate.

Anger.

Excitement.

Gray, crimson, gold, hers to use. To control.

She yanked back. Caliban stumbled forward, cold fear spreading over Astrea's limbs. She pulled on that, too, pushing and pulling the energy between herself and Caliban. He stumbled again, then fell to his knees.

That hate and anger swirled within her, overwhelming. Astrea pulled harder, letting the energy fill her until she was about to burst.

She forced it out. Caliban flew back toward the base, caught in a tidal wave of crimson and shadow. The colors carried him away and away, barreling into Helosian soldiers scrambling toward him.

The wave caught Astrea, too. She crashed back into Jin's hard body. He faltered, then pulled her to her feet and half dragged her to the waiting truck. The other two were already speeding away. Jin shoved Astrea toward the final vehicle, and Adi hauled her inside.

Astrea rolled onto her side, breathing heavily as Jin practically climbed on top of her. Adi pulled the truck's door shut behind them both.

Everything hurt. Every inch of Astrea's skin was on fire, and pain pulsed brightly in her abdomen.

"Civan," she groaned. "Lucian, did he—"

"It's very bad," came Lucian's answer from somewhere in the dark truck.

Astrea pushed to her knees, crawling across the metal floor until she reached Civan and Lucian. A bullet had pierced him right in his abdomen, and as Astrea laid her hands next to Lucian's, sticky blood covered her palms.

"On my count," Lucian said. "One . . ."

Astrea steeled herself.

"Two . . ."

She pulled on her light, its sudden glow hurting her eyes.

"Now."

Energy swirled through her, warm and gentle, before the ghost pain tripled. Mirror healing and pain warred in her gut, echoes of Lucian's pain nearly blinding her. Dark dots crowded the edges of her vision. Adi and Jin said something Astrea couldn't comprehend.

And just as quickly as the pain had overwhelmed her, it receded. A dull ache settled in her bones and abdomen. The blood leaking from Civan's body stopped.

"Fuck," Lucian muttered, slumping back against the bench behind him. "Fuck."

"Is he going to be okay?" Adi asked.

"Yeah," Astrea said as Civan groaned out his agreement.

Civan would live, though he wasn't in very good shape. He'd need days to recover from that. The blood coating Astrea's hands was proof enough. She wiped her palms against her thighs, smearing most of the red liquid onto her pants.

"You two good?" Jin asked Astrea and Lucian.

Astrea would hardly classify herself as "good" in that moment, but she nodded anyway.

The truck swerved to the left, then the right. Tires squealed. Astrea's back slammed into the edge of the metal bench behind her.

"What the fuck is happening up there?" Lucian yelled to the driver in Novarian.

"They're firing on us!" someone called back. The truck lurched again.

"From behind?" Jin shouted.

"Yes!"

Adi flung the truck's rear doors open. Wind blew into the vehicle, so strong it nearly sent Astrea sprawling. Behind them, the base grew smaller in the distance, but gaining on them were two trucks.

"Are those . . ." she asked, then stopped.

People. People were popping up out of the Helosian trucks' roofs, sending massive chunks of flaming earth toward them.

Jin and Adi stood, steadying themselves with the truck's walls. The driver swerved again as a projectile headed right for them. The fire around it expanded as Jin's hands shot forward. Adi punched out, sending the earthen projectile flying back toward the Helosians. It hit the front of one truck, exploding on impact. The Helosian vehicle swerved, toppling over onto its side as the engine caught fire.

The second Helosian vehicle sent another projectile, and again, Adi and Jin redirected it. It smashed into the ground in front of the enemy truck, making them stop short. Then Jin and Adi yanked the doors closed again, blocking out the stench of smoke still coming from the Helosian base.

"How much farther until we reach the border?" Lucian asked the driver.

"We're almost there, Commander."

Astrea slumped against the bench. Jin and Adi did, too. Skies, that had not been the plan at all. Getting Kaius to stand down would have been ideal, but all of *that*? Astrea loosed a shaky breath.

"Everyone else got out?" Adi asked.

"All accounted for, thanks to Astrea stopping Caliban," Lucian said.

"How's my sister?" Civan asked, voice rough. Anxiety pulsed out from him in rough, bright orange waves. "How's Noemi?"

"They're in the other truck with another healer," Lucian said. "They're in good hands."

"They weren't hurt during the fight," Astrea said to Civan when his anxiety didn't dissipate. "Not like you were, at least."

"Alright," Civan mumbled. "Thank you."

"Of course." Astrea touched Jin's shoulder. "And you?" Jin was covered in small burns and bruises, but Adi seemed to be mostly unscathed.

"Nothing that needs immediate attention," Jin said. "Let's just get back to Novaria."

Astrea nodded. And she was glad, not just because she didn't want them to be hurt but because she didn't think she could take anymore. Every inch of her body hurt.

The driver slammed on the brakes, sending all of them in the back sprawling. Jin barely pulled Astrea against him in time to lessen her fall.

"Sorry!" the driver called. "Trouble ahead."

Lucian crawled through the narrow opening between the two front seats and the rest of the truck. He planted himself in the passenger seat, then yelled, "Go around, go around!"

"Lucian?" Jin called.

Gray confusion sparked in the passenger seat. "The . . . Helosians seem to be fighting themselves?" he said.

"Is it more Paragon dressed like Helosians?" Adi asked.

"No, I think it's actually just the Helosians." Lucian pointed to the driver's left. "There, follow our trucks. When they stop, we stop. Not a second sooner."

The driver turned the steering wheel, sending them all in a new direction. Civan grunted and curled in on himself. "Be careful!" Astrea yelled. "Civan's still in pain."

"He's going to be in a lot more pain if we don't get over that border and back to Silverpine," Lucian said.

Astrea grimaced. Surely the commander could still feel that ghostly burning in his own belly. But instead of pushing back against him, Astrea crawled away from Jin and leaned over Civan. Light danced around her hands, and she set them gently on Civan's abdomen.

"There's nothing left for me to heal," she said to him even as echoes of pain slid across her skin. "I think it's just . . . residual."

"Yeah," he muttered. Sweat beaded on his brow. "I suppose getting shot will do that to you."

"We'll get you back to Silverpine, Civ," Jin said. "Just hang in there, then we'll let you lie in a motionless bed for however long you want."

"Sure." The word left Civan as little more than a grunt.

The engine roared as the truck accelerated. Jin and Adi both swore. Astrea braced both herself and Civan as best she could, but the expected swerves never came. Nothing hit them. Instead, the truck zoomed ahead, then began to slow. Mint relief blossomed around the driver just as the vehicle stopped completely.

"Why are we stopped?" Jin asked, pushing up to move closer to Lucian.

"Your sister's truck has stopped," he said. "We're in Novaria."

"She's getting out," the driver said.

Jin cursed under his breath, then climbed out the back of the truck. In the distance, the sounds of fighting and heavy magic and artillery echoed through the forest. Astrea swallowed. *Helosians fighting Helosians.*

"What is it, Ellie?" Jin yelled.

Astrea couldn't make out the muffled response.

"We need to *go, now.*" Jin paused. "No, we most certainly are not going back to the border." Sharp annoyance needled Astrea's skin. "For fuck's sake."

Go back to the border? When Adi shot Astrea a questioning look, she said, "Ellie found a couple of deserters at Kaius's base. They let her go and were surprised that the rumors of her fleeing were true." That must've been why she wanted to go back. If Helosians really were fighting Helosians . . .

"We can't go back," Adi said. "We need to get everyone out of here."

"It looks like General Kanakos is getting out of the truck," Lucian said.

"No way, Zephyrine!" Jin yelled from somewhere outside. One heartbeat passed, then another. "Fine. Be safe!"

"Eliana's getting back into one of the vehicles," Lucian said.

Astrea really didn't need Lucian to narrate every movement for her. She ignored him, focusing on Civan again. His eyes were closed, but the deep furrow between them suggested he was still awake. The truck jostled as Jin climbed back in and closed the doors.

"Zephyrine's going to round up any deserters she can and bring them back to Silverpine," Jin said. "Take us straight back to the fort. Follow my sister."

CHAPTER 13

The ride back to Fort Silverpine had been fraught, Astrea's muscles tense with the thought that Kaius might come after them armed with airships and weapons. But no one came other than an escort of additional soldiers from Silverpine itself.

By the time their truck rolled to a stop in the main courtyard, Astrea wanted nothing more than to check on Cressida and Eliana and go to sleep. She and Lucian had taken turns easing Civan's pain, but between that and the souleating, Astrea was worn out. Even her skin hurt.

So when she hopped out of the truck and found Commander Tarkun standing there expectantly, crimson rage surrounding his stout form, Astrea sighed. *Now what?*

"Prince Varojin—"

"Captain Auris," Jin corrected.

Tarkun rolled his eyes, visible even in the growing darkness. "What is this I'm told about your sister inviting Helosian deserters to Fort Silverpine? On whose authority?"

"On mine," Lucian said as he strode around to the back of the truck.

Astrea pressed her lips together; it was most certainly not on his authority. Eliana had simply wanted it done. Hadn't discussed it with any of them.

"If we are to fight the Helosian emperor," Lucian continued when Tarkun began to argue, "then we will need all the additional numbers we can get. If these soldiers want to support their princess, who am I to deny them that right? They could have followed orders today and attacked her, yet instead they let her go."

"Or is that just a ruse to get into one of our bases?" Tarkun challenged. "First these void mages, now Helosians? What next? Welcome a Zaikudi battalion and give them copies of our battle plans?"

Lucian scoffed. "Silverpine is hardly important enough to be a target of Prince Kaius or Emperor Aelius."

"Hardly important enough?" Tarkun stepped forward, but Jin put himself between the two men.

"Your concerns are valid, Commander. When General Kanakos arrives with anyone who has decided to join her, sequester them for everyone's safety until they've been vetted," Jin said to Tarkun. "Then we'll decide what to do with them. But if they're willingly fighting their own units out there now because they disagree with Kaius? That's proof enough to me."

"You would think that, wouldn't you?" Tarkun snapped. "You're from a country and family that thrives on violence."

Jin's jaw tightened. Astrea was sure he was going to snap back. But he sucked in a deep breath, then said, "You're right about that, but all due respect, Commander, you know nothing about me. Don't assume I'm like them."

Lucian stepped out from behind Jin. "We should get everyone to the infirmary, Your Highness," he said. "I want everyone examined thoroughly before we call it a night. Commander, I'll debrief with you."

Sending one more glare Jin's way, Tarkun followed Lucian into the darkening base. Jin's shoulders dropped. He ran a hand over the back of his neck. When he pivoted toward Astrea, his gaze was still sharp and focused.

"We need to get Civan to another healer," Jin said. "Civ, you good with that? They're going to have to touch you."

From inside the truck, Civan mumbled, "I know how healing works, Captain. I can deal with it."

The corners of Jin's lips twitched up. Adi stomped one foot on the ground, and the earth loosened, creating another makeshift stretcher. He and Jin helped Civan onto it, then Adi began pushing the stretcher through the air.

As they passed the other trucks, Lennor shouted, "Civ!" She hopped down from where she was sitting with Cressida and sprinted to her brother's side. Bright yellow worry pulsed around her in rapid flashes. "Skies, what happened?"

"He got shot," Adi drawled. "In the gut."

"You got shot? Again?"

"Again?" Astrea asked.

"Corsyca," was all Lennor replied.

"Lucian and I healed him," Astrea said, hoping it would help Lennor calm. Not just for Lennor's sake but her own. Skies, every color flashing in the air made her head feel like it would explode. "We were just going to have someone else double-check everything. He's still in some pain."

"I'm alright," Civan whispered when Lennor began to protest.

His sister smacked him on the shoulder. "Don't scare me like that! Don't ever run off like that again!"

"You said we needed to—"

"I know what I said! You know not to listen to me!" That yellow worry spiking around Lennor was joined by orange and steel, anxiety and pain. Her voice cracked as she said, "Of all the times to—"

"Hey," came Cressida's smooth, soothing voice. She wrapped her arm around Lennor's narrow shoulders. "Let's take both Civan and Noemi to a healer, yeah? And you. Get those bruises checked out."

"Yeah, sure." Lennor sniffled and crossed her arms over her abdomen.

Astrea started forward with Adi again, but Jin said, "Az, wait." As she stopped and turned toward him, he said, "Can you get the team settled? I'd like to go talk to Commander Tarkun."

"He was really mad."

"I know."

"You think talking to him is going to help?"

"Honestly?" Jin shrugged. "I'm not sure, but it feels wrong to ignore it. And Ellie's headed their way . . ."

"Right." Eliana probably wouldn't take kindly to the commander suggesting Helosian deserters were just double agents. "Right, sure." Astrea nodded. "I'll make sure everyone has what they need."

"Thank you." Jin pressed a quick kiss to the top of her head, then took off after Nicos and Eliana.

Astrea watched him go, the sureness of his stride, the way he pushed his shoulders back and held his head high. After so many days apart, she just wanted to crawl into bed with him, feel him next to her, and get some sleep. In fact, what she really wanted was to go back to Talmaris.

But there would be no travel that night. No, she needed to go take care of her people, make sure everyone was alright. Especially Noemi. White terror clung to the young woman like a second skin.

Pushing her weary legs to go faster, Astrea caught up to the rest of the team as they neared the infirmary, a two-story building a few hundred feet down from the garages. They were already shuffling inside, and Astrea caught sight of Vernie just before they, too, disappeared inside. Good; at least there'd be one other healer she knew.

Astrea headed into the building. One of the other Lightbringers she'd met, the purple-eyed young woman named Nadia, was barking orders not just to Astrea's people but the Novarian soldiers and healers alike.

"No, you lot go upstairs," she said to Adi.

"But he was shot in the stomach." Adi tilted his head toward Civan, who was now propped up between him and Marko.

"Doesn't look like he's bleeding now. Upstairs."

"Just go up," Vernie said to Marko. "He'll be alright."

They managed to get Civan up the narrow stairs, and Astrea was the last one to make it to the empty second floor. Were they trying to separate the Helosians and the Novarians? Astrea wasn't sure why they'd feel the need to do that. This had been a group effort. She didn't sense any hostile feelings downstairs, either, just a lot of bumps and bruises and aches.

Did Tarkun's anti-Helosian sentiments run deep into the units stationed here? He hadn't *seemed* anti-Helosian to begin with, but . . . but maybe it was the stress of the day. Besides, Astrea *had* sensed a good amount of annoyance in her days at Fort Silverpine. She'd thought that was about the damage the Paragon had caused, though, not their team's presence.

"Here we go, Civ," Adi said as he and Marko helped Civan settle onto a cot. "We'll get you patched up."

Astrea followed Vernie that way, trying to ignore the anxiety and terror vibrating around Noemi. She just needed to talk to Vernie first and get Civan sorted, then she could try to ease Noemi's mind. Besides, Adi was already headed for his sister.

"You got shot?" Vernie said to Civan in accented Helosian.

"Clean through, I think," Civan mumbled.

"Lucian and I healed it, but he's still in pain," Astrea said to Vernie.

"To be expected, even with healing." Warm white light danced around Vernie's long fingers as they placed their palms flat on Civan's abdomen. He grunted. Vernie winced, eyebrows drawing together as they sucked in a sharp breath.

"Is he alright?" Lennor asked. She'd taken her dark hair out of its two usual braids; it was greasy and dirty at the roots, and dust streaked the ends. Her black fatigues looked worse for the wear, too.

"I'm fine," Civan mumbled.

"He is," Vernie said. "I'll get him a tonic for the pain and sleep."

"Is that what you want, Civ?" Lennor asked.

"Yes," he said. "Please."

Vernie strode off to a tall wooden cabinet on the far side of the room. Glass clinked as they sorted through the bottles lining the shelves.

"I'm sure Jin will come talk to you soon," Astrea said, mostly to Lennor. "But what can I do in the meantime? What do you need?"

Lennor dropped onto the cot next to Civan's and buried her face in her hands. Steel pain, deep blue regret, and orange anxiety vibrated around her, almost shocking Astrea's skin with their intensity.

Astrea squatted down in front of her. "Len?"

"I'm sorry," she whispered. "We did *exactly* what we were supposed to do. We went to Rasa when we realized we couldn't make it back to Kalama. There were roadblocks. Checkpoints. And Rasa sent us on our way, but before we could even get to our next pickup location or get word to Jin, Kaius found us. How did he find us?"

"I don't know."

"Skies, maybe if we'd just . . . been a little faster, we could've gotten back to Kalama before the checkpoints were set up. And maybe *this*"—she gestured vaguely to the room—"could've been avoided."

Astrea didn't know how to ease Lennor's concerns. After all, Astrea often blamed herself for such things, too. But this wasn't Lennor's fault. It certainly didn't sound like it.

Setting a hand on Lennor's shoulder, Astrea said, "I truly don't think any of that's your fault. Talk to Jin when he comes up. I'm sure he'll tell you the same."

Lennor nodded weakly.

"Do you want me to heal you?" Astrea asked, though the fatigue weighing her down made healing seem impossible in that moment. A few cuts, bruises, and scrapes marred Lennor's tan skin, but they were by no means emergencies.

"No, save your energy."

"I'll be around if you change your mind."

Lennor tried to muster a smile. "Thanks, Astrea."

Astrea didn't feel like she was accomplishing her task of getting the team settled very well at all. Lennor didn't want healing, Civan was still in pain, and Adi was a ball of anxiety. She met Cressida halfway between where Lennor and Adi sat on beds near their siblings.

"How is she?" Cressida asked, voice low.

"She's blaming herself for all of this, but I don't know what to tell her."

"Did she tell you what happened?"

"Only a little, that Kaius found them after they talked to their commander, Rasa. They were on their way back to Novaria." Astrea hoped Jin would be able to make more sense of the situation and get details. "It might help if you go sit with her. Vernie's going to take care of Civan."

Cressida nodded. "I will, thanks, Az."

With Cressida on her way to see Lennor, Astrea circled the cots separating her from Adi and Noemi. As she approached, she caught sight of Marko whispering with Vernie, then disappearing downstairs. Vernie passed Astrea empty handed; maybe Marko was going to find the tonic?

"Hey," Astrea said to Adi.

He startled, making the cot creak. "Is Civan alright?" he asked.

"He's fine; he just needs some rest."

"Okay, good." Adi's hand rubbed big, smooth circles on Noemi's back. Her face was buried in her hands, and though the fear and worry still circled around her in strands of white and yellow, she didn't seem to be crying.

"Can I do anything?" Astrea asked Adi.

"Noemi?" Adi said gently. She finally perked up, her deep brown eyes darting between her brother and Astrea. "This is Astrea. She's a healer."

"I know . . ." Noemi's full lips curled into a small, tight smile. "It's nice to meet you."

"I'm sorry we're meeting under these circumstances, but Adi's told me a lot about you," Astrea said as she sat on the cot opposite the Kuwat siblings. "I hear you're a student in Kalama?"

"I was."

"And I hear you're studying for two degrees, which is impressive," Astrea said, trying to think of anything to distract Noemi from the situation at hand. "I would know . . . I also got two."

"Really?" Noemi asked. "Everyone thinks I've lost my mind for trying to do two at once."

"Well, based on what Adi's told me, you can handle it."

Bright pink embarrassment flared around Noemi. "How much have you been talking about me, Adi?"

"What?" he asked. "A man can't brag about how smart his kid sister is?"

"I'm not a kid."

"You'll *always* be a kid to me." Adi wrapped his arms around Noemi and pulled her into a hug. "I'm sorry we didn't get to you sooner. That was not how any of it was supposed to happen."

"Lennor and Civan did their best," Noemi murmured. "Prince Kaius's ships came out of nowhere. He said he was—" She swallowed hard as she pulled away from the embrace. "He said he was going to kill me if they didn't go with him peacefully."

"Then they did the right thing," Adi said.

If Kaius was so set on helping his father bring aetherium weapons to the continent, then killing Noemi in pursuit of that goal probably wouldn't have bothered him very much at all. Astrea hated the thought.

As Noemi gave Adi a few more details—very few of which seemed relevant to Kaius or Emperor Aelius's mission—Astrea looked for any sign of injury on Noemi. Like Lennor, she had a few scrapes and cuts, but they were shallow. Her lips were chapped, like she was dehydrated.

And skies, she was basically the spitting image of Adi. They shared the same broad nose, tightly coiled hair, and dark brown skin. Only their eyes were different, with Noemi having two brown and Adi having one green and one brown.

Well, there were other obvious differences, too. Noemi was close to Cressida's height—a couple heads shorter than Adi—and like Astrea, she had a cute, plump figure, all curves.

"Let me heal you up," Astrea said to Noemi, "and then maybe Adi can get you something to eat."

"Oh, I don't need—" Noemi started.

Astrea shook her head. "I insist."

When Noemi nodded, Astrea pushed herself up on tired legs. Her light pulsed around her hands, low and warm and steady. She set a hand on Noemi's upper arm and the other on her cheek. Small needles may as well have been scratching her skin, almost like when she got poked by the thorns on Sarsali's rose bushes. Another heartbeat, then Astrea pulled her hands away.

"All done," she said to the siblings. "You should both get some rest."

"You should too, Az," Adi said.

Astrea nodded; that was exactly what she planned on doing. "See you two in the morning."

Adi shouted his goodbyes to the others, then led Noemi toward the stairs. Astrea checked in with Cressida and the twins again, but none of them needed anything. So Astrea let them be, and after telling Vernie she was going to find food and Jin, Astrea headed downstairs.

Halfway down, Marko started to climb back up. He offered her a tight smile and held up a glass bottle. No doubt that was the tonic for Civan. Like the others, Marko was covered in bumps and bruises, but maybe Vernie would heal him. Or maybe, like Lennor, he didn't feel the need to take care of such superficial things.

"Adi took his sister to get settled in," she said.

"I'll look for him later."

Neither said goodbye as they passed each other on the stairs and went their separate ways. That was something Astrea appreciated about Marko; he was fine to just let things stand sometimes.

Astrea skirted past the Novarian soldiers and healers on the bottom floor of the infirmary, then slipped outside. Cool evening air danced over her skin, making her shiver. There was no sign of Jin, Eliana, or Nicos anywhere, but Saros was making a beeline right for the infirmary.

"Astrea!" he called. "Skies, nobody told me you were back."

It wasn't that she didn't want to see Saros; Astrea also just very much wanted to bathe and crawl into bed. Still, she forced herself to smile as she met Saros a few dozen feet away from the building.

"We haven't been back long," Astrea said. "I was just making sure everyone was healed."

Saros scanned her up and down, much as she'd just been doing to the rest of the team. "And you're alright?" he asked.

"Yes, Uncle."

His whole body relaxed. "What happened?"

Astrea recapped the day for him, focusing mostly on what Kaius had said about the emperor and Helosia's future.

Saros shook his head. "I never should have taken you to Kalama, Astrea."

"I don't think it would've mattered either way." The Paragon still would have found her, and Emperor Aelius still would have been after the aetherium weapons.

"No, but Prince Kaius is right. Helosia has always been aggressive. Taking you there should have been the last place on my list."

Astrea really, truly did not want to have this conversation again. He'd said something similar before, after they escaped Kalama. "I don't think living with that regret is the best way forward," she said. "We are where we are."

"I suppose you're right." He sighed. "You should go rest, my dear. Recover your energy. I'm sure your team's going to need you tomorrow."

"I don't mind taking care of them."

"No, but who's going to take care of you?" Saros asked. "Go get cleaned up, and I'll make sure someone brings food to your room. Should I send some up for Varojin, too?"

This was . . . unexpected. Not necessarily offering to take care of her but to take care of Jin in any way.

"I think he'll be a while," she said. "He'll probably get himself something when he has a moment."

Saros nodded. "Alright, sure."

Closing the small distance between them, Astrea embraced Saros. He ran a hand over the back of her head, much like he did when she was just a little girl. "Thank you," she whispered.

"Of course, my dear. You don't have to thank me for anything."

Warmth seeped into Astrea's bones. She may as well have been under the Kalamian sunshine on a summer morning, soaking in the new day. But something soft cradled her body, and all around her was darkness.

Lips pressed against her neck. Strong arms wrapped around Astrea's, pulling her toward the middle of the bed.

"How long was I out?" she rasped.

"I don't know; I just got back." Jin pressed another kiss to the side of her neck. "Go back to sleep."

Sleep. Sleep sounded so good, but . . .

But everything came rushing back to Astrea.

"Is everyone alright?" she asked. "I tried to get them set."

"Everyone's fine. Vernie was really impressed by your healing, as were some of the other healers stationed here."

"What about Noemi? Did Adi get her settled in?"

"She's shaken up, but she's going to be just fine."

"Good." Astrea rolled over in Jin's arms and rested her head on his chest. He stroked her hair and sighed. "Jin?"

"Hm?"

"What's wrong?" A whisper of shame settled on her skin, delicate and almost impossible to feel.

"I know we did the right thing, but I don't feel good about attacking Helosians."

"They were going to kill us."

"I know, but after fighting alongside so many people like that, people forced into service because of conscriptions or lies . . ." He sighed again. "It's hard reconciling the two things. Even if they didn't want to attack us, it's not like they had a choice. They'd be punished for defying orders."

"Some of them deserted." Even as Astrea said it, though, it sounded lame. "We knew people would get stuck in the middle." That sounded awful, too. "I know it doesn't feel good, but there's only so much we can do. And if we get Ellie into power, those people can have a chance at claiming whatever future they actually want."

"And all the ones bound to die along the way?"

Astrea rubbed at her sleepy eyes and pulled away just enough to look at Jin. Those brilliant golden irises of his were dulled by days of worry and little sleep. His beard was scruffy, his curls messy. She smoothed some hair away from his face. "Where is this coming from?"

As she went to move her hand away, Jin grabbed it and placed a kiss on her palm. "I thought I'd make peace with it by the time it happened. I guess I haven't."

"I don't know that you can expect yourself to. Like you said, you fought alongside people just like that for years. You can't ignore their humanity."

He kissed her palm again. "I never could. I nearly threw up the first time I took a life. A Delian who was set on taking me out."

How much easier would it be to go into battle and not see the *people* on the opposite side? Even Tovan, whom Astrea hated with every fiber of her being, had been a person. A terrible one, misguided by promises of violence and power. And even with all he'd done, when she'd stared him down and made him suffer in Kalama, it hadn't left her feeling anything other than drained, exhausted, bad. Glad he couldn't hurt her anymore, but somehow terrible to know he'd suffered at her hand.

The One had been a person.

Even Victor Nazarov was still a person.

She couldn't think about that too closely. Not now.

Instead, she drew circles around the small mark near Jin's right clavicle, the scar from when he'd almost died on Ilesouria.

"It's never going to be easy, reconciling those things," Jin said, "though part of me wishes it was."

"You're a good person. That's why it bothers you so much."

"Hard to see it that way sometimes." Jin sank down into the pillows, taking Astrea with him. "Sometimes I even wonder if we're doing the right thing."

Unease prickled Astrea's neck. "What do you mean?"

"I just mean I wonder if Helosia should stay an empire. It's not like it's done anyone any good, other than, I guess, offering them protection from the Delians and Zaikudi. But at what cost?"

No Helosian Empire? She saw Jin's point; Helosia had only come to exist mainly through conquest and war. Continued to exist because of conquest and war. That was no good.

"Can Ellie keep the country together and change course? Right those wrongs?"

"I wish I knew," he said. "I know she *wants* to, but . . . but I just don't know if it's possible. I mean, look at us. We're still waging war."

"Because we have to stop your father and the Paragon. That's different."

"I know, Az. I know. It just feels wrong on some level." Astrea's heart squeezed as steel pain bubbled up on Jin's skin. He stroked her hair again. "Maybe I was just naive to think it wouldn't feel like this."

"I don't think it's naive," Astrea said. "You don't want to hurt people. That's not a bad thing."

"It can be a weakness when you're out on the battlefield. That can get you killed."

"Well, we aren't in this moment. Give yourself time to figure it out."

Tipping her chin up, Jin searched her face for a moment, then pressed his lips to hers. He tasted faintly of mint. "You're very wise," he whispered, barely pulling away.

"I try."

Chuckling, Jin kissed her again. That sunshine warmth returned, burning away the last of Jin's pain and easing the ache in Astrea's sternum.

"I love you, Az. So much."

"I love you, too."

"I mean it. I don't think you understand."

Astrea half smiled. "I can feel it, remember?"

"And yet that seems like it must only be a fraction of it. I don't think even magic is enough to show you how much I love you."

"Wow," Astrea whispered, her cheeks burning. "So little confidence in my magic, Auris?"

"No, I have full confidence in your abilities." He shifted so he hovered above her, blocking out the low lamp light. "I'm just so in love with you, Sovna. There's no way to measure it."

"I guess I'll have to take your word for it."

The corners of Jin's eyes crinkled as he smiled. "I guess so."

"I was thinking more about what I want to do after this is all over."

"Oh?" Jin settled on his side and propped his head up on his hand. "What's that?"

"When Saros and I went to visit my mother's old healer friend . . . she lives in this cottage by the lake. You can see the mountains from there. And it just seemed so quiet and peaceful."

"We can certainly visit the mountains."

"Would you ever think about not living in Kalama?" she asked.

"I didn't live in Kalama for eight years, Az."

"I know, but I mean after all this. I think we should try living away from Kalama for a little while. Near the mountains. They're your favorite."

Jin hauled Astrea onto his chest and crushed her to him. "I'd move into an abandoned cabin in the woods if that's where you wanted to go."

She pushed against him, wiggling to regain her freedom. "We can't move if you suffocate me to death."

He placed a wet kiss on her cheek. "Then it was nice knowing you, I guess, because I'm never letting you go."

He hugged her tighter, and Astrea laughed as she settled on top of him, burying her face in the crook of his neck. Just being close to him like this, after the last couple of weeks, helped her heart and mind slow.

They would figure this out, this war and these problems. They would, together and with their friends. Astrea just hoped it didn't cause Jin—or the rest of them—too much heartache.

CHAPTER 14

With Lennor, Civan, and Noemi back where they belonged, Astrea figured she would need to go back to researching her father with Saros. But when she woke up to find Jin curled around her, she let herself stay in bed for just a few more minutes, soaking in his warmth and the feeling of his skin on hers. Even the way his beard tickled her face.

She'd missed this. Missed him.

What she wouldn't give to just stay curled up like that forever with him, hidden away from the world and all the things it wanted to throw their way.

Her mind kept drifting back to what she'd mentioned the night before, about leaving Kalama behind when all this was over and moving someplace different together. She wanted that. Wanted to go find out what life was like with Jin, away from all this. Although really, she'd take any life with him. She couldn't picture a future without him by her side. She didn't *want* a future without him by her side.

When had she become so attached?

And why did it almost feel like a bad thing?

It wasn't. Loving someone and being loved were not bad. Astrea couldn't imagine a world without love. Not just romantic love, but the way she loved Cressida, the Nikaphoroses, Eliana. The way she was coming to love Adi, Marko, the twins. They all made her life so much better, richer.

And yet love could lead to terrible things, like what Kaius had just done. Jin loved the twins and Adi and, by extension, Noemi. And Kaius wanted to hurt Jin, so he'd taken something near and dear to Jin's heart to try to bend him to his will.

It was what the Paragon had done, too, wasn't it? Nazarov had finally dreamwalked to Jin just to bait him, to try to force his hand, because Jin loved her. And Nazarov had known it.

It was a strange thing, love. A strength and weakness all in one.

Astrea sighed and buried her face into Jin's chest. Why did her mind have to go to such topics so early in the day? Why couldn't she just enjoy this?

Jin kissed her forehead. "What time is it?"

"Early."

He groaned. "I should go check on everyone."

"I can go," Astrea said. "You sleep."

"You sure? You used a lot of magic yesterday. You should rest."

"I actually feel mostly alright. Not my best, but not as bad as I expected to." Astrea was groggy, and her limbs were heavy, but that was the worst of it. With every day that she trained, it seemed her tolerance for magic doubled. Was she gaining stamina that quickly, or was her body just getting used to what it had always been able to handle?

"Really?" he asked.

"Yes, I promise."

"Well . . . if you don't mind going. Though I'd like the record to reflect that I'd much rather keep you right here." He pushed up on one elbow and leaned down, kissing her.

Astrea melted back into the bed, the heat of Jin's desire rushing through her and making her blood sing. "I'll make note of it," she said as he finally pulled away.

"I'll come find you soon."

"Take your time."

Astrea slipped out of bed, then changed into a dark green dress, and after cleaning herself up, went off in search of the team. Adi's room was empty. Cressida's was occupied by not one but two sleeping souls . . . Lennor was in there, most likely. Astrea smiled. *Best to let them sleep.* She had no idea where Civan was. The infirmary still, maybe?

She'd just started past another door when it opened. Nicos stepped out, his hair mussed. He looked almost out of place in his black uniform; he'd worn red for all the years they'd known each other.

"Hey," he said, closing the door gently behind him.

"I was just coming to see how everyone's doing," Astrea said. Behind Nicos, energy flickered to life, then drifted off again. "Is she still sleeping?"

"Yeah. She was up all night."

"And you?" Astrea asked. Exhaustion weighed her down.

"The same, but there are things to do. I was just going to get some coffee, if you want to join me."

Astrea had been dining with Nicos for months, technically, but the invitation still felt foreign somehow. They didn't spend much time together alone. If Nicos felt the same, he didn't show it. His emotions were steady, calm, as they headed downstairs.

"So . . . why were you two up all night? Unless I don't want to know."

Magenta embarrassment flooded the stairwell, electric on Astrea's skin, as Nicos laughed. "Skies, no . . . Spent a lot of it just trying to figure out what to do with the people Zephyrine brought back."

"I thought it would've taken longer to get them all here." The border was a couple hours away by truck, let alone walking on foot.

Downstairs, they went to the kitchen and received two thermoses of coffee with little more than an annoyed grunt from the Novarian they'd asked. Part of Astrea wondered if the woman also didn't appreciate "the

Helosians" being around, as Commander Tarkun had implied the night before, but she decided not to focus on it too much. Annoyance didn't mean hostility.

Outside, the morning air cooled Astrea's cheeks. Dew coated the nearby grass and shrubs, and the sky was a beautiful tapestry of pastels. A few soldiers crossed the courtyard, but there was no flurry of activity, no rush of vehicles or shouted commands. The base was quiet.

"We convinced Tarkun to send transport. Well, Lucian commanded it, really," Nicos finally said. He ran a hand through his auburn locks, which hung uncharacteristically loose around his shoulders. "I've got to sort them all out today. Eliana promised *we* would, but I don't want her anywhere near them, just in case."

"Oh. Well, if you want any help," Astrea said, "I can join you."

"Surely you have better things to do than question a bunch of Helosians."

"I need to find Adi and then check on Civan, but otherwise, there's not much for me to do. Where will you be?"

"There." Nicos pointed to a low hangar deeper in the base. "Come by whenever you can."

"I'll be there soon."

As Nicos headed off, Astrea opened her thermos and took a sip of the weak coffee. She'd need it, too; it was going to be a long day if they had to convince Tarkun these Helosians really were on their side.

If someone had told Astrea months before that she would someday be in an empty garage bay on a Novarian base, interrogating Helosian defectors, she would've laughed.

But there she was with Nicos and Jin in exactly that situation. Zephyrine had the other Helosians cordoned off on the far side of the structure. There weren't many, just a dozen, but it was truly more than Astrea had expected. With the chaos of the day—and the threat of Kaius's retribution hanging over their heads—she hadn't been sure anyone would even make it across the border.

And sure, she'd known she was going to help Nicos, but she'd expected the Helosian deserters to be more . . . grateful? Not necessarily. Cooperative? Definitely. The Novarians were putting themselves at great risk of conflict with Prince Kaius by helping these people, and yet half of them had been more than rude.

"Do you actually support what Her Imperial Highness is doing?" Nicos asked one, a brawny middle-aged man with short black hair and tan skin. "Or did you just want to get out of Prince Kaius's station?"

The man tilted his narrow nose into the air. "Of course I support Her Imperial Highness." Rusty annoyance flared around him. "General Kanakos already asked me this."

"And I'm asking you again," Nicos said. "Do you want Princess Eliana on the throne?"

The man's green eyes flicked to Jin. "I support your sister, Your Imperial Highness."

"Captain Auris," Jin corrected.

He grunted. "I support her, Captain. I do. Your brother is no good for the country."

"How far have these rumors spread among the enlisted?" Jin asked.

"That, I can't say, Captain."

Jin stepped up next to Nicos, just a couple of feet from the man. "What's your name?"

The man stiffened, then straightened as he said, "Staff Sergeant Marcellus Marzoli, at your service, Captain."

"Where were you stationed before my brother's unit?"

"Fort Blackrock, Captain."

Astrea perked up. Jin had trained at Fort Blackrock during his time in the military; she knew that from his letters and stories. But Fort Blackrock was also in the Badlands, where Emperor Aelius was digging around for more aetherium.

"I trained there," Jin said. "Brutal place, especially in the summer."

"That it is, sir."

"What do you know about what my father's researching in the Badlands?"

"Research?" Marcellus's thick eyebrows drew together. "What research?"

"What did you think he was doing out there, Sergeant?" Jin asked. "Didn't you see his excavation teams?"

"Well . . ." The man's gaze slid to where Astrea still stood in the back. His annoyance had long since died down. Delicate curiosity brushed over her limbs. "I saw them, Captain, but I didn't ask questions. I'm not supposed to ask questions, just do as I'm told."

"I understand," Jin said. "And I don't blame you. But if you can tell us *anything*, that would be helpful."

"What would Emperor Aelius want in the Badlands?" Marcellus asked. "There's nothing out there but sand and rock."

Nicos barely turned to look at Jin. In turn, Jin set a hand on Nicos's shoulder. "Let's just say my father's not up to any good," Jin said carefully. "We believe what he's searching for would enhance the military's strength and make his war machine nearly unstoppable."

"As if we aren't already?" Marcellus scoffed, then his tan cheeks burned red. "Apologies for speaking out of turn, Captain."

Jin waved the apology off.

"Princess Eliana's not interested in letting her father or Prince Kaius continue on like they are now," Nicos said. "What would you say if we told you she was interested in ending the Corsycan War, or at least Helosian involvement?"

Marcellus hesitated as he studied Astrea again. Why was he so interested in her presence? Mistrust pressed heavily against her body. What could he possibly have to mistrust her about? Or was she misunderstanding . . . did he not trust Nicos's question?

"While Her Imperial Highness's heart is in the right place," he finally said as he looked to Nicos, "simply *ending* the war would be difficult. Who's to say the Zaikudi and Delians will let us move on from it all?"

"A fair question," Jin said. "I fought in Corsyca."

"You did?"

"Yes. I wouldn't wish for anyone to continue on there, but I fought in the Delian-Helosian War, too. I know it's not going to be that simple, and I'm sure my sister knows as well. But she certainly hopes to put an end to Helosian suffering at the very least."

Marcellus nodded. "That's something I can get behind, Captain."

"Good." Jin stuck his hand out to the man for a shake, and Marcellus took it. "If you think of anything strange you saw or overheard while at Blackrock, or even recently while serving under my brother, please tell me, Mister Masalis, or General Kanakos."

Marcellus nodded again. "Thank you, Captain. I'll be sure to."

"And that group's going to need someone in charge," Jin said, tilting his head toward where Zephyrine still had the other Helosians sectioned off. "You're highest rank among them. Help them settle in."

"Not . . . you or the general?" Marcellus asked.

"I'm not sure we'll be in Silverpine permanently," Jin said. "I'll come check on you all when I can."

Marcellus saluted, then headed back toward Zephyrine and the others. As he joined them, a ripple of mint relief and green curiosity pulsed through the air.

"Well?" Nicos asked as he turned toward Astrea. "What did you think?"

"He was a little annoyed with you at first, but his energy leveled out." She shrugged. "I couldn't tell if he mistrusted me or your statements about Ellie's plans, though. Maybe a bit of both based on his answer."

Nicos pressed his lips together.

"I think he was sincere," Jin said. "His reply about not trusting the Delians and Zaikudi was what I expected, honestly. And he's not wrong."

"Ellie knows that, but I don't think she's going to like hearing it from these people," Nicos murmured.

"Why?" Astrea asked.

"She just . . . I don't know. You know how she gets sometimes."

"Tunnel vision?"

He nodded.

Astrea understood that. Ending the Corsycan War was the right thing to do. But if Eliana knew that it was more complicated than that, Astrea trusted Eliana wouldn't do anything to get Helosia into *more* trouble. She'd try to find some solution. It was why she'd been trying to negotiate with the two countries before they'd had to flee Kalama.

"Do you think their ambassadors in Talmaris would be willing to listen to her?" Astrea asked. "Would it be wise to sit down with them?"

"Now?" Jin asked. "We don't even know if we're going to be able to get her into power."

Astrea supposed that was a good point. And it wouldn't do them any good to warn them of the emperor's plans; they'd already discussed that back in Talmaris.

"So, now what?" Astrea asked. "You said we won't be at Silverpine much longer?"

"I think we need to go talk to Ysabel," Jin said. "It might be time to go to the Badlands."

"Going back to Talmaris?" Eliana's fingers drummed against the top of the thick chest of drawers in her room. She'd been given the "finest" room at the base, at least according to Commander Tarkun, and the furniture, though not ornate, was certainly sturdy and well made. "We just got here."

"And now we need to go," Jin said. "We need to talk to Ysabel about mounting a mission to the Badlands. If that's where Father's hunting for this ore, maybe we can cripple his search and at least make this a fair fight going forward."

"Maybe we can take *him* out if we lure him there," Eliana said.

Astrea's eyebrows shot up.

"We did agree to targeted efforts," Eliana continued. "If we strike at the heart of his war effort—*him*—then we should be able to end this before too many lives are lost."

"That sounds more like a coup than anything," Cressida said. She sat with Astrea on the large, soft bed on the other side of the room. "Is that really the best way to go about this?"

Eliana shrugged. "People are going to see it as a coup no matter what I do. Why not take the most direct path?"

"And you think that path won't draw some line in the sand for Helosians?" Nicos asked. "It's still going to divide everyone. I don't think we can take him out without it blowing up in our faces."

"Maybe if we show them proof of what he's trying to do . . ." Astrea trailed off. That would mean exposing aetherium ore's properties and void magic, which could lead to disastrous consequences with the Delians and Zaikudi. "Or we should at least tell them something that explains his intent. Try to explain to people that it's not just about power for you, Ellie."

"Just get Kaius to talk." Cressida lay back on the bed, heavy fatigue and cold regret rolling off her slim frame. "He's always running his mouth, and people would actually believe him."

"*If* we could somehow prove to them what my father's plans are," Jin said, "we could probably sway a lot of people to abandon the fight. But there's no way everyone's going to abandon it. If there's any way to prove this to them, then we need to make sure it's solid. Inexcusable. Indefensible. Get as many of them off the battlefield as possible before it begins."

"Nazarov said he didn't kill those void mages in Sezia," Astrea said. "What if Caliban was actually the shadow man in Kalama? The one who murdered all those people. Maybe they were testing the first bit of aetherium they found with Saros's help."

Jin's eyebrows furrowed.

It made sense to Astrea. If the men who had stalked her on Solstice Night had worked for The One and the Paragon, they weren't the actual shadow man. The murderer, the one who'd killed the ticketer behind the museum and others. That shadow man had run from Jin. And if that really was someone from the Paragon, why would they have abandoned Astrea and Jin, their targets? It would have been the perfect opportunity for the Paragon to grab them.

It had to be that the shadowy murderer had been Caliban or another void mage working for Emperor Aelius, trying to get the book, yes, but also testing the aetherium blade. All the victims had been stabbed.

Maybe the emperor had realized Cressida couldn't discern any specific properties from the meteorite and had decided to try a different kind of test.

"Why do it in the capital, though?" Nicos asked. "Why scare everyone?"

"Because everyone started looking to our father for security measures," Eliana said. "Scare them into thinking there's another enemy, then show we have a way to beat them at their own game."

"Sure," Nicos said, "but that's just in the capital. They'd have to start murdering people all over the empire to convince enough people to care."

"Maybe Kalama was just the testing ground?" Cressida offered.

Astrea's head hurt. So much speculation, and for what? It wasn't like they had any proof either way. And finding proof of . . . *anything* . . . seemed unlikely at this rate. Proof besides the aetherium and Paragon, anyway.

"I still think we need to go back to Talmaris," Jin said. "We should talk to Ysabel about the rumors spreading through the Helosian ranks. See if she'll open the borders to defectors."

"Start gathering more forces?" Eliana asked, and Jin nodded. "Alright," she said. "Let's go back to Talmaris, then. Hopefully Ysabel's going to be receptive."

As Jin and Adi readied the airships that would take them back to the capital, Astrea went to check on Civan. Though he'd been kept in the infirmary overnight, he was returning to Talmaris with them.

She tapped the pocket of her skirt, fingers meeting a hard rectangle. The fact that Eliana had brought chocolate with her at all had been a small miracle, let alone the fact that she willingly parted with it without many questions. Astrea didn't know if Civan would want it, but it was his favorite. And after everything, she thought he might at least appreciate the option.

As she passed through the base's courtyard, she found no sign of the Helosian defectors. So had Zephyrine managed to get them settled? Hopefully. And hopefully they'd remain welcome while everyone else went back to the capital to figure out next steps.

Entering the infirmary, Astrea found it empty other than one Novarian soldier. They sat on a cot on the opposite side of the main floor. A Purifier had her hands set on the man's head, and water glowed around her palms.

Astrea started for the stairs when a familiar voice called out, "Astrea!"

Glancing over her shoulder, Astrea found Vernie approaching, a small bottle clutched in their hand.

"Commander Lucian sent word that you're leaving," they said. "I'm glad you're here. I'm just gathering a few things for him to take on your flight back."

"You're not coming with us?" Astrea asked, following Vernie upstairs.

"No, the commander has asked me to stay and continue evaluating our . . ." Their voice trailed off as they climbed the last few stairs. "Our new recruits, I suppose."

"Right . . ." Even though she didn't know Vernie well, Astrea trusted them to keep a watchful eye over the soldiers now swearing themselves to Eliana's cause. Vernie had proven trustworthy the last few days, and Lucian trusted them. "Well, thanks. I hope you won't miss Talmaris too much."

"Being here is a nice break," Vernie said. "Civan! What are you doing out of bed?"

Following Vernie out of the stairwell and into the room gave Astrea a direct line of sight to where Lennor was helping her brother off his cot. Aside from the four of them, the room was empty.

Lennor hesitated. "You said we were going back to Talmaris today—"

"I didn't mean you had to jump to action," Vernie said with a small sigh. "Please, take a seat. I have some things to go over with you." Once Civan was situated on the bed again, Vernie shooed Lennor away. "I'll release him to you in a few minutes."

Shoulders slumped forward, Lennor shuffled to where Astrea still loitered near the top of the stairs. Yellow worry twined around Lennor's small frame, almost matching the undertones of her skin.

"How's he doing?" Astrea asked quietly. On the far side of the room, Vernie handed Civan two bottles and explained how far apart to take them.

"Oh, he says he's fine and that I'm too worried, but—" Lennor pressed her lips together. "I told him not to go after you all, that Jin and Adi would handle it, but—"

"I understand," Astrea said. That thick fog of yellow surrounding her said it all. "But you've got to trust him and trust me, Vernie, and Lucian. Civan's fine."

"Yeah, I guess."

"Thanks for the vote of confidence," Astrea said, trying to force some humor into her tone.

"No, I mean, I trust you. I just don't understand . . . well, I guess it doesn't matter. He's fine. It's done."

Astrea disagreed; of course it mattered. It was clearly upsetting Lennor, and besides, her brother *had* been shot. If Lucian hadn't been there and if Vernie wasn't a Souleater, too, Astrea wasn't sure they would've been able to get past the Helosians and heal Civan. But Lennor didn't need Astrea to say that.

"And how are you?" Astrea asked. "Beyond being worried about him."

"I'm fine."

The steel pain and orange anxiety bleeding into Lennor's aura suggested otherwise. She watched Civan and Vernie closely, almost like she was expecting something bad to happen. Her fingers flexed, and as they moved, Astrea spotted something familiar and unexpected: a green, purple, and white stone.

The pocket stone Cressida had given Lennor on the boat to Kalama.

Astrea had almost forgotten about that. Cressida had received it from the vendor in Tornama, and somehow, Lennor had kept it safe even when Kaius confiscated everything else. Did Cressida know?

"Alright, you can go now," Vernie said to Civan. "Just remember the schedule, and ask someone at the palace infirmary if you need more."

"I'll remember," Civan mumbled as he stood. "Thank you."

Lennor tucked her stone into the pocket of her black trousers as she looped her arm through Civan's. "Let's go check in with Jin."

As the twins descended the stairs slowly, Astrea turned to Vernie. "Thanks for your help."

Flashing a tight smile, Vernie brushed back a few loose hairs framing their face. "Of course. You heard the instructions for Civan's tonics?"

"I did," Astrea said. The green one every eight hours as needed, and Civan could take the clear one in between. "You think it's necessary, even with the healing?"

"He's still in some pain," Vernie said. "The shock of it all, I think, as I can't find any issues physically, nor can the base healers downstairs. Have him take the tonics for three days, then check him again."

"I will."

"I'll stop by to speak to Lucian before you're off; I'm just going to finish cleaning up here first."

With that, Astrea left Vernie to their task and hurried after the twins. They weren't far outside the infirmary when she caught up with them.

"Len, I think Cress was looking for you," Astrea said. "She should be over by the airships."

"Oh . . ." Green curiosity spiked high in her aura. "Civan—"

"I'm fine," he said with a sigh. "Go see her. I know you want to."

"I'll walk with Civan," Astrea said when Lennor still hesitated.

Some of the yellow worry surrounding her dimmed. "Alright, sure." Lennor walked straight toward the airships across the courtyard, her shoulders and posture tight. Her hand dipped into her pocket, retrieving what Astrea was sure had to be that stone.

"Please don't ask me how I'm doing," Civan said once his sister was far out of earshot.

Up ahead, Jin and Adi rounded the corner of the airships. Noemi wasn't far behind, and as Lennor joined, the two women hugged.

"I wasn't going to ask you that," Astrea said. When Jin caught her eye, he waved. She waved back. "I hate when people ask me that. It's all anyone would ask me for months."

Of course, Astrea appreciated her friends checking up on her, but they worried too much sometimes. She supposed she would feel the same if their roles were reversed, but asking once or twice was different than constant fretting.

"I actually wanted to give you something." As Astrea said the words, she suddenly felt awkward. What if this was an overstep? It was too late to turn back. She reached into her pocket and pulled out the foil-wrapped chocolate.

Civan took it with his free hand. "What's this?"

"I know chocolate's your favorite . . ."

He stared down at the candy as they kept walking.

"And Lennor told me it's sometimes the only thing you'll eat," Astrea continued. "I'm the same. Not with chocolate but some other things. And I just thought that after, well, you know—" She cleared her throat. "Maybe you'd want some? It's just milk chocolate; there aren't any options here. I'm sorry if it's not the right thing."

The tiniest smile pulled at the corners of Civan's mouth as he lifted his eyes to hers. He didn't do that often—look people in the eye. "I didn't realize anyone did the same with food. My grandmother used to get so angry with me."

"Well, I can't speak for her, but I understand," Astrea said. "My uncle and I both do it. One of my favorites is cinnamon pancakes."

"Thanks."

"You're welcome."

They closed the last of the distance to the two airships in silence. Astrea risked one more glance up at Civan; that small smile was still there. She couldn't help but smile a little, too.

"Captain," Civan said as they met Jin near the doors of the larger ship.

"Civ." Jin started forward, then pulled back, almost like he wanted to hug Civan but stopped himself. "Lennor said Vernie set you up with some tonics?"

"Yes." Civan held them up for Jin to see.

"And you'll take them?"

"Yes, I'll take them."

Jin nodded. "Go on inside. We'll take off in a few minutes. We're just waiting for Zephyrine."

Inside the ship, Saros was talking to Adi and Noemi. Civan joined Cressida and Lennor. And outside Eliana's tiny ship, Lucian and Nicos were in deep discussion. It seemed they were all ready to finally get back to the capital, at least.

"What was Civan smiling about?" Jin asked Astrea.

She tucked a few stray hairs behind her ear. "I brought him some chocolate. Lennor said it's the only thing he'll eat sometimes, and I just wanted to make sure he ate after everything."

Warmth pressed into Astrea's skin, pleasant and soft, as Jin circled his arm around her shoulders. "That was very nice of you."

"Is there anything else he and Lennor like?" Astrea asked. "Or Noemi? Do you know much about her?"

Food wasn't the only comfort in the world, but with them being so far away from home, after being kept prisoner for days, what else could she do for the trio? In the weeks following Astrea's ordeal with the Paragon, she hadn't wanted to eat at all, but just passing time with Adi in the kitchen had helped bring some normalcy back to her life. Maybe something similar would help Lennor, Civan, and Noemi.

"Not sure about Noemi, but Len and Civ are also big fans of these dumplings they tried to teach us how to make," Jin said.

"*Tried* to teach you? I thought you and Adi were good in the kitchen."

He gave her shoulders a small shake. "We are, but neither of us has had enough practice pinching the dough. It takes time."

"Do you think Ysabel's staff could make them or find them in the city?"

"Probably. I'll see what they can do."

"And something for Noemi."

"And something for her," Jin said. "I'll ask Adi once we take off."

Someone coughed behind them, then Zephyrine circled around to their front. "Well?" asked the white-haired general. "Are we ready to go?"

"We are if Lucian is," Jin said. "He's up with my sister's ship."

As Zephyrine strode away, Jin tugged Astrea closer to his body until their hips bumped. "Thank you for taking care of them," he murmured as they started for the ship's ramp.

"They're your family, Jin," Astrea said. "Of course I'll take care of them."

Jin was about to reply when Adi shouted for him to meet up near the cockpit. But Jin didn't need to say anything. His soft smile and that familiar warmth making its home in Astrea's heart said it all.

Chapter 16

The Talmaran palace was exactly as it had been every other time Astrea had arrived there after nightfall: a calm, steady light in the dark.

Once their airships landed outside the palace compound's tall walls, a group of guards escorted them into the safety of that perimeter. Ysabel was still keeping the palace under tight guard, with dozens of soldiers swarming around the place.

Was the whole city like this? It had been so long since Astrea had actually been out in the city. The last time was the night they'd gone to meet Nazarov at Club Twilight, and she couldn't remember if she'd seen any military presence in the streets that night.

Even though she'd put more time and distance between herself and what happened under the streets of Talmaris, Astrea's mind didn't feel quite right. It was still slower than she wanted some days, slower than she was used to. Some days, she still had to work extremely hard to keep her focus on the present rather than the past. But sometimes she just couldn't focus on much, like that night at Club Twilight when she'd barely held herself together.

By the time they reached Ysabel's office deep within the palace, Civan's exhaustion lay heavy in Astrea's bones. He'd seemed to perk up after eating some of his chocolate on the flight, but the energy hadn't lasted long. When she peeked at him over her shoulder, he gave her a small smile.

"Adi," Lucian said, "perhaps you'd like to escort your sister and team-mates upstairs? We don't all need to be here for this discussion."

Adi nodded. "Sure. Noemi, Civ, Len, you're with me."

"I'll come find you when we're done," Jin said to Adi.

Cressida's hesitation arced out, rough on Astrea's skin. "Do I need to be here?" she asked Jin. "I'm awfully tired."

Jin tilted his chin toward Adi. "Go. We'll be fine."

As the others split off—Saros joining them—Lucian knocked on Ysabel's office door. When a muffled "enter" came from the other side of the door, Lucian pushed it open.

The warm glow from the chandelier made the grand duchess look almost younger despite the dark circles underneath her eyes. She didn't get up from the chair behind her desk as she said, "You've got your people back, Varojin?"

So much for a greeting. Ysabel was getting harder for Astrea to place as their time in Novaria stretched on. She'd been so welcoming at first, probably more than was appropriate given the situation. But lately? She was colder, less sure, more stubborn.

"Yes," he said. "I just sent them upstairs to get some rest."

"And what did you and your brother speak of?" Ysabel asked, lavender gaze sliding to Eliana. "I must say, I was a bit perturbed when you didn't give me any details yesterday. I thought we'd agreed to that."

"Apologies," Eliana said. "We were busy. And Kaius was exactly as we expected him to be, right, Jin?" Eliana asked with a huff. "Arrogant and not ready to negotiate anything. The only way he was going to release Jin's team was if he took Jin and me into custody instead."

"I hear there was a fight at the border," Ysabel said.

"We didn't attack first, Your Highness." Lucian took a step toward her desk. "Prince Kaius and his void mage did."

"Because I'm sure that will matter to the Helosians." Ysabel pinched the bridge of her nose.

Besides the change in Ysabel's demeanor since their arrival, Astrea didn't understand the grand duchess's reaction to the situation with the Paragon and Helosia. She acted as if it were a constant surprise, like the things they had to do crossed some line she couldn't fathom.

Surely Grand Duchess Ysabel hadn't thought they would get Jin's team out of Kaius's custody without some kind of fight, right? Was there any way she believed they could negotiate with him, give him nothing in return for three prisoners? Astrea didn't think *anyone* would agree to that kind of exchange, especially considering the circumstances and the fact that it was Prince Kaius they were dealing with.

Ysabel had reacted the same way when they'd said they had to go to Helosia to get the Paragon's book. Like it was a huge surprise, an impossible future. Prince Veiko, at least, seemed to have a better grasp of what needed to be done. Was Ysabel just that averse to conflict? She *had* maintained neutrality for nearly three decades . . .

"I would like to speak to you, Eliana, and you, Varojin, along with Commander Lucian and General Kanakos." Ysabel tilted her chin toward where Astrea still loitered in the back, then to Marko, and finally, to Nicos. "Just the four of you. No one else."

"Ysabel—" Eliana started.

"Just the four of you." Ysabel's tone left no room for argument.

Kicking Nicos out? Sure, Astrea could see how she didn't have much to contribute to whatever conversation Ysabel might want to have with the Auris siblings. But Nicos had *always* been by Eliana's side through many other royal discussions.

Jin's shoulders tightened, but he said to Astrea, "We'll be upstairs soon."

"The dreamwalking," Astrea mouthed to Jin. He nodded. Nazarov hadn't shown up since that one night, but whatever it was Ysabel wanted to talk about, Astrea wanted Jin to give her the full picture.

When the three of them were back in the hallway, Nicos asked, "Now what?"

"You may want to settle in for the night," Marko drawled. "I know that tone. Her Highness is going to keep them for a while."

Astrea didn't like the sound of that at all.

Despite the late hour, Astrea found herself unable to get ready for bed. Electricity buzzed just under her skin, making her legs carry her back and forth across the sitting room.

The clock suggested Jin and Eliana had been with the grand duchess for the last hour and a half. Sure, Marko had suspected Ysabel would keep them "for a while," but what could be taking so long? Some new information she had? Was she scolding them for how things had gone down at the base? Astrea didn't see how; Ysabel hadn't been there, and Kaius *had* attacked first.

She huffed. *Just go to bed, Az,* she begged herself. And yet her legs kept carrying her around the room.

So when a knock sounded on the door, she bolted to it. Jin wouldn't knock, but maybe there was news of some kind. Something to settle her nerves.

Pulling the door open, she found neither Marko nor another Novarian guard but someone both unexpected and welcome.

"I wasn't sure you'd be awake," Sarsali said with a smile.

"Can't get myself to rest." Astrea stepped aside to let her into the room. "What's going on?"

"What kind of greeting is that?" Sarsali teased as she waltzed inside.

"Sorry." Astrea ducked her head. "I just wasn't expecting to see you until morning. Is Cress alright?"

"She's fine," Sarsali said. "We saw her a little while ago. She's helping your friend get settled . . . Lan?"

"Len," Astrea corrected. "Lennor and Civan Rusas. They're part of Jin and Adi's team."

Sarsali nodded, as if that was all the explanation in the world she needed.

"So . . . why are you here then?" Astrea asked. "Not that I'm not happy to see you."

"Saros said you made little progress on your search for your father." Dropping into one of the armchairs near the unlit fireplace, Sarsali smoothed out her long violet skirt. "I wanted to see how you were doing, especially considering he's never been the most forthcoming with his information or feelings."

"Oh." Astrea padded over to the sofa and flopped onto it with a sigh. "He was actually more helpful than I expected."

Sarsali's smooth, tinkling laugh filled the space. "Why does that surprise me?"

"Because you're right about him."

"I'm right about many things."

Astrea grinned. "I know."

"You really didn't find much?" Sarsali asked as she sank back into her chair. "He mentioned going to find one of Roxana's old colleagues?"

"Yes, we spoke with her, but my mother kept my father's identity quiet. All Kira knew was that he'd visited Irvina but was from the Helosian side of the border."

Sarsali's eyebrows raised. "Helosian?"

Astrea shrugged. "That's what Kira said. She was going to ask around to see if anyone who still lives in town has anything to add, but we didn't hear back from her before leaving."

On the flight back to Talmaris, Astrea had asked Saros about that. What would they do if Kira showed up at Fort Silverpine with information, as promised? Saros had reassured Astrea that he'd taken care of everything, that he'd sent word to Kira about their next destination.

"Why do you think Mom didn't tell you who my father was?" Astrea peeked at Sarsali through her eyelashes.

"Oh, my dear, I wish I knew," Sarsali said gently. "Your mother and I were great friends, but like Saros, she kept her secrets."

Secrets. Astrea plucked at her skirt. Was that the Sovna family's destiny, to keep secrets?

"Well, that's too bad." Astrea offered Sarsali a tight-lipped smile. "Are you and Balthazar settling in?"

"It's not home, but we're trying. I'm worried about our employees back in Kalama."

"I'm sure they'll figure out what to do," Astrea said, though it sounded lame. What *would* the Lodestar Industries workforce do without Balthazar around? "Hopefully we won't be gone too long. Jin and Eliana are talking about next steps with Ysabel, I think. Some of the Helosians defected to Ellie's side."

"Cressida mentioned it. That's good."

"And how has working with Tomas been?" Astrea asked.

Sarsali pursed her lips, then said, "We've finally got the book back in proper order, and though Tomas has been hard at work going through everything, it's slow. He doesn't trust anyone right now. He barely trusts Balthazar and me to help."

"Really?" Astrea could understand Tomas being reluctant to discuss the topics with an outsider like Professor Shalysko again, but Sarsali and

Balthazar came at Astrea's recommendation. At Cressida's recommendation. "Did he say why?"

"No, and it seems he's in a bit of a tiff with the grand duchess about it all."

"I'll go talk to him in the morning," Astrea said. Grand Duchess Ysabel was already resistant to their goals; they didn't need Tomas putting up roadblocks as well. "I'll get him to come around."

As Sarsali switched topics back to what had happened in northern Helosia and how everyone was faring, then to what she'd noticed about Ysabel's palace, Astrea tried to keep her mind focused. Missions. Politics. Questions about Cressida. It was hard, though. She couldn't help but think about Jin and Eliana and what Ysabel might be saying to them. She also couldn't help but think about how, finally, for a night or two, she might get to spend some real time with Jin. Have some privacy, not just to enjoy each other but to actually sit down and talk about all the things they hadn't been able to in the flurry of activity that was Fort Silverpine.

"Can I ask you something?" Astrea fiddled with the end of her braid. "Something personal."

"You know you can ask me anything, sweetheart," Sarsali said, though gray confusion and green curiosity sparkled around her for a heartbeat.

Heat traveled from Astrea's neck to the tips of her ears, and she was sure her entire face was red. "When did you know you and Balthazar were a good match?"

Sarsali laughed, a light, delicate sound. "What makes you ask that?"

"All this talk about my parents just has me wondering," Astrea lied. "I realized I don't know much about your lives before we moved to Kalama."

"Oh, Balthazar and I . . ." Sarsali's cheeks rounded with her grin, and her eyes crinkled around the edges. "We met when we were so young.

Skies, we were barely twenty-one and twenty-two. We were both actually studying at university in our final year."

"I didn't realize," Astrea said.

"Yes, it was our final year, and I was working on my final project for my advanced horticultural studies course. He was out in the courtyard tossing a ball around with one of his other Metalli friends and completely destroyed part of my project."

"What?" Astrea asked, horrified. That didn't sound like Balthazar.

Warm amusement flowed through Astrea's veins as Sarsali giggled. "He did, but that was long forgotten the second I saw those eyes of his. I swear, I was so smitten."

"Did he at least apologize?"

"A thousand times, and he took me to dinner that night after he helped me fix the project as much as he could."

Astrea had always imagined Sarsali and Balthazar would've had a more peaceful start, not one that involved decimating Sarsali's gardening work.

"We graduated a few months later, then got married a few months after that. Our parents thought we'd lost our minds, but when you know, you know." A dreamy smile settled on Sarsali's face. "Then we moved to Talmaris for a bit so that Balthazar could study with a great engineer—the woman who built the city's train, actually. You've seen it, right? The one with the tracks lifted above the road?"

Astrea nodded. She'd seen that train the few times she'd been allowed to venture out into the city. But her mind kept drifting back to the fact that Sarsali and Balthazar had been together since they were so young.

"After they finished working on that, we actually moved down near Irvina so Balthazar could work on a few civil engineering projects with his mentor. You know, roadways and infrastructure and all that. We met your mother and Saros during our stay, though we ended up moving back to Helosia shortly before I was due to give birth to Cress. Roxana was a few months pregnant at that point, too. We wanted to stay here, but duty called back home in Helosia."

"You really don't think she knew my father was connected to the Paragon?" Astrea asked.

"Sweetheart, your mother loved you long before you were born," Sarsali said. "So much. And though she had her secrets, I truly don't think she would knowingly get involved in something like this. It just wasn't who she was or what she valued. She was always looking for the best in people and situations, and she was always trying to have a positive effect on the world. That's not exactly what the Paragon stands for based on everything you've told me."

Astrea swallowed hard. She wasn't sure if that was better or worse. They'd theorized that Jin's mother had seduced Emperor Aelius to try to birth "the sun" for the Paragon. If that was, in fact, true, then had Astrea's father done the same? That much deceit, that violation of trust . . . Astrea couldn't focus on it, nor could she shake the nausea building in her throat.

"Thanks, Sarsali." Astrea swallowed and forced herself to smile. "That's more than Saros ever told me."

"I'm not surprised."

"No, but maybe if I'd forced him to talk . . ."

"You know there is no forcing Saros to do anything," Sarsali said gently. "I love him like he's my brother, but he's a skies damn fool sometimes. One with good intentions, sure, but a fool nonetheless. If you should have forced him to talk more, then Balthazar and I should have forced him to take you far away from Kalama years ago."

"I'm glad you didn't." As much as Astrea hated all that had happened, had hated keeping her magic a secret, she was grateful for what Kalama *had* given her. The Nikaphoroses. Eliana. Nicos and Adi. Jin.

"Selfishly," Sarsali said with a heavy sigh, "I couldn't let my best friend's child go. We all thought if we just kept holding on a little while longer, things would change."

"I don't blame you."

"No, but I keep wondering what may have been different."

"We'll never know that."

"I suppose not." Pushing out of her chair, Sarsali yawned and said, "And I suppose my husband will be wondering where I've run off to, and I'm sure you're exhausted."

Astrea nodded again. "Yeah."

Sarsali leaned over and kissed the top of Astrea's head. "Good night, my dear."

"Good night," Astrea called after her.

As the door shut behind Sarsali, Astrea slumped into the sofa. She hoped Jin returned soon; she really needed to sleep, and lately, having him close was the only thing that seemed to calm her. And after everything, she needed a chance to be at peace, even just for a few hours.

Chapter 17

"Miss Sovna," a voice cooed. "Miss Sovna?"

That voice was . . . familiar and not. Astrea turned, finding only dark gardens around her. Someone from the palace calling her?

"Miss Sovna? Where did you go?"

Astrea tried to move through the night, but her legs were like stone.

"Miss Sovna, we need you."

Astrea sucked in a sharp breath. Warmth drenched her skin, and as she cracked her eyes open, she found gold ones staring back at her. Jin brushed her cheek with the back of his hand.

"You were asleep when I got back," he whispered.

"Sorry."

"Don't be."

As he kissed the tip of her nose, Astrea relaxed. Draping his arm over her waist, he tugged her closer. Their fronts pressed together. Somewhere in the back of her mind, she knew she should have questions for him. She should ask him about the grand duchess.

But her breath caught in her chest as he kissed her throat, sucking on the delicate skin there. Skies, she'd missed the feeling of his lips on her body. She tangled her fingers in his curls, which only seemed to make his kisses more aggressive.

He trailed his way down to her collarbones, down her sternum to where the neckline of her nightgown dipped between the small swell of her breasts.

"Do you want—" he started.

"Yes."

Heat sizzled pleasantly across her skin. Jin's hands moved to her shoulders, and he pushed her nightgown straps down. Their lips met in a delicate kiss. As Jin moved away, Astrea pulled him back in, hungry. He laughed against her mouth, the deep rumble traveling all the way to her core.

An ear-shattering ring screamed through the room. Astrea jumped halfway off the bed.

Jin laughed again as he rolled toward his side of the bed and reached for an alarm clock. The round silver clock continued its screeching as the bell clanged back and forth. "Sorry about—"

Astrea grabbed her pillow and smacked him on the back with it. "Why would you set that thing?" She huffed. "Skies."

Amusement tickled the end of her nose, and as Jin rolled back toward her, he wrestled the pillow from her with ease. "Because I was exhausted and didn't think I'd wake up in time for the meeting Lucian wants to have this morning."

"*I'm* your alarm."

"Oh, I know. That's why I was already awake. How am I supposed to sleep when you've got your ass pressed against me?"

Astrea brushed her hair away from her face and huffed again. "A meeting with Lucian?"

"Yes. We all need to talk."

"With Ysabel?" Astrea asked.

"No."

"Should I be concerned?"

"No," Jin said again.

"Should I be concerned, then, that we aren't going to finish what *you* started?"

Sure, Astrea would live, but longing weighed her down. A fire smoldered within her, growing with each passing second. Jin's hair was mussed from where she'd been holding onto it, and his lips were a bit swollen. The soft glow of the lamp in the corner of the room made his muscles—especially his arms—all the more defined. And the bright raspberry lust surrounding him and tartness on Astrea's tongue did nothing to help the situation.

She squeezed her thighs together. This was not fair.

"What if I promise to make it up to you later?" Jin asked.

"I'm holding you to it."

Jin leaned down and kissed her cheek. "I promise, we'll pick this up the first chance we get."

Groaning, Astrea pushed herself up and out of bed. It was early yet, at least according to that damn clock. "Why are we meeting now?"

"Lucian's idea."

"And why isn't Ysabel joining us?"

"Skies, you ask a lot of questions before the sun's up," Jin said as he climbed out of bed.

"And you're a shameless tease," she called over her shoulder as she padded toward the bathroom.

Jin's arms wrapped around her waist from behind, and he picked her up. "Am I?"

"Put me down!" she squealed, shoving down the giggle threatening to escape her. As soon as her feet touched the floor, Astrea whirled on him. Part of her was tempted to push him back onto the bed, Lucian's meeting be damned. The more reasonable side of her reined the rest in.

Astrea tried to put on her best serious face as she said, "We've got work to do."

Jin smirked. "I'll say. Let's keep this meeting as short as we can. I think we very much need the rest after the last couple of weeks. Lucian can't argue with that."

Astrea tossed her hair over her shoulder as she started for the bathroom again. "Fine, but you have to be the one to tell him."

"Oh, I'll tell him anything you want me to, Az."

Somehow, Astrea managed to keep her hands to herself and clean up for the morning. She would've preferred a shower, but despite Jin's teasing, he sobered quickly and insisted they needed to get to this meeting on time.

When they arrived at Lucian's office, Astrea pushed her shoulders back and smoothed her hair. Where she'd expected a whole host of energy to meet her magic, the room beyond the door felt strangely empty.

Jin knocked, then pushed inside. Lucian sat behind his desk, and Adi, Marko, Eliana, and Nicos were there. All calm. Neither Zephyrine nor Cressida were in sight.

"Close the door, if you would, Varojin," Lucian said. Then he motioned to the coffee pot on his desk. "I brought breakfast."

A breakfast meeting with Lucian? What was this?

"I don't know where Zephyrine is, but let's get started," Lucian said.

"I'll fill her in on whatever she misses," Jin said.

Astrea accepted a steaming cup of coffee from the commander. A meeting without Cressida just didn't feel right, not after everything they'd all been through. Had Cressida taken the morning off? Maybe to spend time with Lennor?

"As you know, we had a . . . long discussion with the grand duchess last night," Lucian said as they all gathered around his desk. "It was not productive at first, but we reached some level of understanding by the end."

"Is she being stubborn again?" Astrea asked.

Lucian's gaze flicked from her coffee cup to her neck and back again. "Stubborn may not be the right word. Hesitant is more appropriate here."

"Why?" Astrea asked. "She knows what's at stake. Where's this change in position coming from?"

"Honestly, I don't know," Lucian said with a sigh. "I'm trying to understand why she's going back and forth. Even the council is not so indecisive. Nor is she usually."

"Maybe staring down the barrel of war with Helosia is spooking her," Marko said.

"I can understand that," Lucian said, "but she's no fool. She knows there's only one way forward."

Astrea took a sip of her coffee, grimacing at the hot liquid. As she looked up from the cup, she found Lucian studying his desk very carefully.

"I wanted to speak with you all about what our next steps will be. Zephyrine—"

"—is here!" called the general as she strode into the room. The door closed behind her with a heavy thunk. "With the very thing I needed." She held up a thin stack of papers.

"What's that?" Nicos asked.

Eliana, who had turned in her seat to look at Zephyrine, caught Astrea's eye. Her gaze flicked down to Astrea's neck, then back up. Astrea frowned. Then Eliana touched the side of her own neck and mouthed what Astrea swore were the words "love bite."

Astrea's whole face burned. She reached up to touch her neck with her free hand. She couldn't exactly heal it now without getting caught, though Lucian had obviously taken note. He usually forced eye contact instead of avoiding it. Just how much was he judging her? Not that it was a particularly bad thing—it was just a small bruise—but Lucian was still . . . well, it was hard to figure out where he stood when it came to Astrea and Jin.

Although if she was being honest with herself, Astrea might die if Saros ever saw a love bite on her. They just didn't have that sort of relationship, whereas Sarsali and Balthazar might poke fun at her or say nothing at all.

Astrea fluffed her hair, hoping it would be enough to hide the mark for the rest of the meeting. And then she was going to kill Jin.

"Details for my contacts in Helosia and Tornama," Zephyrine said. "I thought you could get the information on Tornama to Prince Veiko, then I'll start finding ways to contact my people in the empire." She passed the papers to Lucian, then took the last cup of coffee from the tray on his desk. "Sorry I'm late."

"Thank you for this," Lucian said as he set the papers down.

"We need to go to the Badlands," Jin said to the group. "Ysabel's not exactly thrilled by the thought, but I'm sure we can stop our father if we go straight to his base of operations. If we can prevent him from finding or obtaining any more of this aetherium ore now, then we can hopefully put a stop to this more quickly. If we catch him while we're there, that's just a bonus."

"And making it look like it's not just a coup?" Astrea asked.

"We'll figure that part out when we need to."

That wasn't exactly a concrete plan.

"I thought we weren't sure of the aetherium's location," Adi said.

"That's why I'm trying to reach out to my network, Adi," Zephyrine said. "See what they know and if they have any intel they can pass along.

It's been hard getting information in and out of Helosia. Even Anjou hasn't had much luck."

Right, Anjou Lazzaro. Zephyrine's "husband," the nobleman and shipping tycoon who had helped them escape the Taipoli Islands. Was he still in Talmaris? Astrea had no idea; nobody had spoken of him since they'd all arrived.

"How long will it take?" Nicos asked.

"Maybe a week, maybe more." Zephyrine shrugged one shoulder. "I don't know for sure. As I said, it's tough right now. Better to be sure than risk the network's safety. They're no use to us if they get caught."

Astrea bit her lower lip. A week or more? Jin had once told her there was a lot of sitting around during war; she was going to have to learn to be patient and let the experts sort these things out.

"And what of our defectors down at Fort Silverpine, Commander?" Eliana asked. "Any word? Is Commander Tarkun being fair to them?"

"Vernie would have sent word if something was wrong," Lucian said. "We'll figure out where to move them soon. Vernie's also on the lookout for anyone else who might show up."

"That's all that was discussed with the grand duchess last night?" Astrea asked.

"That, plus the defector situation," Eliana said. "She says border patrol will funnel anyone who might arrive toward Silverpine."

"Do you think we'll get enough of them?" she asked.

"Hard to say," Jin replied, and Adi echoed his quiet agreement. "There are plenty who *would* if they could, but everything's too chaotic with Corsyca right now. Skies only knows if anyone's going to be able to make their way north."

At least Ysabel's going to welcome them, Astrea thought as she sipped at her scalding coffee again. That was progress, and that was all they could hope for right now.

CHAPTER 18

After their breakfast meeting, Astrea headed out in search of Tomas. It hadn't been all that long since she'd been to the palace library—barely a fortnight—but it still felt like it had been forever. She'd once spent so much time in quiet spaces, surrounded by books. Not anymore.

Jin had stayed behind to talk to the rest of the team about their next steps, and Astrea still hadn't heard from Cressida. That was alright; this might be a conversation better left for Astrea alone. Tomas liked her, or *had* liked her before everything started falling apart. Maybe he'd be more open with her.

Smoothing the skirt of her gingham dress, Astrea pushed her magic out farther. Inside the library was just one presence, calm and steady. That was good. Astrea pushed open the door and headed into the grand room. The dark ceiling and deep-tone wood greeted her like an old friend, familiar and comforting.

"Tomas?" Astrea called as she neared the center of the room. She set her hand on the back of a nearby chair. "Tomas? Are you here?"

Curiosity tickled the end of her nose, then the librarian shouted back, "Astrea?" His blond mop of hair appeared on the mezzanine. "What are you doing here?"

"I wanted to see how things are going with the *Myths and Other Legends* book," she said as he started for the stairs. "Is now a good time?"

"Oh, well . . ." He pushed his glasses up the bridge of his nose. A light blush colored his pale cheeks as he stopped halfway down the stairs. "I suppose."

"I can come back if you're busy."

"No, no, that's fine. I just need to go get it."

Tomas ascended back to the second floor and disappeared into his office. Astrea sat at the nearby table. A couple minutes passed. Nothing in her senses changed, but what was taking him so long?

She was about to go find him when the pitter-patter of Tomas's hurried footsteps returned. He rushed down the spiral stairs in the corner, then pulled out a seat across from Astrea.

"Is everything alright?" she asked, eyeing him. Nothing seemed out of place. Even his charcoal gray waistcoat and olive green shirt were perfectly pressed.

"Everything's fine, thank you for asking," he said. "How was your trip?"

"Eventful."

"I imagine." Tomas let out a nervous chuckle and set the manuscript down. It was bound together by a thick blue cover, no letters stamped on the front or spine. "I just finished binding it a few days ago. Good as new except for the paper being fragile. I took extra care with it." He slid it toward her. "Go ahead and look."

Astrea took the book gingerly and began leafing through the pages. Indeed, everything seemed to be in order. Those unreadable void notes marked up the margin. "Were the Nikaphoroses helpful in getting this put together?"

Hesitation scraped across Astrea's exposed skin. "Indeed, indeed."

"And were you able to find anything on Silya, the old leader of the Paragon?"

"Nothing yet, but something will hopefully turn up soon."

"Right . . . And a linguist to translate the language?"

"We'll find someone eventually."

"But how long do you think that will take?" Astrea pressed. "We don't have forever. Those notes might be important."

Tomas busied himself with picking invisible lint from the sleeve of his shirt.

"Tomas."

He barely met her gaze, only peeking up at her through his pale eyelashes.

"What are we going to do about this language?" she asked. "We need to find someone. This is very important."

"It's not that easy," he said.

"There must be a dozen linguists in Talmaris, probably more. Surely one of them can handle it."

"But who will be trustworthy?" he countered. "Who will not just be another betrayer?"

Astrea huffed. She couldn't make any guarantees, but surely not *every* linguist in the capital city would be a Paragon sympathizer.

"I don't even know if I can trust Lili after what happened with Professor Shalysko," Tomas said, voice low as he leaned across the table. "Friends for two decades, and now I haven't spoken to her in many weeks. We've never gone this long without speaking."

"Did Lucian investigate her?" Astrea asked.

"He ordered people to look into her." Orange anxiety flared in the air as Tomas sighed. "They found no connection to the Paragon, but I don't know that I trust that. They didn't find any link with Professor Shalysko either. What good are these investigations if we can't ever be sure?"

"I'm sorry about your friend," Astrea said gently. She couldn't imagine not being able to trust Cressida or Eliana after all this time, all because of one person's actions.

"So am I. I just hope she's not involved."

"For what it's worth, I doubt she is," Astrea said. "The Paragon's leader would have had her involved, trying to get information or get close to us somehow. Her silence and distance are telling. I'm sure of that much."

And Astrea truly meant that. There was no way Tomas's professor friend Lili would have Paragon connections and never have tried getting close to the investigation. The One or Nazarov would've gotten her involved somehow.

"Maybe," Tomas said, some of that orange bleeding away from his aura. "And I suppose you're right that getting those extra bits translated would be helpful . . ."

"It would be," Astrea said, then pulled the book closer. "Can I look through this for a bit? I'll bring it back when I'm done."

"You won't work in here?" he asked. "I can get you whatever you need."

"I could just use a little fresh air is all," Astrea said. In truth, she was hoping to grab one of her friends to go over it with her, but she had to go find one of them first. And fresh air did sound nice.

"By all means." Tomas gave her a tight smile. "Just please, be careful with it."

"You have my word."

A cool autumn breeze swept through the garden, pulling at Astrea's hair left loose down her back. She kept one thumb pressed to the top corner of the page she was scouring, preventing the wind from playing with that, too.

Tomas may not have been the most helpful, but Astrea was sure there had to be *something* in this book that would help them. Emperor Aelius had possessed the *Myths and Other Legends* book for at least a little while but probably months, which meant he knew about aetherium weapons. And Jin and everyone else were surely right that Emperor Aelius was searching for aetherium in the Badlands, but something nagged at the back of Astrea's mind.

"Are you sure this isn't a waste of time?" Marko asked. "We already know everything there is to know about the Paragon's history."

Lucian had insisted they go back to their old rule, that neither Jin nor Astrea were to be left alone when outside of their bedroom. Which meant Marko—grumbling about her "running off to the library" without him—had found *her* before she'd found anyone else. She enjoyed his company, but Lucian's rule seemed pointless. They might not even be alive for the Paragon to kidnap if they didn't prevent the emperor from developing this weaponry.

And while Marko was right that they'd already pieced together the Paragon's history through this book—information that may have been more useful once upon a time—they had a much more immediate threat to deal with. Aetherium.

"I don't know," Astrea admitted, "but what else am I going to do all day?"

"Right, because rereading the same thing is a perfectly good use of time," Marko drawled.

Astrea glared at him. He leaned against the trunk of a nearby tree, arms folded across his chest. "Don't you think it's a bit strange that the emperor is focusing all his attention on the Badlands, and yet the Paragon don't seem to be operating there at all?" she asked. "I know they have *some* aetherium considering what we found at their ancient sites, but . . . it feels off."

"Is their focus not you and Jin?"

"They wanted this book, too."

He raised an eyebrow. "You think that because the Paragon aren't operating in the Badlands, aetherium isn't there?"

"I just think there's a lot we're missing with all these notes we can't read." She gestured to the book. "Maybe the location of more aetherium. Maybe not. But important nonetheless."

"Did you ask Tomas about a linguist?"

"Skies, not this again," she muttered.

"What?"

"Apparently he doesn't trust anyone after what happened with the professor."

"Can't say I blame him."

"No, but what do I do, go over his head to the grand duchess? Will *she* trust anyone?"

"Why do you ask that?"

"Oh, come on, Marko." Astrea scoffed. "You know she's been so back and forth about these missions and what we need to do in Helosia. You think she's suddenly going to trust someone else from the university?"

Peach amusement sparkled around Marko for just a moment.

"What could possibly be funny about this?" she asked.

That made him laugh, a low, deep chuckle. "You really don't know the grand duchess at all."

"Excuse me?"

"I was *shocked* when Commander Lucian first explained the situation to me months ago. Not shocked about void magic but the fact that the grand duchess had so willingly invited you and your friends into her palace," Marko said. "That she *was* being decisive."

"I was surprised she'd invited us in given who Jin and Eliana are, that she'd agree to work with us so easily," Astrea said.

"Yes, well, that may have been a surprise, too, but Grand Duchess Ysabel has often been slow to decide on a position. I'm glad she's sent Prince Veiko and Princess Delfine out to negotiate on her behalf, otherwise we'd never come to an agreement with the Tornamian or Taipoli governments in a timely fashion."

For all the time she'd spent in Talmaris, Astrea hadn't had much one-on-one time with Grand Duchess Ysabel. A few meetings and conversations over months weren't useful in gauging her decision-making process. And Astrea would be the first to admit she'd never paid that much attention to continental politics. Besides, back in Kalama, basically every news story was about Helosian politics. Any information she knew about the other countries usually came from overhearing gossip on the street or what little Eliana would divulge about her work.

"Alright, fine, maybe she's an indecisive leader," Astrea said. "But that doesn't change the fact that we need to figure something out."

Marko pushed off the tree and squatted down next to where Astrea sat on her blanket on the ground. He gestured for the book. "May I see?"

"Be my guest."

As Marko took the book, he flipped through a couple pages. Rough hesitation scraped over Astrea's cheeks.

"What is it?" she asked.

Marko's gray eyes met hers. "What if we asked that man who translated the journal?"

"Theo?" Astrea's eyebrows furrowed. "You want to ask the Paragon to translate it?"

"They already have the journal translations . . . what could any of this possibly say that would be worse than that?"

Astrea huffed. "Specific locations for aetherium? Some other void magic secret?"

"Or we continue not knowing what it says and possibly miss out on beating Emperor Aelius to a specific source."

"Or we just end up giving the Paragon access to that specific source of aetherium. Marko . . . come on." Astrea gestured vaguely around them and said, "Sure, they want Jin and I for their prophecy, but the journal Theo translated mentioned theories about meteorite having certain properties. That's what Nazarov and Theo had been trying to figure out. They want this book. The One wanted this book desperately. Surely they already know something about aetherium and how it'll help them take down the continental powers."

"Oh, I agree that they know about aetherium, but you said we need this translated," Marko said. "It seems like an obvious solution to our problem, if not a risky one."

"I wouldn't even know how to get in touch with Theo. I can't dreamwalk to him, nor him to me. He's no void mage."

"Nazarov told you to meet him in the Antare Mountains, right?" Marko handed the book back to Astrea. "I'm not saying we must do it, nor that it comes without risk, but at least we know what they want and where their loyalties lie."

"You think the grand duchess won't work with a linguist from Talmaris but will entrust us with a mission to meet with the Paragon again? About *aetherium*? You do realize how senseless that sounds, right?"

He shrugged. "It's just an alternative. A contingency plan in case we have literally no other options. I'd certainly prefer to avoid meeting them again—or giving them more information—if we can help it."

As Marko returned to his tree, Astrea stared at the open book in her lap again. Did he have a point? Could they ask the Paragon to translate this? Would it be worth the risk if it gave them a better chance at stopping Emperor Aelius?

She wasn't sure she wanted to find out.

Chapter 19

A happy sigh left Astrea as she finally stepped under the hot water in the shower. She'd been tense all day. Ever since hearing that Zephyrine needed time to get information. Ever since she'd realized Tomas and Ysabel were both acting strange.

Just give everyone time, she told herself as the warm water splashed against her front. *Lucian wasn't upset about the schedule, nor were Jin or Adi. It's fine.*

Dinner was soon, and she'd promised to eat with her family.

Heavy footsteps sounded in the bedroom, then the bathroom door opened. Through the foggy glass shower, Astrea could make out Jin's body as he began peeling his clothes off.

"Awfully presumptuous," she said as she rubbed at a sore spot at the base of her neck.

"My getting naked is presumptuous?"

"Incredibly."

Jin slipped into the shower behind her, his hard erection pressing into her backside.

"It's a good thing I don't mind presumptuous," Astrea said, leaning back into him and grinding her hips into his.

A low growl rumbled in Jin's chest. "Can I touch you?"

"What do you think?" She ground against him again.

He snaked one of his hands down her abdomen, lower and lower until his fingers reached her entrance. The other slid up to the base of her throat.

"I think I really hate this shower," he murmured as he rubbed her in small smooth circles.

Astrea sucked in a sharp breath. "Why's that?"

"Because I'm too scared of you slipping and falling to fuck you properly."

All the air in Astrea's lungs stilled as Jin slid one finger into her. "So what are you going to do about it?" she managed to choke out. Tart lust exploded on her tongue.

Jin withdrew his hand, and Astrea groaned. Skies, all she wanted was for him to touch her again.

He hauled her up and tossed her over his shoulder.

"What are you doing?" Astrea squeaked.

"You asked what I was going to do about the shower." He stepped out, taking Astrea with him. Chilly air made her skin prickle, but Jin's skin burned under her touch, matching the fire burning in her belly.

"We left the water on," Astrea weakly protested as Jin went back into the bedroom. "And I'm all wet."

He tossed her on the bed. "I really, really don't care. The water's fine, and the blankets will dry you off." Jin leaned toward her, arms bracketing her head. His lips brushed hers. "I missed having you all to myself."

Astrea forced herself to meet his gaze as she whispered, "Prove it."

Raspberry lust and peach amusement swirled around him like a beautiful sunrise. The corners of his eyes crinkled. "Prove it?"

"You heard me."

"Should I give you another love mark? I'm pretty sure that proved it to everyone."

"I can't believe I didn't catch that before we left this morning."

Jin pressed a delicate kiss to the side of her neck. "Is it wrong that I'm a bit proud of that?"

"You're *proud*?"

"I want everyone to know you're mine," he said, kissing her neck again as he fully climbed on top of her on the bed. His thick erection brushed against her. Lowering his voice, he said, "You can give me one if you want, call it even. Tell them all I'm yours."

You're mine. Those two words circled her mind in quick, sharp circles. Jin's desire lit up the room, raspberry and pink and deep purple. *I'm yours.*

"You're mine," she whispered.

Nipping at her neck, Jin brought his fingers back to her entrance. "Say it again."

"You're mine," she repeated, barely getting the words out as he pushed two fingers into her.

"And you're mine."

"I'm yours."

His fingers curled against the right spot. "Again, Az."

"I'm yours." She'd say it a thousand times if he wanted her to. "I'm yours."

Jin smiled, then withdrew his fingers. She wasn't left wanting. He dragged her to the edge of the bed so her hips were perfectly positioned, then pushed into her. They both cursed. Skies, she was so full. So wonderfully, perfectly full.

And as Jin's energy expanded, filling the room, she felt wonderfully, perfectly connected to him. Sunshine flitted over her skin. Purple and pink swirled in front of her half-closed eyes, a myriad of shades. She gripped Jin's shoulder, fingers digging into his muscles.

"Tell me what you want."

"What about what you want?" she asked.

"I already have exactly what I want." He pulled out of her, then slowly pushed back in as he repeated, "Tell me what *you* want."

A thousand things lingered in the back of her mind, just beyond the haze that settled over her. So many things . . . but none of them mattered here, in this moment with Jin.

"I just want to relax."

Jin hummed. "I can help with that."

"Prove it."

A deep laugh started in Jin's chest and traveled to where their bodies were connected. "What is with you and this need for proof tonight?"

"Just keeping you on your toes."

Their hips rocked together in a slow, steady rhythm. Astrea kept her legs tight around Jin's waist, not letting him pull back far at all. Swearing, Jin leaned down and kissed her in quick, sharp bursts.

"I know what I want," he said.

"I thought you already had what you wanted."

He pulled out of her again, joined her in bed, then tugged her on top of him. "I want to see you. All of you as you come undone."

Astrea's skin burned with their mingling desire. She sank down onto him, groaning and letting her head tilt back. She forced her eyes open, taking in the raspberry, pink, gold, and even vermilion filling the air.

Proud. Jin was *proud.*

His warm fingers found their way to that spot between her thighs. She rocked back and forth in his lap, swallowing a cry as pleasure jolted from her core to the very top of her head. Her whole body warmed.

She pressed her hands against his chest, a desperate search for balance as she already felt so close to unraveling. Jin's arms circled her shoulders. He pulled her down and held her there as he fucked into her again and again and again.

Astrea shuddered. Her muscles trembled as she tightened around him, tighter and tighter until she was sure she was going to break.

And she did. The world fell away—the colors, the warmth, everything but the feeling of Jin's body under hers. Even as her head still spun, she kissed his neck. She kissed it again and again, her pace uneven as his thrusts grew sloppier and desperate.

And then he shuddered under her. He cursed in her ear. Warm bliss nestled near her heart as his whole body relaxed and his hips stopped.

"Fuck," he mumbled as he rubbed slow, smooth circles on her back. "Fuck, I don't ever want to go back to that base."

"Why?"

"Because I can't possibly do that with such thin walls and close quarters."

"What happened to letting everyone know I'm yours?" Astrea pushed a few inches off his chest. The raspberry, gold, and vermilion were still there, fading into the background as soft pink arced out from him.

"Maybe I got a bit carried away saying that," he said, that soft, secret smile of his pulling at his mouth.

Astrea giggled. "Maybe."

"Maybe that's not the best way to tell the world."

"Oh?" Her pulse thundered in her ears. "Then what is?"

"I can think of a few things." Leaning up, Jin pressed a quick kiss to her lips. "Let's go finish that shower."

By the time they finished cleaning up, Astrea didn't even want to look at the clock. They'd gotten . . . distracted . . . despite Jin's earlier worries about her slipping.

But there they were, finally dried off, dressed, and nearly ready to go meet her family.

"Are you sure I'm welcome?" Jin asked as he rolled up the sleeves of his black button-down shirt.

"Cress won't care, and I know Sarsali and Balthazar won't care."

"And yet you didn't mention Saros."

Astrea shook out the skirt of her lavender dress. It was the slightest bit rumpled, but she didn't mind. It was just dinner with her family, and none of them would judge a few wrinkles in her skirt.

"Saros has been trying," Astrea said. "This will be a test to see how committed he is to being better about everything."

"Oh, good, just what I wanted with dinner," Jin drawled, "an exam."

"Hey, you're not the one being tested."

"True."

As they left the bedroom and headed for the door, Astrea finally looked at the clock. Cressida had said to meet them at the sixth bell, and it was already ten minutes past. Her whole face warmed. At least none of her family were Lightbringers and wouldn't be able to tell she was embarrassed about *why* they were late.

Astrea just hoped she was right about her uncle, that he'd pass the test tonight. After locking himself away in his room all day, Astrea didn't know what kind of mood he'd be in. But Jin was her partner. Saros had to accept him eventually.

Hand in hand, they walked across the hall to Cressida's room. As soon as Astrea knocked, Cressida opened the door.

Her jade gaze flicked up to Jin as she whispered, "Oh, this is going to be fun." She opened the door wider, revealing her parents and Saros already sitting around. "Come in, though I should kick you out for being late."

"Sorry," Astrea said. "I was—"

"It's my fault," Jin said. "I didn't want to wake Az up from her nap."

Well, that was no better a lie than hers.

"And I hope it's alright that I tagged along?" he added.

"You know you're always welcome, Jin," Sarsali said as she got up and crossed the room to hug them both. "Besides, you're basically part of the family now."

Peach amusement burst to life around Cressida as Astrea's own embarrassment consumed her. Skies. Saros simply gave an easy smile.

Was Sarsali testing him, too? That would have been an easy thing for him to disagree with.

Getting to spend time with her family all in one room again was so nice. Sure, sitting around a foreign monarch's palace wasn't the same as the Nikaphoroses' comfortable dining room. In fact, Jin had to sit on the floor because there wasn't enough seating—not that he minded. He often did that when the team took over their sitting room. But it wasn't at all tense like Astrea had feared.

They talked about how Saros, Balthazar, and Sarsali were settling in. They discussed the food palace staff had brought them and all the tweaks Balthazar would have made to the recipe. It could've been any night they had a Nikaphoros-Sovna family dinner back home.

But Astrea could hardly pay much attention. Her mind kept wandering back to her earlier conversation with Marko.

"Can I get your opinions on something?" she asked, accidentally interrupting Saros as he began to speak.

"About what?" Cressida asked.

"I was talking with Marko earlier—"

"What?" Jin asked.

"You know how I was going to see Tomas this morning?" When Jin nodded, she explained how he was mistrustful of anyone from outside the palace now. "And then Marko and I were talking, and he suggested we try to get Theo to translate the void language bits in the book."

"Theo?" Jin and Cressida asked at the same time.

"That was my reaction," Astrea muttered.

"I'm sorry, Theo Kadis?" Balthazar asked. When they nodded, he said, "I thought Theo had aligned himself with the void mages."

"He has," Jin said before explaining how they'd worked with Nazarov and Theo for the other translation. "Why would Marko prefer that over finding a linguist?"

"He doesn't *prefer* it," Astrea said, twisting her skirt around her fingers and making the earlier wrinkles worse. "He said we already know what Theo stands for and wants. He proposed it as a contingency plan if all else fails."

"A risk we already understand," Jin said. "I get it, but I don't like it. How would we even get in contact with him?"

"You think these translations are that important?" Saros asked, rough hesitation scraping Astrea's skin.

"I don't know," she said, "but I'd rather know everything we can as soon as we can."

"What if I speak with Tomas?" Saros asked. "I used to have friends at the university studying linguistics, among other things. Maybe one of them still works there. I could make a few calls, bring them in for whatever review process the grand duchess thinks is appropriate."

Would Tomas go for that? Astrea didn't know. But it wasn't really up to Tomas. It was the grand duchess's decision.

"I still know a few people in Talmaris, too," Balthazar said. "I can give you their information, Saros. Surely we'll be able to find someone within our network."

"I like the sound of that better than trying to get in touch with Theo," Jin said.

Saros actually smiled. "Then I'll get started on it in the morning."

Cressida shot Astrea a knowing look.

Maybe Saros had tried to get Jin sent away years ago, but this was good. And it was far better than the way Jin and Lucian butted heads.

"Well, with that settled," Sarsali said as she held up a platter of cookies, "who wants dessert?"

<h1 style="text-align:center">CHAPTER 20</h1>

Astrea wanted—*needed*—to do something. Anything.

After dinner with Jin and her family, the next day had passed slowly, spent training with Marko and Cressida while Saros disappeared again and everyone else dealt with the politics of their situation.

And after another quiet dinner and restless sleep, Astrea found herself waiting around. Again.

Maybe Cressida and Balthazar would need some kind of help while they examined more aetherium-meteorite samples? Or maybe Sarsali would be . . . Well, Astrea didn't know. But maybe she needed help. Or Adi; he'd been spending every spare moment with his sister. Maybe she should check on them.

Astrea shook out her pleated dark blue skirt as she climbed off the bed. The shower was still on; Jin had been up early to run through a few drills with Zephyrine. Going to the desk, Astrea grabbed a sheet of paper and scribbled a note about where she was going and left it on the bed.

She was curious about Adi's sister, but she'd wanted to give the poor girl a break after everything that had happened.

As soon as Astrea stepped foot in the hall, Marko appeared by her side. "Where are you off to?" he asked.

"I wanted to check on Adi."

"He and Noemi went outside about twenty minutes ago."

"Do you know where they were going?"

"No, but I'm sure we can find them."

That was good enough for Astrea. They walked side by side through the palace, silent except for the occasional scuff of their shoes on the floors. They passed guard after guard, though none of them paid much attention to the pair.

"Have you talked to Adi much since we got back?" Astrea asked.

Marko sighed. "Some, but I was trying to give him space."

"As was I."

"So what's changed?"

"I don't want Noemi to think she's unwelcome if we aren't being friendly. And I'd like to assess her energy, see how she's doing."

Exiting the palace, they headed into the gardens crawling with Novarian military. It hardly seemed like the place for Adi and Noemi to relax, but maybe Noemi would feel safe?

At Marko's suggestion, they checked a few spots close to the palace first, but neither Kuwat sibling was to be found. They headed deeper into the gardens, and as they crested the hill that sloped down to the lake, she spotted Adi and Noemi walking back toward the palace.

When Astrea waved, Adi's aura lit up with mint relief. The taste coated her tongue as the pair moved closer. Noemi's, however, was filled with orange and yellow, anxiety and worry.

"Az, Marko, hi." Adi wasn't wearing his usual black fatigues. Instead, he wore black slacks and a green shirt that complemented his complexion beautifully. But it was so strange to see him *not* in his uniform. Noemi was in a simple white dress, and she'd pulled her tight curls up into a bun. "What are you doing out here?"

"Just wanted to see how you two are feeling," Astrea said. As Noemi's eyebrows pulled together, Astrea smiled and added, "And Jin's boring, so I thought maybe you'd be up to something more fun."

Adi chuckled. "I don't know that a tour of the palace is fun, but I was just showing Noemi around. Trying to give her a feel for the place."

"It's big," Noemi said. Her full lips pressed together before she added, "I've never been someplace so big."

"Kalama's campus is easily this large," Adi said.

"But it's easier to navigate."

"Would it be alright if we join you on your tour?" Astrea asked, mostly directing the question to Noemi.

"If it's alright with Adi . . ." Noemi twisted her fingers together.

"Of course it's alright with me," he said. "Though Marko might be the better tour guide."

"Would I be?" the Tempest drawled, making Adi chuckle again. Mint relief and pink desire twined together in both the men's auras, arcing out toward each other.

Adi's so-called tour of the palace kept them busy. He explained the guest house and why they were no longer staying there, then took Noemi to the guardhouse and showed her where Lucian's office was in case she ever needed the commander. He even took Noemi to the library, which was when her eyes finally lit up and her aura shifted from orange to green. Curiosity danced over Astrea's skin like a gentle morning breeze.

"This place is amazing." Noemi stopped in the middle of the room, tilting her head back to look at the painted ceiling. "It's so beautiful."

"I'm sure you're welcome to come in here whenever you please," Astrea said. "I'll put in a good word with the librarian for you. His name's Tomas."

"Is he here?" Noemi asked, gaze drifting to the mezzanine.

"No." Astrea couldn't sense his energy anywhere in the room; it was just the four of them. "He usually is, though."

"You would've liked a couple of the places we've been in the Macadian and Antare Mountains," Adi said to his sister as she circled the room and examined the different stone busts of old Novarian rulers. "There are these void mage ruins—"

"I still can't believe all that's real," she murmured.

"Oh, you'd best believe it is," Marko said. Astrea glared at him, but he simply shrugged.

At least Noemi seemed to be relaxing a bit, though her stiff posture and the faint sheen of orange anxiety stuck to her skin said she still wasn't entirely comfortable. Astrea didn't blame her. She'd need time to settle in and adjust after everything.

"Grandmother would never believe this," Noemi said to her brother. "To see us in a place like this. Neither would Father."

"I know," he said tightly.

Noemi glanced at where Astrea and Marko loitered a dozen feet away. "I can really come in here whenever I want?"

"I don't see why not," Marko said as he looked first down at Astrea, then over to Adi. "I'll let the staff know."

For the first time that morning, Noemi's round cheeks lifted in a smile. "Thank you. I can see why my brother likes you."

Marko's entire face turned pink. "Well . . . I, uh—"

The library door swung open, and anxious surprise slid over Astrea's limbs as Tomas exclaimed, "Oh!"

"Hey, Tomas," Astrea said. "Sorry to scare you."

"Astrea," he replied with a nod. "Adi. Marko. And . . . I'm sorry, I don't believe we've met?"

"This is my sister, Noemi," Adi said. "We were just showing her around and trying to get her settled in after coming here from Kalama."

Tomas shifted the two books tucked under his arm. "I see."

"I've already promised Noemi she can visit the library whenever she wants," Marko said. "I hope that's alright."

"I'll try not to be too much of a bother," Noemi said. "And respectful, of course. It's a beautiful space."

"That it is," Tomas said with a small nod. Rough hesitation scraped Astrea's skin.

"You've got my promise that it won't be an issue," Adi said. "Noemi's spent plenty of time in libraries. She's getting two degrees right now from Kalama's—"

"You're a scholar, too?" Tomas interjected.

"Oh . . ." Magenta embarrassment flared around Noemi. "I don't know about a *scholar*—"

Adi nudged her. "I think you're a scholar."

"You have to say that. You're my brother."

"Well, it's also true," he said, vermillion pride swelling around him. "The top of your class currently in both archaeology and history."

"A scholar indeed," Tomas said. "You're welcome here any time, Noemi." He turned to Astrea. "Any luck with the *Myths and Other Legends* book? I assume not so much since you didn't leave me a note when you returned it."

"It's as I said the other day, that we need a linguist to help us with the translation," she said. "My uncle was going to reach out to some folks he still knows in Talmaris. Has he spoken to you?"

"The grand duchess and Prince Varojin mentioned something of the sort yesterday," he said, pushing his glasses up the bridge of his nose. "And your uncle gave me the contact information for one person earlier this morning. I suppose it's something we need to get a jump on."

Astrea forced herself to smile. They should've had a jump on this weeks ago, when they'd gotten an entirely translated notebook from Theo. That would've helped any linguist begin building the language out. And if not then, surely Tomas could've been working on that with someone while the rest of them were trying to rescue Jin's team. But harping on that wasn't going to do any good.

Instead, Astrea said, "Great. Would you like some assistance?"

"That's alright. I was just going to make the call now," he said. "I'll let you know what they say."

"Let me know, too," Marko said. "The commander's going to want to clear them before we let them into the palace."

With the way Tomas pressed his lips together, it was obvious he was trying to hold back another comment about how the last background check had failed. "I'll let you know," he said to Marko. "Anything else?"

Adi shrugged. "I suppose we should let Tomas get back to work and continue on with our tour . . ."

"Very good," Tomas said. "It was nice to meet you, Noemi. Marko, Astrea, I'll be in touch." He circled their group and started up the stairs to his office.

"What else could you possibly have to show me?" Noemi asked. "I thought this was the last important spot."

Circling his arm around her shoulders, Adi said, "We haven't even been to the kitchen yet. Let's see if we can snag you some of the Kalamian coffee my old commander brought with her."

"Well, I guess that'd be okay," Noemi murmured as they headed out the door.

Astrea smiled. Yes, Noemi would need time to settle in, but Astrea was sure she would. And with Saros, Jin, and the grand duchess getting Tomas back on track, they'd surely have their answers about the void language soon, too.

Despite the cool afternoon breeze, sweat beaded down Astrea's back and forehead. She barely pivoted away from Jin's fire. Its heat scorched her skin, a warning not to slow down.

Training *with* Jin was new, something they hadn't done before. Well, they'd trained before, but it had never involved his fire, nor did it involve Adi trying to pummel Astrea with his earth.

"C'mon, Az! Show 'em what you're made of!" Cressida shouted from somewhere behind Astrea. Lennor's amusement slid over Astrea's skin, like someone tickling her with a feather.

"Shut up!" Astrea called. She didn't need the distraction.

Adi punched. There was too much distance between them for his fist to get anywhere near Astrea, but the ground under her feet rumbled. She jumped back, forcing her shield to life as grass and rock shot toward her. Heat roared to her right. Astrea turned, her shield barely absorbing the flames.

She was supposed to try that souleating ability on them. The whole point of this exercise was to have them try to cut off the connection once she started it.

But Jin and Adi's walls were tight.

And unlike how she could reach past the Paragon's veil, there was no way into Jin and Adi's energy.

"You know," Astrea said, huffing with the effort of continually dodging them, "I don't think that blocking me out is actually the point of this exercise."

"So find a way in," Adi said as he stepped closer.

The wind gusted, rustling the weeping willows near the lake's shore. Astrea gritted her teeth as she pivoted away from Adi's next attack. How was she supposed to find an opening? There were no cracks in their walls, no diminishing focus. Not even when Cressida yelled taunts from the sidelines.

"Prince Varojin!" Commander Lucian called from back near the palace.

"What's he doing here?" Adi asked, gray confusion swirling around him as he stopped and relaxed.

Jin stopped, too, the faintest hint of yellow worry clinging to his skin.

Astrea reached forward. Their energies buzzed along her palms and up her arms. She clenched her fists, pulling back. Both men stumbled forward, crying out in surprise as they tried steadying themselves. Pain sizzled in Astrea's sternum, making her nauseated, but she didn't let go.

"Fuck," Adi grunted, voice rough.

"So find a way to shut me out," Astrea said. And despite it all, Adi's amusement brushed the end of her nose.

Jin cut the connection first, blocking her out once again. The electricity dancing along her palms lessened. Shoulders drooping, Jin put one hand to his sternum. Another heartbeat, and Adi cut the connection, too. With a grunt, he shook out his arms and legs. Astrea let her head roll forward and blew out a deep breath.

After clearing his throat, Jin called back to Lucian, "Yeah?"

"I need to speak with you."

"Somebody's in trouble," Adi whisper-sang.

"Shut up," Jin grumbled. He snatched a small towel from the ground, then jogged up the hill to meet Lucian.

"Do you really think he's in trouble?" asked Noemi.

Like Cressida and Lennor, Adi's younger sister had come out to watch their training. She wasn't a mage, but Astrea figured she didn't want to be left alone in a foreign palace, so she'd invited her to join them.

"No," Astrea said as she walked toward the three women and accepted a flask of water from Cressida. There was no way Jin would be in trouble.

"Hopefully he's not long," Cressida said. "I was really looking forward to you kicking his ass."

"Yeah, you almost had him there at the end," Lennor said.

"Oh, I don't think so." Astrea closed the flask lid. Sure, she'd managed to avoid getting hit, but that tiny hold she'd had over him didn't mean much as far as she was concerned.

"Dirty fighting to attack us while distracted, Az," Adi said.

"You told me to find an opening."

"I didn't say fighting dirty was a bad thing." He grinned, making his dimple appear. "It's the only way sometimes."

Shrugging, Astrea scratched at the waistband of her pants. Skies, some days she really hated wearing them. More than she hated using her souleating on her friends for practice. She was mostly used to trousers by now, but she longed for her quiet days spent in loose dresses and library alcoves.

"You want to get in there, Cress?" Adi asked.

"No, thank you." She tilted her chin up into the air. "I'm fine right here."

His dual-tone eyes flicked over the group. "Az, you and me?"

"Can we take a break? Just until Jin's back?" She tugged at her pants again. It was like once her mind recognized the uncomfortable feeling of something tight on her waist, it couldn't let it go. "Skies, you'd think someone would've made a dress you could exercise in by now. I'd pay whoever made that a million lire."

"You don't have a million lire," Cressida said.

"Like you've never heard of a figure of speech?" she shot back.

"Some regions in Zaikud used to wear something similar to dresses into battle," Lennor said. "Not for a long time, but they used to."

"How do you know that?" Cressida asked.

"Our father used to read a lot of Zaikudi history books to Civ and me. They were Civ's favorite; he'd look at them for hours. I just liked the pictures of all the different armor."

With a small sigh, Astrea dropped into the grass. "Well, it sounds like they had the right idea."

"I could make you something, Az," Adi said as he sat next to her.

"What?" Her cheeks burned. "No, that's alright, I just meant . . ."

"It wouldn't take me long, and it beats sitting around all day," he said quickly.

"Well . . ." Astrea hesitated as she watched him. Nothing spiked in his aura. Instead, calmness settled on her skin. "It's not like I can pay you. That doesn't seem right."

"You don't have to pay me."

"I can't just have you do all that work for nothing in return."

"Alright, well, how about you just heal me whenever I need it? Indefinitely."

"Adi!" Noemi exclaimed, the first time Astrea had heard her voice rise above a quiet, soft tone. "*That's* not fair!"

He laughed, a warm, deep sound. Lennor and Cressida joined in. "What did you say earlier, Az?" he asked. "Haven't you ever heard of a figure of speech?"

"I don't think that's a figure of speech," Noemi mumbled. "But if you're making Astrea a dress, I want one, too. Something like I wore back home, not this." She plucked at the white dress she wore. "Something pink."

"Fine, fine," Adi said, peach amusement snapping in the air around him. "Let me see if I can get my hands on some supplies. And you have to cut the patterns."

"Deal." When Noemi smiled, her right cheek dimpled just like her brother's.

"Should I put my order in, too?" Cressida asked.

"I'm fairly certain you have enough clothes," Adi replied.

"Do I, though?"

Adi had just started to argue when Jin appeared at the top of the hill again. Gray confusion undulated around him. Hesitation scraped Astrea's skin. Pushing to her feet, she jogged over and met him halfway.

"What did Lucian want?" she asked.

"Word's finally gotten around," Jin said. "The Delians and Zaikudi both want meetings with us."

CHAPTER 21

It should have been no surprise to Astrea that the Delian and Zaikudi governments were finally demanding a meeting with Eliana and Jin.

And it wasn't. Not really. What did surprise her was how quickly things began moving once it was decided that they were going to take the embassies up on their offer to meet. So did the fact that they were going to meet these other countries off Ysabel's property.

The grand duchess had been incredibly strict about Eliana's and Jin's movements, especially Eliana's. In fact, Ysabel didn't want any of them leaving the compound. For safety, yes, but also to conceal the fact that they were even in town as best they could.

So how had the Delians and Zaikudi found out? Through whispers from some of the soldiers or staff at the palace? Or could this be some kind of strange retribution by Emperor Aelius for Eliana and Jin defying his orders to stay out of his business? No, that didn't seem to make much sense.

The ambassadors had said they wanted to discuss why Eliana and Jin were in Novaria and what was happening in Corsyca. Eliana hadn't wanted to refuse the meeting, saying that would look suspicious at best, and easing their suspicions was "ideal."

Astrea swallowed her reservations as she clasped on the opal necklace Jin had gifted her. Paired with her plum blouse, pleated black skirt, and brogues, she looked a bit too casual. But it was either that or an evening gown. And Astrea may not have had all that much experience around dignitaries, but even she knew that was inappropriate.

As Jin came out of the bathroom, dressed in black slacks, a black shirt, and wingtip shoes, Astrea finished putting the top layers of her hair in a braid. She tied it off with a ribbon. Hopefully their group's lacking appearance wouldn't signal their lack of preparation or strength to the Delians or Zaikudi.

Neither Jin nor Astrea said much as they left their room and joined Marko in the hallway outside. He led them through the palace halls, past soldiers and staff alike, until they reached a door Astrea hadn't seen in months. He opened it, then motioned for them to step into the tunnel first. It led from the palace directly to the garages.

"Lucian's already there, right?" Jin asked Marko.

"Yes, he's already on site with a team. He would have radioed if he thought this unsafe."

That made Astrea's shoulders relax a fraction.

"And do you happen to know where my sister is?" Jin asked.

"No, but we have two cars ready and waiting."

"Thank you for helping with this."

"You don't have to thank me, Jin. It's my job."

"Yes, well, it feels a bit strange to me to have a friend running my and my sister's security detail," Jin said.

Astrea swore Marko perked up ever so slightly at the mention of "friend." Did he not see it that way? She certainly considered him a friend. They'd been through too much together.

"And just so you know," Jin said as they neared the end of the tunnel, "I haven't seen Adi so happy in a very long time."

"Skies," Marko murmured, bright pink embarrassment flaring around him. "Is now really the time for this?"

"I'm just going to bring it up this once," Jin said. "And only because I haven't had a chance yet. But Adi's my brother, and I like seeing him happy, so thank you. I'm done now, I promise."

Marko cleared his throat, murmured something incoherent, then opened the door at the top of the stairs. As he held it open for Astrea, she didn't miss the slight smile pulling at his mouth.

They were, unfortunately, not bringing the team with them. But as Jin and Eliana had said, there wasn't much for Adi, Cressida, or the twins to do even if they joined in the conversation. The Delians and Zaikudi wouldn't listen to anyone but Princess Eliana Auris, Prince Varojin Auris, and General Zephyrine Kanakos. Which had just made Astrea question twice why they were bringing *her*. She thought Lucian would've made the better candidate to study the foreign diplomats' reactions, but both Jin and Eliana had insisted they needed her there. Two Lightbringers at the meeting table were better than one, they'd said. And with Lucian there on Ysabel's behalf, Astrea would have to pay more attention than usual.

Fresh air tickled Astrea's cheeks as they neared the open garage bay doors. Two sleek black cars waited, already idling. Zephyrine stood near one, arms folded loosely across her abdomen. She'd certainly dressed the part, with her white hair tied in a braided crown and her emerald wide-legged trousers and silver silk blouse. Even her jewelry—small but sparkling with gems—hinted at her status.

"Finally dragged yourself out of bed?" she called to Jin.

He waved her off. "I'm hardly late."

"Not that we can leave ahead of your sister."

"No, we can't." Jin surveyed the garage. "Where is she, anyway?"

"Coming, I think," Astrea said. The energy in the air behind and below her—in the tunnel—shifted into electric anxiety. It zapped her skin, first distantly and then more powerfully as several people moved closer. "That must be her."

Jin's eyebrows furrowed. A moment later, Eliana stepped through that narrow door leading to the tunnels. Her crimson tea-length dress, gold jewelry and hair pins, and red lipstick all screamed Helosian. Smart or stubborn? Astrea couldn't decide. Would the Delians and Zaikudi see it as a testament to Eliana's desire for the throne, or would they just see her as another Helosian ruler to take down?

Nicos, thankfully, hadn't put on his old palace uniform. Instead, he was dressed similarly to Jin but had swapped a black shirt for a maroon one. Still tied to the Auris family, but at least he was being a bit more subtle about it.

"Ready?" Eliana asked with a hesitant smile.

"Let's get this over with," Jin said.

"With that attitude, things aren't going to go well," she chided as she swept past him. Her heels clicked on the garage's cement floor. "We must look strong and united."

"We *are* strong and united," Jin said as he opened the closest car's door. "I just think it's going to be a bunch of bullshit on their end."

"We'll see!" Eliana called over her shoulder, her tone much lighter than that anxiety still pulsing around her in fits of orange.

Astrea sucked in a deep breath, then climbed into the car.

She really hoped Jin was wrong for once.

Winding through Talmaris's streets had taken a while, thanks to morning traffic. But it had begun clearing out eventually, and the closer they got to downtown Talmaris, the more Astrea's nerves buzzed.

Jin and Zephyrine didn't say much, other than agreeing to let Eliana's tone set the meeting. She had more experience with the Zaikudi and Delian governments than any of the rest of them, as did Nicos. After all, she'd been meeting with their representatives in Kalama to try to find some solution to the Corsycan War.

Marko pulled their car onto a quiet street lined with large buildings and tall metal fences that gleamed in the morning sun. Set far behind those fences were beautiful white buildings, all with flags flying high above them. The green, blue, and white Delian flag. The green and white Zaikudi flag.

A guardhouse sat a few feet down the sidewalk, the guards dressed in a dark green that matched the colors on the Zaikudi flag. Lucian stood nearby, dressed in his formal commander of the guard uniform, the one trimmed with silver and all those tiny badges above his heart.

"Well, here we are," Marko said as he shut the engine off.

Astrea let her magic spread wider and wider until her head ached. There were her friends, of course, and Lucian and the Zaikudi guards. Toward the embassy itself, there were flickers of annoyance, outrage, calm. Certainly not unexpected among politicians and bureaucrats.

Zephyrine climbed out of the car first, then Jin. Astrea took Jin's hand when he offered it to her. She squinted against the morning sun, trying to see the Helosian or Tornamian flags somewhere farther down the line of buildings. But she couldn't see past the tall trees and glaring sun. Would those Helosian ambassadors, the ones who had delivered Emperor Aelius's ultimatum, be snooping around? Would they even still be in Talmaris after the way Jin and the rest of them had broken into Kalama?

Once Eliana and Nicos joined them on the sidewalk, Marko escorted them all up to where Lucian stood.

"Commander," Eliana said in Helosian. "Are we ready?"

"Yes, Your Imperial Highness." His midnight blue gaze flicked to the Zaikudi guards, and in Novarian, he said to them, "Their Imperial Highnesses are ready."

The guards' expressions hardened as they assessed Eliana and Jin. But they nodded, then pushed the ornate black gate open on squeaking hinges. It was at least six feet taller than even Jin, the tallest of the group.

While the embassy's exterior gardens and architecture were all Novarian in style, the inside was a different story. The same dark wood accents as the palace covered the floors and trim, but comparisons stopped there. Shades of green and white mixed with blues and golds. Everything from the art on the walls to rugs on the floor stuck to the color palette. Several Zaikudi flags hung from the tall ceiling.

A woman around Eliana's height stepped out of a line of guards. Unlike her counterparts, though, she wore a simple dark gray dress. "Your Imperial Highnesses," she said in heavily accented Helosian, "welcome to the Zaikudi embassy of Talmaris."

"Thank you for inviting us," Eliana said.

The woman tilted her head in acknowledgment. Distrust prickled Astrea's skin as the woman's narrow blue eyes flicked over the group. Would she be a mage? And if so, what type? Tidebacker or Tempest, like Lennor and Civan? Perhaps a Stargazer or Lightbringer? There was no way to tell without seeing her show off her magic—if she even had any.

"My name is Marel, Your Imperial Highnesses," she said. "I work for Ambassador Tahere. The others are waiting down the hall. I'll escort you there."

The line of guards parted as Marel turned on her heel and started down the corridor. As they passed by the guards, more of that distrust radiated off them and lanced Astrea's bones, painful and unyielding.

"I don't think they're very happy to see us," Astrea whispered to Jin.

"Not surprised," he murmured.

Marel led them down one hallway, then another, deeper into the embassy. As they walked, Astrea spotted some of Lucian's people in their Novarian blue standing alongside guards in Zaikudi green and the much lighter Delian blue. That made her feel a bit better.

Finally, they stopped at a set of arched double doors, both carved with an ornate scene of a forest, mountains, and the rising sun and moon.

Marel tilted her head at them again. "Ambassador Tahere of Zaikud and Ambassador Sirras of Delia are waiting for you."

"Thank you," Eliana said. "We're ready."

It all seemed a bit redundant to Astrea; couldn't they just get on with it? But she held her tongue as Marel opened the doors to the meeting room.

Inside was the same beautiful design as the rest of the embassy, the same mix of cool tones and gold accents. Paintings of Zaikudi leaders in their extravagant formal regalia lined the walls, as did maps of the continent. The thick mahogany table shone under the chandelier's light, and though the table could easily seat twelve, just two sat at it, one on either end spot.

"Princess Eliana Auris, Prince Varojin Auris," said a woman as she pushed out of her seat. She couldn't have been much younger than Zephyrine, perhaps in her thirties. Her silky dark brown hair lay over her shoulders, and a few freckles dotted her light brown skin. Her small eyes crinkled as she smiled, but from her distance, Astrea couldn't catch the color. "Welcome to my embassy."

"Ambassador Tahere," Eliana said with a small nod. "Thank you for inviting us to speak." Then she turned to the man who was still seated at the far end of the table. "Ambassador Sirras."

"Your Imperial Highness," he said to Eliana, not even deigning to look at Jin. He gestured with one pale hand for them to sit down. His auburn hair was streaked with white, and his wrinkles suggested he was probably close to Ysabel's age.

Astrea hadn't expected a warm welcome, but that was cold. Jin didn't seem bothered at all.

As Eliana sat at the seat in the middle of the table, Jin circled and sat opposite her. Astrea, Lucian, and Marko joined him. Nicos and Zephyrine sat with Eliana while Marel took a seat near Ambassador Tahere. Tense silence settled over the room.

"I must say, Your Imperial Highnesses," said Ambassador Tahere, "news of your being in Talmaris was quite the surprise, especially given how long you've been in the city. We'd heard of the rumors in Kalama that your life was threatened by our people, but I want to assure you, our governments made no such directives."

"It makes one wonder how Grand Duchess Ysabel has managed to keep such news a secret," drawled Ambassador Sirras. Distrust and annoyance scraped Astrea's skin, rough like tree bark. "Especially given that the Novarian government's official position is neutrality. To find out she's been hiding not one but two Helosian heirs is . . . concerning."

"Grand Duchess Ysabel and the Novarian government did not mean to keep secrets, Ambassadors," Lucian said. "Rather, she was providing refuge to two young royals expelled from their home country."

"Refuge," mused Sirras. "Right. And the scuffle at the Helosian border several days ago? The increased military activity on both Novaria's and Helosia's parts?"

Astrea swallowed past the lump in her throat. Had Kaius tipped these embassies off about Eliana and Jin? But why would he do that? Wasn't Emperor Aelius trying to conceal Helosia's true actions? She risked a look at Lucian, but his neutral expression didn't change.

"I'll admit," Eliana said, all smooth politeness, "I was surprised by this invitation. It's not like our countries are very good friends, after all."

"We're concerned, Your Imperial Highness." Tahere's gaze softened. "Our countries may not be friends, but I appreciated the work you were doing with my counterpart in Kalama. I don't enjoy war."

"Nor do I," Eliana said. "It seems the Corsycan conflict serves no one."

"No one?" spat Sirras, rusty annoyance flickering around his lanky body. "Your father cannot be allowed to expand his borders."

"Ambassador." Eliana smiled tightly at the older man. "I don't agree with the war effort at all. I think Corsyca should be left to determine what it wants for itself, and the rest of us should back out. It's not our business. Let them do as they please."

"The Corsycans don't know what they want or what's good for them." Sirras waved a dismissive hand. "Delians have ruled Corsyca on and off for centuries. It's time we formally bring them into the fold."

"While I disagree with you on that," Eliana said, "I think I need to make it clear that I have no say in what the Helosian government does at this moment. As Commander Lucian said, I have been exiled."

"There has been no formal announcement," said Tahere.

"No, but I would not have been living in Talmaris for months if I had been welcome and safe at home," Eliana replied.

"And what a miracle it is that we've found you now," Sirras muttered. Astrea's eyebrows furrowed.

"I believe what Ambassador Sirras is *trying* to say," Tahere cut in, "is that we're curious to know what could get both of you sent into exile."

At least they aren't dragging this out. Astrea didn't particularly care for the line of questioning, but in a social circle that usually danced around the hard questions and played games instead, it was nice to get to the point.

But how would Eliana answer that question? They couldn't exactly reveal what the emperor was actually doing—or what they thought he was attempting to do.

"Well . . ." Eliana leaned back in her chair and sighed. "Frankly, Ambassadors, it's my disagreement over Helosia's Corsycan policies that drove me to leave the country. It's become increasingly clear since the spring that my brother—*our* brother, Prince Kaius—is unwell. Unstable, really."

"He's been unwell for years, but our father, of course, doesn't want to admit that about one of his children," Jin added. "That's what the skirmish at the border was about. He kidnapped one of our friends and was holding them hostage, demanding that we turn ourselves over even after our father told us that if we stayed out of his business, he'd leave us alone."

Ambassador Tahere looked at Marel, who had started writing on a notepad. What, did Eliana and Jin hope to portray Kaius as unstable in order to either sway these ambassadors to their side or to make Kaius a target? They had not told her about this plan.

"We don't know what Kaius's goal is," Eliana said, her emotions calm even as she lied. They knew *exactly* what Kaius was attempting. "An unstable Helosian heir, though, is a danger to us all. I hope you can see that."

"Of course," said Ambassador Tahere. "An unstable heir to any throne is not ideal. An unstable leader of any country, really."

Eliana nodded sagely. "Another thing we're in agreement on."

"Now hold on." Ambassador Sirras leaned forward almost conspiratorially. "You expect me to believe that Emperor Aelius Auris is simply ignoring one of his children losing their mind and acting out in such . . . peculiar ways? That's not the Emperor Aelius Auris we all know."

"Perhaps not the one *you* know, Ambassador," Eliana said. "But our father has always placed Kaius on a pedestal. We aren't even sure if he knows what Kaius is up to. That kind of information is . . ." She pursed her lips. "Hard to come by."

Ambassador Sirras steepled his bony fingers in front of his mouth as he leaned back in his seat. Distrust still radiated off him in harsh waves, but Ambassador Tahere was surrounded by green curiosity.

"You would tell us this about your family?" she asked Eliana.

"What's happening with our father and brother is largely an internal family problem," Eliana said. "Notwithstanding what someone unstable could do with that kind of power, of course. I hope you can respect that Varojin and I are working hard to get Kaius the help he needs."

"Largely an internal family problem?" Sirras laughed, his tone mocking. "Why should we leave you to it?" he asked. "Taking out Emperor Aelius and Prince Kaius would ensure Delian victory in Corsyca. All I'd need to do is call a few contacts back in Mematos, and we would be set."

"Novaria will not stand for that kind of intervention," Lucian said.

"Oh? And what's the grand duchess going to do? Send her half-assed army to invade Delia?" Sirras chuckled as wave after wave of red contempt rolled off him. The heat of his frustration singed Astrea's skin. "No, I don't think so. She'll sit on her hands, as she always does, because she knows Novaria is weak."

"Weak?" Lucian snapped. "Novaria is far from weak, Ambassador. All due respect, but you've been as uninvolved in Novarian and Delian relations as your predecessor. You know nothing about our country."

"I know you sit up here in the north, happy to watch the rest of us gain strength and power."

"You think conquering small neighboring countries is power?" Lucian laughed. "Arrogant like your predecessor, too. Why am I not surprised?"

"Commander, Ambassador, please," Zephyrine cut in. "What I think is important here is that Their Imperial Highnesses see the threat their father and brother pose to the continent. Might there be some way we can all remain neutral, at least toward each other, while Helosia sorts itself out?"

"Neutral?" Sirras spat. "I—"

"What of Prince Apelo?" Ambassador Tahere asked, leaning forward. "What is his situation like? Could he be counted on to take over Helosia?"

Eliana and Jin exchanged what seemed too curious of a glance, at least to Astrea.

"We've not been able to discuss it with him directly," Eliana said carefully, "but Apelo has always been levelheaded. Perhaps he would be a good choice for the job."

That was the play. They'd all been worried that Eliana might seem like she'd been plotting a coup this whole time. If she positioned herself as supporting Apelo and wanting to get Kaius help, perhaps later, if they really did manage to stop the emperor, they could paint Eliana in a softer light, someone who had tried all other options first.

"I don't buy it for a second," Sirras muttered. "He abdicated years ago."

"That was merely a rumor," Eliana said coolly.

"And the rumors of you and Prince Kaius being top picks to inherit the throne?"

"Our father has always valued magical strength above other attributes," Eliana said. "With Apelo not inheriting the Auris family fire, our father refused to see all the good qualities Apelo does have."

"Family," Tahere mused. A faint smile pulled at her mouth as she leaned back in her seat. "It always complicates matters, doesn't it?"

This didn't seem to be getting them anywhere. The ambassadors still hadn't truly said why they'd called this meeting; it couldn't just be for a chat. Astrea glanced across the table to Nicos, whose emotions were locked down impressively tight. He didn't move a muscle.

"That it does," Eliana said.

Marel looked down at her wrist, where a small gold watch caught the light. She leaned over to Ambassador Tahere and whispered something too low for Astrea to make out. The ambassador nodded, then Marel headed for the door.

"Apologies for my secretary," she said as the door shut behind Marel. "There are some things she must attend to, and we both lost track of the time."

"That's quite alright," Eliana said. "Though I must admit, I'm not sure what else we have to discuss, Ambassador. I'm hoping you see now why I'm in the city and that we can leave it at that."

"I don't think we can, unfortunately," Ambassador Tahere said before Sirras could jump back in. He huffed. "My government has asked me to find out more about that attack on the Novarian palace months ago." Tahere's attention drifted to Lucian. "Commander? Is there anything you can share?"

"We believe the operatives were sent by Prince Kaius," Lucian lied. "Sent to try to retrieve Princess Eliana and Prince Varojin."

"Some might see that as an act of war," Tahere said. "You have not retaliated?"

Lucian shrugged one shoulder. "One lone act of aggression is not something that would drive us to war. If he attacks again, the conversation may have to change."

Tahere pursed her lips.

"And that's why we've set up so much security around the city," Lucian continued. "My office should have notified your office about this weeks ago."

"We were told about the security but not the culprit."

Sirras drummed his fingers against the table. He sucked in a breath as more annoyance radiated from him in bursts of rusty red.

"I suppose it's reassuring to hear that the grand duchess will not jump to immediate retaliation," Tahere said.

The back of Astrea's neck prickled.

"Reassuring, indeed," Tahere continued, "to know that she is still the same after all these years. That some things never change."

The goose bumps traveled all the way down Astrea's body, from her neck to her toes.

Void mages.

Chapter 22

The legs of Lucian's chair scratched against the wood floor as he stood and announced, "We need to leave."

"Commander?" Eliana asked.

That cold wrongness surged in the air as a muffled boom echoed through the halls.

Astrea shoved to her feet, too. "Now, Ellie."

"What is going on?" Sirras demanded, the heat of his anger burning Astrea for the umpteenth time. She gritted her teeth. "What was that?" Orange fear and gray confusion formed a tight knot around his body.

"The embassy is under attack," Lucian said.

"How could you know that before the explosion?" Tahere asked. Something in her energy, some sense of ticklish curiosity mixed with stone-like certainty, made Astrea pause.

"You know," she said to the ambassador.

"I'm sorry, who are you?" Tahere asked.

"She knows," Astrea said to Jin and Eliana. Another boom echoed above them. The ratta-tat-tat of automatic gunfire followed. "It's—"

Lucian prowled around the table. Tahere scrambled out of her seat and sprinted to the door, shouting in Zaikudi as she ran down the hall.

Energy exploded in Astrea's senses: pain, anger, panic, rage, pride, and that cold, cold, cold she hated so much.

Lucian followed Tahere into the hall, shouting orders in Novarian. Marko ran after him. Astrea made to follow both of them, but Jin pulled her back.

"Ambassador Sirras," Zephyrine said, "we need to get you out of here. This was obviously some kind of setup."

"What is going on?" he asked, orange fear pulsing around him as the gunfire continued creeping closer. "I don't understand."

Astrea actually believed him. Sirras may not have liked Eliana or Jin very much, but he didn't seem to be the one working with the void mages.

"We'll explain later," Zephyrine said. "I need to get you and Princess Eliana out of here. Do you know if there's a rear exit?"

"A tunnel that leads to the other embassies," he said quietly. All of his earlier anger and annoyance bled away. "In case of attack or emergency. It's the same in all the embassies."

"Then let's go. Lead the way."

Sirras called for some of the Delian guards standing outside, and three filed into the room, joining him as he headed for the far corner of the space.

"What about Ambassador Tahere?" Astrea asked Jin as Eliana and Nicos followed the ambassador. He pulled on a candelabra, and one of the wall panels loosened. "We can't just let her go."

"Lucian and Marko are going to take care of it," Jin said.

"We can't let them go alone."

"Lucian's team is in the building."

"So? I can help, Jin. More than most." If she and Lucian could use their souleating on the void mages, just like they had near Kaius's base, everyone might stand a chance.

"There could be void mages waiting for Ellie down there," Nicos said, tilting his head toward the secret doorway.

"There aren't," Astrea said. "I don't feel any."

"And what if they show up?" Nicos asked. "We need you, Az. Ellie needs you."

Astrea's fingers twitched. He had a point, but she couldn't just let Lucian and Marko go out there with so little backup. So few Lightbringers could actually do what she and Lucian did.

Another boom echoed through the embassy. The floor shook.

"Nic, we'll be fine; we can fight them," Eliana said, then turned to Astrea. "Go help Lucian. Get as many Novarians as you can to safety, and try to figure out what the Zaikudi are doing with the void mages. Please."

Before any of them could argue, Eliana shoved Ambassador Sirras in first, then followed. Heaving a sigh, Nicos ran after her.

"I'm not leaving you here, Jin," Zephyrine said. "I'll get Eliana on the way to the palace, then come back. Be safe." Then Zephyrine disappeared and pulled the secret door closed behind her.

Astrea hated to see Eliana and Nicos leave, to not go with them, but Zephyrine would protect them. They would protect each other.

Now, Astrea needed to go help the Novarians. And the Delians, it seemed. And figure out why the skies the Zaikudi would side with the void mages.

"How many void?" Jin asked as he crept toward the doors leading to the hall.

Astrea tried to count, but separating so many strings of energy proved fruitless. "I don't know, maybe ten? Twelve?" There was too much interference, too much to sift through. "It's all blending together."

"And how close are they?"

"Not too close."

He grabbed her hand, then pulled open one of the doors. Outside, two Novarian guards in blue dress uniforms stood, hesitating as they stared down the now-empty hall. "Where'd Commander Lucian go?" Jin asked them.

"That way," said one, a young woman with sepia skin and bright purple eyes—another Lightbringer. Her companion, a tall, older man with blond hair, had brown eyes. "He told us to stay here," she added. "For the princess."

"My sister's on her way out. Come with us," Jin said. "We need to help him round up the Zaikudi. We think they're working with void mages."

Were *all* of them working with void mages, or was it just the ambassador and her assistant? It'd be nice to know so they could maybe recruit some more people to their side, but Astrea supposed they'd just have to figure it out later. She ran after Jin, the Novarian guards at their backs.

The embassy's hallways, cluttered with narrow hutches, tables, and paintings, offered no cover and no stealth. No bodies littered the ground, though bullet holes riddled the floors and walls. No blood. Had they pretended to attack just to draw the Helosians out? What did that mean for Eliana? Should Astrea have gone with her after all?

Focus, Astrea scolded herself. She had to stand by this choice.

"Go right!" she called to Jin. That was where the most cold was, where the most pain was. It pinged around in her chest, searing her from the inside out. That had to be Lucian controlling someone, maybe even the void mages.

Jin veered to the right at the next break in the corridor and found stairs. They ascended as quickly as possible, Jin always multiple steps above Astrea. The stairs turned twice before leading to the next floor.

A large, open space spread out before them. Lucian's back was to the stairs, as was Marko's and another Novarian's. Several Zaikudi guards stood with the ambassador, and behind them . . .

Faces Astrea had hoped to never see again.

Masked faces, their obsidian features trimmed with red, white, and gold.

Paragon.

Lucian's hands were stretched out before him. Pain and cold lanced into Astrea. Color and shadow swirled in the room, tying together in a messy knot between the two groups. He had them.

He had them!

"He cannot . . . maintain this . . . forever . . ." said one of the masked figures, a voice Astrea swore she'd heard before but couldn't place. It wasn't Solana, nor was it Nazarov.

Lucian's arms trembled. His knees were too straight, like he could barely hold himself up.

Astrea readied herself, lowering her stance and stretching her arms out. They could not lose these Paragon or this ambassador, not today. If they were even a second too slow, they might disappear, jump away. Then how would they get answers?

Lucian's arms overextended. Pain ripped through Astrea, like muscle being torn from bone. All that energy directed at Lucian burst through the room, nearly knocking her back. She reached for the cold, *through* the cold. Goose bumps prickled her skin. Bile crept up her throat.

But there it was, anger and rage and frustration. She grabbed it all, again and again as she poked through the Paragon's veils. The Zaikudi ambassador stumbled to her knees, and so did two of her green-clad guards.

Against her wishes, Astrea's eyes closed. But the pull was too much, like a thousand strongmen were yanking on the other end of the rope she clung to desperately. Wind gusted around her, and the room's temperature jumped. Several bodies hit the floor.

Determination pulsed somewhere behind Astrea, bright and strong. Minty relief filled her mouth. Rushed footsteps clambered up the stairs.

Zephyrine—at least it sounded like the general—barked out an order to take prisoners alive.

Energy seared Astrea's skin, her veins, her bones. No part of her was left untouched by the burning anger and hatred of these people she held captive. She was too hot, overloaded.

More footsteps. Reinforcements. *Good.* They could end this.

A deafening pop exploded behind Astrea. Pain followed, and the other Lightbringer and Lucian both cried out. Pop after pop deafened Astrea until her ears were ringing. Her shoulder, side, and arm burned with unbearable pain.

One by one, the void mages slipped from her grasp. One disappeared in a swirl of shadow, then cold blasted behind Astrea's back.

Astrea's vision blurred. Her knees met the hard floor with a crack.

Behind Astrea, someone growled, "You weren't supposed to shoot *her*, you fool!"

And then a second body hit the floor. That unbearable hot and cold surged under Astrea's skin, then shut off. *Aetherium.*

Someone screamed. Stars danced in Astrea's line of sight, obscuring the box beam ceiling above. Another gunshot, more wind and fire. All that cold blinked out one by one . . . except for one. A familiar voice said something about surrender.

"Az?" Jin's panicked tone forced Astrea's eyes open. White terror blinded her vision, obscuring the darkening embassy. "Az, hey. Come on, look at me. Eyes on me."

Her lids fluttered closed, then opened again.

"I want this place locked down!" came that familiar voice again, rough and grating.

"Is everyone okay?" Astrea asked.

Jin laughed, a tight sound. "They will be." When her eyes drifted shut again, Jin said, "Hey, come on, look at me. Open your eyes."

"You're bossy," she whispered.

"I know." Jin gathered Astrea up in his arms. Pain sliced through her with every step he took, with every shuddering breath she sucked in.

"I can heal it," she said weakly. She just needed fresh air, a moment to think and gain her bearings after being shot.

"I'm getting you to the palace."

She didn't want to go to the palace. She wanted to heal it herself. Astrea forced one hand to move, bringing it to rest on her abdomen. Sticky blood covered her palm. Energy fizzled under her skin, dying before it even had a chance to grow. She pulled harder on it, wincing as her magic resisted.

"Stop, Az," Jin said.

She sucked in a deep breath, squeezing her eyes closed as light built around her palm. Mirror healing and pain warred on her skin, an uncomfortable clash. She whimpered.

"I'm getting you help," Jin said. "Don't heal it. I don't know if it was a clean shot."

Astrea's hand fell away from her side. Even in her cloudy mind, she knew that was at least enough. Enough to stop the worst of the bleeding there. She desperately wanted to sleep. To just let her eyes close . . .

"Az, come on, keep them open. I know it's hard."

The dark ceiling above her changed to late morning sunshine and blue skies. Fluffy white clouds drifted by overhead. Sirens screamed through the streets as untold emotions and walls bombarded Astrea. She couldn't pull her barrier back even if she wanted to; she couldn't hold focus long enough to reach it.

"Where's my sister?" Jin shouted.

"Gone, Your Imperial Highness, to the palace." Astrea didn't recognize that voice.

"We need to go. Now. Stay with Commander Lucian. He has prisoners in his custody."

"Yes, Your Imperial Highness."

"Marko, with me," Jin said.

Astrea's head lolled back. Skies, Cressida was going to kill her when she found out what had happened.

"Should've been watching our backs," Astrea whispered as Jin laid her down in the back of a car. The same car, it seemed, as they'd arrived in.

"No kidding, smart-ass." Jin turned over his shoulder. "Marko, can you drive?"

"I'm on it." Marko's gruff, muffled voice called out more orders, then car doors began closing.

Jin kneeled on the floor of the back row of the car, tearing his shirt open. He shucked it off, then ripped the fabric.

"How inappropriate," Astrea said.

"Are you really making jokes right now?" Jin asked as he pressed fabric against her side. She cried out, her body jolting off the bench seats. "You're worse than Adi."

Astrea's half-closed eyes followed the colors bursting from Jin, the white terror as it receded, the orange anxiety, the mint relief, even the faintest sheen of peach amusement. "You like it."

"I like *you*," Jin corrected. Her eyes fluttered closed again. "Hold on, Az. We're going as fast as we can."

Astrea kept her eyes shut that time, welcoming the cold relief of sleep as it pulled her under.

CHAPTER 23

"Miss Sovna!" Someone gasped. "Miss Sovna, what happened?"

Darkness enveloped her on all sides.

"What happened?" the shadows asked again.

"I got shot."

Someone clicked their tongue. "That was not supposed to happen. We need you, Miss Sovna."

"What happened?" a light, familiar voice asked.

Panic surged through Astrea's body, sharp and bright. She gasped as she tried to sit up, then cried as fire burned through her.

"Lie down," said that light voice. Astrea's vision focused long enough to see Ivy, the Purifier from the palace infirmary. "What happened?" she asked again.

"Shot," Jin said. "The embassy was attacked." He started explaining how the Zaikudi and void mages seemed to be working together, how Lucian had stayed behind, and how they'd certainly lost several Novarian guards.

Astrea's throat burned. Her eyes burned. Her whole body burned. She stared up at the blue sky high above her. Her fingers flexed, finding grass under her hands. She was . . . on the ground?

"And you didn't have him heal her there?"

"They were Paragon, Ivy. We couldn't stay. Not even for this."

"Right . . . well . . . we'll get this taken care of," Ivy said. "And Commander Lucian?"

"Had plenty of help on scene to do what had to be done," Jin said.

Ivy's hands settled on Astrea's shoulder and upper arm. Cool relief poured into her veins, crashing through her as her heartbeat and breathing calmed.

"Where's Ellie?" Astrea asked. The sky above her still danced and swirled. Even with her arm and shoulder healed, her side pulsed painfully.

"Already going to speak with Ysabel," Jin said.

"We can't tell Sar—"

"Astrea!" A panicked voice again shouted, "Astrea!"

"Saros," Astrea mumbled as Ivy pulled her hands back. "Thank you," she said to the other healer.

"Don't thank me yet," she said. "We need to get this bullet out of you. It shattered." Her gaze shifted to Astrea's left, and she gave a small shake of her head, making her coily curls bounce. "Incoming."

"Astrea!" Saros exclaimed again. "What happened?"

"I need to get you back to the infirmary," the Purifier said, ignoring Saros entirely. "Is that okay?" When Astrea nodded, Ivy said, "Then let's have Prince Varojin take you."

Astrea hated this feeling, this weakness. This knowledge that a bullet was stuck inside her. No wonder it hurt so much. And Saros's terror made her head spin even more than everything else.

"I'm fine, Uncle," she said as Jin hoisted her up in his arms. She clung to his neck, trying to keep her head upright as they headed for the palace. Vomit crept up her throat. She focused on his warm skin, the way his muscles flexed. "I'm fine."

"It's not fine!" Saros cried.

It was hardly the worst thing to happen to Astrea these last months, but she wasn't going to tell Saros that. Not now.

Jin explained again what had happened at the embassy, much to Saros's continued horror.

"How can you say you're fine after being shot three times?" Saros asked as Jin stepped into the infirmary just behind Ivy.

"Well, I'm alive," she muttered.

Truth be told, Astrea wasn't fine. Her breath was starting to grow shallow, not from pain but from reality settling in. The Paragon seemed to be working with the Zaikudi.

"You weren't supposed to shoot her." That was what that void mage had said. If not her, then who? Jin, maybe? Zephyrine? Lucian? Any of them could've been the target . . .

"Just give her some space, Saros," Jin said gently. "Let Ivy do her work."

He set her down on one of the cots. The sheets were cool and crisp under Astrea's fingers, and she hated the thought that her blood was going to get all over them.

The high ceiling. Ivy's blue eyes. Jin's chestnut curls. Astrea sucked in a shaky breath. *Laundry soap. Rubbing alcohol. Vanilla.* Another breath. She couldn't focus her mind on any of the small sounds around her, drowned out by the panicked energy out in the hallway.

Cressida burst into the infirmary, Adi right behind her. Bright white panic exploded in the room, making Astrea flinch. Her ears buzzed, muffling out Ivy's exact words. Something about a Metalli.

"Calm down, Cress, it's too much," Astrea whispered.

She wasn't sure anyone would hear her, but the terror and panic pulled back. The suffocating feeling stopped, at least enough that Astrea was able to steady her breathing.

"Do you need me to take the team down to the embassy?" Adi asked Jin. "Ellie told me some before she ran off to find Ysabel."

"Take Marko and Lennor—and Civan if he's feeling better—and see what Lucian needs," Jin said. "Zephyrine stayed with them."

"You got it." Adi smiled down at Az and said, "You really are one of the team now."

"Getting shot makes me one of the team?" Astrea managed to ask.

"Yup." Adi grinned at her, and she actually smiled back.

"I could use your help, Cressida," Ivy said. "A bullet shattered in her side, and some of the pieces are still there. It'll be far faster if you get them out."

"Me?" Cressida swallowed hard. Her eyebrows furrowed. "Az?"

"Just do it."

"It's going to hurt," Ivy warned.

"Just do it," Astrea said again.

"Varojin, hold onto her hand," Ivy instructed as she circled to the opposite side of the bed from Cressida.

Jin took her hand, and as Astrea watched him, she couldn't help but find it a little funny that he still had no shirt on, long abandoned as makeshift bandages. She tried to focus on his warm skin again. The way his thumb traced the same line on the back of her hand over and over again. The way he stared down at her with those beautiful eyes. Unreadable to her magic but face contorted up in pain.

"You can't sedate her?" Saros asked.

"Everyone just needs to stop talking and let me work," Ivy snapped, the first time Astrea had ever heard her tone sharp like that. "Please."

"Just do it," Astrea said for a third time.

At first, Astrea wasn't sure anyone was doing anything. Nothing changed. But then pain ripped through her side again. Astrea cried out, her hips lifting off the bed as she tried to squirm away. Squeezing her eyes shut, she gripped Jin's hand so tight she thought she might break it. Saros pushed her shoulder down on the other side, and Cressida used one hand to pin her leg down, forcing Astrea to stay mostly still.

Metal clinked against metal. Blood leaked down Astrea's side. Then a soft hand settled on her abdomen, and that cool, healing relief took over again. Astrea's muscles relaxed, and Saros and Cressida pulled back.

"Sorry," Ivy said as she pulled her hand away. "Far quicker than doing any kind of surgery."

"Well," Astrea said past the bile in her throat, "I'm part of the team now, and you're a healer, Cress."

"Shut up, Sovna," Cressida said, but the only thing rolling off her best friend was cool, minty relief. It coated Astrea's tongue, chasing away that awful taste of vomit.

Jin's hand brushed Astrea's forehead. "She's freezing, Ivy."

"Give her body time to settle and put a couple more blankets on her," the Purifier said gently. "I'll keep an eye on her. Do you want a tonic, Astrea? Something to help you sleep?" When Astrea hesitated, Ivy said, "It'll make this easier for both of us."

"Alright." Astrea certainly didn't want to make this harder on Ivy or herself.

Glass bottles clinked together, and Ivy murmured something to herself too low to hear. Astrea forced herself to look up at her family, at Saros's terrified expression, Cressida's knitted brows, and Jin's gentle smile as he settled two blankets on top of her.

Astrea tried to wait for Ivy to return, but her eyelids grew heavy. The darkness pulled her under and didn't let go.

The Novarian palace infirmary was hardly the first place Astrea wanted to be. She'd rather be in her own bed, tucked away from prying eyes and the rest of the world. But ever since Ivy's tonics had worn off, Astrea had been bombarded with all manner of things, mostly Saros's, Cressida's, and the Nikaphoroses' hovering.

She hadn't seen Jin in hours. She'd woken up shortly after losing consciousness the first time, only for Ivy to force not one but two tonics on her. Jin had been there, but she hadn't seen him since falling asleep shortly after. Nobody mentioned him or where he'd gone off to, and she hadn't wanted to ask. She didn't want to come across as needy. And it wasn't that she *needed* him, but the one person she really wanted to have there was her partner.

Ivy had gone to the kitchen in search of dinner for herself, and Saros and the Nikaphoroses had only gone away when Astrea begged them for some quiet.

She reached for the cup of water Ivy had set on her bedside table. As she grabbed it, pain exploded between her shoulder blades. Shadows encroached on her vision. The cup fell from her hand as she slumped over, water and glass shattering on the floor.

Am I interrupting? Nazarov asked.

Despite not being able to see him, Astrea could hear the smile in his voice.

Attacking us today wasn't enough? she retorted.

That was not me, little Lightbringer.

Why do you still call me that?

He chuckled. *It has a nice ring to it, don't you think?*

Astrea gritted her teeth. *What do you want?*

To make sure you're alive. As I said, it was not me.

It sure looked like the Paragon.

Oh, it was the Paragon, but I wasn't there.

It was a technicality, but Astrea wasn't going to argue the point with him. It would just be a waste of her time. Maybe that was what he wanted.

In any case, the reckless oaf who shot you has been taken care of, Nazarov said. *No need to worry about him anymore.*

Was that who she had felt die by aetherium? She wanted to ask, but instead, she said, *Why are you working with the Zaikudi?* That seemed like the more important question.

Perhaps we want some of the same things. Or perhaps they're just a means to an end.

Why should I believe you when your people have kidnapped me, shot me, and blown my friends' airships out of the sky? she asked.

Oh, testy, I see. That smile returned to his voice. *Still feeling sore after what happened this morning?*

Fuck off. Astrea didn't know why Nazarov bothered talking to her at all. What reason could he have to contact her like this other than to torment her?

I thought I'd made it plenty clear that you needed to come see me in the mountains, Nazarov said. *It's not a far journey for you. What's taking so long?*

Why would I do that? she asked. *Your people nearly killed me today. You were going to kill me the last time we saw each other.*

You want to stop Emperor Aelius, and so do the Zaikudi. So do I. The darkness surrounding Astrea pushed in closer, suffocating her. *So come meet me, little Lightbringer, and I'll make a deal with you. I'll help you stop Emperor Aelius and halt all Zaikudi attacks on Helosian targets if you—*

No.

No? Nazarov scoffed. *You foolish, strong-willed girl.*

Accepting your deal didn't work in my favor last time.

You got the book, didn't you?

And you sent Tovan and Solana to kill me! You shot us out of the sky!

Nazarov scoffed again. *You're spirited, little Lightbringer. I'll give you that. But there is only so much one woman can take. Meet me in the mountains, or we'll just have to see how quickly I can break you.*

As Astrea's vision cleared, she flopped back onto the thin pillows. Groaning, she scrubbed at her face with both hands. Was Nazarov manipulating the Zaikudi now? To what end? Get them and Helosia to destroy each other? And probably drag Delia into it—their ambassador had at least an inkling of something being wrong.

But why get involved? They were on the brink of destroying each other in Corsyca anyway. Hasten their collapse?

Astrea had been reluctant to take Ivy's tonics at first, but now she wished she had more. Anything to just make this awful day go behind her more quickly.

And it was only getting worse. Two balls of energy were moving her way. Quick footsteps in the hallway outside made Astrea push up to a sitting position. Cressida and Eliana walked into the infirmary, their auras thick with relief and worry.

"Oh, you *are* awake!" Eliana said.

"What, like I'd lie about that?" Cressida retorted as they wove their way through several rows of cots.

"No, but I thought you might not want me to worry."

"Where's Jin?" Astrea asked.

Eliana's hands went to her thick hips. "Where's Jin? *That's* the first thing you're going to say to me?"

"Sorry." Astrea huffed. "Nazarov just dreamwalked to me, so I'd like to know Jin is at least safe."

"He's around," Eliana said as she dropped onto the cot next to Astrea's. "What'd Nazarov say?"

"He's *around*? What the skies does that mean?"

Eliana shrugged. "I think the dreamwalking is more important."

"Answer my question and I'll answer yours," Astrea said as Cressida sat on the foot of her bed.

Eliana and Cressida exchanged a long look, something silent passing between them as the same relief and worry danced in their auras. Finally, Eliana sighed.

"Commander Lucian returned with several people in his custody," she said. "The Zaikudi ambassador and her secretary, one Zaikudi guard, and one of the void mages they managed to nab."

"Why hasn't the void mage jumped away?" Astrea asked.

"I don't know."

"And Jin?"

"Well, he's . . ." Eliana gestured vaguely. "He's with Lucian."

"Oh." With Lucian. "They're not . . . ? Are they?"

"Torturing them?" Cressida asked. "I don't think Jin would let Lucian."

"And if Jin's not there?" Astrea asked. Sure, getting information was important, but Astrea didn't want Lucian to resort to violent means. She'd been through it. Even if these people were guilty, what would that accomplish?

"I figure that's a problem for us to deal with if it even arises," Eliana said.

Shuddering, Astrea shoved back against the image of those tunnels trying to force its way into her mind. She swallowed hard. "Nazarov wanted to ensure I hadn't died," she said. "And he mentioned the Zaikudi are just a means to an end for him."

"A means to an end?" Eliana's eyebrows furrowed. "What end? Getting Zaikud, Delia, and Helosia to turn on each other?"

"As if they haven't already turned on each other," Cressida murmured.

"I can't think of any other reason," Astrea said. "Maybe he needs their resources to gather aetherium or launch another attack?"

"Bold of him to launch one in the embassy. What was that, just to stoke tensions?" Cressida asked.

"Probably," Eliana said.

Astrea flopped back onto her pillows. At least Lucian, Jin, and the others were on the case. Hopefully they'd learn something, although she really didn't like that one of the mages seemed to have stuck around of their own accord. But Lucian and Jin would know that was strange and certainly try to take precautions.

"How's everyone else doing?" Astrea asked.

"Ysabel's livid about the whole thing," Eliana said.

"At us?"

"No, at the Paragon and Zaikudi. She's been speaking with the Delian ambassador since we returned to the palace."

"What does that mean for . . . everything?"

"I don't know yet, Az." Eliana pressed her lips together. There was no trace of her red lipstick now nor any of her other usual makeup or baubles. Her hair was pulled back in a simple braid, and she wore a plain blouse and skirt. "We should know more in the morning."

"Shouldn't you be helping her with all that?" Astrea asked.

"I've helped as much as I can. I've assured Ambassador Sirras of as much as I can from Helosia's side." She shrugged. "It's up to Ysabel now to cover the Novarian side of things. He's quite shaken up about all of this."

That didn't make Astrea feel much better at all, but maybe this would force Ysabel to take a stronger stance. To finally hasten some action:

recruiting a linguist, going after the emperor, and whatever else they were going to need to accomplish to put an end to this madness.

"Thanks for coming to update me," Astrea said.

"Update you? As if that's the only reason we would come find you?" Cressida teased. "No, we're here to take you back upstairs. Ivy gave us the all clear."

"Did she actually?" Astrea asked. "She didn't mention it to me when she left a while ago."

"We ran into her in the hall."

Astrea arched an eyebrow.

"Really, we did," Eliana said. "I may have had to argue a bit, but I thought you'd rather be in your own room than down here all night."

"Yes, I suppose I would."

"Then let's get you up to bed!" Eliana hopped off her cot and offered her hand to Astrea. "Or maybe a shower first." She grimaced. "No offense."

"None taken," she said as she grabbed Eliana's hand. She was, after all, still in her blood-stained blouse. She'd seen better days. "Thank you."

Eliana wrapped her arm around Astrea's waist as soon as she was on her feet. "Of course, Az. You don't have to thank me. Let's put this awful day behind us."

Chapter 24

Astrea groaned as she rolled onto her side and pulled the blanket over her head. She had no idea what time it was, but she felt like she'd been run over by a streetcar. Her whole body ached.

But something smelled good. Very good.

Like cinnamon. And coffee.

She pulled the blanket down only to find Jin sitting next to her on the bed in nothing but his underwear.

"Morning," he said.

"What time is it?"

"A little after the eighth bell. I managed to convince the chef to make cinnamon pancakes, though they aren't quite the same as the ones in Kalama."

Astrea rubbed her tired eyes. "You did?"

"I figure getting shot three times in one day warrants something special for breakfast," he said with a tight smile. Orange anxiety and white terror wove around his body in thick, opaque spirals.

"I'll say."

Astrea pushed up into a sitting position as Jin carried a tray over to the bed. He set it between them and poured Astrea a cup of coffee.

"How do you feel?" he asked.

"I've felt worse." And she had. She'd felt far, far worse in the last few months.

"I don't know if I should hate that or not."

Astrea shrugged. There wasn't anything either of them could do about it. Instead, she swiped one of the pancakes from the tray, the sticky cinnamon sugar coating her fingers. She didn't care. Jin was right; they weren't quite the same as her favorites back home, but they were still delicious.

"Stay in bed as long as you like," Jin said as he picked up his own mug of coffee and stood.

"Why? Don't we have things to do today?"

"I don't know that there's anything for you to do."

"What's that supposed to mean?"

Jin took a sip of his drink, then set the cup on the bedside table and went to the wardrobe. "I mean there's nothing to do."

"Well, what are *you* going to do?"

His shoulders tightened, but he kept his back to her as he picked out a black shirt. One of his training shirts. "I need to talk to Cress, then I'm meeting with Lucian and Nicos."

"Why?"

"To talk about what happened yesterday and how we missed that connection between the Paragon and Zaikudi."

"No, I mean why talk to Cress?"

"Uh . . ." He cleared his throat as he grabbed a pair of black slacks. "She's been spending a lot of time with Lennor and Civan. I wanted to see if she has any insights on how they're doing."

"You can't just talk to them directly?"

"They don't always want to be open with me." He tugged his pants on first, then his light gray shirt.

"I can read them for you if you want."

"No, no, that's fine. I'll just ask Cress."

"Is this because I got shot?" Astrea huffed. "I'm serious when I say I've felt worse. Honestly, moving around would do me some good."

"No, it's not about that at all."

"I'm not a porcelain doll, Jin. I can help where needed."

"If you really want to do something, maybe you can go to the library," he said. "Focus on Zaikudi and Paragon overlap during the Great Wars. See if there's some precedent for them working together."

"You didn't find out anything from the ambassador or the Paragon member you captured?"

"Ambassador Tahere claims the Paragon offered her a deal she couldn't refuse to ensure Zaikudi victory in the Corsycan War. And the Paragon member, well, he's been spouting the usual nonsense."

"Like?"

"That the Paragon will restore balance through chaos and so forth."

"Why hasn't he jumped away?"

"Not a void mage, actually," Jin said. "I don't know if they left him behind on purpose or not."

"Did Ellie tell you Nazarov dreamwalked to me last night?"

"Yes, I'm all up to date."

Up to date? That was all he had to say about the issue? No questions? Nothing about Nazarov or the mountains?

Jin took another large sip of coffee, then circled the bed and leaned down, placing a gentle kiss first to Astrea's lips, then one to the top of her head. "Adi will stay with you today. I've got to go talk to Lucian."

"I thought you were meeting Cress first," Astrea said as Jin started for the door.

"Oh . . . right." He chuckled, and all the anxiety still wrapped around him disappeared as his heavy wall returned. "I'll need to have more coffee, I suppose. I'll see you later."

And then he was gone.

Astrea looked down at the half-eaten pancake still in her hand, then the door. Why was Jin so out of sorts? Was this just him being spooked about her injuries, or was there something he wasn't telling her?

Getting up and moving around had loosened Astrea's body up, helping some of the achiness subside. She didn't feel quite like herself, and just walking about made her heart speed up, but it wasn't the worst she'd ever felt.

Besides, if Jin needed her to look into possible Zaikud-Paragon connections from history, having help would be great. And who better than not just Adi but Noemi, resident scholar, and the twins?

"Alright, here's everything we've already looked at for the Paragon during the Great Wars," Tomas said as he set a stack of books down on the large circular table Noemi had chosen for the group. "And I found a few more in the catalog that might be useful. Adi? Astrea? Care to help?"

"Sure," Adi said.

Astrea followed him and Tomas to the far end of the library.

"Several of them are down there," Tomas said, gesturing down one of the wide, dimly lit aisles. He passed Astrea a scrap of paper with a few titles written on it. "I have one more in mind, but it's upstairs. I'll be back shortly."

As Tomas hurried away, Astrea started down the aisle, Adi not far behind. She passed him the scrap of paper, and they got to work looking for the right authors and titles.

"Hey, Adi?" Astrea asked as she squatted in front of a lower shelf. Of course that was where her book would be. "Can I ask you something?"

"You can always ask me anything," he said.

"Did you talk to Jin this morning?"

"Yeah, why?"

"Was he acting strange?"

"Strange?" Adi studied Astrea, confusion pulling at his mouth and eyebrows. "In what way?"

"Just . . . strange? I don't know. He was being awkward and indecisive about what he was doing with his day."

"He's probably just anxious after what happened yesterday."

"I suppose." Astrea yanked one of the books off the shelf, then frowned to see it was the second volume in a set. The first was nowhere in sight, and Tomas hadn't specified which one she'd need. "He mentioned that the ambassador only said the Paragon offered to help them win the Corsycan War when she was questioned last night. Did they learn anything else?"

"Not that I know of. Why?"

Astrea didn't know what to think. Was Jin meeting with Lucian to try some more aggressive tactics to get information? That wasn't the Jin she knew. Yes, he'd been upset about her getting shot, but still . . .

"Never mind," Astrea said. "You're probably right; it's just the stress of everything making him lose his head."

"Do you want me to talk to him?" Adi asked.

"No, no, that's alright. I'll see how he's feeling tonight."

"The offer stands if you want me to."

"Thanks, Adi."

They found the last book needed, then headed down the aisle and back to their table. Noemi smiled from ear to ear, electric excitement dancing over Astrea's skin. It looked like she had the Paragon's book in front of her along with a stack of papers Astrea hadn't seen in a long time.

"I thought bringing out some of our primary sources would be useful," Tomas said, gesturing to what Noemi was leafing through. "I didn't spot anything on the Zaikudi last time, but I also wasn't particularly looking for it. Perhaps I missed something."

"Good idea," Astrea said as she set the books on the table. "Let's get to work, then, shall we?"

Being back in research mode after so long away made Astrea's head hurt. Her eyes strained to read so many words so quickly, and just beyond that, her mind was tired. It still didn't feel quite right after all this time, despite how much distance she'd put between herself and the tunnels under that house.

But it also felt good, being surrounded by books and *doing* something, anything.

She leaned back in her chair and folded her arms over her stomach. They'd learned a little in the hours they'd been in the library, finding no direct ties between the two groups but still finding an old tale about powerful mages living in the mountains and fighting the early Zaikudi kingdom in the Great Wars. No alliance, sure, but that seemed to point to direct contact between the early Paragon and Zaikudi.

They'd reasoned that it was possible for the Paragon to either have formed some kind of connection with that early government or embedded themselves in it, just like they'd embedded themselves in Novarian social hierarchies with the Seviya family. Maybe Ambassador Tahere's family was the same, from a long line of Paragon sympathizers. Maybe it was just that Nazarov had approached the Zaikudi government, and they'd accepted his offer.

Concrete? No. But nothing ever was when it came to the Paragon.

"I missed the library!" Noemi exclaimed as she stretched her arms high above her head. "Skies, it's so much better than being locked in my room upstairs."

"You're hardly locked in, Noemi," Adi said.

"Fine, not locked in, but it's not like I want to just wander around some foreign palace by myself," she said.

"It's strange, being in the palace," Lennor said as she lowered her voice. "Especially with all the guards. I feel like I'm being watched."

Astrea shrugged. She'd gotten somewhat used to it, especially after being sent away from the palace. Even surrounded by friends, Astrea had still felt like she was under constant watch, if only for her own safety. And, in a way, she'd felt that way her whole life, being able to sense the whole world.

She glanced at Civan, who had kept to himself the whole time they worked. She hadn't wanted to bother him while he was recovering from the ordeal with Kaius. He was impossible to read now, completely surrounded by his wall. Lennor, at least, seemed to be in better spirits. Her pocket stone was out again, and she spun it around on the smooth tabletop.

"Az, if you're not busy, I was going to get to work on that dress I promised to make," Adi said.

"Oh, I'm sure you have better things to do."

"Like?" he asked with a laugh. "We've done what we can to answer Jin and Lucian's question."

"Surely you could be out . . . I don't know. Training someone? Working with Jin and Lucian on the Paragon problem?"

"Honestly, I don't have it in me to be around the commander today," Adi said. "He was a nightmare yesterday at the embassy."

"Right . . . I forgot you all went down there," Astrea murmured. "He was that bad?"

"Well, he did lose two of his people, and the Delians lost some, too."

Astrea pressed her lips together. Someone had mentioned casualties, but she hadn't even thought to ask about any of it now that her head was clearer. How bad of a person did that make her, to get so caught up in her own feelings and fatigue?

"Anyway, I'm going up now if you want to join me," Adi said. "I started it yesterday but want to see what you think."

"Sure, yeah, let's go."

They all shuffled around the table, fixing the books into three neat stacks for Tomas to deal with when he returned from his afternoon tea break. Lennor offered to go on a walk with Noemi in the gardens, and Civan tagged along.

"You really don't mind making me something different to wear?" Astrea asked as she followed Adi up one of several staircases that would take them back to their rooms.

"Not at all. It's a nice break from everything else." Adi opened his door, then motioned for Astrea to go in first. His room was tidy except for the pile of cloth on the coffee table. "I already told you I used to sew with my grandmother all the time. Noemi, too."

Astrea wished she'd learned something useful like that. But Saros didn't like working with his hands, and the closest Astrea had ever gotten was learning a bit of gardening from Sarsali.

"What do you think of the fabric?" Adi asked as he passed her a thick piece of black cotton. At least, it felt like cotton to her. "Careful of the pins."

Astrea fingered the material and nodded. "It feels like what we usually wear."

"That was the idea. You'll still need some kind of pants under it. Or leggings, more or less."

She supposed that was reasonable; she couldn't very well go into battle with only her bloomers underneath, especially with winter around the corner. "Can you make the waistband thicker than the ones I have now? And softer? I think that'd make them more bearable."

"Won't take me long at all," Adi said as he took the fabric back from her. "And how do you want it to fit?"

"A bit loose and boxy."

"You got it."

"I really appreciate it, Adi," Astrea said. "I feel like I need to give you something in return. You've been doing so much these last few months . . . I'm sure it wasn't ever what you imagined getting dragged into."

"I told you the other day that I don't need anything," Adi said. "And no, I never imagined any of this, but I don't think any of us did."

"I guess not." Astrea fidgeted with the end of her braid. Maybe she could still find a way to pay Adi back, find something she could do for him in return. No, she couldn't do anything useful like bake or cook or sew, but there had to be something.

"My grandmother always taught Noemi and me to pay forward what we could to others," Adi said as he began sorting through the fabric pile again. He set aside a pretty orange swatch. "My father's gambling problems left us without all that much, but my grandmother always wanted us to do good when we could."

"She sounds like a lovely person."

"She was. It was a lesson her own grandmother had taught her, back when she still lived in the Taipoli Islands. She said it was the most important lesson she'd ever learned."

"When did she move to Helosia?"

"Oh, when she was just a kid. Her parents—my paternal great-grandparents—moved because, at the time, Delia was interfering with trade routes on the Islands and had caused a lot of economic troubles."

"That's awful."

Adi shrugged. "Yeah, but they also built quite the life for themselves. My father kind of ruined all that, but he just . . . well, he didn't do well after my mother died." Blue sadness flashed twice around him, replaced by his usual calm.

"And your mother's family?"

"From the Islands as well, but they left several generations back just for a change, no particular reason. Growing up, I was told they always looked forward to the next adventure. They lived in Tornama and Novaria before settling in Helosia."

"And now you've been to all those places, too," Astrea said. "Though I suppose for far less fun reasons."

Adi's deep laugh reverberated through the room. "I'll say. Less of an adventure and more of a headache."

"The world's worst headache."

"Skies." Shaking his head, Adi set aside the rest of his fabric. "Anyway, point is, I'm paying it forward to you, and I know you'll pay it forward to someone else."

"How can you be so sure about that?"

A wry smile tugged at Adi's lips. "We may not have known each other for as long as you've known Jin and the others, but you're a good person, Az. I have no doubt you'll help people whenever you can. I already see you doing that."

Astrea nodded. She wanted to do good for not just people but the continent. The world. Maybe finding a way to stop the Paragon and Emperor Aelius would be her first big way of paying some good forward after all the kindness the Nikaphoroses and now Adi and everyone else had shown her over the years. She could only hope.

CHAPTER 25

Waking up to a breakfast invitation from Grand Duchess Ysabel was almost unnerving. With her recent hot-and-cold behavior, Astrea wasn't sure why Ysabel would want to speak to their group at all—barring Eliana and Jin, of course. But not only was their original group of six invited, but so were Zephyrine and Saros.

"Please, sit," Commander Lucian said as palace staff moved about the dining room.

Astrea sat down as instructed by one of the servers, Jin on her left side and Cressida on her right.

"What's all this about?" Jin asked as the staff closed the dining room door behind them.

"I have no idea," Eliana said.

"Nor do I," Lucian said.

"Is it about what happened at the embassy?" Astrea asked.

"I don't see why it would be," the commander replied as he settled into his chair. "Unless the Delians gave her more information overnight, but Ambassador Sirras was already being cooperative, and as of just a few minutes ago, the Zaikudi we have in custody have stopped talking and asked for legal counsel."

"What right do they have to legal counsel when they're the ones who tried to kill Az?" Cressida muttered.

"They weren't trying to kill *me*," Astrea said lamely, something she'd already told everyone in this room. They all knew about Nazarov's latest dreamwalking escapades.

"Well, they were working with the cult trying to kill someone who was in that embassy, so . . ." Cressida shrugged one slender shoulder. "Seems pretty straightforward to me."

"Everyone has a right to counsel in Novaria," Lucian said. "Even if they are *obviously* guilty. Anyway, all I know is that the grand duchess wanted to speak with us."

That didn't make Astrea feel any better at all. If anyone was to know what this meeting was about, it would be Commander Lucian, right?

Under the table, Jin's leg bounced up and down, occasionally brushing Astrea's. She set her hand on his knee, partially annoyed by the movement but mostly just concerned. Jin never fidgeted like that. His emotions were locked away, but what would have him so nervous? Even the others were more curious than anxious, with green occasionally snapping into their auras.

Jin set his hand on top of Astrea's, giving it a light squeeze as the dining room doors opened again. Grand Duchess Ysabel strode in, the skirts of her long gray dress almost getting caught around her legs. Behind her came Mariya, her cane thumping lightly on the hardwood floor.

"Your Highness," Lucian said to Ysabel as she sat at the head of the table, "what's all this about?"

"Straight to the point, Commander." Ysabel gestured to the palace staff entering the room, each of them carrying either a tray of food, tea, or coffee. "Let's give everyone a moment to settle."

Jin's knee bounced up and down again, and again Astrea set her hand on it. He smiled down at her. What, was he still upset over her getting shot? Astrea felt fine today; Ivy was a strong and talented healer.

As the doors shut again and all the staff disappeared down the hall, Ysabel said, "Now, I've asked you to meet this morning because Mariya's had a vision."

Eliana snatched a scone from a nearby tray. "Of what?"

"Well, Your Imperial Highness, it came to me before sunrise. It woke me up, actually." Mariya smoothed her hand over her hair, checking that her bun was in place. "It was of masked figures attacking a Novarian base, a munitions stockpile, it looked like."

Unease prickled Astrea's skin.

"Do you know which base?" Lucian asked.

"No," Mariya said just as Saros mumbled, "That's not often how it works."

Lucian's eyebrows raised as he turned to look at Saros. "I'm sorry, Mister Sovna, what?"

Saros glanced at Astrea, his thin lips pressed into an even thinner line. He looked better than he had in months, his cheeks fuller and skin not so sallow, and yet his eyes were . . . exhausted. Had he been up to his usual tendencies again? Not sleeping?

"I was just saying that Stargazing is not so specific most of the time," Saros said.

"Indeed, it's not," Mariya said. "There wasn't even a glimpse of the surrounding environment to hazard a guess."

A soft clink cut through the silence as Ysabel set her teacup down on a saucer. "I've put all of our bases on high alert."

"Is that all we can do?" Eliana asked. "If Nazarov is moving in on Novarian military targets now—or is planning to—I'd feel much better knowing that we've exhausted all options."

"Yes, about that . . ." Ysabel's lavender gaze settled on where Astrea sat, stirring sugar into her coffee. "We had several airships fly over the ruins in the Antare Mountains multiple times, Miss Sovna, the ones where Nazarov instructed you to meet him. We've done near daily sweeps."

"And?" Astrea asked.

"We found nothing."

Nothing. If Astrea was honest with herself, that didn't come as a shock. After all, it was Victor Nazarov they were talking about. But why would he demand she go meet him if he wasn't there? Perhaps he was monitoring the ancient Paragon site somehow and would only show up if she did?

"Alright . . ." Astrea looked across the table to Lucian, then back at the grand duchess. "And?"

"And I'm now hoping you might have more insight into where we can find him. If we can locate him before he attacks one of our bases, maybe we can prevent Mariya's vision from coming true."

"If he's not where he said he wanted to meet me, then I have no idea. It seems he's strong enough to dreamwalk from very far distances. Couldn't he be in Zaikud if he's working with their government now?"

"Possible, I suppose, though can Zaikud really fight a war both against the Helosians and against us?" Ysabel mused. "I don't know that they'd go along with attacking a Novarian base. Surely they could just give Nazarov whatever weaponry he wants. Varojin, what do you think?"

Jin almost choked on his coffee. He swallowed hard, then echoed, "What do I think?" When Ysabel motioned for him to continue, he said, "I think it's unlikely he's in Zaikud, but he's probably hiding out somewhere near the Antare ruins. Maybe north or east of there, where it's harder to access."

"We have no bases near there . . ." Ysabel took another sip of her tea. "And we saw no sign of the stolen Helosian airships."

"He could deconstruct them with a Metalli's help," Cressida said. "Obviously their ranks are made up of more than just void mages. Surely he's got a couple of Metalli on hand."

"If we assume he's hiding the airships somehow—perhaps deconstructed them—and that he *is* able to gather the weaponry he may want, what would be his first target of attack?" Zephyrine asked.

"Maybe he'd go after Helosia this time," Nicos said. "Last time, he used stolen Helosian equipment to attack a Novarian base. Maybe this time, he's going to try to steal Novarian equipment to attack a Helosian base. Stoke conflict between the two countries. Make Novaria seem like the aggressor."

Jin's knee bounced up and down again. Astrea set her hand on his thigh, and he stopped.

"Or use our munitions to attack another country," Lucian mused. "He wants to take down all governments, or at least, that was what the Paragon told Astrea. He may be looking for a way to make us destroy each other. Less work for him in the long run."

"I will see if the stars tell me more," Mariya said, "but I'm not sure they will."

"I know we've been reluctant to share our intelligence with the other countries," Eliana said slowly, "but I think we must. What have Delfine and Veiko shared with the Taipoli and Tornamian governments?"

"I had them keep things vague," Ysabel said. "A faction not connected to any government that's been trying to gain power, plus suspected Helosian aggression."

"Well, we must tell them *everything* we know, not just of my father's plans but Nazarov's, too. And after what happened at the embassy, it will be impossible to hide it for much longer anyway."

With a heavy sigh, Ysabel said, "Then I suppose I need to call the council and decide where we're starting. Eliana, would you like to be part of those conversations?"

"Yes," she said.

"General Kanakos?"

"Of course," Zephyrine replied.

"Varojin?"

"How soon will we meet?" he asked.

Astrea's eyebrows furrowed. She'd expected him to simply agree; this was clearly important. The most important thing they could have to do.

"In an hour or two," Ysabel said. "Why?"

"Just curious. I'll be there."

"And do we have any news from your people, General?" Ysabel asked. "Anything we might tell the council or that could help Mariya or Saros as they stargaze?"

"I haven't received any communication, but with the current situation, I'm not sure how easily they'll be able to get me information. Do *your* people in Kalama have anything to share?"

"Just that they're trying everything they can to meet with the Helosian government to see what people know about Kaius's movements," Ysabel said.

Astrea wished they could just show up and demand answers from those trying to start wars and cause trouble. Like the Paragon, just jump into Emperor Aelius's office and get whatever information they needed. Short of breaking into the capital and abducting him, though, there wasn't much more they could do. Diplomats and spies would have to do the work for them, and Astrea hated feeling like her hands were tied.

Ysabel's presence at breakfast had been cut short by her needing to summon the council, but the rest of them had stayed and discussed everything more. Round and round they went, making the same point: Nazarov was surely trying to provoke the continental powers into attacking Novaria, and they still needed to decide what they were going to do to stop Emperor Aelius from finding more aetherium, particularly in the Badlands.

The conversation proved fruitless. Zephyrine and Lucian didn't want to act without more intelligence to go off, which Astrea could understand. Part of her agreed. But the other part hated sitting around while the world fell apart.

And here she was, literally sitting on her bed, watching as Jin rerolled the sleeves of his forest green shirt. His forearm muscles flexed with each movement.

"What do you have to do before you go to the council meeting?" she asked.

"Hm?" He continued fidgeting with the fabric, as if it required all the attention in the world.

"You asked Ysabel how much time she'd need to get the council ready. I assume you have something to do?"

"Oh." When he finally looked up at her, his golden eyes seemed almost cloudy, distracted. "I need to talk to Cress about something."

"Didn't you speak with her yesterday?"

"Uhm . . ." He headed for the bathroom, returning just a moment later as he fussed with his hair. "I did, yeah. I've been trying to see if she knows any more about the aetherium."

"Right . . ."

Jin often said Astrea was a terrible liar, but everything in Astrea's gut screamed that Jin was lying to her now. But why would he lie about going to see Cressida?

"Lennor and Civan seem to be doing alright, by the way," Astrea said.

"Huh?"

Skies, he was distracted. "Yesterday, you said you wanted to talk to Cress about how Lennor and Civan were doing since she's spent so much time with them lately," Astrea said. "Well, they were helping me and Adi. I think they're managing."

"Oh, right." Jin smiled softly. "Thanks, Az."

Closing the distance between them, he leaned down and kissed her lips. Astrea wrapped her arms around his neck, pulling him in deeper. He moaned against her mouth, resting his forehead on hers as he pulled away.

"I love you," she whispered.

"I love you, too." That ever-present warmth on her skin doubled as he said the words. "This council meeting will probably take all day, so I'll see you tonight."

Astrea's belly twisted as she watched him walk out the door. She knew he loved her—she had no doubt about that—but why wouldn't he just talk to her about whatever was bothering him?

She may not have had any real answers from Jin, but that didn't mean Astrea just had to sit around and wait. Once she was sure Jin and the others would be meeting with the council, Astrea left her room in search of Cressida.

Marko leaned against the wall opposite Astrea's bedroom door. He raised an eyebrow at her. He didn't even move a muscle, as if he knew she wasn't leaving the palace.

Astrea ignored him and went to Cressida's room first. But as her magic spread out and came up empty, she headed for the Nikaphoroses' room at the far end of the hall. Only there, where she'd thought she might find three people, her magic sensed just one.

Astrea knocked on the door, and Sarsali opened it a moment later. She'd pulled her long, dark hair into one braid and donned a light green linen dress. Even the floral bandanna tied around her head was familiar, something she often wore in Kalama while gardening.

"Oh, this is a surprise," she said with a smile, her aura lighting up with golden joy. "Come in, my dear, come in. I was just about to order some tea, if you'd like any."

"Actually, I was hoping you know where Cress is."

Sarsali's lips pursed, then she laughed. "Not only have my husband and one daughter abandoned me, but now you are, too?"

"I just really need to talk to her." What Astrea needed was answers. See if Jin was telling her *any* of the truth.

"She's down in the gardens with Balthazar," Sarsali said. "She mentioned a forge by the Stargazer's tower?"

Astrea nodded. "I know where it is."

"Do you want me to come with you?"

"If you want, sure," Astrea said. If Cressida was indeed with Balthazar, Sarsali being there would hopefully give Astrea and Cressida a moment to talk.

They headed out of the palace in silence, Marko just a few feet behind them. Astrea hadn't gotten to talk much with him these last couple of days, but she'd grown used to his silent companionship at that old base. And Sarsali had never forced a conversation on Astrea, even when the silence dragged on and on. It wasn't that Astrea *wanted* to be silent, but she didn't know what to say or how to explain to Sarsali that something seemed off.

The midmorning sun warmed Astrea's cheeks and exposed arms, and the breeze played with the strands of hair she hadn't captured in her braid. It was the perfect morning, and Astrea had spent many like it with Sarsali and Cressida over the years, usually in their back garden or wandering Kalama's busy streets. Despite her family's presence in Novaria, Astrea's heart still ached for those days, before everything got so messy and dangerous.

"Oh, there they are," Sarsali said as they entered the more shaded, overgrown section of Ysabel's garden.

Mariya's stone tower broke up the foliage, which was beginning to change from green to golds and reds. Smoke and steam rose up from Cressida's makeshift forge, where a crucible sat on top of a fire, much like when Cressida had first smelted down the aetherium with Jin's help. Maybe Jin really had gone to talk to Cressida, to help her.

And not only were Balthazar and Cressida there, but Mariya and Saros were, too.

Great. Getting Cressida alone to talk was only going to be a thousand times more difficult—or awkward.

"Ah!" Balthazar's aura lit up with gold when he turned and saw them walking up. "My beautiful wife has finally come to join me?"

"Oh, stop." Sarsali smacked his chest with the back of her hand. "We just came to see what you were doing out here, and I can already tell I don't like the look of it."

"Doing as Eliana has asked," Balthazar said, his mood sobering quickly. "She wants these aetherium weapons, or at least some. We're doing what we can without a real facility."

"The grand duchess won't let you work someplace in the city?" Marko asked. "We have plenty of factories and forges."

"Doesn't want questions being asked right now," Cressida said, her shoulders and voice tight. Rough annoyance scraped Astrea's skin, but it certainly wasn't annoyance with the grand duchess. Cressida didn't want to be making these weapons. "We settled on bullets and daggers. Easiest to make out here."

"In all my life, I never thought we'd discover something like this," Saros said from where he stood near the long work table. Light danced around his fingertips as they hovered over a bar of dark, dull metal. "So much time wasted. I can't believe we didn't figure this out months ago."

Wonderful. Saros was in one of his moods. Deep blue regret twined with the green—the curiosity—surrounding him.

"At least we know what it does now." Cressida pulled a cloth from the back pocket of her tight black trousers and dabbed at the sweat on her forehead. "Now if only we knew where to find more of it. You really didn't feel any of it in the Badlands, Saros?"

"It's difficult to say," he replied. "There was what Emperor Aelius had already found, but it's not like I could feel the entire region. There may be more, or there may not be. I'd have to go back and search."

"Just wonderful." Mariya sighed. "If you lot need me, I'll be inside." She headed back into the tower with another heavy sigh.

"She's been annoyed all day," Cressida murmured as Astrea stepped closer to her. "I think she's frustrated with Saros."

"Why?" Astrea whispered.

"Because he's being Saros."

"Right." They'd have to sort that out themselves; Astrea wasn't getting involved in whatever tiff Saros and Mariya were in. She glanced at the forge, which Balthazar was tending while speaking with the others. "Can we talk, Cress?"

"Sure, about what?"

"Away from them."

Yellow worry sparkled around Cressida. "Ma, Dad, I'm going to take a quick walk with Az."

Her parents waved them off. Saros, however, watched Astrea for a beat too long. His eyebrows furrowed with a silent question. She smiled at him. If he started to worry about her, it was only going to make him more moody. And maybe it wasn't her job to worry about his moods, but she really didn't need him breathing down her neck.

As they started down the path past Mariya's tower that would take them deeper into the gardens, Marko's light footsteps followed. Astrea sighed.

"Marko, can we please have five minutes?" she asked. "I know you're just doing your job, but this is private."

He held his palms up in surrender. "Don't go far."

"We won't."

Astrea trudged forward, trying to ignore the overgrown grass and shrubs slapping at her shins.

"What's up with you?" Cressida asked. "You're just as snappy as Saros today."

"Sorry." Astrea deflated; she didn't mean to be snappy with anyone. "Why has Jin been having secret meetings with you for two days?"

At that, Cressida laughed. "Secret meetings? How are they secret?"

"He keeps making up reasons he's come to speak with you. What's he on about?"

"He was just checking up on Len and Civ and the weapons, and you know, helping with the smelting." But as she said the words, Cressida's aura shrank and dimmed, like she was trying to block Astrea out.

"Then why's he being so strange about it?"

"Strange in what way?" Cressida asked.

"Evasive and distracted."

"He's probably just worried about everything. I mean, Len and Civ got abducted, you got shot . . . the man's got a lot to worry about."

That didn't explain why he was acting the way he was. Jin was hardly ever so distracted. He hadn't been this distracted when all the other terrible things had happened. Was all the worry of the last few months just catching up with him?

Was he avoiding asking her things about the twins because he was trying to spare her from using up her energy? If that was his goal, it was silly. They'd gone over this. They'd made so much progress, and he'd been sharing more.

"Would you tell me if something was wrong with him?" Astrea asked. "Or if something else was going on?"

"Of course I'd tell you, Az," Cressida said. And though Astrea could no longer feel any of Cressida's emotions, she believed her best friend. "Just give things a few days to settle."

"Yeah, I guess." Maybe Astrea needed to be more sensitive to the fact that Jin was spooked after what happened at the embassy. After all, it might have even reminded him of the time he got shot in Corsyca—not all that long ago. "Maybe I should talk to him tonight after dinner."

"I think that's a great idea."

Astrea smiled tightly as they turned back toward the tower. "Sorry I'm being grumpy. You shouldn't have to deal with two grumpy Sovnas in one day."

Cressida chuckled, her amusement washing over Astrea in a strong, fruity wave. "Then you owe me for *years* of both of you brooding," she teased as she slung her arm around Astrea's shoulder.

Astrea nudged her in the ribs. "Name your price."

"Eh, I'll figure out what I want someday."

"A real first date with Lennor?" Astrea asked. "Or maybe your bakery back home?"

"You don't have the means to finance my bakery."

"Fine, organizing your first proper date, then."

"What, you're playing matchmaker now?"

"You like Len, and she clearly likes you. How is that me playing matchmaker?"

"How about you let me worry about my love life," Cressida said as they walked, "and you can work on figuring out how to pay for this bakery instead. I think I'm going to need a big space. The biggest bakery in Kalama."

"Don't you have an inheritance or something from your parents?" Astrea teased.

Cressida waved her hand dismissively. "You told me to name my price! And my price is your help."

"You'll always have that, Cress. With anything."

"Good, because I'm going to need it if Saros is sticking around the rest of the day."

Looping her arm through Cressida's, Astrea said, "Well, let's get this over with, then. I think we both know this isn't going to be the most enjoyable afternoon."

"At least we're all together again," Cressida said. "I think I even sort of missed Saros's brooding. Makes it feel a little more like home."

Astrea smiled. "Me too."

Chapter 26

It had been one more long day in a series of never-ending long days. After watching Cressida and Balthazar work for a while, Astrea had spent a few hours with Adi, Noemi, and the twins. And it was only after several more hours that Jin and Eliana finished up their meeting with the council, who agreed that they needed to get ahead of whatever tale the Zaikudi might be spinning for the other continental leaders.

After a quick and quiet dinner with Cressida, Adi, and Noemi, the three had disappeared, leaving Jin and Astrea alone. Astrea stretched out on their bed. Jin had still been acting oddly since returning from the meeting, though Cressida had been mellow all through dinner.

The sink running in the bathroom turned off. Jin's wingtip shoes clicked gently against the bedroom's wood floor.

Astrea didn't know whether to be mad that he wouldn't tell her what was really going on or worried about what it might mean. Yes, she'd thought she needed to be more sensitive if he was simply trying to process everything, but her mind was starting to spiral. Was it something he didn't want to tell her? News about Raela's fate? Something else? But why go to Cressida?

"Can we go for a walk?" Jin asked.

Pushing up on her elbows, Astrea caught a hint of orange anxiety vibrating around him before it disappeared. Her pulse jumped.

Was it truly bad news of some kind?

She wiped her palms on her skirt before taking Jin's outstretched hand. He laced their fingers together, and despite all of Astrea's frustration, she leaned into his side. Getting to feel his skin on hers and just be close after a long day was nice.

One of the Novarian guards stationed outside their door—not one Astrea was familiar with—followed them at a short distance. She tried to ignore them, just as she tried to ignore her pounding heart and the way her mind whispered a dozen awful pieces of news Jin might have to deliver.

Outside, the last hints of sunlight had finally dipped below the horizon. The dark blanket of night settled over the palace, decorated by hundreds of stars. Astrea breathed in deep, a familiar hum unfolding under her skin.

"You're tense," Jin said quietly.

"Because you've been acting strangely the last couple of days."

"I suppose there's no hiding that from you."

"There's no hiding it from anyone," Astrea said, though the words lacked any edge.

"Trust me for a few more minutes?" Jin asked. "Then I'll tell you."

"Is it bad news? I'd rather just know now if it's bad."

"I don't think it's bad."

"You don't *think*?" Astrea scoffed. "That gives me no confidence."

"Skies, will you just trust me?" Jin asked, tart amusement coating Astrea's tongue as he tugged her down the hill toward the lake.

She tried incredibly hard to keep her mind from wandering too far from his words. *I don't think it's bad. Will you just trust me?* It was a struggle, her worries a siren song her mind desperately wanted to follow.

They'd walked a quarter of the way around the lake before Jin said, "Ysabel finally told the council about my mother."

That . . . that was not where she'd expected the conversation to go. "Why? I thought she wanted to keep it under wraps."

"I don't know. I think our meeting would've taken far less time, but they started going into succession laws and all sorts of nonsense."

"But you don't want to be a ruler."

"I know, and they didn't believe me for the first hour and a half I tried to tell them that," Jin said with a tight laugh. "Skies, you'd think rejecting that kind of power wouldn't be such a big deal."

"Maybe they see it as a threat to the dynasty," Astrea said. "Ysabel said you were one of the last descendants."

"Yes, well, Veiko and his children seem like enough security to the family line. Or maybe a change in governance wouldn't be such a bad thing."

Peeking over her shoulder, Astrea found the guard was no longer trailing them. Had Jin somehow waved them off without her realizing it? Still, she lowered her voice as she said, "You didn't tell them that, did you?" If that was what the Novarian people wanted, then far be it from her to disagree with them, but surely the council would be frustrated by that kind of talk.

"No, no. I was on my best behavior."

"Good."

Jin laughed. "Once I convinced them I really, truly did not want an ounce of power in this country, they drew up a binding document." Relief rolled off Jin in bright, minty waves. "I signed it this afternoon. I'm off the hook, even if Ysabel and the rest of them will always be family."

"I'm happy for you." Astrea squeezed his hand. "It must be a weight off your shoulders."

"That's not all. It means nothing until Ellie's in power, but she drew one up for the Helosian side, too. Both thrones are truly, fully off limits to me now." Another laugh escaped him. "One of the only things I've ever wanted, and Ellie actually gave it to me without a fight."

Astrea squeezed his hand again. "I'm glad." For years, Jin had always told Astrea that he dreamed of leaving palace life behind, of seeing other places and meeting other people, doing things without being tied to his family. And while a couple pieces of paper didn't rid him fully of those ties, to be somewhat legally separated . . . "I mean, it sounds so silly and, well, trite, but I'm really, really happy for you," she said.

Jin lifted their joined hands, then pressed a kiss to the back of hers. "I know. I don't think there's much else to say." Sighing, his shoulders relaxed. "Skies."

"What will you do with this newfound freedom?"

All that relief bled away, replaced by bright, unwavering anxiety. Orange lit up the night, so bright Astrea had to look away.

"Jin?" she asked. The intensity of his worry faded, but the orange remained. "What's wrong?"

As his steps slowed, Jin gestured out to the lake. "Do you remember when we first came here?"

"It feels like forever ago," she admitted. Months before, Jin had taken Astrea out to this very lake, sat her down, and asked if she wanted to explore whatever it was between them. And now here they were. Summer was gone. A chilly wind swept in from the north, a preview of the winter to come. "It feels like it could've been a year ago."

"A lot has happened," Jin said. "A lot of hard things."

She swallowed thickly, gaze fixed on the water as it bobbed up and down near the shore. So many hard, awful things. But good things, too. Jin meeting family he didn't know he had—one that seemed to accept him as he was. Their partnership. All the things Astrea had learned about herself, and, of course, reuniting with their families.

"And I'm sorry all the bad has happened," Jin said, "but I'm glad we've faced it together. Honestly, I didn't know what to expect when I got called home, not from my father but especially not us. I thought you'd hate me."

"I don't think I could ever hate you," she said, glancing up at him. "I was just a little mad at you."

He laughed, a quiet, nervous sound. "Well, I'm very glad to hear that. I just . . ." He sucked in a sharp breath. "I love you so much, Az. And I don't feel like I always do a good job showing you that."

"What do you mean?" She felt Jin's love every moment of every day, even when there were questions or issues between them. Not just that sunshine feeling but all his little actions. Her nightlight, the pancakes and coffee, and everything in between. "Of course you do."

"Yes, well, you've *always* seen the best in me, even when I don't see it in myself," he said. "You've forgiven me, welcomed me home. I know it's not been an easy road for either of us. I know that. But everything I went through was worth it because you're here. You're here for me. With me. And that makes everything"—he gestured around them—"that makes all of this, alright."

"Jin—"

"I know you're going to think I've lost my skies damned mind . . ." Jin shifted, kneeling on one knee as he squeezed her hand.

What was he—

Oh.

Oh.

That was why he'd been acting so strangely. Not war. Not bad news. *This.*

Astrea sank to the ground in front of him, legs weak.

"I've lost so much in the eight years since I left home." Jin reached into his pocket with his free hand, revealing a narrow band of silver and gold braided together. "I don't want to wait for this, Az. My feelings won't be any different a year from now than they are today."

Tears burned her eyes.

"I want to marry you, Astrea Sovna," Jin said. "I want to be your husband, and I want you to be my wife. Partners, always."

Kalamian couples didn't have long courtships, most lasting little more than a year before they ended in marriage or the partners parted ways. But they had not been together that long. And though they'd danced around the topic a few times, they'd never seriously talked about this step. With the rebellion and trying to find the Paragon, it just seemed so far away. So impossible.

But here Jin was, bent on one knee before her, offering her a ring. Asking for that commitment. Asking to be bound together.

And what reason did Astrea have to say no?

She didn't want to say no.

She, too, was confident her feelings wouldn't be any different if they waited a year or even more. And she'd known him for so long. She knew Jin, and he knew her. Nothing was going to change when they finally dethroned Emperor Aelius. Nothing was going to change when they finally defeated the Paragon. They knew each other, and they wanted similar things out of life.

And she loved him. She loved him so much more than she thought possible.

Maybe this dream they'd had, of building that life together, didn't have to be so far away. Maybe it wasn't impossible, even with all the bad happening around them.

"Yes." She barely breathed the word, afraid this would be some cruel dream about to end if she said her answer loudly.

Lavender pulsed around him. "Yes?"

"Why are you surprised?" she whispered. "I said yes."

He laughed, warmth spreading over Astrea's skin as his love washed over her again and again. Jin pulled Astrea toward him, kissing her long and deep, so hard Astrea somehow found herself nearly sitting in his lap on the ground.

He pulled away, both hands cupping her face. "Astrea Sovna, my wife."

"Not yet."

"Not soon enough."

"And you say *I'm* impatient."

Jin chuckled, a warm, deep, beautiful sound Astrea could listen to forever. "I stand by that assessment," he said, one thumb stroking her cheek. "And I don't care. You can be as impatient as you want."

"Then let me see this ring."

Laughing again, he dropped his hands from her face. He'd slipped the ring onto his thumb at some point but now took it off again. Sliding it onto her left ring finger, he said, "Cress made the matching set."

"Oh, skies." Astrea's face burned as she stared down at the ring in the dim moonlight.

"What?" Jin asked.

"Now I see why you and Cress were both acting so odd the last couple of days." And that was surely why Cressida had been trying to shut Astrea out earlier in the day. To keep the surprise for Jin.

Magenta embarrassment danced in the darkness as he said, "Guilty."

"Where's yours?" Astrea asked.

Jin reached into his pocket again and retrieved a thicker ring, this one gold with silver splitting the middle. Astrea snatched it from him and slipped it onto his left ring finger, then Jin was kissing her again. He kissed her until she couldn't think straight.

My wife. Astrea pressed her body into his. He groaned into her mouth, his fingers threading into her hair.

"We should go inside," he said as he finally pulled away.

"Do we have to?" Astrea leaned against his chest, trying to soak in the joy and love washing over her magic again and again. She didn't want to leave this moment. She wanted to stay there, under the stars, and pretend the rest of the world didn't exist for just a little while longer.

"I can't very well let my wife freeze out here all night."

"You say that as if we're already married."

"Like you said, I'm impatient." Jin kissed the side of her neck, then helped her stand. "Come on. I'll keep you warm all night."

Chapter 27

A glint of silver and gold caught Astrea's eye as soon as she woke, not just on her hand but on Jin's, too. She hadn't meant to sleep with the ring on—she didn't like jewelry on her body while she slept—but after Jin had completely worn out the last of her energy and forced her into the shower for a few minutes, she'd simply fallen asleep as soon as she collapsed back into bed.

She wasn't even in any clothes. Her bare skin pressed against Jin's.

Astrea couldn't help but laugh. It came out as a mix of a giggle and a groan, her body reacting to the feeling of Jin behind her. Hadn't she gotten enough the night before?

"Az?" Jin's rough voice asked in her ear.

"Go to sleep," she whispered. "Sorry."

As Jin stirred behind her, sour and sweet lust exploded on her tongue. His body reacted, too, and one hand drifted to the curve of her hip.

"Don't be sorry."

"Aren't you exhausted?"

"Completely." His lips brushed the side of her neck. "Absolutely, completely exhausted, and yet all I can think about is ravishing you again."

"I don't think I'll be able to walk at all if you do that."

He hummed. "I suppose that would be a problem. We've got a lot to do today."

"Like?" Astrea turned in his arms so their fronts were pressed together. "Does Ysabel have something planned?"

"No, but . . ." As he lifted his left hand, his ring caught the light. "I thought we'd tell our families."

"Oh, right. Of course." Why hadn't she thought of that? Of course they were going to tell their families the good news. "Oh, skies, what is Saros going to say?"

"Only good things, I'm sure." Jin kissed the end of her nose.

"Have you met my uncle?"

"Probably only good things."

Astrea nudged Jin's chest. He grabbed her wrists, rolled her over, and climbed on top of her in one swift move. Her breathing turned ragged as his gaze roamed her body and that raspberry flared higher, brighter.

"Hm." He pinned her wrists among the pillows, the cool metal of his ring brushing her skin. She could get used to that feeling. "It's really too bad we have a schedule to keep."

"Since when are you the responsible one?"

"Since I know you like to get a punctual start to your day." Jin let go of her wrists, then helped her off the bed. "Come on," he called over his shoulder, already headed for the bathroom.

Rolling her eyes, Astrea finally took the ring off her finger. It was lightweight, smooth. Perfect, really. She set it on the bedside table next to her opal necklace, then joined Jin for a proper shower. Despite his insistence that she needed to hurry up, Astrea took a few extra moments to heal the love marks Jin had left on her neck and collarbones the night before.

Astrea slipped on a dark purple dress, then her brogues. She left her hair long and loose around her shoulders; she couldn't be bothered to braid it. As soon as her ring was back on her finger, Jin grabbed her hand and tugged her toward the door.

"What has gotten into you?" Astrea asked. "They're all still going to be available even if we walk a little slower."

She'd kept her magic pulled closer to her body the night before and all the time she'd been awake, selfishly wanting to focus just on Jin despite the Paragon's threat still hanging over their heads. As they stopped in front of Eliana's door, electric excitement raced over Astrea's skin.

"Did you already—" she started.

The door opened, and Eliana flung herself into Astrea's arms. Laughing, Jin steadied them both.

"Finally!" Eliana shouted. All the guards in the hall turned to look. "Oh, skies, I'm getting another sister!"

And then Eliana's tears started.

The world grew louder as Cressida, Adi, and Nicos all yanked the rest of them into Eliana's room. Excitement, pride, joy, amusement—it overwhelmed Astrea so much that she couldn't separate the colors or see much past the thick fog clouding her vision. She pulled her barrier back, closer and closer to her body, until she felt nothing at all.

"And this was about *my* punctual start to the day?" Astrea asked Jin as he grinned down at her.

"Maybe I told Ellie to have the wine ready."

"It's barely the ninth bell."

"Never too early for that," Eliana called over her shoulder as she sauntered toward her sitting area. "What do you want? Bubbly wine and orange juice?"

"Just the juice," Astrea said.

"I want all of it," Cressida said, and Eliana gave her a thumbs-up.

"I can't believe you didn't tell me you were planning this," Adi said, grabbing Jin by the shoulders and shaking him gently. "I would've helped!"

"He didn't tell me either," Eliana called over her shoulder. "Or Nicos."

"Now I'm suddenly feeling very special rather than a convenient Metalli," Cressida quipped.

"I can't believe you managed not to tell me," Astrea said to her.

With a smile, Cressida accepted the cocktail Eliana handed her. "I couldn't very well ruin Jin's surprise."

As Eliana finished passing out everyone's drinks, Jin snaked his arm around Astrea's waist and pulled her into his side. "Do you mind that I told Ellie early?" he murmured.

"Of course not. Did you tell anyone else?"

"Not yet."

For that, Astrea was grateful. She wanted—needed—to be the one to tell Saros.

"A toast," Eliana said, lifting her glass filled to the brim. "To Jin and Az, for finally finding their way to each other. May you have a long and loving life together."

"To Jin and Az!" the others said, lifting their glasses.

"I'm surprised, Ellie," Astrea said.

"Why's that?" She took a sip of her drink and nodded approvingly.

"That your toast didn't become borderline inappropriate."

"Hey!" Peach amusement bubbled up around her. "I'm saving that one for the wedding."

"Please save it for never."

Eliana stuck her tongue out.

"Not to interrupt, but . . ." Cressida glanced down at her watch. "We need to get going."

"Now what?" Astrea asked. She just wanted a chance to talk to Saros, Balthazar, and Sarsali before the rest of the day got started.

"We"—she gestured to Eliana—"may have asked a few people to gather downstairs for breakfast."

"Who counts as a few people?" Jin asked, the question mostly directed toward his sister.

"Saros, Sarsali, Balthazar," she said.

"That's a given."

"Lucian, Marko, your team, and Noemi."

"Anyone else?"

"You mean like a certain royal?"

"That's exactly who I mean, Ellie."

"I said you had something to tell her." She shrugged. "But I asked her to meet us a half hour after everyone else. Family first."

Astrea hadn't even considered the fact that they'd have to tell Grand Duchess Ysabel.

No, Astrea hadn't considered that, nor had she considered the fact that she'd be marrying into two royal families. She just saw Jin and the future he wanted away from it all. And sure, Jin had signed away his political rights the night before, but that didn't change the connection Astrea was about to have to the grand duchess.

Oh, that was far more worrisome than telling Saros.

She stared up at Jin. "Were we supposed to get permission?"

"Permission?" He chuckled. "Ysabel has no say over what I do, Az. This is about what we want."

Astrea swallowed hard. Sure, Jin said that, but Ysabel was all over the place these days. Could it really be that simple?

The dining room Eliana had everything set up in was shockingly understated, especially considering it was the very same one they'd dined in when meeting Jin's cousins for the first time.

The grand duchess's opulent decor hadn't changed, but everything else was simple. Two bouquets of fresh flowers sat in vases on the long table, and trays of pastries, coffee, tea, and juice were all out, but nothing about the setup screamed "I set up a secret engagement party for my best friend."

And that was good. Astrea was sure that, in a different time and place, Eliana would have made this far more elaborate. Over the top. That was Eliana's favorite way to throw a party, after all. That was the Kalamian way.

Astrea paced back and forth in front of the lit fireplace, where she'd once stood with Jin while he met Prince Veiko and Princess Delfine for the first time. The night he'd introduced her as his partner, the night Delfine had asked if they were already married.

Was Delfine secretly a Stargazer?

Astrea almost wished the nosy princess was there; she would love to see Delfine's shocked face.

"I thought everyone was supposed to be here by now," Astrea said to Cressida. Jin was a few feet away, speaking with Adi.

"Give them a few minutes before you panic. We staggered them all so you could tell Saros first."

Astrea huffed. Right. And Saros was generally not the most punctual person on the continent.

She stared down at the ring on her finger, twisting the braided metal around and around.

"You like the ring?" Cressida asked.

Astrea smiled. "I love it, really. I'm just nervous about Saros and Ysabel."

"He wanted stones added to it, but we didn't know how to get them without somehow telling Ysabel what was going on. Figured it was best to avoid making waves."

"That's alright," Astrea said. "It's perfect."

"I'm really happy for you," Cressida said, reaching for her hand. "You deserve to be happy."

"We all do—"

"Yes, but this is *your* moment." When Cressida squeezed her hand, Astrea squeezed back. "You and Jin deserve to be happy."

"We will be." Of that, Astrea had no doubt.

"And if he doesn't make you happy," Cressida said, a wicked grin spreading across her face, "we'll get revenge."

"I don't like the sound of that," Jin said as he returned, a glass of water in hand.

"Consider it your first and only warning, Auris," she quipped. "I may have helped you with the rings, but don't think I can't take them back just as easily."

"Noted," Jin said, but when Astrea looked up, she found him watching her. Pink vibrated around him. As he started to say something else, the door opened.

"What's all this?" Sarsali asked as she led the way inside. Balthazar and Saros trailed in behind her.

Eliana jumped out of her seat at the table as she exclaimed, "Astrea and Varojin have some wonderful news!"

Skies, Astrea might as well have died right there where she stood. Her whole face heated. Why did it almost sound like Eliana was announcing they were expecting a baby?

A smile tugged at Sarsali's mouth, her aura reflecting green curiosity the same color as her eyes and her dress. She circled the dining table, Balthazar and Saros still at her heels.

Jin's hand moved to the small of Astrea's back, the weight familiar and comfortable.

"Well . . ." Astrea smiled. "Last night, Jin asked me to marry him, and I said yes."

"Oh!" Sarsali closed what little distance remained between them and threw her arms around both their necks. "Oh, wonderful news indeed, you two!" Warm joy washed over Astrea again and again, settling near her heart.

"Finally, something good around here," Balthazar teased as his wife stepped away. He pulled both Astrea and Jin into a warm hug. "Congratulations."

"Thank you," Astrea said to them both, wanting to revel in that joy forever. But she made herself focus on Saros, on his slightly rumpled gray shirt and the wrinkles around his eyes. "Uncle?" she asked.

His expression softened. "Oh, my dear." Saros stepped forward and pulled her into a tight embrace. "I'm glad to see you so happy."

"Really?" she whispered.

"Of course." He pulled away, hands still on her shoulders. "Of course, Astrea. Congratulations to you both." Teal approval danced around Saros's head as he turned toward Jin. "You'd better take the best care of her."

"I wouldn't dream of anything less, Saros," Jin said. "I promise."

Saros extended his hand to Jin, and as they shook, Saros's shoulders relaxed away from his ears. "It's a good thing I know you're a man of your word, then."

As Eliana began passing out coffee and tea, their next guests arrived. Lennor couldn't stop smiling at the news, and Noemi commented about "loving weddings." Civan didn't say much, but he gave Astrea a quick hug and genuine smile, and that was enough for her. From him, that meant everything.

When the dining room doors opened next, it wasn't Zephyrine like Astrea had expected. Marko strode in, impossible to read aside from his furrowed eyebrows.

"What's going on?" he asked.

"We're celebrating!" Adi called from the far side of the room. He lifted his coffee cup in a one-man toast.

"Celebrating what, exactly?" Marko asked as he shut the door behind him. "We're at war."

"Az and Jin! They're getting married!"

One side of Marko's mouth quirked up. "Congratulations," he said.

Astrea couldn't help but laugh, especially as she noticed him looking not at her or Jin but across the room toward Adi. "Thanks, Marko."

"Does the grand duchess know?" he asked, finally giving them his full attention.

"Not yet," Jin said. "Apparently my sister told her to show up a bit later than everyone else."

Marko nodded. "Probably for the best."

"Why, you think she'll be upset?"

"Not upset, but I'm sure she'll have more pragmatic concerns. She's never been much of a romantic."

Astrea didn't need the grand duchess to be romantic about the situation; she just needed Ysabel to support their union without any questions or remarks. Simple support of Jin—her cousin—as he looked to build a life for himself. Could that be so much to ask?

The dining room doors swung open again, revealing not just Grand Duchess Ysabel but Zephyrine and Lucian, too. They were entirely shut off from Astrea's magic, empty spots amid all the warm joy still filtering through the room.

"Good, you're all here," Ysabel said, her face like stone. "We have a problem."

Chapter 28

"A problem?" Eliana squared her shoulders. "And what might that be?"

"There's been an attack," Lucian said.

"Multiple attacks." The grand duchess's face pinched up like she'd eaten something sour. "Across multiple cities. Mematos, Thasia, Katavena, Talmaris . . . Kalama. And others."

Cold horror swept through the room, making Astrea shiver.

"It seems the Paragon have attacked," Ysabel continued, "although it was not with Novarian weapons as we anticipated. Everything is still accounted for here."

Eliana set her half-empty glass on the dining table, voice quiet but firm as she asked, "What kinds of attacks?"

"Bombings," Lucian replied.

"Where?" Eliana asked. "I mean, where specifically in the cities?"

"Markets mostly. Crowded places," Zephyrine said. "Civilian targets. It's despicable."

"Do we know it was the Paragon?" Jin asked. "How are we sure?"

That was Jin's question? How were they sure it was the Paragon? Bombing crowded marketplaces had Victor Nazarov written all over it. Chaos. Fear. Destruction. It fit perfectly with his way of doing things.

"Their symbol was painted at several of the sites," Ysabel said. "I have not been able to confirm this with Delian leadership."

"It could be a false flag operation by my father, to throw us off," Jin said. "We've . . . I . . . I've seen it before."

"Don't think that's what it is this time." Zephyrine shifted her weight to one leg and crossed her arms over her chest. "There's no evidence of an attack in Zindir."

"They didn't attack the Zaikudi?" Eliana asked. "Is it possible my father would somehow know of Zaikudi involvement with the Paragon and is trying to misdirect us?"

"I don't think so, El," Nicos murmured.

Chills rippled over Astrea's skin. If the Paragon were attacking everyone but the Zaikudi, not only did that reinforce the fact that the Paragon had an ally—a powerful empire—but it meant Nazarov was escalating.

As he'd always intended. But they'd been too slow. They hadn't stopped him.

She hadn't stopped him. Why hadn't she been able to kill him the last time she saw him? Why hadn't she agreed to meet him in the mountains?

"Was it aetherium?" Astrea asked.

"No," Lucian said.

Her shoulders sagged. At least he didn't have that. Unless he was just saving it for a later date . . . Astrea's lungs tightened painfully, and she tried to shove the feeling away.

"But there were many casualties," Lucian added quietly. "Many. Both here and abroad. Mostly civilians, mid-ranked government officials . . ."

"And there's no sign of Nazarov or his people anywhere?" Jin asked. "No trail to follow? We still haven't found them in the mountains?"

"No sign," Ysabel said. "No sign at all."

"Damn it," he muttered. "How the fuck does he keep getting away?"

It was a good question. Every time they got close to Nazarov, he got away again. Every time he got near them, he managed to escape just in time. The ability to move through the void was too strong, even with its limited range. It made running that much easier. And he obviously had resources beyond just his magic. Skies only knew what the Zaikudi were providing him with.

"Do we know when he formed the alliance with the Zaikudi?" Astrea asked. "Would the ambassador say?"

"She's refusing to speak more on the subject," Ysabel said. "Useless."

Tense silence settled over the room. Astrea chewed on her lower lip. If Nazarov—or even The One—had begun setting up some kind of alliance with the Zaikudi even a month ago, it would surely be enough time to get their hands on some weapons. But how could they anticipate his next move without even an inkling of where the Paragon were? If they were allied with the Zaikudi, then logic would follow that the Paragon—or some of them—were using Zaikud as their new base of operations. But with them targeting every other capital city . . . Just how many resources did they have?

As Astrea folded her arms over her chest, Zephyrine's gaze flicked to her, then Jin's hand. Lavender surprise and teal approval swirled around her body. "And it seems you two have news?"

Jin cleared his throat. "Yes, although now hardly seems like the time for it."

Zephyrine's expression softened. "Maybe not, but congratulations. We'll find another morning to celebrate."

The grand duchess, however, scrutinized the two of them. "Varojin?"

His hand found the small of Astrea's back as he said, "I've asked Astrea to marry me, and she said yes."

Ysabel nodded. That was it. She *nodded*.

Sure, they had bigger concerns, but that was it? Astrea shoved the question deep, deep down.

"So, what do we do now?" Eliana asked. "What's our next move?"

Pushing her shoulders back, the grand duchess said, "We make ourselves visible. I show our people that we will not be pushed around by some power-hungry interloper, that these—"

"Make yourself visible how, Your Highness?" Lucian asked, one eyebrow raised.

"By going to the site of the attack downtown," she said curtly. "The military and police should have locked it down by now. Will you please arrange transportation, Commander? I cannot wait too long to go to my people."

"Your Highness—" Lucian began.

She sighed, a harsh, almost violent sound. "Victor Nazarov cannot think he has intimidated me or any of us, Commander. Ready my car and ensure the perimeter of the attack site is secure. I'll be at the garage within the hour."

The muscle in Lucian's jaw ticked, but he inclined his head to his leader, then headed out the door. Only when the door clicked shut behind him did Ysabel speak again.

"Varojin, you and I need to talk."

"About?" Jin asked.

"You and Miss Sovna will come with me." Her tone suggested there was no room for argument. "Come along." Ysabel's long black skirt swirled around her legs as she turned and walked out of the dining room.

With a huff, Jin took Astrea's hand and started after the grand duchess. Peering over her shoulder, Astrea caught Eliana's eye. The princess shrugged, gray confusion flashing around her and just about everyone else in the room.

Great. This had to be about their engagement, right? Unless there was some news about the attacks Ysabel felt she couldn't share with everyone else? But why hide something like that?

"Do you think she's mad?" Astrea whispered to Jin as they hurried down the hall.

Ysabel disappeared around the corner.

"Honestly, I don't know," he said.

Selfishly, Astrea wanted just one single day where something could go right. One day to be happy and just bask in this next step she and Jin were taking together. Yes, securing alliances after Nazarov's new attacks was important. So was ensuring the people of Talmaris were safe. But couldn't she have even just half a day?

Don't be like that, Az, she warned herself as they stepped into Ysabel's office.

"Close the door behind you," Ysabel called as she circled her desk.

"As if I wasn't already going to do that," Jin muttered under his breath. He smiled tightly when the task was done. "What would you like to speak about?"

"I genuinely mean my congratulations when I say them," Ysabel said. "But I must warn you, Varojin, and you, Miss Sovna, that the timing of this is going to look very bad to the council. You signed away your rights to the throne just a few hours before getting engaged?"

"I fail to see the issue," Jin said. "Especially considering we have much bigger things to worry about. We should be focused on finding Nazarov and the Paragon."

"You signed those rights away just a few hours before getting engaged," Ysabel repeated. "The council is going to see this is a mistake made by a man in love, not a rational decision."

"How can you know that?" Astrea asked before she could think better of it. Warm pride burst in her chest, and she was sure that feeling wasn't coming from the stone-faced grand duchess. "You can speak for every person on your council?"

"I know them well enough, Miss Sovna. I've known most of them for longer than you two have been alive."

"Let them think what they want," Jin said. "It was always my plan to sign those documents the moment they were offered to me. You know that. Veiko and Eliana know that."

"And your first act of official freedom was to plan a wedding?" Ysabel drawled.

"I still don't see what the problem is."

Ysabel turned toward Astrea. "I like you, Miss Sovna. You're a kind, smart young woman. But the optics of this—"

"I'm sorry," Jin said, "you're worried about the optics of my private life, in a country I don't live in, while said country was just attacked? While multiple countries were just attacked? There were civilian casualties, and yet you're worried about the *optics* of our engagement?"

"That's the thing, Varojin." Ysabel leaned forward on her desk. "You've lived here for months. And while you surely plan to return to Helosia someday, you're involved with my government now whether you like it or not."

"Sure," Jin said, "but why would the timing of my choices make the council question my motives? That I am not still devoted to this cause, as I have been for months? I fail to see the connection."

Astrea fiddled with her necklace, running her finger over the smooth opal. What *was* Ysabel trying to get at? She could see how the timing might seem rushed to the council, but as Jin said, their other problems were far bigger.

Ysabel sighed. "They are furious that I hid your heritage from them for so long. This is not just about you signing away your rights."

"Then what is it?" Jin asked.

"They worry you may be a liability because of your familial connection to the Paragon. And now with this attack . . ."

Surprise whispered over Astrea's skin just before rage burned her.

"They think I'd turn against Novaria?" Jin all but growled.

"After the attack on the embassy, and now the attack downtown, they aren't sure what to think anymore. We've always had a good relationship with Zaikudi leadership."

"Do we know how deep the Paragon connection runs in their government?"

"No."

"Did the Paragon leave any message for Astrea or myself at the attack site?"

"Nothing that has been found."

"Hasn't Jin proven his dedication to the cause?" Astrea swallowed hard. "How can they not see that, Your Highness? He's done everything in his power to help."

"I signed away my rights to any legal claim to power in this country, and the council still thinks I could turn? And do what?" he asked. "Just use my closeness to the palace in some way?"

Ysabel shrugged.

"You may want to get yourself new advisors," Jin muttered. "Their concerns are barely rational."

"You let Nazarov get away down near Irvina," Ysabel began. "You bring Helosian defectors to our borders. You insisted on going back into Helosia, which got several Novarian soldiers seriously injured. Both sides of your family have been trying to destroy Novarian sovereignty for generations, and now you want to tie yourself to the other half of the Paragon's obsessions on the same morning of these attacks." Her expression and voice hardened as she said, "*I* do not question your loyalty, but the council isn't sure what to think anymore."

When it was spelled out like that . . . no, it didn't look great. But that was all being taken out of context, not in consideration of Jin's intentions and plans. The council didn't know his heart or his mind.

And besides, how could they not see the situation for what it really was? That Nazarov had barely escaped in Irvina and only with help from another void mage? That Helosian defectors were always going to be part of the rebellion the council had agreed to back? That Jin had said he would go into Helosia alone, yet the Novarians had approved a joint mission? That he could not be held responsible for the choices of his Seviyan grandfather and the Auris dynasty that didn't even respect him?

"What do you suggest?" Astrea asked. "That we call off the engagement publicly just for optics? Wouldn't painting Jin or me as a scorned lover just fuel any suspicions? The council already suggested we be forcibly separated, and we said no."

That warm pride seeped out of Jin again, and Astrea stood a little taller. No, she would not let the council ruin this for them, optics and poor timing be damned.

Ysabel deflated, though Astrea sensed nothing from her now. Dark circles had made their homes under her lavender eyes.

"No, I don't think that's the route to go," Ysabel said. "But there is one way you might be able to save some of your reputation with the council."

"And how is that?" Jin asked.

"Join me today downtown. Show them that you care about the people. If you could even heal some of the survivors, Miss Sovna—"

"Our being hunted by the Paragon somehow makes us suspicious to the council, and yet now, if we go to the site where they attacked, *that* won't be seen as bad somehow?" Jin scoffed. "I told you they weren't rational."

"As I was saying," Ysabel continued, "several of the councillors will be there, and if they see Miss Sovna healing the survivors, and if they see you there, supporting your betrothed, it may paint you both in a softer, more generous light. I say this not to upset you, Varojin. I want you both to be aware of the council's concerns. Tread carefully. Try to put their minds at ease."

"Or what?" Jin asked.

Ysabel's lips pressed into a thin line. "Let's not find out."

Chapter 29

The grand duchess's words ran circles in Astrea's mind as she trudged through the palace with Jin. *Tread carefully.*

Every hallway they walked down crawled with soldiers and guards, and though so many people being around hadn't always been comfortable, it had once been reassuring. A sign of strength, proof that the Novarians weren't going to let the Paragon attack again.

Except they had.

And now, every pair of eyes on them made Astrea's skin crawl.

Jin was right. The council's concerns seemed illogical. Sure, the two of them were the objects of Victor Nazarov's obsession, but why would Jin and Astrea spend so many months trying to solve this problem if they were really just working with the Paragon?

Why fight Nazarov so many times?

Why go back to Kalama?

Why do any of it?

Could the council have loyalties other than to Ysabel and Novaria? What if the Paragon had corrupted not just the Zaikudi but Ysabel's very own advisors? And if someone on the council—or multiple people—now had ties to the Paragon, what could that mean for these very soldiers and guards sworn to protect everyone in the palace?

After all, if someone was accusing you of something so far from the truth, it was usually because they were capable of that very thing.

And Astrea knew so little about the council, just that the ruler of Novaria needed majority support on certain initiatives. She'd spent so little time with the councillors.

Jin's thumb traced circles on the back of her hand, like he knew she was on the verge of panic. Astrea sucked in one deep breath, then another, and willed her pulse to slow as they reached their bedroom.

As soon as they entered, Jin shut the door behind Astrea, then pulled her to the far wall near the fireplace.

"Do you think—" she started.

"I don't know what to think," Jin said. "If I were truly some stranger, I could understand the council's concerns, but they've been talking to me for months. No, we're not the best of friends, but the fact that they see me as disloyal?" Steel pain flared around Jin. "It's insulting."

The Novarian Council may have had the right to their own opinions, but Jin was right. Astrea may not have had much interaction with them, but he had. He'd been discussing things with the council for months, since their very early days in Novaria. He'd kept his familial connections secret at Ysabel's suggestion. And as for Nazarov, it wasn't fair—or accurate—to suggest Jin *let* him get away.

"Do you think anyone on the Novarian Council might actually be in the Paragon's pocket?" Astrea asked. "Like the Zaikudi ambassador. Could they be trying to split the government, make them turn on us?"

"I'd like to think no, but honestly? I have no idea, Az."

"So now what?"

Sighing, Jin ran a hand across the back of his neck. "I think we have to do what Ysabel suggested. Go with her and Lucian today. Let them see your work, and show them we truly want to lend our support."

"You think it's safe?"

"I don't think anywhere is safe anymore. Not if Nazarov's attacked every capital."

Pressing her lips together, Astrea fiddled with her engagement band. "I suppose you're right."

"Hey." Slowly, Jin tilted her chin up so she had to look into his eyes. They were warm, molten. Concerned. Full of love and pain both. "We'll go, and we'll do what Ysabel's asked. The team will be there, and we'll make sure nothing happens. And we'll tell Lucian all of this."

"Alright."

"Let's get ready, then," Jin said, glancing at the clock above the fireplace. "Ysabel said she'd be at the garage within the hour, and time's almost up."

After stopping by Eliana's room to let her know about the issue with the council, Astrea and Jin went to collect Adi and the twins. Once in the palace garage, they'd found Ysabel waiting, along with Marko, Commander Lucian, and Zephyrine. The grand duchess had said little as she climbed into her waiting car, Lucian giving them a quick glance before climbing into the driver's seat and driving away.

Now, Astrea sat in another car with Adi, Zephyrine, and Jin, with Marko at the wheel. Lennor and Civan had gone with Lucian at his request.

"What's got you two so upset?" Zephyrine asked as she leaned back in her seat. "Shouldn't you be feeling better with your news?" When no one answered, she said, "Already do something to make Astrea call it off, kid?"

"No." Jin huffed. "Ysabel's warned me that the council apparently doesn't think I'm loyal and is going to further question that loyalty once they learn of my engagement to 'the other half of the Paragon's obsession.'"

Adi's thick eyebrows shot up. "What?"

"Apparently the fact that I 'let Nazarov get away' down in Irvina means I am not to be trusted."

"It's hardly your fault he can disappear in the blink of an eye," Marko drawled from the front of the car.

"So now what?" Astrea asked. "What do we do?"

"You stand your ground," Zephyrine said. "Neither of you has done anything wrong except be the target of some very delusional people."

"The council apparently doesn't see it that way," Jin said.

"We can worry about the council if they even say anything."

"I think they will," he said. "Ysabel basically said Az showing up this morning to heal some of the bombing victims is the only way the council will slow their reaction to the engagement news. That's the only reason we're here."

"I'm happy to help," Astrea said. "I want to help."

Jin's hand settled on her knee, and he gave it a squeeze. "I know. I just hate that you have no choice if we want to save any face politically."

Astrea shrugged. What was she going to do? Not go help Nazarov's victims? Not try to keep the Novarian government on their side?

"We were wondering if the council may be corrupt, or if someone on it may have been swayed by the Paragon," Jin said. Lavender surprise exploded around Adi. "Zephyrine, do you think there's any chance of that?"

The general sighed. "Honestly, kid? Anything seems possible right now."

Great. That didn't make Astrea feel any better at all.

"I'll tell the commander of the situation once we arrive downtown," Marko said. "It's best he's made aware . . . if the grand duchess isn't telling him as we speak."

Astrea settled back in her seat as they continued on. The closer they got to downtown, the more the world morphed from the calm near the palace to the pandemonium expected after such an attack. Sirens whined in the distance, and several police cars were at every corner they passed. Some officers and soldiers stood together in the street, directing both vehicular and pedestrian traffic.

And even as they moved through the city at a quick pace, panic and pain reached out to Astrea in waves. Gritting her teeth, she pushed back against the energy. Surely there would be plenty more where that came from.

Her heart ached for the people of Talmaris. For the people of every city that had been attacked.

This wasn't just about Astrea anymore. It wasn't about Jin. It didn't even seem to be about that Stargazer's prophecy. No, this was about Nazarov's desire for power and the Paragon's creed to bring chaos and destruction.

Something nobody could have predicted until recently. After all, even scholars at prestigious institutions hadn't a clue about the Paragon. Their leadership had successfully hidden themselves away, relegated themselves to the shadows and spun their part in the Great Wars to nothing more than fables and bedtime stories.

Nazarov had unleashed himself upon the continent, and these civilians were now caught in the crossfire.

Jin's hand brushed hers as Marko pulled the car to a stop along a curb. Several police officers and palace guards were waiting outside.

"You sure you're up for this?" Jin whispered.

"I'm sure," she said.

She would not let her healing go to waste. Not when people needed her help.

Zephyrine and Marko got out of the car first, and Adi quickly followed. Jin climbed out next, and as he extended his hand to Astrea, his engagement band caught some of the morning sun, which was half obscured by gray clouds. Astrea took his hand.

The police officers and palace guards on the sidewalk signaled for their group to wait. A few steps ahead, Lucian and the twins were exiting the grand duchess's car and scanning the street. At the next intersection, the road was blocked off by barricades, and a mixture of police dressed in blue and medics in white rushed around. Wave after wave of panic and pain crashed against Astrea's body, making bile climb up her throat. She couldn't see anything beyond the crowd of emergency personnel.

"I'm sorry this day can't be more happy," Jin murmured to Astrea. "It wasn't supposed to be like this."

With a sad smile, Astrea said, "Hardly something for you to apologize for."

"I know, but still."

As Ysabel exited her car, all the officers and guards stood at attention. She waved them off as she approached Astrea and the others.

"Councillors Tarsaya, Kanirva, and Fresan will already be on scene," Ysabel said, voice low. "They should be waiting near some of the medical tents. That's where we'll go first if you're ready, Miss Sovna."

"I'm ready," Astrea said.

As they walked down the sidewalk flanked by the police and royal guards, Astrea searched her mind. She remembered Councillor Tarsaya; he'd been involved in some of their discussions of stealing the *Myths and Other Legends* book from Kalama. But Fresan and Kanirva? She couldn't specifically remember who they were, and now certainly didn't seem like the appropriate time to ask.

Ysabel walked with regal purpose, head held high and shoulders pushed back. She wore no crown, but her dark blue skirt and black blouse were made of expensive material, and her sturdy heels were somehow both elegant and no nonsense. She *looked* like a leader, so perfectly put together and serious.

The officers near the barricade saluted the grand duchess's approach. One of the officers, a stout man wearing a shade of blue darker than the rest, stepped out of line and joined their procession onto the busy street beyond.

"Commander Lucian, Your Highness." The man's thick mustache was filled with as many gray hairs as on his head. He seemed to be around Ysabel's age, with light brown skin and deep wrinkles around his mouth. "We secured the perimeter over an hour ago. Only medics and patients have been permitted to leave the premises for further treatment, but the nearby hospital is full."

"I've brought additional healers," Ysabel said as they passed by a group of civilians covered in dust and tiny bits of debris. They huddled together, but none of them seemed injured. "Please, take me directly to where my councillors are."

"Right away, Your Highness," the man said.

They continued on, weaving their way through the overloaded street. People were beginning to set up white tents, where the blue and white glow of healing shone out in the cloudy morning. Astrea risked a glance over her shoulder; several buildings on either side of the wide street were damaged, just messes of brick and metal. Debris crowded the sidewalks and road, and Earthmovers and Metalli were working together to move it out of the way. Dozens of white sheets covered the bodies of the victims. Astrea turned back around and squeezed Jin's hand.

They passed by more medics, this time healing people out in the open. It all seemed to be minor from what Astrea caught quick glimpses of: bruises, shallow cuts, concussions. And yet there was still so much more pain around her, so much that the cores of her bones ached and nausea built in her belly.

"Here we are, Your Highness," the officer said as they approached an open-sided tent. Underneath, three people in expensive-looking clothes spoke quietly among themselves. "My officers are all nearby if you need anything."

"Thank you, Chief Rizvan," Ysabel said. "You've done Talmaris a great service today. Thank your officers for me." As Chief Rizvan wandered away, Ysabel stepped up to her councillors. "How bad is it?" she asked, voice low.

Councillor Tarsaya's deep brown eyes flicked first to the grand duchess, then to where Jin and Astrea stood not far behind. "Prince Varojin, Miss Sovna." He turned back to his leader. "It was wise to bring them?"

"Miss Sovna's healing talents will be of great use today, Reimo," Ysabel said. "Tell me, how bad is it really?"

"Bad," said the female councillor as she brushed her black corkscrew curls away from her face. "Worse than Chief Rizvan indicated on the phone. Fifty dead, many more wounded."

"How is that possible?" Ysabel asked. When the councillor didn't reply, she said, "Please, Sinni."

Sinni; that was right. Astrea knew Sinni. Councillor Kanirva, one of the councillors who hadn't been completely hostile toward Astrea and Jin in their time in Talmaris. And as she glanced at the third councillor, the one with skin and hair so pale they looked like they were covered in snow, Astrea remembered them, too. Councillor Jules Fresan. They were one of the more reasonable members of Ysabel's council.

"They hit one café and one restaurant, Your Highness," Jules said. "Plus trolleys on opposite sides of the road, and they also attacked one of the department stores. All at rush hour. Slightly staggered, according to witnesses."

"Do we have anyone in custody?" Ysabel asked. "When I spoke with Chief Rizvan this morning, his people were just trying to piece together exactly what had happened."

"They were . . ." Reimo pressed his full lips together. "Your Highness, bombers seem to have died in the attacks as well."

Ysabel paled.

"You're sure?" Jin asked.

"Multiple witnesses confirmed it," Reimo said.

"The bombers didn't jump away through shadows?" Jin asked.

"No one reports such a thing," Sinni replied. "They're still trying to figure out the specifics."

Astrea looked over her shoulder again, at all the civilians laid out on sheets and tarps as they waited for healers to reach them. From what she could gather, there were far more people in need of healing than there were medics.

Ignoring whatever Ysabel and her councillors were discussing, Astrea tugged on Jin's hand. He followed her away from the tent and toward where a mother and child sat on the ground nearby. They both shared the same pinkish complexion and light brown hair.

"Has a healer been by to see you yet?" Astrea asked as she knelt down next to them.

The mother peered up at Astrea, her light blue eyes filled with tears that reflected the orange fear tangled around her body. "Who are you?"

"I'm Astrea," she said. "I'm a Lightbringer."

"You're not dressed like them," the woman said, tilting her chin toward one of the medics across the way. They wore a crisp white uniform while Astrea was in her casual purple dress, fit for that silly engagement party, not this.

"No, I'm not," Astrea said. "I came with the grand duchess, as we heard there aren't enough healers to go around. How can I help?" With so much pain and no good reason to close herself off, Astrea couldn't parse out where anyone's particular injuries were. Her skin and muscles pulsed in time with her heart.

"Her ankle," the mother said, gesturing to her daughter, who couldn't have been older than three or four years old. "I think it's broken. She only stopped crying after one of the medics gave her a tonic."

"May I look?" Astrea asked.

With a nod, the woman adjusted to give Astrea and her daughter space. The little girl even had her mother's blue eyes. They were cloudy, though. Unfocused.

"How much tonic was she given?" Astrea asked.

"Probably more than she needed," the woman admitted. "She wouldn't stop screaming."

Frowning, Astrea said, "Hi there." The little girl barely paid her any mind. "I'm Astrea. I need to look at your ankle, alright?"

When the child gave a quivering smile, Astrea took that as consent. She reached for the blanket covering the girl's lap and tugged it away. Sure enough, her ankle was swollen and bruised, and her shins were both covered in cuts and blood. Astrea would've been crying, too, if her legs were in such bad shape.

"I need to touch you to heal you, alright?" Astrea said to the little girl. "It won't take long."

"Do it," her mother said. "Please."

Next to Astrea, Jin knelt, too. Footsteps shuffled behind them, and curiosity tickled the end of Astrea's nose. Adi, maybe? Or one of the twins?

Setting her hands on the child's legs, a soft glow built around Astrea's palms. She gritted her teeth as the pain in her ankle doubled, then tripled.

But the little girl's body relaxed, and the mirror pain and relief in Astrea's joint eased. When she pulled her hands away, the child's ankle was almost back to normal except for a faint yellow bruise. The cuts remained, but they were shallow enough, and Astrea couldn't use all her energy on the inconsequential things given all the people still in need of treatment.

"Thank you," her mother said, her relief minty in Astrea's mouth.

"You're very welcome," Astrea said, still kneeling on the ground. She rested her hands on her thighs as she tried to regain her composure.

"Varojin?"

That voice was not Adi. No, it sounded like Councillor Tarsaya. When Astrea looked up, she found him staring at her hand. At the ring on her finger.

"A discussion for another day," the councillor mused.

"There's nothing to discuss," Jin said quietly. "We're getting married, regardless of what you or your colleagues may think."

That was not the delicate way Astrea expected him to handle this situation. Not when he'd agreed with Ysabel's plan to try to soften their image to the reluctant council members.

"You're getting married?" the woman asked. When Astrea nodded, she said, "May your union be a blessed one. Your future children will be very lucky to have a healer as a mother."

Astrea's entire face heated. *That* was not something she wanted to discuss in public, not with a stranger and certainly not around one of the Novarian councillors.

"Thank you," she managed to say as Jin helped her stand up. "If you need more help, please come find me. I'll be here for a while."

As they moved away from the woman and toward the next waiting patient, Astrea tried to ignore Councillor Tarsaya's hovering. But that was what she was supposed to do: soften her and Jin's image. And they played the role well, she thought. After all, both of them genuinely cared about these civilians who were just in the wrong place at the wrong time, left to the Paragon's mercy.

After her first couple of patients, Grand Duchess Ysabel joined them. She made a big show of talking to each person as Astrea healed them, complimenting Astrea's work and the bravery and strength of all the medics present on scene. Ysabel also commended the survivors for their tenacity and mentioned several times that Novaria was a tough country, one that would not be taken down so easily.

It seemed to help. Each person Ysabel spoke with sat up a little straighter, and warm pride flowed off them by the time Astrea's healing was complete. Even the councillors, who had all joined by that point, seemed to be in better spirits after the first hour had passed.

Astrea, though, was dead on her feet. Lucian didn't seem to be faring any better; he was helping with healing where he could, though his focus had remained on security. Together, they healed everything from broken bones to concussions to burns and deep gashes. It was too much, both healing and leaving herself open to feel for any Paragon stragglers who might show up to the scene of their crime.

"You doing alright?" Jin asked, his hand rubbing smooth, gentle circles between her shoulder blades.

Ysabel was a few paces ahead of them, talking to Councillor Fresan and a Lightbringer with auburn hair.

"Fine," Astrea said. "Managing."

"We could go."

"We can't go."

As Astrea surveyed the crowded street before them, all she could see were all the people still waiting for healing. Some nurses and non-magical medical personnel were practicing first aid and passing out tonics. Jin, Adi, Civan, and Lennor had all administered some first aid, too, where they could. That had really seemed to impress the council. But even if Astrea needed a break, she couldn't leave.

And besides, she was glad she could help. These people were unaware of what she and Jin represented, that they were part of why the city was under attack. Spending a little time healing them was the least she could be doing.

"Alright, maybe not," Jin admitted with a small smile, "but we can at least see about getting you a coffee or some water."

"There's a tent set up a few hundred yards down," Lucian said as he came up to them. "Just don't take too long," he added, voice low. "Councillor Fresan is very pleased with the way you two have shown up. Keep it up. They're a good ally to have in the palace. A very good ally."

"No pressure," Astrea muttered.

"You're doing great, Az," Adi said from half a step behind her.

They were already heading in the right direction, so Astrea prepared herself to heal the next few patients along the way. Then she could take a short break. She stayed behind Ysabel and the council, figuring they would lead the way.

"Do you think that—" Adi started.

Pain pierced the spot between Astrea's shoulders, right where Jin's hand was. She stumbled forward a step as her vision blurred and went dark.

Miss Sovna, Nazarov cooed as Astrea gritted her teeth. The shadows seemed to swirl around her, crawling up her limbs. *Twice I've invited you to visit me, and twice you've rudely declined. Yet here you are, out and about. Obviously you're not ill, so what could be the cause of this delay?*

Nazarov, Jin growled. *What the fuck do you think you're doing, attacking civilians?*

This is war, Varojin. I thought you'd know that.

Even war has rules, Jin said. *Civilians are off limits. Don't you have any humanity left?*

Humanity doesn't get you what you want. You'd best learn that lesson soon, Varojin, Nazarov said. Astrea could almost hear the smile in his voice. *I told you not to cross me, Miss Sovna. But you've done so again. Just what are we going to do with you?*

The shadows disappeared like a tide rapidly rushing out to sea. The real world snapped back into place around Astrea. The sun, still half obscured by clouds, made her squint. The grand duchess and councillors were looking at Astrea and Jin with confused expressions.

A crack rang through the street. Pain lanced the back of Astrea's head, then dissipated. Something wet covered her face, and as the grand duchess tumbled forward, horror and ice-cold terror spread over Astrea's limbs.

Her insides burned with cold fire. Ysabel lay on the ground in a heap, shadows flickering across her skin. There one second and gone the next, like someone had flipped off the lights.

Aetherium.

The grand duchess . . .

Jin grabbed Astrea and pulled her to the ground as someone shouted about a sharpshooter. Then another crack rang out through the streets, and an echo of pain pierced the side of Astrea's head. Councillor Tarsaya fell to the ground. Shadows crawled up his face. Icy fire swallowed up Astrea's insides again, and then his energy slipped away.

Grand Duchess Ysabel and Councillor Reimo Tarsaya were dead.

Dead.

People began screaming. White terror rippled in the air, painful and bright.

Astrea tried to move, but shadows clouded her vision again, holding her in place. Then Nazarov whispered, *Cross me one more time, little*

Lightbringer, and you'll see what happens when you push me too far. Now, I know I've made a mess for you to clean up. Meet me in the mountains within a fortnight. The earlier, the better.

And just like that, Nazarov was gone again.

Before Astrea could even gather her bearings amid the panic unfolding before her, Jin hauled her to her feet. The team circled around them—Adi, Marko, Lennor, Civan, Zephyrine.

"Go, now," Adi ordered, propelling them both forward.

Jin pulled her along so fast she had no choice but to sprint. They scrambled past the police barricades and back to their parked car so fast that Astrea didn't even have time to see where the commander was.

"Where's Lucian?" she asked, breathless, as Jin shut the car door and Marko started the engine.

"He'll take care of the grand duchess and councillors," Marko said. The car lurched away from the curb.

"We're just leaving them here?" she asked, horrified. "We're just leaving everyone here?"

"I have my orders." Marko's voice was cold as ice. "Trust the commander. We need to get back to the palace."

As soon as Marko had turned the car around, they sped back toward the palace, putting more and more distance between them and the scene of Grand Duchess Ysabel's assassination.

Chapter 30

Cold static had taken over Astrea's entire body by the time the car pulled into the palace drive.

Dead.

Grand Duchess Ysabel was dead.

Councillor Tarsaya was dead.

Killed just feet from where Astrea had stood.

The car stopped at the bottom of the palace steps. Marko turned the engine off and jumped out, shouting, "Lock this place down! Lock it down!"

Zephyrine climbed out next, following up Marko's order with more shouts.

"Find my sister," Jin said to Lennor and Civan. "Please."

They left without a word, scrambling out of the car and toward the palace.

"Jin?" Astrea whispered, gaze trained on her hands in her lap. "Adi?"

Adi shook his head. "I can't believe . . ."

"I can," Jin muttered. "Nazarov's a dead man. As if he didn't already have the Novarian military hunting him. He won't be able to run from this."

"We don't even know where he is," Astrea said. "He could be *anywhere*. He again told me to meet him in the mountains. He said it had to be within a fortnight."

"He's offering us *time?*" Adi asked. "He assassinates two leaders and gives us *time?*"

"He said it was because he gave me such a mess to clean up," Astrea said. "As if he was being gracious. He . . . he did this because I 'crossed' him again . . ."

"This is not your fault, Az," Adi said. "Nazarov is unhinged. What do you think he's planning to do in the next fortnight, Jin?"

"I have no fucking idea, but I know it's not going to be good. This isn't about giving us time." Huffing, Jin glanced out the car window. Soldiers and guards flew down the palace steps, heading to new posts. "We should go inside," he said, opening his car door. "I need to talk to Ellie."

Cool autumn air met Astrea's blazing cheeks as she scrambled out of the car after Jin. Adi wasn't far behind her.

"Just like that, back to business?" Astrea asked, making Jin stop in his tracks. "The grand duchess is dead."

Astrea wasn't the grand duchess's biggest fan, but she hadn't deserved *that*. She'd been trying to stop Nazarov, stop the emperor. She'd been trying to do something good, even if she was indecisive and too concerned with optics.

In fact, she might still be alive if she hadn't been so concerned with her image. If she hadn't insisted on going out to the site of the attack. Tears pricked Astrea's eyes.

"I know, Az." Jin finally turned to look at her. Blood had splattered on his face. The grand duchess's blood. He stalked toward her, keeping his voice low as he said, "I *know*. And right now, neither of her heirs are in the country, and the council already apparently thought poorly of us. Now she's dead, and we were standing two feet away from her."

"They can't seriously think you'd have *anything* to do with that," Adi said. "You wouldn't even gain anything!"

"I don't think it's about gaining anything," Jin said. "It's about us being the Paragon's targets and putting Ysabel in danger. And if Az is right, that maybe someone on the council is compromised, then maybe they tipped Nazarov off somehow. Or will use this to just further divide the government. They already sent Az and me into exile once, even if it was for our protection. They already tried to split us up. Whatever their next move, we need to get ahead of it. We need to find my sister."

What was Eliana going to do about any of this, exactly? It wasn't like she had any real political power in Talmaris. Maybe she could bring some logic back to the council, but she wasn't Ysabel's heir.

Jin grabbed Astrea's hand, then all three of them hurried up the steps and into the palace. Inside was an explosion of color and emotion, fear and panic and deep, deep sadness. How was Lucian faring? Were the other councillors alive? What if Nazarov had attacked them, too?

Adi broke off from their trio to help Marko with whatever the next steps were going to be. Astrea and Jin continued on, upstairs and to the wing of the palace where their rooms were. Just as they entered the hallway, Eliana burst out of her bedroom, Nicos and Zephyrine right behind.

"What happened?" Eliana cried as she ran up to them. "Skies, Az, you're covered in blood. You too, Jin."

Her raised voice made others open their doors. Cressida, Lennor, and Civan came out next. The Nikaphoroses out of another room. Noemi and Saros were the only ones missing.

Jin tilted his head, a silent signal for Eliana to follow. *Everyone* followed them into Jin and Astrea's room, and Balthazar shut the door behind them with a heavy thunk.

"Zephyrine said Ysabel is dead?" Eliana half whispered. Orange fear and deep blue sadness twined around her limbs. "And Councillor Tarsaya?"

"What?" Cressida asked. "You're serious?"

Swallowing hard, Jin nodded and said, "It had to have been the Paragon. Nazarov dreamwalked to me and Az, and then it happened."

"He came back to me . . . after," Astrea whispered. Sarsali walked into their bedroom, eyebrows furrowed. "He told me not to keep testing him. Blamed me for this." Shaking her head, she reached up to scrub at her face, only to touch the blood there. Pulling her hand away, she added, "He gave me a fortnight to meet him in the mountains."

"Why'd he give you time?" Cressida asked.

"We've already talked about that," Jin said. "He's probably planning something else."

"Maybe it's a trap," Nicos said. "One he needs time to set up first, especially after the kind of attack he just pulled off."

"It was an aetherium bullet that killed Ysabel and Councillor Tarsaya," Jin said to the others.

Sarsali's soft footsteps returned. She approached Jin and Astrea, two damp washcloths in her hands. "For the blood," she said quietly. "It's all over your faces."

Astrea tried to take her washcloth, but her hands were trembling so badly that Sarsali had to clean her face up for her. She worked in quick, careful strokes. Her eyes glistened with unshed tears by the time she was done.

"What do we do now?" Cressida asked.

"That's why I wanted to find you, Ellie," Jin said. "Do you know where Veiko and Delfine are?"

"Surely they got on the first airships back to Talmaris after the initial attacks," she said. "I doubt they know about Ysabel yet."

"What about Veiko's wife and children?" Jin asked. "Where are they?"

"At an estate in the country, I think."

"They need to be brought back to the palace immediately," Jin said. "I wouldn't put it past Nazarov to track them down. At least here, surrounded by Lightbringers and extra military, they stand a chance."

Jin said it with such calmness that it almost didn't sound like him. This was Captain Auris, the man who knew how to survive war.

Victor Nazarov had declared war on Novaria the day he first attacked the palace and captured Astrea. But this? Assassinating not just the head of state but one of the most prominent people in the government? Attacking civilians?

This was different.

"Where are Saros and Noemi?" Astrea asked.

"They were with Tomas in the library," Sarsali said. "They have been since you left this morning."

"I can go fetch them if you want," Lennor offered quietly.

Astrea shook her head. "That's alright." As soon as Saros heard of the assassination, he'd be sprinting upstairs to try to find Astrea anyway. And Adi might've gone in search of his sister if Marko didn't need any more help.

"We need to get ahead of this, Ellie," Jin said. "You know the council already views Az and I as a problem simply because the Paragon are obsessed with us. If they think—"

"There's no way they can see you at fault for this," Eliana snapped.

"They can," Zephyrine said. "It's easier to blame it on Astrea and Jin than to accept that Nazarov has once again gotten the better of us. That their grand duchess made a mistake in venturing outside the safety of these walls."

"Then we need to talk," Eliana said to her brother. "We need a plan."

"We contact Veiko and Delfine, as well as Letizia and the kids," Jin said. "We get them all here as quickly as possible. As soon as the other councillors are back, we find them and try to see where they stand. And we get Lucian's help when he returns to the palace."

"That simple?" Nicos muttered.

"Not like we have any other choices," Jin said. "We can't leave. Our best bet is to stay here."

"Veiko won't believe you two are to blame," Eliana said. "I'm sure of that much. He can always convince the council."

"And we need a way to determine whether anyone on the council might be connected to the Paragon," Jin said.

Just how were they going to do that?

"Let's go call Veiko," Eliana said. "We'll start there, then go down the list. We'll figure this out."

As Eliana and Nicos headed for the door, Jin turned toward Astrea. He took her face in his hands, then kissed the top of her head. "I'll be back," he whispered before following his sister out of the room.

Astrea watched him leave, catching a glimpse of his engagement band as he reached for the doorknob. She let out a long, slow breath.

Just last night. Just last night, they'd gotten engaged.

Just that morning, they'd been attempting to celebrate.

Just hours before, and now everything was horribly, terribly wrong.

As Astrea cleaned up in the bathroom, cold fear bit her skin and rippled through her muscles, mimicking the thunk, thunk, thunk of her heart. She scrubbed the soap and water from her face, trying to let the movement bring her back to reality.

Ysabel was dead.

Astrea grabbed the towel she'd set near the sink and patted her face dry. Her eyes were puffy, a bit red. She'd barely managed to get her tears under control in the few minutes she'd been alone in the bathroom.

The Nikaphoroses were just outside. Balthazar had volunteered to keep watch for Saros, who would undoubtedly lose his mind when he found out what had happened. Jin had left not even ten minutes before, so Saros was surely going to arrive soon. News would travel quickly.

A knock sounded on the bathroom door, then Cressida nudged it open. "Hey."

Astrea set the towel down. "How are your parents?"

"Shaken up. Worried about you."

"I'll be alright." Astrea didn't even believe that lie, but Cressida didn't say anything. She just smiled weakly.

A new wave of anxiety washed over Astrea. It moved closer and closer, drowning her.

"I think Saros is—"

"Where is she?" Saros shouted.

"—coming," Astrea mumbled to Cressida. Then, she called, "I'm right here!"

Sarsali and Balthazar's jumbled words came next, and as Astrea stepped back out into her bedroom, Saros launched himself at her. He wrapped his arms around her, holding her tight. She tried to relax, but the warring panic and relief swirling around him made it impossible.

"Fucking skies, Astrea," he said as he pulled away, still gripping her shoulders. "You should have come to find me immediately! What's this about the grand duchess being assassinated? You were there?"

"We had things to discuss," Astrea said lamely. "We couldn't just come find you. But I'm safe."

As she went on to explain to Saros what had happened, from all the destruction downtown to the grand duchess's assassination, more of that cold horror bled into the air. It seeped out of Saros, of Balthazar, Cressida, and Sarsali. Her whole family. Astrea held onto the fact that they were there, that *she* was there with them.

Unlike so many people whose families had just been torn apart all across the continent.

"I can't believe it," Saros murmured. He'd long since sat on the bed, hands buried in his hair. "I can't believe they killed the grand duchess. Nothing like this has happened in Novaria in a very long time. Generations."

"Is Noemi with Adi?" Astrea asked.

"Huh?" Saros straightened, his eyes bloodshot. "Oh, uh, yes. Adi came and found us."

"Any luck in the library?" Cressida asked half-heartedly.

"Actually, the grand duchess gave orders to Tomas this morning to contact the linguist I know . . . before breakfast." Saros shook his head. "We were trying to reach out to him when news of the attack came."

"Did you actually get in touch?" Sarsali asked. When Saros nodded, she said, "I'm surprised Tomas was willing to go through with it."

"Well, he is receptive to directives from those in charge," Saros replied. He shook his head again. "I suppose we'll need to see if Prince—Grand Duke Veiko approves . . ."

"Do it anyway," Astrea said. When her uncle gave her a questioning look, she said, "We've waited long enough. Just make sure to coordinate with Lucian's security teams. I'd rather ask Veiko's forgiveness than permission."

"If you think it's best," Saros said.

"I do."

"Alright then. We'll get back on it."

Nazarov may have orchestrated a devastating blow today, but Astrea would be damned if she didn't figure out a way to stop him, whether that was getting those translations or taking an army to the mountains. She could not let this day and all its suffering and death mean nothing. No, she would stop him if it was the last thing she did.

Chapter 31

By the time night fell, the harsh reality of the day's events had fully set in.

What should have been a happy day was just one full of pain. So much pain. Astrea hated it. Her heart ached not just for herself and Jin but for Veiko and Delfine, who had lost their aunt. All the civilians downtown who had either lost their lives, lost a loved one, or been injured. For Novaria as a whole, now reeling from the assassination of two of its political leaders.

Her stiff fingers stayed wrapped around her coffee mug, long since cold. The others in the war room were deep in discussion about next steps: Veiko's ascendance to the throne, Ysabel's funeral, what Veiko would need to tell the nation, where to pull troops from to increase security.

"Letizia and the children should be here soon," Marko said, glancing over at the clock on the far wall. "They left the estate a few hours ago."

"Has anyone had contact with them since then?" Jin asked.

"Yes, one of the guards on their detail was able to radio about an hour ago. They were close to Talmaris."

Jin nodded. "And Lucian?"

"He was supposed to return to the palace about an hour ago as well. He should be around here somewhere."

"Are we done for the night?" Cressida asked.

"Have we sent aid to the Talmarans hurt in the attack today?" Astrea asked. Surprise whispered over her skin as everyone looked her way. It was the first time she'd said a word in at least a half hour. "I might've missed it if you already said, sorry. I'm just tired."

Not only was the shock from earlier starting to wear off, but Astrea had done so much healing earlier in the day. It had finally caught up to her, and now, she could barely sit upright.

"Healers and nurses will remain on scene and have begun transferring patients to another hospital on the south side of the city," Marko said. "We're taking care of them."

"What about other things?" Astrea asked. "Food, clothes, accommodations for family?" Healing was just one of the few things those people would need. "Do we need more healers? Would it be safe for me to go back?"

"Everything's being taken care of," Marko said gently. "We're getting them everything they could need."

She gave a brief nod. If Marko said everything was taken care of, she would believe him. And if she found out it wasn't, well, Astrea would just have to take matters into her own hands. Those people could not suffer because of Nazarov. Because of her.

One of the war room doors opened, and a blonde guard stepped inside. "Marko," she said. "Princess Letizia and the children are here."

"And Commander Lucian?" Marko asked as he stood.

"Handling some things. He's asked you to tend to the princess's needs."

"I'll be right there. Make sure Cari is on their detail at all times. They are to go nowhere unprotected." With a nod, the guard returned to the hallway. Marko glanced at the others. "I can take it from here, unless any of you want to join me."

"I'll go," Eliana said.

"So will I," Jin said.

Adi excused himself to check on Noemi, and Cressida, Lennor, and Civan all decided to go for a walk to clear their heads. Zephyrine offered to rendezvous with the commander.

With Jin's help, Astrea stood. Her joints cracked and protested the movement. As a group, she, Eliana, Nicos, Jin, and Marko started through the palace. Guards and soldiers roamed around, some armed with guns and other weapons while some went without. Astrea suppressed a shiver. Would this truly help keep them safe?

They continued on through the halls, eventually descending into the tunnel that would take them over to the garage. There was just as much activity there, perhaps more. Walls and emotions met Astrea's senses, heavy grief and confusion dominating everything else. And there, surrounded by a retinue of guards, was the fair-haired wife of the new grand duke. Her two children, Helena and Leo, clung to her legs.

"Princess Letizia," Marko called out.

She turned, searching among the crowd. "Marko," she said as they drew nearer. Her guards parted enough for Marko to step into the circle. "Varojin, Eliana. Is it true? Is Grand Duchess Ysabel"—she lowered her voice—"gone?"

"I'm afraid so," Marko replied quietly.

One of Letizia's pale hands covered her mouth. The fear swirling around her tripled, white overtaking the air. Helena and Leo peeked up at the group, their attention settling on Jin in the back. "And the attacks?"

"Also true," Eliana said. "I'm sorry, Letizia."

"Where's my husband?" she asked, voice shaking. "Where's Veiko?"

"On his way," Marko said. "Come, Commander Lucian has asked me to make sure you and the children are settled."

"I can't believe it," Letizia whispered as she moved to follow Marko. "I didn't believe it, honestly, when the staff at the estate told me. Is it wise for us to be back here? Where it happened?"

"This is the safest place you can be right now," Jin said. "I promise."

"Those who attacked Ysabel won't strike here next?"

"No, we don't believe so," Marko said, ushering her toward the tunnel. "Safer for you to be here, surrounded by the military and all these Lightbringers, than out in the middle of nowhere."

Letizia scooped Leo up in her arms, balancing him on one hip. She took Helena's hand with her free one before they began their descent. "We should speak after we get the children settled."

"Where are we going, Momma?" Helena asked. "Where's Papa?"

"Oh, my sweet girl," Letizia said, "it's as I told you in the car. We need to be here to be safe. Papa is coming soon. We'll go to your room, alright?"

Turning in his mother's arms, Leo stared at Astrea and Jin with tear-filled eyes. "Aunt Ysabel went back to the stars?"

"She's safe now, up in the sky," Eliana said. "She's with my mother, too."

Astrea's heart broke a little more, watching Leo—only a few years old—as he tried not to cry. He buried his face in his mother's hair.

How many other children were out in Talmaris—in Thasia, Mematos, and other cities—trying to understand what it meant to lose family? To lose friends?

"Cari's going to be on your detail while you're at the palace," Marko said as they exited the tunnel again. "Ah, speaking of." A young woman with tan, freckled skin and dark wavy hair approached. "This is Cari. One of our most talented Lightbringers."

"I know Cari, I'm—" Letizia started.

Cari bowed her head. "Grand Duchess Letizia." Her words held a certain lilt to them, almost like Raela's. Was she from near the mountains bordering Tornama, then, just like Astrea's old boss?

"Grand—" Letizia shook her head. Even after a car ride with two small children, her hair was impeccable, styled in a braided crown. She was dressed casually, just a thin sweater paired with a long skirt. "We'll discuss that later."

Cari gave a curt nod. "If you'll follow me, Your Highness."

"Find me if you need me," Marko called after Letizia. As the Novarian royal family headed down the guard-filled hallway, Marko sighed. "Skies. Grand Duchess Letizia."

"We'll need to get Veiko crowned as soon as he's back," Eliana said.

"Not exactly something I'm qualified to deal with," Marko muttered.

"You won't have to," she replied. "I'll help. However I can. However much Veiko wants me to."

"Right, well . . ." Rubbing the spot between his eyebrows, Marko said, "You all should get some rest. Someone will let you know as soon as Veiko's returned or if there's anything you need to know about."

"I want to know if there's even a hint of where Nazarov might've gone," Jin said. "I don't care if it's two in the morning."

"You will be among the first to know," Marko said. "Now go to bed."

Exhausted as she was, Astrea didn't think she could go to sleep. No, her mind buzzed, wary of everything around them in the palace. The walls, the sadness, the rage, the fear.

Taking her hand in his, Jin tugged Astrea back toward their rooms. Eliana and Nicos were right behind them. Although she was going to ask them to stay to talk, Eliana and Nicos both murmured excuses and good nights as soon as they were back in their wing of the palace. Astrea wasn't going to push them.

No, instead, she let Jin lead her into their bedroom. And as soon as the doors were shut and locked, he wrapped his arms around her waist and pulled her closer.

"Fuck, Az," he whispered into her hair. "Skies, I can't believe this."

"I know." All day, Astrea had felt that disbelief, that grief and confusion freely flowing from him. "Me either."

"I don't even know what to think anymore."

"Me either," she said again. It was all too much.

"And the day after our engagement. Some timing I have," he muttered as he finally pulled away.

"*That* is not something you could ever have predicted," she said. "Ever."

"Is it wrong of me to wish this hadn't happened today? Or ever, of course, but skies . . . it's like Nazarov can't even let us have one thing, one moment of peace."

She smiled sadly. It didn't seem wrong; it seemed human to be sad for oneself while holding space for all the other pain in the world. "I thought the same thing earlier."

With a heavy sigh, Jin said, "I don't think I have it in me to talk about this anymore. Can we just go to bed?"

"Whatever you want."

As they got ready for the night, Astrea couldn't stop her mind from replaying everything that had gone on that day. That horrible, terrible, impossibly long day.

When gentle hands shook Astrea awake in the middle of the night, she wasn't upset. No, she was grateful. She'd been waking up every hour, it seemed, with images of the dead grand duchess and all those people looping through her mind.

"Az," Jin said, nudging her again. "Lucian wants to talk to us."

"Now?" She tried to blink the sleep from her mind. "What time is it?"

"Three. He's in the other room."

What could Lucian possibly want to talk about at three in the morning? Rolling out of bed, Astrea smoothed her messy hair and slipped her sweater on over her thin nightgown. Jin opened the door to their sitting room, where just the table lamps were on. Lucian loomed like a specter near the fireplace.

"I'm sorry to wake you both," Lucian said. Deep blue sadness filled his aura. That grief sat so heavily on Astrea's chest she could barely breathe. "But it's important."

"What's going on?" Jin asked.

Lucian motioned for them to sit on the sofa, and only once they were settled did he say, "Councillors Fresan and Kanirva have made it back to the palace safely. They're under tight guard."

"Unharmed?" Jin asked.

"For the most part." Lucian rubbed a hand over his pale face and sighed. "They know you two are not connected to this. Not in the way others on the council might think. I was able to speak with them more, and it's Councillor Reis who is trying to spread doubts about your loyalty, Varojin."

"That's what this is about?" Jin asked. "Politics?"

"I want you to be prepared for the morning," the commander said, voice low. "Councillors Fresan and Kanirva may understand what truly happened yesterday and your loyalties, but Reis has moved to question you both, but specifically you, Varojin. Tomorrow."

"Question him?" Astrea asked, suddenly very awake. Her pulse pounded in her ears. "Like a trial?"

"Not a trial," Lucian said. "An inquiry."

"So basically a trial," Jin deadpanned.

"There can be no punishment with an inquiry. But you must convince them you are not connected to Nazarov."

"Logic would dictate I'm not. I already told Ysabel that yesterday . . ."

"I know that very well," Lucian said. "I know the kind of man you are, Varojin. We may not always agree on the means, but it's clear you have a good heart."

Was that . . . support from Lucian? Was he actually defending Jin?

The faintest hint of hope bloomed in Astrea's veins. After so many disagreements between the two, maybe things would finally settle between them.

Or, at the very least—and more importantly—Lucian was on their side.

Jin pressed his lips together, then asked, "And what does this inquiry involve?"

"They'll task one of the other Lightbringers in the palace with reading your emotions as they question you. Don't put up any barriers. Let them see what you feel. Be truthful. Councillors Kanirva and Fresan will speak on your behalf."

"It seems Councillor Reis is the big problem," Jin said. "What do we know about him?"

"Pascal Reis's family has served the Novarian government and military in many ways going back generations," Lucian said. "I've never had a reason to investigate him."

"Could he be connected to the Paragon?" Astrea asked. "We know the Paragon supposedly planted spies into noble families and royal courts. Could the Reis family be one such house? Like the Seviyas?"

"Possible, I suppose," Lucian said. Blue regret spiked high above the commander's head. "I won't be able to conduct a thorough investigation before the inquiry. I'll need time."

"And so you need me to not screw this up is what you're saying," Jin muttered.

"Even if I could investigate it all in a few hours, Varojin, convincing the council is crucial. We're going to need them to continue being on our side, come what may."

If Councillor Reis's family had been connected to the Paragon, or even if his connection was more recent . . . Astrea shuddered at the thought.

"Then I'll do what I can," Jin said. "I promise."

Chapter 32

Even with Lucian's warning that the council would be calling on Jin to testify about what had happened, Astrea almost couldn't believe it when guards arrived to escort him to the council chambers.

She was going with him, of course, as were the rest of their friends. Surprisingly, Lucian had asked the Nikaphoroses, Saros, and Noemi to assist him that morning, saying he'd take them to the library. To look for anything they could find on Councillor Reis.

The council chambers were grand like the rest of the palace, a smaller version of the throne room. The ceiling ended with a dome, allowing light into the room. Rain pattered against the glass. Situated upon a dais at the far end of the room was a long table with six chairs. Only five were filled, and only three of the councillors were readable. Midnight blue grief surrounded them like storm clouds.

"Please, sit, Prince Varojin," said Sinni Kanirva. Her light brown eyes almost glowed in the warm chandelier lights. "All of you, please, have a seat."

A small table had been set up in the middle of the room, just two chairs tucked underneath. Behind that were more chairs, almost like a gallery in a courtroom. Astrea took the one closest to where Jin sat at the lone table, and their friends filled in the rest.

Aside from a few guards near the doors, there were no other Novarians in the room. No Marko. No guards Astrea was more familiar with. No

Lucian, for obvious reasons. Letizia wasn't even there. Shouldn't she be, though? As Veiko's consort and with him unavailable? Astrea's palms began to sweat.

"Please join Prince Varojin, Miss Sovna," said Councillor Kanirva. She tucked a few stray curls behind her ears.

Astrea's heart thundered up her throat as she went over to Jin. She pulled out the chair next to him and sat.

Councillor Kanirva gave them a tight-lipped smile. "Do you know why we asked you here, Prince Varojin?"

"Because the council is concerned I may somehow be aiding Victor Nazarov," Jin said.

"*Some* members do question your loyalty," said Councillor Kanirva, shooting a pointed look down the table at a man with features so light he looked like he was made of snow—Councillor Pascal Reis. "But not all of us. Can you please tell us why you and your betrothed were with the grand duchess yesterday morning?"

"She asked if Astrea would be willing to help the injured," Jin said. "And, if I'm being completely honest with you all, she knew some on the council were questioning my loyalties. She thought it would be good to show us involved, trying to help."

"Would you have gone to the victims' aid without such a suggestion?" asked Councillor Fresan, their deep blue gaze flicking to Astrea, then back to Jin.

"Of course," Astrea said, trying to steady her voice.

"What happened yesterday is a tragedy and a crime," Jin said. "All we want to do is help."

"You would take your fiancée to such a scene?" asked Councillor Kallis. A heavy furrow formed between her eyebrows.

"I thought, given the heavy police and military presence, it would be safe. Especially considering that Councillors Kanirva, Fresan, and Tarsaya were going, and because Ysabel was going."

"And yet you brought your entire military team with you?" asked Councillor Kallis. "That almost seems like you didn't trust Novarian security."

"Not at all," Jin said. "Your people have done an exceptional job these last couple months. But in a situation like this, can there ever be too much security?" When the councillors murmured among themselves, he added, "And as Councillors Kanirva and Fresan can attest, my team is trained in first aid. While not the same as powerful healing like what Astrea can provide, we were able to help keep people comfortable while they waited for the real medics. We wanted to help where we could."

"It's true." Councillor Fresan tapped their long, pale fingers against the table. "They were all assisting yesterday. Miss Sovna especially. It would seem she has an immense capacity for healing. Thank you for what you did."

"Of course," Astrea said. Councillor Reis's jaw tightened slightly, but still she said, "Wherever we can put my talents to use, just let me know, Councillor."

"It's our understanding that Victor Nazarov dreamwalked to the both of you just before the assassinations," said one of the councillors, a woman with red hair and sun-kissed skin. Councillor Tory Makivna. "Why would he do this?"

"To distract from what his sharpshooter was about to do," Jin said. "But he only dreamwalked to Astrea the second time."

"Miss Sovna?" Councillor Makivna asked.

"Well, he . . ." Astrea plucked at her dark blue skirt. "He said that what happened yesterday to the grand duchess and Councillor Tarsaya was just a fraction of what he would do if I did not comply with his demands to meet him."

"His only demand was for you to meet him?" asked Makivna.

"Within a fortnight, yes."

"Why would he offer you time?" asked Makivna.

"I don't know," Astrea said, glancing at Jin. He nodded. "We were wondering the same and thought perhaps Nazarov wants or needs time to set something up. Honestly, I assume he's going to try to force my hand into helping him somehow."

"And he hasn't told you how you are to help him?" asked Councillor Fresan.

"No," she said. "He has not. Will not, even when I've asked."

"We assume he wants to use our magic somehow," Jin said. "It's the only thing that makes sense given the prophecy the Paragon follow and our unique strength."

"Ah, yes," said Councillor Reis, the first words he'd spoken at all. "Your *magic*. Tell us, Prince Varojin, what exactly is *your* magic?"

"I'm a Fireweaver."

"And what about this Sunreaper and Souleater nonsense Tomas was exploring in the book you stole from Kalama?" asked Reis.

Jin's shoulders tensed slightly. Astrea didn't dare move a muscle.

"That is what the now-dead leader of the Paragon called us," Jin said. "And what we believe we are, based on what we've both been able to do."

"And what is it you're able to do?" pressed Reis.

"You already know what they can do, Pascal," said Councillor Kanirva. "We've all read the texts."

"But I would like to hear Prince Varojin tell us."

"It means I have stronger fireweaving than what would be expected," Jin said. "I generate more power. More fire."

"Generate more power . . ." Reis steepled his fingers in front of his mouth. "That's a mild way of putting it. It seems to me that you're just a ticking time bomb, one that will endanger us. Continues to endanger us."

"I can control it," Jin said tightly.

"Whether or not you can control your oh-so-powerful magic is an entirely moot point," Reis said. "What counts is who you use it for."

"Why do you think I would help him, Councillor Reis?" Jin asked. "I don't understand your concerns. The Paragon have done nothing but hurt me and the people I love and care for. I want to stop them more than anything."

"I am not the one on trial here," the councillor spat.

"I didn't think I was exactly on trial either," Jin said. "But here we are."

"Answer the question, Pascal," said Councillor Fresan, their soft voice hardening. "You have been evasive at best when trying to convince us that Prince Varojin is a threat."

"What reason could he have to tie himself to Miss Sovna?" Reis asked, gesturing to them both. "He refused the grand duchess's orders to split up. He's let Nazarov escape several times. His mission into Helosia to rescue *his* people hurt Novarians and continues to put us in a precarious position. In fact"—Reis's attention shifted to Eliana—"the Auris siblings being here continues to put us at risk. At risk of an attack by Nazarov. At risk of an attack by Helosia. They have only brought problems with them since arriving this summer!"

That's what this was about? Novaria's position rather than some strange alliance with Nazarov? Or was Reis bluffing? Astrea couldn't tell; his emotions were tightly locked away.

That commander down at Fort Silverpine had some of the same concerns, as had some of the soldiers stationed there. It didn't seem unreasonable that Reis was being honest now. It also didn't seem unreasonable to her that he could just be hiding behind that facade to sow discord and distrust.

"We were supposed to turn away these young people who needed sanctuary and had information?" asked Councillor Kanirva. "That's not who Novarians are."

"No, but we know who Helosians are," spat Reis. "Troublemakers. Warmongers. Bringing destruction with them everywhere they go. When have Helosians ever done anything good for Novaria? Ysabel was a good woman, but she did not always think things through. We all know that."

"Your mistrust of my father's regime is justified," Jin said. "And frankly, I don't blame you for being wary of me and my sister. We were raised in his household, after all."

"At least you're a smart man," Reis said.

Jin raised his chin. "Do you want to see exactly what I've suffered at my father's hand? I know how cruel he is. I have the scars to prove it."

Lavender surprise flickered around a few of the councillors as Councillor Fresan said, "That won't be necessary."

"So have our actions not proven that we are not on his side?" Jin asked. "Not on the Paragon's side?"

"Never trust a Helosian," muttered Reis.

"Unbelievable," Cressida whispered loud enough for Astrea to hear. Rough annoyance scraped her skin.

"With all due respect, Councillor Reis, if you were so distrustful of us from the beginning, why not say something sooner?" Jin asked. "I've had multiple meetings with the council since my arrival."

"I was willing to give you a chance," he replied, "but given recent events . . ."

Wariness prickled Astrea's skin as the councillors murmured among themselves.

"Is this how all of you feel?" Jin asked.

Councillors Kanirva and Fresan immediately dismissed Reis's ideas. Councillor Makivna hesitated. Councillor Kallis, though, said, "My colleague makes a fair point, Prince Varojin."

"Even after you just witnessed me signing away my rights to power here?" Jin asked.

"Being in line to the throne is not the only way to maintain power and influence. Surely you recognize that, Prince Varojin," Kallis replied. "Your family has tried to destroy our country many times over the centuries. Maybe this is a more subtle way of doing so."

"What can I do to prove to you that I'm on your side? That I want nothing more than to stop the Paragon and my father?" Jin asked. "What else can I—can all of us—do to make that clear?"

As the councillors talked among themselves again, Astrea risked a glance back at Eliana. She was the picture of cool, calm, and collected. Nothing flared in her aura. She was locked down, impossible to read.

"What most of us here can agree on is that you both"—Councillor Kanirva nodded at Jin and Eliana—"obviously do not want your father to succeed in his goals. You would not have come to Novaria in the first place with such information if that were not true."

"But," continued Councillor Kallis, "given recent events and lack of findings, we aren't sure how to proceed with any of you."

Lack of findings? As if figuring out the Paragon's motives, the existence and power of aetherium, and more were no findings at all? No, they hadn't found all the answers, but to suggest that they'd been entirely useless?

What had all of this been for, then, if two on the council were going to view it all that way? With such a narrow lens?

"As such, you are to remain on palace grounds at all times," Kallis said. "No trips to hospitals, to the attack site, or anywhere. No access to the library. No more smelting this . . . aetherium. Not the lot of you, nor your friends and family you brought back from Kalama."

Astrea blanched.

They were just going to tie their hands? Halt *everything*?

"We will discuss this with the new grand duke when he arrives," said Councillor Reis. "We will make a joint decision at the appropriate time. You're dismissed."

The councillors stood, then began exiting one by one through a narrow door at the back of the room.

Eliana jumped out of her seat and muttered, "This is absolutely ridiculous."

"I know, Ellie." Jin scratched his beard. "But it's the time Lucian asked for. They aren't kicking us out or throwing me in prison."

"Maybe, but how can any of them even think their claims are valid?" Crimson anger bled into the air around Eliana. "Skies, after all we've done for and with them . . ."

"Prince Varojin."

Astrea jumped. Behind Jin, both Councillors Fresan and Kanirva had approached. She hadn't even noticed them.

"We're sorry for our colleagues," said Fresan. "This is something Pascal has been harping on about in private since your arrival. He has not trusted any of you from the beginning."

"I understand being wary of Helosians, but I stand by what I said," Jin replied. "That our actions should be enough. I don't know what else we can do."

"Nor do we," said Kanirva. "We will try to sway Jade to see reason again. In the meantime, please do as the council has asked. Keep to yourselves. Don't interfere. That will only make Pascal more suspicious."

"Right," Jin said. "Of course."

Astrea ground her teeth together. The politics of it all was infuriating. But if obeying the council's request until Veiko returned and could convince them otherwise was necessary—if that was the only way to repair the fractures in this alliance—so be it.

Chapter 33

With their hands tied by the Novarian grand council and the skies open with a flood of rain, there was nothing to do. Astrea was beyond bored. Frustrated.

She'd spent time dissecting the "inquiry" with the rest of her friends, then again with the Nikaphoroses, Saros, and Noemi once they'd been herded away from the library. Lucian, too, joined in, infuriated with the turn of events.

But they all agreed on one thing: either Councillor Reis was simply anti-Helosian, or he may have been trying to stall progress to help the Paragon. None of them had proof of the second, but Lucian had set out in search of it again.

So by the time the eighth bell rolled around and a knock finally came on Astrea and Jin's bedroom door, she raced to it, eager for whatever news Lucian might have.

Instead of the dark-haired commander, though, she found Marko. He ran a hand through his blond locks, left loose around his shoulders.

"Prince—Grand Duke Veiko has returned," Marko said. "His car just arrived at the garage. Lucian sent me to get you and the others."

Veiko was finally back?

After making themselves presentable, Astrea and Jin followed Marko, Eliana, Nicos, and Zephyrine downstairs and through the palace. They moved quickly through the halls, eventually reaching the war room. Veiko was already there, hunched over a map spread out on the table.

"We're working to track down Victor Nazarov, as you've requested, Your Highness," Lucian was saying, "but he is once again missing."

"Missing," Veiko muttered, shaking his head. He glanced up, his lavender eyes framed by dark circles. His chestnut hair was a bit mussed, and his white skin was somehow paler than usual. Had he slept at all? "Varojin, Eliana."

"I'm sorry." Jin's first words to his cousin, an apology. "I'm so, so sorry, Veiko. We—"

Veiko held up his hand. "It's my understanding that everyone on every security detail thought the site of the attack was secure," he said. "Hardly anything for you to apologize for, Varojin."

"Still, she was your aunt."

"And your cousin."

"I didn't know her like you did."

With a sigh, Veiko said, "It's a tragedy, but Novaria has seen tragedy before. We will get through this." He sighed again. "What else do I need to know, Commander?"

This was not the Veiko Astrea had expected. He was . . . hard. Not callous, but more distant. Midnight blue grief snapped into his aura occasionally.

"The council . . ." Lucian shook his head.

"What about them?" Veiko asked.

"They interrogated me this morning," Jin said.

Veiko straightened. "They *what*?"

"Councillor Reis—" Eliana started.

"Of fucking course," the new grand duke muttered. He shook his head. "He's still on this? The anti-Helosian sentiments? He's never liked Helosia, but this . . ."

"I hardly blame him for not trusting my father's government," Jin said slowly, "but I have to admit, that after everything we've been through together, with Novaria, it's insulting that he and Councillor Kallis consider *me* a threat. Even after I signed away my legal claims to the throne here."

"What?" Veiko asked again, cold fear prickling Astrea's arms.

Jin's mouth drew into a hard line. "Just a few days ago, before the assassination, I gave up formal claims to power here. Ysabel had all the documents. The council has them, too. For both here and Helosia. I gave up my power entirely."

Blinking slowly, Veiko ran a hand over the stubble on his chin. "Then why does Reis think you're up to no good?"

"The fact that Nazarov's escaped Varojin several times," Lucian said. "That Aurises aren't to be trusted. We even questioned if he might actually be in the Paragon's pocket somehow."

"Reis?" the grand duke asked. "I can't imagine . . . well, frankly, I couldn't have imagined any of this, so I suppose that doesn't count for much."

"We were looking into his family, but the council has essentially sequestered us to our rooms," Eliana said. "Stopped us from helping, anyway."

"They did *what*?" Veiko swore under his breath, red rage spiking high above his head. "Skies damn it. Are they still in the palace, Commander?"

"They are, Your Highness."

"Then I need to go see them."

"Shall I call a meeting?" Lucian asked. After getting an affirmative, he slipped out of the room and closed the door behind him.

With a groan, Veiko buried his head in his hands. "None of this was supposed to happen. I wasn't supposed to take over for at least another decade."

Astrea didn't know all that much about Veiko, but he wasn't much older than Jin, maybe in his early thirties. She didn't think that was too young to help lead a country, but how distressing that must have been, to not just lose his aunt but now be shoved into a leadership role, all within a few days.

"Whatever you need help with, I'll help," Eliana said.

"So will I," Jin said. "It's the least we can do after the kindness you and your family have shown us."

"Our family, you mean," Veiko said, peeking up at Jin with a sad smile.

"Hard to remember that sometimes," Jin said gently. "Still getting used to it."

"And you're family now, too, Miss Sovna," the grand duke added.

Astrea's entire face heated, but Jin cut in and said, "And that. Is our engagement going to be a problem?"

"Not at all," Veiko said. "No, of course not."

"Reis wasn't thrilled about it."

"Of course he wasn't," muttered Veiko. "I'll need to handle the council on my own, and of course, you're not confined to your quarters. You're welcome to move about freely." With another sigh, he said, "But we'll still need to plan Aunt Ysabel's funeral, and then of course there's my own coronation to think about . . . skies. And of course the investigations must continue . . ."

"Whatever information you need, just ask," Jin said. "Lucian also has our testimony about what happened yesterday if you'd rather speak with him."

Veiko waved a hand, his gaze unfocused. When the war room door creaked open again, cool relief coated Astrea's limbs, making her shiver.

"Papa!" shouted Helena and Leo in unison.

They scrambled around the table, and Veiko barely managed to kneel on the floor in time to wrap them both in a hug. The two children practically tackled him. Letizia swept past their small group and to her family. Prying himself away from his children, Veiko stood and embraced his wife.

"Come find us if you need us, Veiko," Eliana said.

As he called out his goodbyes and promises to speak to the council immediately, Astrea followed the others out of the room. Jin kept close to her, his hand pressed to the small of her back. She didn't know what would come next, but hopefully Veiko would be able to help them figure out where Reis really stood and how to get around the council's restrictions and alleviate their concerns.

At least, no matter what happened, they would be together. All of them.

By the time they got back to their rooms, it was already past the ninth evening bell. Astrea changed into her nightgown, one with narrow straps and light fabric. She slipped a sweater over her head, cursing the temperature. They were deep into autumn now, and the weather was turning colder by the day.

"Well, that went about as well as I could've hoped," Jin said, undoing the buttons on his shirt with one hand as he walked out of the bathroom.

"At least Veiko knows you aren't a threat," Astrea said.

"Yes, I suppose Reis could've gotten his claws into Veiko . . ."

"Let's just be glad he didn't."

Humming his agreement, Jin started to take his shirt off. But a knock sounded on the door. "Now what?" Pulling his shirt back on and buttoning it back halfway, he went out into the sitting room and opened the door. "Zephyrine?"

"Hope this isn't a bad time," the general said as Astrea also went into the sitting room.

"Not a bad time," Jin said, closing the door once Zephyrine was inside. "What's going on?"

"I heard from Anjou."

Jin moved toward the fireplace, summoning a small flame over his palm. He sent it toward the waiting logs. "Where's he been, anyway?"

"Oh, here and there," Zephyrine replied casually. As she took a seat, Astrea wandered over to the fireplace, letting the growing heat warm her bare legs.

"That's not very specific," Jin said.

"No, but it's as specific as I'll be, given"—she gestured vaguely—"everything."

Everything. Like what was going on with Reis? Did Zephyrine think he might have guards spying on them?

"Anyway," the general continued, "he's finally gotten in contact with a few people in Helosia. Things have really tightened up at the borders. Kaius and your father are making this difficult."

"But not impossible," Jin said.

"Not impossible." Zephyrine smiled. "Anyway, Anjou will be back in town in a few days. Said he had a rendezvous down near the southwestern edge of Novaria."

Jin shook his head. "Mysterious."

"And he thinks this will get us something we need?" Astrea asked.

"Ideally," Zephyrine said. "Anjou rarely goes to meetings himself unless he thinks it's worth his time."

Folding her arms across her abdomen, Astrea focused on the flames dancing at her feet. It was strange, having just met Anjou Lazzaro the one time in the Taipoli Islands, and now having to trust him to get the information they were after. Information about what Emperor Aelius was up to. With a little luck, they might finally be able to plan their next move.

"But what of Nazarov?" Astrea asked. "Where does he fall in all of this? We can't focus on both of them."

"No, but with the Novarians aiding us, and hopefully swaying some of the other countries to help in the search for Nazarov, that might free us up to go after Aelius," Zephyrine said. "If we have the resources to split our attention, we should."

"And if we can't?" Jin asked.

"Then I suppose we'll just have to figure it out."

How were they to pick if they had to? It seemed impossible when both threats were so large. Let Nazarov run around unchecked just to go after Emperor Aelius? Or leave Emperor Aelius unchecked just to try to locate Nazarov? Both were threats too big to ignore. Maybe Lucian would have better insight.

Or maybe Astrea would actually need to go meet Nazarov in the mountains, as he'd demanded. Maybe that would buy them some time if nothing else. She hated the thought of placating him, but if it would make him stop his senseless violence, then she would do it.

"Az?" Jin asked.

She peeked over her shoulder, only to find both Jin and Zephyrine watching her closely. "Sorry, what?"

"I just asked if you had any questions before I leave. I'm exhausted," Zephyrine said.

"Oh, sorry. No, I don't have any questions." Well, Astrea had questions, but none of them seemed worth asking that night. If she'd thought of those possibilities, there was no way General Kanakos and Captain Auris hadn't.

"Then I'll let you two get back to your evening." With one last tired smile, Zephyrine showed herself out.

Jin followed her to the door, then locked it. When he rejoined Astrea by the fire, he slid an arm around her shoulder and tugged her into his side. "We'll figure it all out, Az," he whispered. "I promise."

She leaned into him. "I know."

After all, they didn't really have a choice. One way or another, they needed to stop both Nazarov and the emperor. That was the only way there might be any semblance of peace on the continent again.

CHAPTER 34

The weight of the grand duchess's assassination had fully settled over the palace, leaving Astrea's bones aching with the intensity of the grief, fear, and anger tangled in the air. She couldn't escape it, not unless she hid her magic away.

Leaning her elbows on the dining table, Astrea rubbed at her temples. Veiko had called them downstairs for a breakfast meeting but had yet to show up. It was already the tenth morning bell, well past the breakfast hour in the palace. Was it another meeting with the council? Had he changed his mind after his promises the night before?

"I don't care if he's the new grand duke and has a ton to deal with," Cressida murmured from beside Astrea. "This is just rude. Couldn't he have sent someone to tell us?"

It couldn't be an emergency, whatever was keeping Veiko. Someone would've alerted them to that, right? Unless he really had changed his mind . . .

"We could just leave," Adi said.

Eliana pinned him with a look. "We're not leaving. Not when Veiko needs us."

"I hardly think he *needs* us," Cressida said. "I mean, he's got the entire country backing him."

"He's a brand new monarch who only rose to power thanks to violence and murder," Eliana said. "He needs friends right now, and so do we."

There it was. Surely Eliana saw some of her own situation in Veiko's. Not that Eliana was wrong.

"And friends he will continue to have in us," Jin said. Under the table, his hand rested on Astrea's thigh, a heavy, comforting gesture. They'd both been restless all night, worried about what was to come. "If any of you want to leave, you can. Ellie and I will stay."

"I don't want to be rude," Adi said. "My point is just that he can't keep us here."

Nicos shot Astrea a questioning look from across the table. She shrugged one shoulder. What did he want her to do about any of this?

Just as Astrea brought her delicate coffee cup to her lips, the dining room door opened in a rush. She startled, barely avoiding spilling coffee on herself.

Veiko stormed in first, a blur of chestnut hair, a black suit, and deep blue grief. And behind him strode a face Astrea hadn't seen in months: Princess Delfine, his younger sister. She was far calmer, just a thin haze of blue sadness tinting her black dress.

"Sorry to meet again under such circumstances," Delfine said as her brother went straight for the coffee tray in the middle of the long table.

"And apologies for the delay," he said. "I wasn't expecting Delfine to return so soon."

"We caught some good winds. Better to be back sooner," she replied with a wave of her hand. "Nor did I return alone. The Taipoli government agreed to send an emissary back with me, to discuss not just the Paragonian threat but the Helosian one, too."

"That's good," Eliana said quickly. "Great, actually. What about the Delian ambassador? Is he still willing to speak with us?"

"He is," Veiko said as he settled in with his freshly poured coffee. Exhaustion rolled off him in heavy waves, and Astrea had to fight not to slump over in her seat. "And President Sikori is sending up several Tornamian representatives. They should be here tonight."

At least the siblings were wasting no time after being so late to breakfast. Astrea took another sip of her coffee, steadier now that no doors were slamming open.

"Do you think they'll be open to some kind of alliance?" Nicos asked. "Do you think we can even tell them about aetherium? Or will they be too interested in getting it for themselves?"

"Always the question," Delfine mused. "It's too big of a risk not to tell them if you ask me. Besides, Helosia is too big for us to go after alone, never mind the Paragon *and* Zaikudi. We need help."

"The Taipoli and Tornamian governments have never been keen on expansion or wars," Eliana said. "They seem to pose little risk, at least based on that. Not telling them puts us at a much more certain threat."

"Then we will brief them as soon as things are more settled," Veiko said.

Eliana nodded.

"And what is this my brother tells me about the council laying all the blame on your shoulders, Varojin?" Delfine asked.

With a sigh, Jin explained the situation to Delfine.

"Councillor Reis is not a friendly man," said Delfine, leaning across the table almost conspiratorially. "Doesn't care much for Helosians, Delians, or Zaikudi. Always said they can't be trusted. Honestly, he's often cold toward our Tornamian and Taipoli friends as well."

"So, he basically doesn't like anyone who isn't Novarian," Nicos said, half question and half statement. Delfine nodded.

That surely explained why Councillor Reis didn't seem to like Astrea very much either. She may have been a Novarian citizen by birth, but she'd spent more than half her life in Kalama. He probably didn't see her as Novarian anymore—not to mention the Paragon connections, of course.

"How do we get him to trust us again?" Eliana asked. "How to trust Jin specifically? And Astrea? And even the Delians if they agree to ally with us?"

Delfine pursed her lips. "I don't know."

"Helpful," Cressida whispered, so low Astrea barely heard her.

"I can try speaking with him," the princess offered. "Or we can talk to Councillors Fresan and Kanirva. They're reasonable."

"They promised me they'd work on getting their colleagues in line," Jin said.

"Then it sounds like there isn't much to do until we can get Reis back on our side, though I'll still see what I can do about all this," said Delfine. She glanced up at her brother. "And we need to get you coronated and plan Aunt Ysabel's funeral."

"Letizia's started planning the funeral," he said. "It will be ready tomorrow. Smaller than what she deserves, but I don't think we can take on that security risk right now. I'm afraid of what Nazarov will do."

"Aunt Ysabel would understand."

He nodded slowly.

"Let me talk to the council about the ceremony for you," Delfine said gently. "We can always do something proper when things are settled."

He nodded again. "Thanks, Del."

Delfine made to stand up, but her sharp lavender gaze flicked toward Astrea's hands. A sly smile pulled at her lips. "News, Varojin?"

"Astrea and I got engaged a few days ago," he said.

"Good. Took me up on my advice?"

"What advice?" Jin asked, though his words lacked any edge. "The way I remember it, months ago, you assumed we were already married, then insinuated we might take that step someday. That's hardly advice."

"Insinuation, advice . . . I gave you the idea, didn't I?" she asked with a wink.

"Hardly," Jin said, leaning back in his seat.

Delfine grinned. "Either way, congratulations to you both."

"Thank you," Astrea said.

Those small traces of humor disappeared, and Delfine's face sobered. "You're family now too, Astrea. If you need anything, please ask."

With a rough swallow, Astrea nodded. Delfine was already doing so much for them. She wasn't sure what else she could even ask for.

Delfine stood and headed for the door, and as Jin began to stand as well, Veiko held his hand up. "Can I speak with you?" he asked. "You and Astrea, alone?"

"Oh . . . sure." Jin sat down again.

Eliana, Nicos, Cressida, and Adi made their way to the door. Cressida turned over her shoulder and mouthed "library" to Astrea.

Once they were gone, Jin asked, "What did you want to talk about?"

"I reviewed the documents you signed for my aunt just before she died," Veiko said slowly. "The formal renouncement of your rights as a Novarian royal family heir."

"Was something wrong with them?" Jin asked.

"No, no, nothing like that. I was just . . ." He pinched the bridge of his nose. "I know you don't want power in this country, or anywhere, but is there anything I can do to persuade you to reconsider?"

"Reconsider?" Jin echoed, gray confusion spiking over his head. "I already signed the paperwork."

"Nothing my signature couldn't undo."

Jin tapped his fingers against the table. "Why?"

"Our family is small, Varojin. You are one of the last descendants of our royal house. With you stepping out of line, that only leaves Helena, Leo, and Delfine. My sister doesn't want children, which is fair enough, of course, but . . ."

"You're afraid something will happen to them," Astrea said quietly. That was clear as day, not just in his words but his aura. White terror, orange anxiety, and yellow worry snapped out amid that ever-present midnight blue grief.

"Indeed I am. Look at what happened to my aunt. There's no promise of safety. I suppose there never was, but the risk has only grown."

Shifting in his seat, Jin said, "I can appreciate that concern, Veiko, but I'm not the man to lead a country."

"What makes you say that?" Veiko asked. "You're smart, loyal, driven."

"How am I the right person to rule Novaria, should it come to that?" Jin asked. "I've been living here for a couple of months. I know nothing of your rules, customs, people."

"That can be learned."

"I don't want power."

"And that is one of the things that makes you a good candidate," Veiko said, palms flat against the table as he leaned forward. "Despots like your father *want* power. People like you—like Eliana—who see the struggle and risk behind that kind of power are the ones to be trusted. The ones who know just how easily it can corrupt."

"I'm sorry, Veiko, but I can't do that," Jin said, voice tight. "I cannot."

"Should you have children," he said, looking right at Astrea, "don't you want them to have a stake in what is theirs?"

"Oh—" Astrea's face heated. She and Jin hadn't talked about that, other than someday, far from then, bringing new life into the world. But placing their child in line for power? "I think that's an awful lot of responsibility to place on a child, one who might not even be a good leader."

His eyes narrowed. "Leaders can be taught."

"Sure," Jin said, "to some extent. But I saw what that did to our family and the toll it took on my siblings. That's not the path I want for my future children. They should have a choice about being part of an institution like that."

"There's no choice when it's in your blood," Veiko said.

"There's always a choice," Jin replied coolly. "Always."

Hanging his head, Veiko sighed. "I understand. I do. Honestly, I worry about what that responsibility is going to do to Helena and Leo."

"Do everything you can to protect your family, Veiko," Jin said. "We'll help however we can. But stepping back in line for power is just something I can't do for you."

"I understand," Veiko said again.

"Thank you."

"You're a good man, Varojin."

"And so are you," Jin said. "You're going to be a great leader, Veiko, and a good father. Don't doubt yourself. Don't let Nazarov intimidate you."

"Easier said than done, I'm afraid," Veiko murmured.

"We'll find him," Jin said. "I promise, we'll find him before he hurts anyone else you care about. With a little luck and help from our potential new friends, we can get this done."

With a small smile, Veiko said, "At least one of us is confident."

Astrea didn't know where Jin got that confidence from. As desperately as she wanted to stop Nazarov, she was beginning to doubt they'd ever catch him. He seemed to slip away so easily, to always be several steps ahead somehow.

But maybe Jin was right. With their potential new allies, maybe they would finally stop him.

CHAPTER 35

After their discussion with Veiko the day before, Astrea and Jin had gone to the library, only to find Cressida and Adi with Noemi, Saros, and Tomas. With Veiko's approval of their continuing activities, they'd finally set up a meeting with the linguist Saros had once known. It wasn't until the following week due to the background check Lucian wanted his team to run, but it was progress.

Rain had returned to Talmaris overnight, and it wasn't letting up even with the new day. While the Novarian royals and Eliana and Nicos welcomed the foreign diplomats to the palace, final arrangements for Ysabel's funeral had been made. And there they sat, in the palace's throne room, with a closed casket in front of the dais and rain pitter-pattering on the glass dome high above them.

Not only was their Helosian group there, but so was the entire Novarian royal family, the diplomats from Tornama, the Taipoli Islands, and Delia, as well as the council and all the palace staff Astrea had come to know. It was surely a fraction of what a true royal funeral would be like, but given the circumstances, it was the best they could do to honor Grand Duchess Ysabel.

"Esteemed guests and beloved family," Veiko began from his position at a podium near the casket, "today, we must bid farewell to a remarkable ruler, my aunt, Grand Duchess Ysabel Volara. But in the midst of our sorrow, let us find solace in the knowledge that her spirit now mingles with the stars."

Astrea held Jin's hand loosely in hers, a tether as the grief swirling in the cavernous room threatened to consume her. Tempted as she was to close herself off from the waves of blue, she forced her magic to stay open.

"Ysabel graced our lives with her wisdom, kindness, and unwavering strength. When our parents died"—Veiko motioned to Delfine—"when we were barely adults, she took us in and cared for us, just as she always cared for the people of this country. She did so much for this country, and her work was her greatest pride."

As Veiko began to recollect some of Ysabel's achievements, from staving off the aggression of the empires to guiding Novaria into an age of prosperity, Astrea shifted closer to Jin. He stroked the back of her hand with his thumb in small, calming circles.

"Cross me one more time, little Lightbringer, and you'll see what happens when you push me too far." Nazarov's words from that awful day swirled around Astrea's mind. And as she glanced down at the line of mourners and caught Letizia's tear-filled eyes, Astrea sucked in a deep breath. They couldn't let this happen again. They couldn't let Nazarov take someone else.

"Though she is no longer here with us, Ysabel's legacy lives on," Veiko said. "Through me, as I seek to build on her policies. Through my children, my sister, our wives. Through the entire Volara family." He glanced at Jin for a split second. "And through all of us here in this room, all of us who seek to find the ones who did not just to her but to families all over the continent. She would want us to be resilient and continue the fight we now find ourselves in."

Red determination and orange fear exploded in the air, momentarily overtaking that heavy, impossible grief. Astrea's lungs tightened painfully, like she couldn't breathe, as the energy in the room surrounded her. Her pulse sped up.

"As we mourn her passing, let us take comfort in the knowledge that she is now watching us from above, an eternal light in the vast void. Let her memory inspire us to live our lives with the same grace and courage she exhibited every day."

Turning to face her casket, Veiko said, "Grand Duchess Ysabel Volara, you may have journeyed beyond this realm, but you will forever guide us, reminding us that even in the face of darkness, we can shine as brightly as the stars."

After Veiko's speech, more followed. Delfine gave one, providing anecdotes about how "Aunt Ysabel" always took care of the whole family. Stories about her wedding to Katerina and the way Ysabel had been so excited for their union full of love. Letizia and Katerina had made small speeches, too, as had some of the councillors.

And now, as the Novarian royal family exited the room with the procession taking the casket outside, palace staff moved about, changing out the somber white flowers to blooms of purple, light blue, and what looked almost like silver. They began laying out very specific items—for Veiko's coronation, no doubt.

It would be a busy afternoon, one of emotional whiplash from the funeral to the crowning of Novaria's new monarch.

And to make it even more strange, palace staff had laid out refreshments in the large foyer outside the throne room, tables filled with pastries, tiny sandwiches, pots of tea and coffee. All the decorations were blue, purple, and silver, the colors of Novaria.

Astrea leaned against Jin as they lingered in the corner with their friends. Eliana had gone to mingle with the foreign emissaries, Nicos just half a step behind her at all times and Marko hovering nearby.

"It was a nice speech," Cressida said. "Veiko's, I mean."

"It was," Astrea said absently. She scanned the room, watching for any dangerous changes to the mood. Voids, rage, anything. But everything remained calm, as calm as it could given the situation.

"How long do you think it'll be until Veiko's back?" Adi asked.

"Not long, I suspect," Saros said, peeking around the corner through the open doors. "The staff look like they're almost done setting up."

Though Astrea knew this was a historic moment—the coronation of a new monarch—she was eager to get everything done with. Set them back on track. Get away from this much grief and pain.

Eliana, at least, seemed to be hitting it off with the diplomats, even the Delian ambassador who had been present at the embassy attack. Nothing unpleasant flared in anyone's auras, the best sign Astrea could hope for. She'd tell Eliana later.

Eventually, they were herded back into the throne room by some of the palace guards. Everyone took their places again, with Eliana, Jin, and the rest of their group in the front row of the right aisle. The councillors took the front row of the left aisle. And as a hush fell over the room, the Novarian royal family entered through the door at the back of the dais.

Delfine and Katerina went first, followed by Letizia, Helena, and Leo. Their outfits had all changed, from the black of mourning to a range of purples and silvers. And finally, out came Veiko, dressed not in his somber black suit from before but a much more intricate one of midnight blue brocade.

"Esteemed guests," he called out over the room, "though it is with great sadness that I stand before you today, we're on the precipice of a new era. One filled not with the peace Novaria has known for decades but one with war on the horizon. And it is with great honor and humility that I, Veiko Volara, become your new grand duke. I take on this mantle with a deep sense of purpose and commitment to restoring peace to not just Novaria but beyond our borders, too."

Delfine stepped forward, taking a small aubergine pillow from a podium. On top sat a shining silver crown, delicate but strong.

"As I ascend to this revered position," Veiko continued, "I am acutely aware of the trust you have placed in me. I pledge to uphold the values that define our great nation: unity, justice, and compassion. Together, we shall strive for a future where every citizen has the opportunity to thrive, where fairness prevails, and where the strength of our communities knows no bounds. And together, we shall fight for this future. We will not let external factions tear it away from us."

Removing the crown from the pillow, Delfine brought it to her brother. He bowed slightly, and she nestled the crown among his wavy chestnut hair. Vermilion pride swirled around the family, overwhelming the dais.

Lifting his head, Veiko gazed out at the crowd. "May the blessings of our ancestors guide us, may the strength of our people sustain us, and may the future we create be a testament to our collective spirit."

The guests broke into loud applause. Astrea clapped slowly, the roar of the crowd making her wince. But Veiko's words washed over her again and again.

The collective spirit. That was what they would need if they were to be successful in stopping Nazarov and Emperor Aelius. They would need everyone involved. And as Astrea stole a glance over her shoulder, she caught Lucian's eye. He was just one row behind, solemn as ever. He gave her the smallest of nods.

Together. They would all find a way through this together.

CHAPTER 36

"Az, wake up."

Groaning, Astrea rolled over and covered her face with the blankets. "Go away."

"Az, please, I need you to wake up."

Jin's voice was just urgent enough that Astrea pulled the blankets back down. A sheen of orange anxiety swirled around him.

"What's wrong? Was there another attack?"

"No, but Anjou met with Zephyrine late last night."

"Is he at the palace?"

"No, he's staying elsewhere."

Astrea frowned, her tired mind trying to conjure a reason for that. Instead, she asked, "What did he find out?"

"There's a large deposit of aetherium in the southern Badlands that my father's found and is actively seeking to mine."

Panic pulsed through her as she sat up straight in bed. "What?"

Jin's lips pressed into a thin line. "Not entirely unexpected, but Veiko's called a meeting. Us, the council, and the diplomats. It's time to lay it all out on the table."

Scrambling out of bed, Astrea cleaned up in record time. The palace was still chilly, not just thanks to the autumn air but to another morning of rain. Dressed in her dark blue pleated skirt and black sweater, Astrea figured she was as presentable as she'd get when meeting with a bunch of politicians. And appropriately somber given the mood still settled over the palace.

They met up with their original group from Helosia as they headed for the war room. Astrea couldn't stop thinking about this news. It was as Jin said; they'd known Emperor Aelius was finding sporadic locations of aetherium—or what they assumed was aetherium, based on what Saros and Balthazar had told them. But a large deposit?

Despite the fact that the old Paragonian book spoke of the need for both a Sunreaper and Metalli to create aetherium weapons, all the advances in technology meant there were now forges hot enough to bypass those steps. Cressida and Balthazar had made a few more weapons without Jin's help. Emperor Aelius wouldn't need a Sunreaper's help, even if there were surely more of them on the continent besides Jin.

Within half an hour of Astrea's abrupt awakening, she was seated once again in the cold war room, surrounded by not just her allies but the diplomats from the other countries. There was Ambassador Jai from Tornama, a woman with light brown skin and silky black hair. Then there was Ambassador Nehali from the Taipoli Islands, a tall man with dark brown skin and his hair styled into long locs. And finally, Ambassador Sirras from Delia, who looked every bit as tired as Astrea felt. She could only imagine what he'd been trying to process since that attack at the Zaikudi embassy.

"I won't beat around the bush this morning," said Veiko as he pulled at the cuffs of his black shirt. "As we've been alluding to, the threat against our countries is not just some outside, country-less faction. No, it is far worse."

As Veiko began explaining void magic, the history behind it, and the current threat of the Paragon, disbelief, anger, and confusion spread through the room like wildfire. The diplomats had questions—and lots of them. Questions about aetherium, about why Ysabel had kept all of this hidden, about Eliana and Jin's intentions. The Taipoli ambassador had even thrown out a comment about how Nazarov, new leader of the Paragon, just *had* to be Helosian on top of it. That had riled Councillor Reis up, but Veiko had gotten control of the room once again.

"I wish I could say my aunt made all the right choices," Veiko said, "but we all know that is impossible, even though leaders must try to do so. She was doing her best with the information we had. Surely you all can understand why we were cautious about who we told. Void magic? Lifestealers? This aetherium?" He shook his head. "That power in the wrong hands would be catastrophic."

"But in *your* hands it's fine?" asked the Taipoli Ambassador Nehali. "In the hands of two *Auris* children?"

"It's hardly in our hands, Ambassador," Eliana said coolly. "I would love to find a way to avoid what's to come, but surely you don't need to be Stargazers to see the very obvious future. If my father's allowed to continue on, or if Nazarov is allowed to continue on, the recent attacks will be nothing in comparison."

The mood quickly sobered, and even Councillor Reis and Ambassador Nehali didn't argue further.

Zephyrine tossed several thin brown folders on the table. "Emperor Aelius is reported to have found a huge cache of this aetherium ore recently," she said. "Messages came in very late last night. Soldiers are talking about 'something unstable' that he's attempting to mine in the Badlands."

"So what do we do?" asked Councillor Kanirva. "What would you recommend, General Kanakos?"

"We need to stop his operation," Zephyrine said. "Even if we only delay him, it buys us time. And trust me"—she looked around the table, holding eye contact with each person for a moment—"we do not want Emperor Aelius Auris successfully forging aetherium weapons. What's going on in Corsyca will be like a sunny springtime stroll compared to what he'll do with an army backed by this new material."

Reaching for one of the folders, Eliana flipped it open and asked, "Do we know for certain that he's found aetherium? Could it be something else?"

"*Could* it be?" Zephyrine mused. "Of course it could be something else, but based on what's been reported, and based on chatter, this points to aetherium. Something secretive and powerful."

"Cressida?" Eliana said.

"I can't imagine what else it might be," Cressida said, glancing across the table to where Astrea sat with Jin. "No other known element would need to be kept secret."

"Which begs the question of how we proceed," said Veiko.

"Hold on, Your Highness," said Ambassador Jai. Her voice was smooth and cool, reassuring. "I understand your desire to move, but this is quite a lot to take in. We haven't even seen this magic," she continued. "Who's to say this isn't just going to get us locked into a war with the Helosians? Who's to say you aren't using this as some excuse to rush into attacking the emperor?"

"This is hardly us *rushing*, Ambassador Jai. This has been in the making for months."

"So you claim," she replied with a demure shrug.

Pushing his shoulders back, Veiko said, "I thought our discussions in Thasia were great progress, and now you think I just want to attack Helosia for some undisclosed reason? Because I'd really, truly prefer to *not* drag my people into war, but there is no other way forward."

"I know President Sikori would feel more comfortable supporting the war effort if there was some proof of void magic that you could show her," said Ambassador Jai.

What proof could they give? They could show them the *Myths and Other Legends* book, but a book was just that. A book. It didn't prove anything, nor did a chunk of aetherium. The only way they could prove what aetherium did was killing someone with it, which certainly wasn't a line Astrea was willing to cross.

"How do we know this isn't some ploy to draw us into Helosia, only to give Emperor Aelius a reason to attack our nations?" asked Ambassador Nehali. "No offense intended to you, Your Imperial Highnesses, but the timing of this? The way Grand Duchess Ysabel kept this from us? She was always friendly with our government, always."

"And ours," said Ambassador Jai.

Heavy disbelief pushed against Astrea's body, almost pinning her back in her seat, as Eliana huffed a laugh. "You think this is some incredibly elaborate lie just to provoke you all into attacking my father first?" she asked. "All due respect, Ambassadors, but have you lost your skies damned minds? There are far more efficient ways for my father to attack you all if he wanted to."

"Would speaking to the Helosian defectors change your attitudes?" Veiko asked. "Or the Novarian soldiers who have seen void magic first-hand when one of our southern bases was attacked?"

Some tiny part of Astrea wished that Nazarov would dreamwalk to the whole table full of people in that moment. As much as she hated him and that power, such a display would surely prove what they needed to prove.

"As I said before, Your Highness," Ambassador Jai said, "if you give President Sikori proof, then I believe she will support your efforts." She arched one eyebrow. "Perhaps send in a joint team to try to confirm these reports the general received."

"I believe my government would agree to that as well," said the Taipoli diplomat. "If it's good enough for President Sikori, it will be good enough for them."

Veiko glanced at the Delian ambassador. Sirras shook his head and muttered, "I don't know what my leaders will want to see, but sending a Delian agent in will only heighten the team's risk and the risk to my country in the Corsycan War. I will try to convince them of whatever the Tornamian agent sees."

Councillor Reis clicked his tongue. "Sending more Novarians into the line of fire?" he asked. "Your Highness, is that how you want to begin what should be a long, prosperous, and peaceful reign? By sending Novarians toward certain death in Helosia?"

"It's not certain death if they're good at their jobs, Councillor," Veiko replied. "You know war is inevitable just as well as I do."

"Be that as it may," Reis said, scanning the table, "sending in Novarians does not sit well with me."

Veiko dragged his fingers through his hair and sighed. "Then what would you have me do, Councillor? Surely you aren't suggesting we sit around and do nothing."

A chill ran up Astrea's spine as the councillor glared at her and Jin.

"Prince Varojin and his friends have insisted they're here to help us," he said, voice hard. "They have experience with these kinds of missions, or so he's claimed in past meetings. He wants to prove his dedication to the cause, so why don't we put him to the test?"

Astrea's entire body went cold.

"Councillor," said Commander Lucian, "with all due respect, you don't exactly have the most trust in Prince Varojin and his friends, nor do you, Ambassadors. Why send him?"

"The way I see it, we can't lose," said Reis with an easy smile. "If he succeeds, it proves his dedication to the cause and gets us the proof we need to move forward. And if this mission proves to be too much and he doesn't come back, then we don't have to worry about this problem anymore."

Astrea blanched. Not worry about this problem anymore? She stole a glance at Jin, but he was entirely still, stone faced, as he stared at the Novarian Council seated just across the table.

"And what if you're right to be suspicious, and Prince Varojin and his friends really are here on behalf of the emperor?" said Veiko, red anger bursting around him. "What then, Pascal?"

Murmurs broke out around the table, yellow worry and green curiosity weaving between the foreign dignitaries.

"If Varojin really is still loyal to his father, sending him home is the least of our worries," said Reis. "We still have everything else to deal with. He'd be out of our hair."

"Question my loyalty to Novaria if you must," Jin said, voice cold, "but don't you ever, *ever* think I am loyal to my father. That man is a monster."

"And so might be you," the councillor drawled. "That's what I'm trying to figure out."

Jin barely smiled. "I've already offered to show you what I've endured at my father's hand over the years. Shall I show the room? Tell you each and every terrible thing he did to me?"

"That won't be necessary," Reis said. "So what say you, Prince Varojin? Will you go?"

"That's not up to him," Veiko said. "I'm still the grand duke, Councillor. This is my decision." Still, Astrea didn't like the way Veiko was appraising their group. "Would you agree to go, Varojin, if we also sent Novarian and Tornamian agents with you?"

Jin tapped his pointer finger on the smooth table. He was rigid as wood, still as stone, as he surveyed the politicians. His jaw tightened, then relaxed. "Councillor Reis, you're right that my team and I have the skills, and you're right that we want to help." His gaze flicked down the table. "I can't speak for all of us, but I'll go."

"I'll go," said Adi.

"And so will I," Zephyrine said.

The twins echoed their agreement, and so did Cressida and Astrea.

Astrea didn't *want* to go back to Helosia. Skies, she didn't even know if she trusted Reis's logic for sending them in. Could this be another ploy by the Paragon? But even if he was in Nazarov's pocket, it was clear enough that the foreign leaders sitting across the table needed proof. And their team had fought void mages before. Had encountered aetherium. They were better equipped for whatever was to come than random soldiers.

"So there you have it," Jin said. "We'll go. We'll get your proof."

"And if Reis is right, that they're all actually the emperor's spies?" asked Ambassador Nehali.

"Councillors, Ambassadors, you have my word that Varojin will not return to his father," Veiko said. "He's proven himself time and again. And if *I'm* wrong, then I will abdicate this throne immediately, and it will be the end of the Volara reign."

Astrea barely held back her gasp. To know Veiko so steadfastly supported them was reassuring in the face of Councillor Reis's distrust, but to put such stakes on this mission . . . what would happen to Veiko if they failed?

"That is a bold stance to take, Your Highness," remarked the Tornamian ambassador.

"Because it's the right stance," he replied. "I know Varojin. I trust him. You all should, too. I hope this mission proves it to you once and for all."

Councillor Reis pursed his lips. "Time will tell, I suppose, Your Highness."

After Veiko adjourned the official meeting, Lucian managed to pull their Helosian group and Marko into his office. The room was hardly big enough for the nine of them, but they squeezed in anyway.

"You're sure you really want to do this, Varojin?" Lucian asked as soon as he sat behind his desk. "You know what your agreement means, don't you? If you come back with nothing?"

"I won't come back with nothing," Jin said. "I won't fail Veiko or Novaria."

As if it's that simple, Astrea thought ruefully.

"What are the odds we'll be able to take Rami?" he asked. "Is she on good terms with the Tornamian government? Could she be their 'agent' on this mission?"

"I'll reach out to her today," the commander said.

"If not, she has connections," Marko added.

"That's all well and good," Astrea said, "but what about the Paragon and the Zaikudi? What about Nazarov demanding I meet him in the Antare Mountains?"

For the whole meeting, the group had fixated on the news about Emperor Aelius. Not unreasonable with the new developments, but certainly not prudent. Nazarov was the one who had orchestrated the attacks across the continent.

"Stopping the Paragon is crucial," Lucian said, "and yes, they attacked us at the embassy. They've attacked so many people. But it still seems Nazarov isn't operating from the mountains, and we don't even know what's happening now that their hereditary leader is dead."

"Maybe that's what Nazarov wants to talk to me about," Astrea said. "If I really am The One's niece, and a descendant of Tytas Ramkas by extension, what if Nazarov's learned about that and wants to talk to me about who the next leader will be?"

"Or he could just kill you to take you out of the running and secure his position," Marko said.

"Maybe," Astrea said past the lump in her throat, "or maybe he now thinks that's how I'm to help the Paragon. He keeps insisting I'm meant to help him. Maybe my blood relation—"

"Astrea," Lucian said gently, "I understand your concerns. But we cannot send you to meet Nazarov. Even if we didn't have this mission with Emperor Aelius, we could not risk it. That man is unstable at best, bloodthirsty at worst."

"I know, but if I don't go, he might—"

"He might very well do *anything* even if you comply," Lucian said. "He is not to be trusted or listened to."

"But—"

"We"—Lucian gestured to those in the room—"focus on going to the Badlands. I'll have Vernie take up the investigation into the Paragon, and we all know Veiko will fight for support and resources from the other countries to look for Nazarov, even if they aren't so sure about void magic. He's still the man who attacked their people. Let them handle it while we deal with this threat in the south."

Astrea ground her teeth together. Maybe splitting their time and resources was the right idea, but Nazarov had given her just a fortnight to meet him, and that had been four days earlier. The clock was ticking. What if he really did attack again when she didn't show up?

Jin's hand settled between her shoulder blades, like he knew what she was thinking about. Sighing, Astrea relaxed into his touch. There was no way Lucian hadn't already considered all of that.

"What do we need to get started?" Eliana asked.

"If my father's really got aetherium weapons, or at least the possibility of having them," Jin said, "I'd like to reinforce our armor. Cress, do you think you and your father could work on that?"

"Reinforce it how?" she asked.

Astrea's palms began to sweat.

"Thin steel plates to insert?" Jin asked Cressida. "Would that stop an aetherium blade?"

"I'd have to test it, but it might at least give us a chance," she said.

"As soon as you can start, please do," he said. "I don't want to wait too long to leave. We should start drawing up our plans immediately."

Chapter 37

After an agonizing night of discussing the possibilities of what was to come—more attacks by the Paragon, an escalation of violence by the emperor, some combination—Astrea had managed to get little sleep. Jin had been out most of the night to continue planning. She'd slept in Cressida's room, wary of being alone.

She'd gotten a few minutes with Jin that morning, but he'd quickly left to go back to planning the mission. And now, Astrea found herself standing in Adi's room again, not for the purposes of planning an operation in the Badlands but for a fitting. She hadn't had a proper one in years, as she'd managed to avoid them as much as possible. But Adi needed to make sure everything fit with her armor, and Astrea was a little curious about how everything was going to come together.

How unfair it was that her and Jin's special day had been ruined by Nazarov, and now it continued to be ruined by Emperor Aelius. And he didn't even *know* he was ruining it. He'd probably be pleased, though, considering he obviously didn't even like his own son.

Astrea sighed.

"You don't like it?" Adi asked. He'd just helped her get her body armor on and finished adjusting it to fit her snuggly.

"Sorry, it's not that. I like it a lot, actually."

The woman in the mirror staring back at Astrea was hardly recognizable. It was her, and yet it wasn't. The black cloth and leather covering her body made her look paler than usual, a sharp contrast against her white skin and pink undertones. And she was covered head to toe.

Instead of the lower-cut boots she'd originally been given, Adi had somehow gotten her knee-high ones that laced up the front. The leggings had a thicker waistband—just as she'd asked Adi for—making them bearable. And the dress . . . well, that part was perfect.

Its sleeves were long, and with her armor on top, the skirt flared out from her hips. It ended mid-thigh and was reinforced with thin leather strips.

"Is the padding in the knees good?" Adi asked as he walked around her in a circle. "Thought it'd be better if you need to get on the ground to heal anyone."

"Yeah, I don't mind it, actually." It was such a thin, flexible layer that Astrea barely noticed it. "Good idea."

"I can't take all the credit," he said. "Noemi suggested it first."

"Well, please tell her I said thank you."

"I will." He smiled, but it was distracted. "Everything else feels good?"

"It feels great," Astrea said. No more dealing with tucking a shirt into her trousers—a major bonus, no fabric to bunch up and distract her. "Way more comfortable."

"That's good."

"Are you alright?" Astrea asked as he moved back to the desk and started packing up his sewing supplies into a small metal box. Its silver exterior caught the light.

Adi shrugged. "Oh, you know."

No, Astrea *didn't* know. That was why she was asking. "What, going to the Badlands?"

"The Badlands, Noemi, the twins, everything." He exhaled sharply. "I don't know, it's all just a lot. My mind hasn't felt right since we found out they'd been captured. Even having them back . . ."

"I get it." Astrea fiddled with the end of her skirt, fingers running over the fine stitches. Adi had done a really good job. "I still don't feel right after being with the Paragon."

"Really?"

She shrugged one shoulder. "My mind's cleared up some, but I still don't fully feel like myself."

"I know exactly how that feels." Adi shoved a few more objects into his sewing kit, then secured its clasps. "Like I'm trying to run underwater."

"Exactly."

"I know it gets easier with time," Adi said quietly. He slipped the box into his knapsack. "It's not the first time I've felt this way, and I certainly doubt it'll be the last. I just hope Noemi's going to be able to cope when we leave."

"It's safer here," Astrea said.

"Right, but I'll be gone again, and she'll have to be alone after the ordeal with Kaius *and* try to not worry about me back out on the battlefield."

"I imagine that was hard on both of you, all your years being away from home."

"Yeah, though she's only admitted it once." Adi pushed his shoulders back. "I want to make sure no other family has to go through that. Or at least, doesn't have to go through it through coercion but the soldiers' choice to join. People should always have a choice, not last resorts or conscriptions."

How many times had Astrea felt that very same way? That Saros had never given her a choice, not when it came to hiding her magic and suppressing who she really was. And she'd been *safe*, at least for the most part. How awful it must have been to actually be forced into the military at the emperor's demands, forced away from family and whatever lives those people dreamed of for themselves.

"We'll do our best to make sure no one else has to go through it, Adi," she said. "I promise."

"Oh, I know." His lips barely quirked up. "Just hard to imagine that day when there's so much left to do."

"Maybe we'll get lucky and be able to take out Kaius or the emperor while we're down there," Astrea said. "Targeted strikes, like Ellie said."

"Yeah . . . maybe."

"You don't sound confident."

Picking up his knapsack with one hand, Adi trudged toward the wardrobe. "I wouldn't bet on Emperor Aelius being in the Badlands, but we might be able to get an upper hand on Kaius if he's there and doesn't expect us." He pulled a stack of red fabric from the wardrobe, deep Auris red.

"Are you making something for Ellie?"

"You, actually."

"What? You already made me this." She plucked at her skirt. "And I don't really wear red."

"You do when we go into Helosia," Adi said. "Make ourselves look like part of the military."

"Oh . . ."

"And I figured I might as well make it the way you like it, that way you aren't distracted when we get out there."

"That seems like a lot of work," Astrea said. "I'll be fine."

"Noemi already helped me cut the fabric out last night, so it won't take me long."

Now Astrea just felt bad, making so much extra work for him *and* Noemi. "Really, I'll manage. Where's everyone else getting their red gear?"

"The royal family's tailors are on it. And really, I don't mind, Az. It gives me something to do."

"Shouldn't you be helping Jin or something? I don't want to take you away from where you're needed."

"You're bad at accepting a gesture from a friend," Adi said with a tight laugh. "And no, I don't need to be helping Jin right now. I need to clear my head, and this is . . . meditative. He knows I need a break."

"I guess if it makes you feel better . . ." Her voice trailed off, and Adi laughed again as he set the stack of fabric on the coffee table. "When was that decision made? To go in disguised as Helosian military, I mean."

"Late last night."

Jin and Astrea hadn't gotten to talk all that much the last few days. Not with so much going on, from the inquiry to the funeral to all these new potential allies they had to speak with. And now this plan. They'd stolen a few moments when they could, but neither had really been in the mood to discuss any of this.

"Well, I guess I'd better let you get to it," Astrea said as Adi dropped onto his couch.

"I was actually thinking I might go down to the lake for a while if you're interested. I could work off some stress."

Training? Astrea supposed it would be the smart thing to do, even if all she really wanted was to crawl into bed and wait for Jin to get back.

"Sure. Should I see if Cress wants to join us?"

"Cress and the twins, if they're all around," Adi said. "Meet me at our usual spot in twenty. And keep the new armor on! Let's give it a test run."

Tiny metal spikes whizzed past Astrea's head, so close she could hear them whistle through the air. She pivoted right, away from where Cressida was already moving in.

Her light burst to life in front of her, growing denser and wider at her command. Astrea brought it up just in time to absorb the blow of Civan's water whip.

"Good, Az!" Adi called from the sidelines.

Colors danced in the air: green curiosity, rust red annoyance, vermilion pride. Anticipation lay heavy in her bones. Cressida and Lennor's energies were open for Astrea's taking. Civan's? Not so much.

Astrea pivoted again, her shield taking the bulk of Lennor's wind as it gusted through the area. She dropped her arm, her starlight bleeding away onto the breeze. Concentrating on the rust red and vermilion, Astrea reached for the colors. Her own anxiety and anticipation lurched forward, twining with her friends' energy and pulling them back.

Lennor and Cressida stumbled at the same time, falling to their knees. Echoes of their pain reached Astrea, but she didn't pull on that. The point of this was to help them practice shutting out a Souleater, not hurting them as much as she could.

"Hold it, Az!" Adi called as he circled the perimeter of the group. "Civan, stand down while they do this."

Astrea didn't dare glance at Civan for even a moment, keeping her focus on Lennor and Cressida. Cressida's eyebrows furrowed. Lennor squeezed her eyes shut, both palms flat on the ground.

"Shut her out!" Adi called to them. "Pull your energy back!"

Astrea hated this.

But practicing was important. She'd already done this five times with Adi alone.

"Just like we went over earlier!" Adi yelled. "Shut Astrea out!"

Cressida's body strained, and she let out a loud grunt as the energy around her faltered. Astrea staggered forward a step, keeping her tight grip on Lennor's energy. Cressida fell onto her hands and knees, breathing heavily.

Lennor's face screwed up in pain. Astrea resisted the way her magic wanted to pull harder on Lennor's energy, the way it tried to surge forth. Astrea pulled it back, trying to keep her strength in check.

"Len!" Adi shouted. "Now!"

When Lennor still hadn't moved, Astrea released the connection. Lennor sucked in one shaky breath, then coughed. Cressida reached her first, and Astrea dropped to her knees at Lennor's side moments later.

"Len?" Cressida asked, her hand resting between Lennor's shoulder blades.

"Sorry," Lennor whispered. "I'm sorry."

"Hey, it's alright," Cressida said. "It's fine. It's just practice."

Lennor bent forward, her head resting on the grass. Pain echoed through Astrea's whole body, pinging particularly rough in her sternum. She set a hand on Lennor's shoulder, holding back a curse as the pain doubled, then died off.

"Sorry, Adi," Lennor said as he approached and squatted near them. "I was trying."

"You know you don't have to apologize," Adi said gently. "It's just practice, like Cress said. We'll get you there. Maybe you need a break?"

"But I just started." Lennor finally lifted her head, and though her eyes were bloodshot, she wasn't crying. "That was my first drill. I can do better."

"Maybe today's just not your day," Adi said.

"What if we run into a Souleater in the Badlands?" Lennor asked.

"Maybe you should focus on keeping your energy locked away rather than shutting me out in the moment," Astrea said. "You know, like going into the fight with armor on. It should keep you protected for the most part."

Astrea had given Lennor and Civan that lesson long ago, back at that old decommissioned base. Civan found the exercise far easier than his more expressive sister, but Lennor had picked it up eventually. She just didn't practice all that much as far as Astrea could tell.

"I need to be able to do this," Lennor whispered. "I need to."

"If the other way works, then why?" Astrea asked. When Lennor pinned her with a look, Astrea said, "I'm being serious. If you can't learn a new skill in just a few days, then do whatever you can do to protect yourself instead."

"Wow, Az," Cressida said with a tight laugh. "I never thought I'd hear you say something like that."

Astrea shrugged. She'd demanded perfection from herself for too long. And sure, she still wanted to do everything the best, most correct way she could, but Astrea was just too damn tired to keep reaching for the impossible. If just having a tight wall would protect Lennor for the time being, why not do that until she had more time to practice shutting off a Souleater's connection?

"Astrea's right," came Civan's rumbly voice. He'd stopped a few steps away from his sister. Lennor peeked over her shoulder. "Do what you can now. We'll keep practicing when we can."

Lennor's chest heaved. "Alright," she said. "Yeah, I'll do what Az said."

"Good," said Adi. "Then let's reset, but you'll practice keeping her out while Cress practices shutting her out. Let's go."

With a few loud claps from Adi, the four of them reset their positions. Astrea kept her attention trained on Lennor, who shook out her arms before bending her knees. She just hoped Lennor wouldn't be too hard on herself. None of this was easy. None of it.

"In three, two . . ." Adi called. "And one!"

Astrea bent her knees, bracing herself for the onslaught of elements to come. It was going to be a long morning.

Chapter 38

After running through a few more drills at Adi's direction, Astrea had returned to her room and cleaned herself up for the rest of the day. Civan's water mixed with Cressida's earth resulted in a lot of mud. Astrea had also given her new armor to one of the palace staff to clean. It was still strange, relying on anyone else to do such tasks for her.

She sat in bed, brushing out her damp hair. Not only did the mud get all over her armor, but it got all mixed up in her hair, too. And that had not been fun to wash out once the mud had begun to dry, nor was it fun working out all the tangles.

After Lennor's mishap—if it could be called that—during the drills, Astrea hadn't been able to concentrate as much. She'd kept trying to watch Lennor carefully, gauge her mood and assess how well she was practicing with her barrier. And though she'd had some success, Lennor was so expressive naturally.

Astrea knew just how hard it was to start holding all of that energy back. It sometimes made her feel like her chest was about to burst, like a tiny pulsing star had replaced her heart and was threatening to explode.

With any luck, Lennor would keep practicing and be able to at least protect herself that way. Or, with *more* luck, maybe they wouldn't even run into any Souleaters down in Helosia. It was impossible to say. They didn't even know how many void mages they might encounter under Helosian command.

With her hair finally smoothed out and tangle-free, Astrea set her brush aside and began braiding her hair into one long plait. She'd just started to tie it off with a purple ribbon when a heavy wall pressed into her awareness, followed by a tight swirl of anxiety and another steady barrier. A few moments later, the bedroom door cracked open.

"Az?" Jin called. He kept the door mostly closed, and she couldn't even see him.

"Yeah?" She climbed off the bed, smoothing out her dress. "You can come in."

"The guards said you were showering." Jin poked his head into the room and smiled. "Something about a lot of mud?"

"Adi's fault," Astrea said. "What's going on?"

"We need to have a team meeting," he said as she met him near the door. "We were just going to do it here." Jin motioned to the sitting room behind him, where Eliana and Nicos were making themselves comfortable. "If that's alright."

"Sure, I don't mind."

As Jin excused himself to go round up the others, Astrea padded over to one of the armchairs and plopped down into it. "So, we actually have a plan?" she asked Eliana and Nicos. "Or is this about something else?"

"We have a plan," Eliana said.

"I don't think anyone's going to like it," Nicos added, "but we have a plan."

Astrea folded her legs up under her, then adjusted her skirt to cover her shins. "Well, now I'm nervous." Not that anyone was inherently going to like a plan that involved trying to take down a core part of Emperor Aelius's war machine, but what could Nicos possibly mean?

"Don't be," Eliana said. Her aura told a different story; bright orange anxiety twined around her entire body.

As they waited for Jin to return with everyone else, Eliana and Nicos filled the silence with talk of dinner and a few questions about what drills Adi had put the rest of them through. Astrea would've just preferred silence, but the chatter seemed to help Eliana's worries lessen. That intense orange faded, just a sheen of it left hovering over her skin when Jin returned.

Astrea had thought he was just going to get the rest of his team, but no. It was everyone. The entire Nikaphoros clan, Noemi and Adi both, the Rusas twins, Saros, Lucian, Marko, and Zephyrine. They all shuffled inside, scattering around to wherever there was space to sit or stand.

Jin went to the head of the room, in front of the fireplace and right next to Astrea's chair. Lucian and Zephyrine joined him.

"Alright," Jin said as a hush fell over the group. "We've finally straightened out the biggest details. We're leaving in four days."

A thousand questions jumped to the forefront of Astrea's mind, but she forced her mouth to stay closed.

"Veiko's secured us a meeting with President Sikori of Tornama ahead of the mission, so we'll meet with her and her agent first," Lucian said, "and then we'll travel into Helosia from there. It won't be a comfortable journey, but heading in from the Tornamian border closest to the Badlands is going to save us time and trouble."

"I'll be joining you on the first leg of the journey," Eliana said, "but after that, I'll remain in Thasia to continue discussing things with the Tornamians. The rest of you will continue on."

"Not *all* of us," Jin corrected. His gaze flicked behind Astrea, to where the Nikaphoroses stood. "Balthazar, Sarsali." He looked toward Noemi, who stood behind Eliana and Nicos. "Noemi. I'm asking that you stay here."

Noemi nodded quickly. But behind Astrea, the energy shifted into intense worry and . . . was that frustration? Yes, it scraped over her skin for one heartbeat, two, before it receded.

"Jin, I think I'd be an asset out there," Balthazar said. "If we're dealing with that much metal, well, it's too much for one Metalli to handle on their own. It just doesn't make sense to only bring Cressida."

Jin pressed his lips together. He crossed his arms over his chest, the lamplight catching on his engagement ring. "My understanding is you've got very little training for these situations, Balthazar. I'd hate to throw you into the deep end. I thought we might see if the Tornamians wanted to send an additional Metalli with us."

"Maybe Balthazar's right," Zephyrine said. "I'd rather have the two Metalli we know."

"I'd rather have him there, too," Cressida said. "Someone I can really trust to have my back."

Jin's arms remained crossed, his expression almost neutral except for that tiny crease between his eyebrows. He nodded. "Alright, Balthazar, you're with us. That'll leave you here with Noemi, Sarsali."

"How can we help while you're gone?" she asked.

"Noemi," Astrea said, "maybe you and Sarsali can work with that linguist? And take over some of Tomas's research for him? Anything to find where the old Paragon might have gotten all their aetherium from, or any clues as to where it may have gone . . ."

Noemi's posture straightened, and she pushed her shoulders back. "I can do that."

"Varojin," Saros said from behind Astrea, his voice tight, "I notice you didn't say I was staying behind."

"We need you down there with us," Jin said. "Besides having already seen some of my father's excavation sites, you're the only person in this room who can feel the different properties this metal has. We're going to need you to actually find the aetherium, or at least confirm that's what we're dealing with."

Saros was silent for a long moment, but then he said, "Of course."

"We're still trying to pinpoint the operation's exact location," Zephyrine said, "but regardless, we'll be going in disguised as Helosian soldiers."

Right. The red uniform Adi was making for her. Astrea had almost forgotten about it.

"This mission is about two things," Jin said. "Finding proof to bring to the other governments and finding a way to at least slow my father's operation down, if not cripple it. That may be something we have to figure out when we get there, depending on what we find."

Astrea didn't love the sound of that. And no one else in the room did, either. Orange clouded Astrea's vision, a heavy smoke in the air.

"We'll be done with final preparations in a few days," Lucian said. "I suggest you all get some rest while you can. This trip is going to be taxing. It's going to test us all."

Though Jin had disappeared again after their meeting to tie up a few loose ends with Lucian and Zephyrine, and then he'd gone on a run with Adi, he'd finally returned. After twenty minutes, the shower finally cut off. Its rhythmic sound had been lulling Astrea's eyes closed.

She couldn't believe Saros and Balthazar were both going to the Badlands with them. Of course, she understood why they were going, but she just hoped they'd be able to navigate the situation with little trouble. As far as she knew, they had even less experience with this type of thing than she did.

Although . . . Saros had held off Nazarov that day at the Kalamian palace. He'd shown mastery over his light on that boat in Tinale Bay while they were under attack. Balthazar had shown he could keep calm in that kind of situation, too. He'd helped Cressida control missiles, after all. He'd helped her do that even after being forced away from his home and suddenly coming under attack.

Maybe she needed to have a little more faith in them.

As Jin came out of the bathroom, the smell of eucalyptus and a blast of humid air followed. Astrea watched him carefully as he moved around their room, gathering up clean clothes. His back muscles flexed as he finished drying himself off, making the scars on the left side grow and shrink with each movement.

It was still hard for her to think of herself as being at war, but wasn't that what this was? Maybe not in the way war was being fought in Corsyca, but this was a very targeted mission, going on intelligence the former general had compiled. A mission to strike at the heart of Emperor Aelius's growing war machine. If they could stop him, or at least cripple this part of his empire, it would make overthrowing him that much easier.

"Jin."

He finished tugging on his underwear before turning toward her. His wet towel dangled from his hand. "Hm?"

"I want to get married."

The corners of his mouth quirked up. "I'm pretty sure I've already asked for your hand."

"No, I mean now."

"Now?" He hung his towel over the top of the wardrobe door, leaving them both ajar. "Like tonight?"

"Not tonight but before we leave."

"I know I said I wanted to marry you as soon as possible, Az, but I didn't mean we had to right this moment." He crossed the short distance to the bed and sat down next to her. "I don't want you to give up having a proper wedding just because I'm impatient."

"You think I want some big ceremony and a party?"

Helosian wedding celebrations were big to-dos, with even everyday couples having at least two hundred people in attendance, usually more. They were joyous occasions, not just the ceremony but especially the party after. Full of color, food, and so many people. And for Jin? Part of two royal families? She didn't even want to know what that might look like.

"Well, I suppose *you* wouldn't want those things."

"Do you?"

Taking her hand in his, he said, "Az, if all we did was sign the paperwork and call it a day, I'd be happy with that. I just want to be your husband. No parties or lengthy ceremonies needed."

"Then let's get married," she said. "Before we leave. I've waited so long to do anything—everything—in my life." Holding his gaze, she whispered, "I want to be your wife, Jin. For the rest of my life. I don't even want to let a day of it go to waste. I don't want to wait."

Maybe she was holding onto this one good thing too tightly. But so much bad had happened in such a short time. The embassy attack. The Paragon's assaults across the continent. Ysabel's assassination. Every other single skies damned thing since early summer.

And every time Astrea looked at Jin, every time she saw her ring or his, she couldn't help but think of making it official. She wanted this. Him. So badly. They would always be committed to each other, even without marriage or a wedding; Astrea was sure of that. But the thought of making it official, of getting to tell the world about this commitment, made her so happy.

A slow smile spread over Jin's face. "Not a single day?" he mused.

"Not one."

Cupping her face in his hands, Jin pressed a gentle kiss to her mouth. "Me either. Let's get married."

Chapter 39

Trying to plan a wedding in less than two days was going to be a nearly impossible task.

Astrea and Jin had stayed up late the night before, agreeing on what they wanted. A small ceremony with their family and friends to honor Helosian tradition, and of course, something to celebrate. Though neither of them felt the need to do something enormous, they'd both agreed that a little fun might do everyone else some good.

And so now Astrea sat not just with Sarsali but Eliana and Delfine, a selection of tableware and fabric laid out in front of them on a long empty dining table.

This seemed . . . entirely unimportant.

"I don't know why Varojin doesn't want to be involved in this," Delfine mused as she dragged her fingers over a white chiffon table runner. "Do men care so little for their own weddings in Helosia? Veiko was heavily involved in the planning of his."

"Of course Jin cares," Astrea said. "He's busy."

Busy going over preparations with Lucian and Zephyrine. Busy checking over airships, supplies, everyone's gear, the new metal plates Cressida and Balthazar were making. Busy with something of much greater importance.

Because at the end of the day, all Astrea and Jin cared about was being together. As Jin had said the night before, if all they did was the paperwork, he would be perfectly content with that. So would she. She'd be content if they had to get married in an abandoned old military fort with no one around but the officiant. She just wanted to be with him. Tablecloths hardly mattered.

"What I think Astrea's trying to say," Eliana cut in as she examined an overly ornate place setting, "is that my brother is not one for the usual customs of royalty, Delfine. Or customs at all, quite frankly. Surely you know that about him by now. I mean, he doesn't even want to wear a full suit to dinner."

"Indeed," Delfine said with a small smile. "And you won't give us more time to prepare something grander, Astrea?"

"No," Astrea said. "Will that be a problem for the council?"

Scoffing, Delfine waved her hand. "If Varojin wants to get married now, I'll ensure Councillor Reis doesn't interfere. My brother won't let him screw this up, either."

"Thank you," Astrea said, and she meant it.

"Of course."

"The council won't see this as inappropriate given . . . recent events?" Sarsali asked quietly. "Not that I think it is, but I worry about that Reis fellow."

"We could all use something a little happy after what's happened, could we not?" Blue grief floated around Delfine's head for just a moment, but then she straightened in her seat and said, "Well, if the two of you aren't that specific about what you want for tomorrow, do you just want me to decide? You should've *seen* the wedding Katerina and I had. Flowers for days, everything pink and green and off white, just stunning."

"No." Astrea didn't know where the quick answer came from, but there it was. "No, I'd like to pick it out." After all, she was only going to get married once. She might as well select what matched her taste.

"Then where shall we start?" Delfine asked. "You've given me no direction thus far."

"Jin likes blue. And I like purple. And flowers."

"You don't think he'll want any red for the Auris family?"

"Skies, no," Eliana said with a laugh. Then she ducked her head and said, "Sorry, Az. I don't mean to cut in."

"Well, you're certainly not wrong," Astrea said. "No red."

"What about something like this?" Sarsali set a lavender table runner on top of a white table cloth. "And then we can do bouquets with a bit of blue mixed in, maybe a hint of pink, too?"

"I like that," Astrea said. It sounded simple, and simple was good.

"Maybe we could do something with flowers to mimic your necklace." Eliana gestured vaguely toward Astrea. "The opal, I mean."

"Oh, Eliana." Sarsali's teal approval lit up the room. "Oh, yes, I can work with that if you like it, Astrea. I can relax some tulips to open them up and—" She paused. "I'll need to cut some things from the garden, Your Highness. I'll be sure to replace it all."

Delfine waved a hand. "If Astrea's happy with it, then by all means. At least we have a direction now. I'll even go out to help you gather the flowers. Maybe Helena and Leo can join us."

"You like the idea, Astrea?" Sarsali asked.

"It sounds pretty," she said. And Jin would like the colors, especially if he realized the necklace he'd gifted her had inspired the choice. "Let's do it."

"Oh!" Sarsali pulled Astrea into a quick embrace. "Alright, leave everything to me."

"I can help—"

"Nonsense! Let me handle this. You still need a dress."

"I've already told the seamstresses to be ready," Delfine said. "They're waiting for you."

Astrea held back a groan. She *hated* fittings. The one with Adi had been alright, but that had barely been a fitting at all. But at least this was a dress and not more armor.

"Sarsali, if you want to get started on the flowers, I'll take Az upstairs," Eliana said.

"Consider me on it!"

Eliana wrapped her hand around Astrea's arm and tugged her toward the door. "Come along, Az. Time to get you wedding ready."

As Astrea finally got back into her loose gingham dress, she let out a happy sigh. The four seamstresses and Eliana were waiting on the other side of the privacy screen, chattering away.

She'd been trapped in this grand workroom for several hours, forced to examine bolts upon bolts of fabric, everything from stiff white satin to pink lace to sparkly tulle. And when that was done, choosing the cut and style of the dress had taken even longer.

When Astrea stepped out from behind the screen, one of the seamstresses, an elderly woman with gray hair and pale skin, said, "We shall have you something in the morning. Come by first thing for a final fitting."

"And remember, fitted but not tight," Astrea said. "Just fitted enough."

"Yes, yes." The woman waved her away. "Now go, let us handle this."

With a reluctant huff, Astrea followed Eliana out into the hall. They were in a different part of the palace than normal, a hallway Astrea had never been down before. Eliana looped their arms together and started pulling Astrea down another unfamiliar corridor.

"Where are we going now?" Astrea's stomach rumbled.

"You'll see."

"Ellie, it's supper time. Can't we go eat? That took forever."

"You'll see. Now come on!"

"Is this another engagement party?" Astrea asked skeptically as she pulled her arm away. "You really don't have to do that."

"An engagement party of sorts," Eliana said.

"Oh, skies." Astrea knew exactly what this was. "We really don't—"

"We really do!" Eliana grabbed Astrea's hand again. "Adi and Nicos are handling Jin for the night. Let Cress and I handle you."

"'Handling' me doesn't sound very fun."

"You know what I mean."

Did she, though? Astrea had never attended a wedding, let alone any of the pre-wedding festivities friends and family took part in. And now Eliana wanted to split them all up for the separate spouses-to-be celebrations?

"I really wanted to just spend a quiet night—"

"It *will* be quiet," Eliana said. "It's not like we can go out. If we were in Kalama, I'd do it up right. But since we're stuck in here"—she gestured to the palace and the now-familiar stairwell they climbed—"let's at least have some time, just us three."

It *would* be nice to be able to sit with her best friends, just the three of them. Like old times, before everything went completely off course.

"Alright, but you'd better have food because I'm starving."

Eliana grinned. "Of course I have food. I'm not an animal, Az. I know how to throw a party."

They reached their wing of the palace, and as Eliana tugged Astrea down the hall, Astrea and Jin's bedroom door opened.

"Adi, come on—" came Jin's voice.

"No, *you* come on!" Adi, like Eliana, was forcing Jin out of the room. "Oh! We weren't supposed to see you two. We coordinated this, Ellie." He looked down at the watch on his wrist. "You're ten minutes early."

Eliana just shrugged.

All Astrea could focus on was Jin, though. A piece of black silky fabric was tied around his eyes. Adi had blindfolded him.

As Jin moved to take it off, Adi smacked his hand.

"Ow!" Jin cried, indignant. "What was that for?"

"You aren't allowed to see the bride," Adi said. "And my precautions have paid off, thank the skies."

"This is ridiculous," Jin muttered.

"It's tradition," Eliana corrected.

"Az, tell them this is ridiculous." Jin huffed, and as he went to move the blindfold again, Adi smacked his hand away. "Ridiculous!"

"Oh, come on, Jin," Eliana chided. "One night apart won't kill you two. You have the rest of your lives to share a bed."

"Then at least give us a minute," Jin retorted. "Alone."

"You can have one minute with Az," Adi said. "One. And you can't take the blindfold off." As he pivoted toward Astrea, he said, "If I find out you two broke the rules, then I'll make sure your new armor is fitted painfully tight."

"That's rude," Astrea said, making Adi grin.

Still, she took Jin's hand and led him into their bedroom. As soon as the door was closed, Jin wrapped his arms around Astrea and pulled her close.

"If I'd known they were going to do *this*," he said, "I would've made sure we had time together this morning."

"Oh, I think we should just let them have their fun," Astrea said as more sweet amusement stretched for her through the door. "They're enjoying themselves."

"And I'd really prefer to enjoy myself with you tonight." He sighed, a heavy sound, even as raspberry lust, peach amusement, and light pink love tangled around him. "I really can't take this blindfold off?"

"No," she said. "I won't let your lust result in me having uncomfortable armor, thank you very much."

Astrea pushed up on her toes and pressed her lips to Jin's. His hands cupped her face, holding her in place as he kissed her back. His tongue teased her bottom lip, and when she groaned, he nudged her back against the door. He pressed into her, his body heavy and warm. What she wouldn't give to be pinned under him on the bed instead.

"Still want to let them have their fun?" he murmured as he barely pulled away.

"Yes," she said, breathless. "It's good for them."

"You're a bad liar." He nipped at her neck. "Such a bad liar, Sovna."

"I think you like it."

"I like *you*," Jin said. "A lot."

"Hm . . ." She ran her fingers over the bottom edge of his blindfold, right at the tops of his cheekbones. He sucked in a sharp breath. Her belly tightened as she whispered, "And I kind of like this. Maybe you should keep it."

His lips twisted into a wry smile. "And just what will you do with me—"

A forceful knock on the door made Astrea jump. With a laugh, Jin pulled her away, fumbling with the handle for a moment. When he opened it, Eliana stood on the other side, hands on her hips.

"Alright, say goodbye for real," she said. "We're going now."

Jin pressed a kiss to the top of Astrea's head. "I love you."

"I love you, too." She wanted just one more second to lean into his warmth, but Eliana snatched her hand and tugged her away. "Hey!"

"Yes, I love you, I love you, too, making eyes at each other even with him blindfolded, we get it," Eliana drawled. Then she shouted over her shoulder, "Bye!"

"See you tomorrow!" Adi called.

Astrea tracked Jin's amusement, frustration, and sunshine love as far as she could as they were dragged apart. Oh, she hated this tradition, too.

As soon as they were in Eliana's room, Cressida pushed up out of her seat and said, "What's all the shouting about?" It was just her in the room, and several covered trays sat on the coffee table, as did a bottle of unopened wine and a carafe of water.

"We ran into Adi and Jin," Eliana said, finally dropping Astrea's hand.

"You weren't supposed to let that happen!"

"Excuse me," Astrea said, "you were going to whisk me away from my fiancé without even letting me say good night to him? In what world is that acceptable?"

"Because we all knew it'd be a struggle to pry you away from him," Eliana said. "He's obsessed with you, Az. In a good way, sure, but let me guess: he was telling you how much he didn't want to be separated tonight."

Astrea's cheeks heated. "He said nothing of the sort."

"She's lying," Cressida half sang as she pulled one of the silver domes off a plate. Steam rose up, and the smell of pan fried potatoes met Astrea's nose. "Damn, those look good."

"We got all your favorites," Eliana said as Astrea took a seat. "Potatoes, chicken with that spicy green sauce you like, and—"

"The sauce is my dad's recipe," Cressida said.

"*And*," Eliana continued with a huff, "we couldn't get the chef to make guava tarts, but we did get them to make these raspberry and chocolate cream—"

"Thank you," Astrea whispered. "I know I was just complaining about this a few minutes ago, but thank you."

Astrea didn't know where the sudden emotion was coming from or why it was overwhelming her. Gratitude, sadness, anxiety—all her own—swirled inside her. Eliana and Cressida had been there for her so much over the years. Birthdays and graduations. The day Jin left for the military. Solstice Night and everything that had happened since then.

So much bad had been happening lately, and though Astrea had been wrapped up in her own problems, Eliana and Cressida hadn't wavered in their friendship or support. They'd been there. They'd stayed. Even when she was struggling to talk to them. Even when she should've tried to check in with them more.

"I'm just really glad you're both here with me right now. That you've both always been there. I can't thank you both enough for everything." Astrea wiped at her tears with both hands. "Sorry, I know this is supposed to be a fun night, and here I am, crying."

Cressida's laugh rang through the room, peach amusement filling the air as she said, "You owe me, Ellie."

With a sigh, Eliana said, "I figured it'd be at least twenty minutes into dinner before one of us started crying. I think we've barely been sitting down for two."

Astrea wiped away the last of her tears. "I don't mean to be sappy right now, I'm sorry."

"Oh, I think a girl's allowed to cry a little the night before her wedding," Eliana said.

Rolling her eyes, Cressida said, "That sounds entirely too morbid, Ellie."

"I just mean that emotions are running high. I'm sure someday I'll be crying before my wedding, too."

"Oh, Nic's going to pop the question?"

"Only I'm allowed to call him that." Eliana chucked a throw pillow at her, but Cressida caught it with ease.

"Territorial," Cressida mused, more of that amusement flaring in the room. "I bet he likes that."

"How about you be quiet and pass me the potatoes?" Eliana shot back. "I'm starving."

As they settled in, each with their own plate and glasses of white wine, Astrea asked, "Where's everyone else tonight?"

"Oh, Adi's putting on something much bigger for Jin." Eliana waved her forkful of potatoes in the air. "His whole team, plus Zephyrine."

"Where's Noemi?" Astrea asked.

"I think she was going to stay in tonight," Cressida said. "I saw her going into her room with a book. Mentioned something about finally having time to herself without Adi hovering."

Part of Astrea was tempted to go knock on Noemi's door to see if she'd want to join them; it seemed rude to leave her out. But having time alone? Without that hovering? Astrea very much understood wanting and needing that. She didn't want to intrude.

"Do you think we're doing the right thing?" she asked.

Cressida's eyebrows furrowed. "What, this? I know we can't do the traditional—"

"No, me and Jin. Getting married."

"What kind of question is that?" Eliana asked with a laugh. "It's right if it's what you two want."

"We do, but just . . . the timing?"

"If not now, when?" Eliana shrugged. "When you know, you know, right?"

"No, I mean . . ." Setting her plate on the coffee table, Astrea sighed. "With everything with the council. I don't want us doing this to cause some kind of political damage."

"Delfine said she'd handle it."

"But—"

Looking pointedly at Cressida, Eliana said, "Do you want to smack some sense into her or should I?"

"Nobody needs to resort to violence," Astrea muttered.

"Look, Az . . ." Eliana smiled gently. "I've dealt with plenty of people like Councillor Reis, and they're *never* happy with what other people do politically or personally. If he gets upset, he gets upset. We're all—especially the lot of you—going out on a very precarious limb to prove our dedication to the cause."

"A *very* precarious limb," Cressida said. "Is it even safe for you to leave Talmaris, Ellie?"

She shrugged. "Do I have a choice? Tornama's got a strong military. We need them on our side, and I've met President Sikori before. Speaking with her in person might get us somewhere."

"And if the Paragon track you down there?"

Sucking in a shallow breath, Eliana said, "I know it may seem like it sometimes, but I don't see the world through rose-tinted glasses. I know exactly what kind of position I'm in. That we're all in. I know the risks. I think what happened to Ysabel is proof enough."

"Ellie . . ." Astrea pressed her lips together.

"Don't *Ellie* me," Eliana replied with a small smile. "Please, for the love of all that is good, let's just have some fun, alright? There's been enough pain the last few months. I'd really like to think about something happy, and this wedding is happy."

Astrea regarded her for a moment. That particular set in her jaw. How she held her head high, even as a mist of orange anxiety floated around her.

"Alright," Astrea said. "I think I can put my moods aside for a couple of days and do happy."

"Excellent!" Eliana set her half-finished plate of food on the table and stood. "Because we've got presents to open, and I won't take no for an answer."

"I don't need presents," Astrea said.

"What did I just say?" Eliana called over her shoulder as she strode to the wardrobe. Opening the doors, she reached up toward the small shelf at the top. "I won't take no for an answer!"

"C'mon, Az," Cressida said. "This is the one tradition we can actually do, so let us do it. We didn't go overboard."

Astrea didn't even know where they'd manage to get gifts at a time like this. Sent the palace staff out to a store, maybe? She fidgeted in her seat as she watched Eliana walk back over holding three presents wrapped in lavender paper.

Back in Kalama, pre-wedding parties varied widely but were always big to-dos. Some chose to have joint banquets with the friends and family of both spouses-to-be. Others involved a night out on the town with friends. There were always gifts and pieces of wisdom passed on to those getting married. Astrea supposed they could've had one big joint dinner party, but Eliana and Adi seemed keen on mimicking the second option instead.

"Open mine first," Eliana said, handing Astrea the biggest present.

As she carefully unwrapped it, Astrea's fingers brushed the cover of a book. She flipped it over, revealing the title, *Whispers of the Heart*, stamped on the front in ornate silver letters.

"It's poetry," Eliana said. "A collection to remind you about love, friendship, and the beauty of life."

Astrea's lips quirked up. "Eliana Auris, finding a *poetry* collection for me? You hate poetry."

"I don't *hate* it," she protested. "It's simply not what I prefer to read. But I thought you'd like it."

"I do."

"Do this one next!" Cressida shoved another box into Astrea's hands. "It's from me, my parents, and Saros."

"All of you?" Astrea's eyebrows furrowed. What could they possibly all go in on together?

This box was much smaller and lighter. Inside was a small silver locket engraved with an *A*. With delicate fingers, Astrea opened it. One side was empty, and on the other was a handwritten note of love. She sucked in a sharp breath.

"Ma wanted to put a family photo in, but obviously we don't have any here . . ." Cressida trailed off. "So we thought that was the next best thing. Ma specifically wanted me to tell you that we'll add a family photo as soon as we can get one taken."

"I love it," Astrea whispered. After all, it was a piece of her family she could always have near her heart.

"Alright, the final gift!" Eliana exclaimed, handing Astrea the remaining box. "From the both of us."

This one was also small and light. Opening it, Astrea found not one but three bracelets, delicate silver chains that glittered in the lamplight.

"One for each of us," Eliana explained. "So we're always together, even now with you gone off and married."

"Gone off?" Astrea asked with a laugh. "I live down the hall from you!"

With a grin, Eliana said, "Well, still."

"Made them myself," Cressida said.

Astrea plucked one out of the box. "I'd expect nothing less."

And so their night continued on, indulging in more food and sweets as they talked about their childhoods in Kalama and all the years they'd been friends. They eventually settled in bed, all three of them, as the wine took over and Eliana grew sleepy—as she always did when she'd had too much wine. She curled up against Astrea's left side while Cressida stretched out on the right, her chest rising and falling slowly.

So much had gone wrong since the start of summer. And yet, with autumn's arrival and this change on the horizon, Astrea was . . . happy. There was still so much that could go wrong, so much they had to figure out, but Astrea was grateful. Grateful for her friends, her family, this new alliance that seemed to be brewing. Grateful for Jin.

And most of all, she was grateful to herself for stepping out of her comfort zone and being all in. All in with stopping the bad actors on the continent, all in with learning about her magic, all in with Jin.

For once, she was making decisions. She was doing what she wanted, when she wanted, all with the support of the people who loved her most. And there was no better gift than that.

CHAPTER 40

Astrea ran a hand over the front of her dress. Her wedding dress. It was traditional for Kalamian brides to wear a bright color, so Astrea had chosen blue. Jin's favorite.

It wasn't bright, exactly, but instead a dusty blue lace lay on top of a silver slip. She'd never really imagined her wedding dress before, but it was perfect. The palace seamstresses had followed orders, making the dress gently fitted to Astrea's curves. The neckline dipped down in a V shape, and the long lace sleeves poofed out a bit before tightening at the wrists, as was popular in Kalama. Her opal necklace lay just below her collarbone. Even her hair—in long, loose waves down her back—and light makeup were perfect for the night.

All day she'd waited for this, and now, it was here. Butterflies fluttered through her belly as she made her feet carry her back into the bedroom where Sarsali and Cressida were waiting. Sarsali had opted for her favorite color, sage green, while Cressida had chosen a vibrant pink.

"Oh, Astrea." Bright teal approval and marigold excitement danced around Sarsali as she pressed a slender hand to her mouth. "You look beautiful."

"Blue was a good choice," Cressida said.

"Roxana would be so happy for you," Sarsali said as she pulled Astrea into a hug. "*I'm* so happy for you, sweetheart."

Astrea melted into Sarsali's embrace. She'd never really imagined herself getting married. Even in the rushed planning for this day, it hadn't quite seemed like her wedding. But she was going downstairs to marry Jin. Her mother may not have been there, but Sarsali was. Balthazar and Saros were. Cressida was.

"Now, as you know," Sarsali said, pulling away, "it's my duty to give you some advice as you enter this next phase."

Smiling wryly, Cressida muttered, "Ma . . . save it. Eliana's already down there waiting for us."

"Fine, fine," Sarsali said. "I'll give you and Jin my advice *after*, since my daughter's in such a rush."

"I'm hardly the one in a rush!" Cressida exclaimed. "Ellie's waiting, and we need to get started."

Astrea steeled herself as the three of them made their way to the gardens. It was not only where they'd have the ceremony but their reception, in the quiet Novarian night. Thousands of stars sparkled above them, and deeper in the gardens, warm lights lit up the trees.

Of course, scattered around were soldiers and trucks, but Veiko had ordered them to move to give the wedding party space.

Balthazar and Saros were both waiting near a large hydrangea bush, both dressed in simple slacks and collared shirts.

"Here she is!" Sarsali announced proudly. "Our bride."

"Oh, my dear," Balthazar said as they approached. "Astrea, you look so lovely." As Astrea thanked him, he walked over to her, his smile warm. Then he pulled her into a hug and whispered, "I always knew you and Jin would be together."

"What?" she asked, half laughing. "How could you possibly have known that?"

The wrinkles around Balthazar's eyes deepened. "Because you two have always looked at each other the way Sarsali and I look at each other.

We got married after a few months, too, you know. And look how far we've come. I think you and Jin will be just fine."

"I think so, too." Astrea hugged Balthazar again, then he joined his wife and daughter.

"My dear," Saros said as he gently placed his hands on Astrea's shoulders. "Your mother would be so happy to see you like this."

"What about you?" she asked. They hadn't really talked about this, not since they announced their engagement. The focus had all been on the assassinations, the attacks, the next steps and mission. But when she'd told Saros the wedding would happen immediately, he hadn't even batted an eye. He'd just offered to help if it was needed. "Are you happy to see me like this even knowing it's Jin waiting for me?"

"I trust him to take care of you as much as I trust the Nikaphoroses," Saros said.

That was high praise coming from Saros. Astrea smiled as she asked, "Have you had any visions of us? Do we seem happy in the future?"

"Oh, my dear, I don't need a vision to know that will be true. Varojin has always made you happy. I don't think that's going to change."

Astrea threw her arms around his neck, and Saros's warm pride washed over her again and again.

"Now," Saros said, "let's not be late, alright?"

The five of them headed toward that light deep within the garden. Astrea couldn't see anyone through the maze of hedges and trees, but she could hear them and feel them. Eliana's laugh. Nicos's chuckle. Zephyrine, Lucian, Marko, the twins, Noemi, and even the Novarian royals. All waiting.

"We'll see you in a few minutes," Cressida murmured to Astrea before ushering her parents and Saros down the dimly lit garden path and out of sight.

Astrea pushed past the excitement of everyone and felt Jin's wavering wall. He was nervous. Excited and nervous and headed her way. She smoothed the front of her dress, suddenly so anxious.

A few moments later, Jin and Adi rounded the corner. Adi passed Astrea quickly, nudging her with his elbow as he slipped past.

"Hi," Astrea whispered as Jin strode up to her.

"Skies . . ." He reached for both of her hands. "You look beautiful, Az. Stunning."

"Thank you." Her heart thrummed in her chest. She hadn't gotten to see Jin at all since their kiss the night before, and now, just seeing him there in his black suit, the way he watched her . . . "Are you ready?"

"I've been ready for a long time." Jin cupped her cheek with one hand as he leaned down to kiss her.

"Hey!" Adi shouted from up ahead. "Get your asses out here!"

With a huff, Jin pressed his forehead against hers. "I don't think we're supposed to do that until after the vows," she said as their friends' amusement danced across her skin.

"All these fucking rules," he said wryly. "I suppose we should go out there. It is our wedding, after all."

Lacing her fingers through his, Astrea started into the gardens. The whole place smelled of sweet roses, peonies, and hydrangea, all her favorites. How had Sarsali managed it?

They rounded a corner, entering a clearing. Someone had set up an arch, and Sarsali had decorated it with blue, pink, and white flowers, mimicking the colors of an opal. Someone else had recreated the traditional Kalamian wedding setup in front of the arch. Flower petals scattered in a circle, symbolizing the earth. Four lanterns lit by candles, symbolizing fire. The fountain behind the arch for water. Outdoors, of course, for air. And at night for the stars shining high above them.

"Are you nervous?" Jin whispered.

"A little."

She wasn't nervous about marrying Jin. No, she was so certain about this decision. But with everyone's eyes on them, especially Veiko's and Lucian's, Astrea's breath turned shallow. What if Veiko stopped this at the last minute, by some pressure of the council?

Still, she moved with Jin to stand in the middle of the floral circle. They faced each other, still holding hands. As Eliana positioned herself under the arch, their family and friends formed another circle around the setup.

"Hi," Eliana said unceremoniously, drawing a laugh from everyone. "As some of you here know," she continued after flashing a smile at Astrea, "I've wanted these two to get together for an eternity. And I thought they might have had things not changed eight years ago."

Had Astrea been that oblivious? Everyone, apparently, had expected this outcome except for her. She tried to push that thought aside, instead focusing on Jin as he watched her. That orange anxiety vibrated in the background of his aura, but she could barely see it as deep purple reverence took over. Marigold joy, pink love, and even raspberry lust swirled around him, a beautiful sunset just for her. And the warmth of his love, that sunshine, washed over her again and again, overpowering the chilly breeze.

"The last eight years—the last few months especially—have been hard on all of us for many reasons," Eliana said, "but we're here now. And we're here to support and celebrate Jin and Astrea as they commit to building a life together. Now, this is usually where there would be some long, drawn-out explanation of what that means by the officiant," she continued, "but I wanted to do something different."

Astrea frowned. What would Eliana want to do differently?

"I want to skip to the good part," Eliana said. "The part where you two explain why you want to marry each other. Would you like to go first, Astrea?"

"I don't know where to start," she admitted, and Jin chuckled. But she really didn't know where to start. She'd been thinking about this part all day, and she hadn't come up with anything.

It wasn't because she didn't love him. No, not at all. She loved him so much. But how could she convey those feelings? How could words ever do them justice? Especially with all these people standing around. What if she didn't say the right thing?

"Hey," Jin whispered, more of that gentle warmth gliding over her skin. "Look at me. Just tell me."

"You make me feel safe." Astrea swallowed past the lump in her throat and the burning in her eyes. It was Jin. Just Jin. She could tell him, just as she could tell him anything. "Lately, the world feels unsafe at every turn, but you make me feel safe. I mean, you even made me a nightlight."

That earned her another laugh from Jin, and from somewhere in the circle of their friends was amusement and approval and even a hint of confusion. That was fine. Only Jin had to know what she meant. She wasn't going to explain.

"And you've accepted me as I am since the day we met all those years ago," Astrea continued, warmth building in her chest. "You've seen some of my best and worst days, Jin, and you're still here walking beside me. I've never really known what I wanted or had the courage to take it, but you help me feel courageous. I know what I want today." She sucked in a breath, then said, "I want to marry you."

Those final five words were the intent spoken by each party, required for the ceremony. But they were so true, deep in Astrea's bones.

"Jin," Eliana said, "your turn."

Jin adjusted his grip on Astrea's hands. "You've always seen me for who I am," he started. "Not Prince Varojin, not Captain Auris, but just me. Just Jin. And though finding my way back to you wasn't easy, it was all worth it because now, you're here with me. I might do a few things differently to avoid some of that long road, but I will always fight to come home to you, Astrea Sovna. I want to marry you. I'm pretty sure I've always wanted to marry you."

The last sentence earned a chorus of emotion from their friends and family, and Astrea's entire body heated. But she focused on his words, letting them wash over her again and again. She focused on that warmth, those colors of love and respect that flared so brightly around him.

"Now, repeat these vows together," Eliana said. "I take you to be my spouse, my partner in life, and my one true love. I will cherish our friendship and love you today, tomorrow, and forever."

"I take you to be my spouse," Astrea and Jin started in unison, "my partner in life, and my one true love." Astrea's voice shook. He squeezed her hands. "I will cherish our friendship and love you today, tomorrow, and forever."

"And now, who has the rings?" Eliana asked. Across from Astrea, Cressida smiled, and two rings shot through the air toward Eliana. She passed them to both Jin and Astrea, then said, "Wedding rings are an unbroken circle of love, signifying to all the union of this couple. Repeat after me, Astrea."

Astrea held tightly onto the wedding band she was to slide onto Jin's finger, trying hard to listen to Eliana's words and memorize what she had to repeat.

"Jin," Astrea said once Eliana was finished. He reached up and wiped away the tears pooling at her lash line. "This ring is my sacred gift, my promise that I will love you, cherish you, and honor you all the days of my life." She slid it onto his right ring finger, a perfect match to the engagement band on his left. "I will always choose you."

And when it was Jin's turn, a few tears slipped down his cheeks, too. "Astrea," he said, his voice somehow steady as stone, "this ring is my sacred gift, my promise that I will love you, cherish you, and honor you all the days of my life." He slid her matching band onto her right ring finger, the twining silver and gold glinting in the candlelight. "I will always choose you."

Eliana gave a happy sigh before she said, "I now pronounce you wed. Jin, kiss your wife, for skies sake! We all know you're dying to."

Everyone around them laughed and cheered as Jin leaned down and kissed Astrea. It was gentle, chaste even, but Astrea's whole body still tightened pleasantly. And when Jin pulled away, she grinned up at him, lost in that soft, secret smile of his. The one she'd loved for years, the one she loved even more now.

"I love you," he whispered.

"I love you, too." Then, with a giggle, she added, "Captain."

Jin's smile turned wry. "Devious," he murmured, but the smile remained. "You haven't called me that in months."

"Yes, well, teasing you is fun."

Jin's arms circled her waist as he pulled her in for another kiss, and this time, Astrea wrapped her arms around his neck. The kiss was hardly any more intimate than the first, but being pressed up against Jin set Astrea's whole body alight.

"Enough of that, you two!" Cressida called. "Let's party!"

Astrea twisted her new wedding band around and around on her finger, watching as the metal caught the light of the candles flickering on the table. The remnants of their dinner were still strewn across its surface: serving dishes now emptied of vegetables, bread, and meat; dinner plates; wine glasses that had been refilled multiple times; and even the half-eaten cake that Cressida had so lovingly made with Balthazar. It had been filled with strawberries and topped with airy icing.

As a wedding gift, Delfine's wife Katerina had brought out a large camera to take family portraits, even promising to make small copies for Astrea so she could put them in the locket Cressida had gifted her. Lucian and the Novarian royals had returned to the palace, but everyone else was still scattered around the garden, chatting and eating. It was nice, getting to revel in everyone's happiness, even just for this one night.

"So," Cressida said as she leaned toward Astrea, "how does it feel to be married?"

"The same," Astrea said. "Ask me again in a few months."

"Think they're next?" Cressida asked, tilting her chin toward Eliana and Nicos. They were across the table, and tonight, they only had eyes for each other. They'd kept their relationship so private the last few months, but now, there was no denying it to anyone who might be watching them.

"If they want to go there, yes," Astrea said. It was, unfortunately, not quite so simple for Eliana and Nicos. She was fighting for the throne. Politically, it made more sense for her to ascend alone, then marry. Helosians knew her. They didn't know Nicos yet. "Once the war is over, yes. I would be very surprised if they parted ways."

"And you're happy?" Cressida asked.

"Very happy." She took Cressida's hand and squeezed it gently. "Thank you for helping organize all this for us."

"What was I going to do, *not* plan my best friend's wedding?" Cressida teased. "And you're far easier to work with than Ellie, so this was my one shot to actually have fun with it."

Astrea grinned.

They sat like that in silence, watching the rest of their friends and family continue the festivities, which were really now just about the food and wine. Astrea even indulged in a little more, taking a glass when Cressida offered it to her.

Eventually, Zephyrine, Sarsali, Balthazar, and Saros broke away from where they were speaking with the twins and Noemi. Zephyrine made some silent signal to Jin, and Balthazar one to Astrea. Curious, she stood and wandered toward where they were gathering. Jin passed his whiskey glass to Adi and joined her.

"It's been such a beautiful evening," Sarsali said, "but I'm afraid I can't keep up like I used to. I'm going to bed."

"Oh, you didn't have to stay this late," Astrea said.

"For you, my dear, I'll always skip bedtime." Sarsali beamed. "Now, remember what I said earlier? That I had some advice to pass on?"

"We'd love to hear it," Jin said, his arm circling Astrea's waist.

Sarsali's smile relaxed, the glow of nearby candles flickering across her soft features. "Be open and honest with each other, alright? Share your thoughts, fears, and dreams. That trust and understanding will be the foundation for your partnership."

Astrea nodded. She could do that. She and Jin already did that.

"And remember to pursue your own interests and passions," Balthazar said. "Sarsali and I may do just about everything together, and we always work as a team, but we also honor our differences. You should do the same."

"Wise words," Jin said. "Thank you both." He stuck out his hand for a shake, but Balthazar pulled both him and Astrea into a tight hug. Jin laughed.

"Good night," Sarsali called over her shoulder as she and Balthazar started back for the palace.

Saros hung back a ways as Zephyrine stepped up next. The general looked resplendent in her forest green dress, and her eyes twinkled as she said, "Don't screw this up, kid."

Jin laughed, half amused. "Why is that the first thing you say to me?"

"I'm teasing, mostly," she said, winking at Astrea. But her mood sobered quickly. "Although my marriage is not the most authentic of unions, I do know one thing. Love requires nurturing. It's easier than you might think to let life get in the way and come between you. Cultivate what you have. Always approach each other with kindness, understanding, and patience."

"Thank you," Jin said to her, taking her hand as she offered it for a shake.

And when Zephyrine offered to shake Astrea's hand next, she took it, feeling only a little awkward. Balthazar's bear hug was more her speed.

As Zephyrine followed the Nikaphoroses, Saros shuffled forward with an awkward laugh. "I know I'm supposed to have advice for you two, but I've never been very good at personal relationships," he said. "But I think what I can offer is this: Remember to embrace the quiet moments. Life gets hectic if you let it. A little balance never hurts."

That, Astrea could do. She loved quiet moments.

"No, it certainly doesn't," Jin said. "I look forward to many quiet moments for all of us once this is over."

"As do we all, Varojin. And I just . . ." Saros smiled tightly. "I know I haven't always been the kindest to you, but you've grown into quite the man. You're making Helosia proud, even if they don't know it."

Jin sucked in a sharp breath. "Thank you, Saros. That means a lot."

"It's the truth," Saros said. Then he turned to Astrea. "My dear, you've chosen a good partner. Listen to all the other advice you've received tonight, and you'll both be just fine."

He pulled Astrea into a hug, and she leaned against him. She couldn't believe it . . . Saros saying that to Jin. It meant so much to her. To Jin, too, she was sure. And then Saros actually pulled Jin into an embrace, too. Lavender surprise flickered around him as he patted Saros's back.

"Alright then," Saros said when he quickly let go. "See you two tomorrow."

And then he was gone, disappearing into the dark garden.

"Wow," Jin said. "I never thought I'd see the day Saros actually liked me."

"Well, you're very likable," she said. "He just has trouble seeing that about people sometimes."

Grinning down at her, Jin twined their fingers together. "I'm likable, huh?"

"I mean, I did marry you. You must have *some* redeeming qualities."

At that, he laughed. Pink love and peach amusement swirled around him, bright against the night. "I should hope so."

"What are you two still doing here?" Cressida called out. "Jin, take your wife to bed!"

If it had been anyone other than Cressida or Eliana suggesting it, Astrea might've died right on the spot. But she wanted that more than anything. She wanted Jin to help her get the dress off and use his fireweaving to warm her skin all over.

"Want to get out of here?" Jin asked, voice low.

"Take me to bed, Jin."

"Yes, ma'am."

"Just don't eat all that cake!" Astrea called to Cressida. "I want some in the morning." It had been too long since she'd had Cressida and Balthazar's baking, and besides, a little cake for breakfast never hurt anyone.

Cressida saluted in response, and Astrea was about to make a gesture in return when Jin swept her off her feet.

"Hey!" she exclaimed, clinging to his broad shoulders. "I can walk."

"Not a chance," Jin said. "My wife's not going to walk anywhere if I can help it."

"You do realize that's incredibly impractical, right?" Astrea asked as he started for the palace. Their friends shouted a chorus of goodbyes. "I have to walk at some point."

"Do you, though?" Jin mused as he picked up his pace.

"You're ridiculous."

"Ridiculous, eager to get you to bed—what's the difference?"

They made it to the palace in record time, and somehow, Jin wasn't even out of breath or breaking a sweat. No, every step he took was sure, steady, calm. He didn't set her on her feet until they were in their bedroom, door closed.

Jin switched on the nightlight in the corner, then started a low fire in the fireplace. When he was done, he turned toward Astrea. "Now," he said, "where shall I begin?"

"Can you take my dress off?"

"I'll take off anything you want me to. Turn around."

Astrea turned, holding still as Jin undid the buttons on the back of her dress. She, however, did not hold still as Jin pushed her sleeves down her shoulders and trailed his fingers along her exposed spine. She did not hold still as Jin started pushing the dress off her hips.

"Unfair," she said, though she didn't mean it. "I'm freezing."

"I'll warm you up." Jin reached for her hair clips next, taking them out carefully before running his fingers through her hair. His hands trailed lower until one cupped one of her exposed breasts and the other teased the waistband of her bloomers. "Are you tired?"

"No." Astrea palmed him through his pants, and Jin hummed in her ear. "Are you?"

"Not the least."

Astrea wiggled out of his grasp and pivoted toward him. "Good."

With one hand, Jin undid the buckle of his belt and pulled it off. She swallowed, watching as his forearms flexed with every button he undid on his shirt. His rings—one on each ring finger—glinted in the firelight.

Married.

They were married.

Her husband.

He was moving so slowly, like he knew it was torturing her. Peach amusement and raspberry lust tangled around him, and a fire burned in Astrea's belly.

"Could you be any slower?" she asked.

Jin tsked. "Impatient."

She just wanted his hands on her body. She wanted to run her hands all over him, tangle them in his hair, guide him to exactly where she wanted to be touched.

"Now . . ." He reached into his pocket, pulling out something black and silky. The blindfold from the night before. "I think it's only fair that you wear this for a little while after what happened last night."

Her breath hitched. Not because she didn't want to try it, but that would mean being in the dark.

"Only if you want," he said gently.

As if that had to be said at all. Jin would never make her do anything. She licked her lips. "Yes."

"You're sure?" he asked as he took a step toward her.

"Yes."

"We can take it off whenever you want," he said, and she nodded. "Turn around." She turned. "Close your eyes."

As she did, Jin slid the cool, soft fabric over her eyes. He tied it behind her head, then smoothed some of her hair back.

"How's that?" he asked.

This darkness wasn't so bad. Not when it was Jin right there next to her, when she could feel his warmth and all the energy around him. "What now?" she asked.

Jin hoisted her up again, and this time, Astrea squeaked. He set her on the bed. "Get on your stomach and wait."

"I can see why you weren't a fan of this yesterday," she said, listening to his movements. Footsteps. Fabric rustling. Part of her desperately wanted to see him, but another part liked not knowing exactly where he was or what he might be planning. Butterflies danced in her belly and chest. "You're *so* slow."

He chuckled, the sound making its home near her heart. The mattress dipped, then Jin straddled her hips. "And you're impatient. I want to focus on you right now."

"Touching me would be focusing on me."

His hands moved up her exposed back, his palms growing warm. "How's that?"

"Good."

Jin worked his way to her shoulders, then to the base of her neck. His hands drifted lower again, and Astrea relaxed into the bed. Jin followed that pattern for a while, making her pleasantly warm. Her whole body tingled.

His hands moved lower and lower, skimming her waist. That heat pooling in Astrea's belly turned into an inferno as his hands lingered there, delicate but possessive. The rough pads of his fingers moved toward her bloomers.

"Jin," she whispered, wiggling her hips. "Please."

"I don't think I'm done yet."

"Well, I am."

With a satisfied growl, Jin tugged her bloomers off. "Spread your legs for me."

Astrea did as instructed, immediately rewarded with Jin's fingers trailing her exposed heat. He sucked in a sharp breath as he worked her, every movement gentle but firm. Just how much raspberry might she see in the air should she take the blindfold off? Her skin tingled pleasantly. Was that her magic trying to tell her what Jin was feeling in a different way? She wasn't sure, but she liked it. Sweet and sour filled her mouth.

Astrea arched her back more, a silent plea. Then he was gone.

The bed shifted, and Astrea was about to ask what he was doing when he settled behind her again, tugging her hips up off the bed. The tip of his erection pressed right into her entrance.

"Ready?" he asked.

Pushing back, Astrea took him right down to the hilt. He cursed, and a satisfied tremble worked its way down her body. Jin held her hips in place, controlling their rhythm and speed. He took his time, each stroke purposeful, drawn out. Astrea's fists curled into the sheets as he pulled all the way out, then pushed back into her.

"You're teasing me," she whispered.

"Am I?" It sounded like he grinned. Something light and airy tickled her skin, delicate like butterfly wings.

One of Jin's hands slid to her shoulders, tugging her up. His arm slid around her, pulling her back against his chest and holding her there. His other hand moved from her waist down between her thighs, moving in smooth circles over that extra sensitive spot.

Astrea barely choked out his name, her nerves on fire as he made quick, shallow thrusts. "Jin," she whispered again, her muscles tightening like a coil.

"Yes?" he asked.

"I'm—"

The half confession just made Jin work faster. He kissed the side of her neck, sucking on the delicate skin there. Raspberry, pink, vermilion, purple swirled behind Astrea's eyelids. Sweet and sour coated her tongue. Her whole body heated. She was on fire in the best way, and she never wanted it to be extinguished.

Trembles rolled through her. She clenched around Jin, so tight it seemed like he could barely move. A satisfied laugh rumbled behind her, traveling from his chest into hers.

He pulled out of her, then helped her lie down on her back. Pulling off the blindfold, Astrea pushed hair out of her face and sucked in a deep breath.

Jin hummed as he hovered over her, his golden irises molten. "How was that?"

"Intense, in a good way." She fingered the blindfold. They would definitely be using that again; she wanted to find out what else she might feel when her magic couldn't feed her those colors.

"Good, because I was *thinking*," he said, nudging her legs apart, "we could play a game tonight."

"A game? Don't I need to know the rules?"

"It's very simple." He lowered his mouth to hers, capturing her lips in a delicate kiss. "It's called 'How many times can I make my wife climax in one night?'"

"How is that a game?" she retorted. "A game implies two players."

"Well, I believe my previous record is . . . four?" His fingers moved down to her entrance, and she sighed happily. "So that means I need to score three more points tonight, minimum."

"I can't take that many," she whispered. No, she was sure she would simply be a puddle of goo.

He chuckled. "How about we see how you're feeling after the next one?"

"Deal."

The soft, secret smile returned, and then Jin kissed her, slow and sweet. She drank him in, trying to taste the subtle hint of whiskey on his breath, trying to memorize the flex of his muscles as she grabbed his shoulders. His fingers moved in slow, steady circles as his tongue explored her mouth. He dipped one finger inside her, then another, his thumb pressing right into the apex of her thighs.

"Fuck," she breathed. Every muscle in her body grew tighter, tighter, tighter as Jin continued.

"Skies, I don't think I've ever felt you this wet," he murmured against her throat.

The hint of praise in his voice made Astrea's stomach curl.

"My beautiful wife."

She didn't want it to end, didn't want it to stop, but she couldn't take much more. Her fingers dug into his back, and then he had her tumbling over the edge again. Her muscles clenched around Jin's fingers still buried inside her, her thighs trembling and shaking.

"I believe that's two," Jin whispered. "Can I get another?"

Astrea was already melting into the mattress. Lust and pride danced around the room, coloring everything bright pink and red. "I'd like to see you try," she said.

Jin's eyebrows shot up as sugary amusement coated Astrea's tongue. "You'd like to see me *try*?" he asked.

She smirked. "You heard me."

"Then tell me," Jin said as he hovered over her, "do you want to be fucked like this or get on top?"

"Like this."

Nudging her legs wider, Jin settled between them. Astrea reached for him, wrapping her hand around his erection and pumping up and down. He sucked in a breath, then pushed her hand away and buried himself deep inside her.

"Fuck." He groaned. "Fuck, Az. I'm never going to get tired of this."

He moaned as Astrea tangled her fingers in his hair and pulled on his bottom lip with her teeth. His thrusts sped up, setting her sensitive body alight. Skies, she was so close again . . .

Jin slowed only to move her legs from his waist to on top of his shoulders. He trailed kisses along her calf muscle, out of breath as he said, "Show me. Let me see you touch yourself."

Astrea's fingers drifted right between their bodies. The gentlest of touches sent a jolt through her. He moved her legs again, gripping the undersides of her thighs and pushing her hips back.

Raspberry, vermilion, deep purple, pink. That sunshine. Her whole body heated.

"Eyes on me, Az. Look at me."

Through hooded lids, Astrea looked up at Jin, focusing on those brilliant golden eyes and the pink reflecting in them. The softness in his expression, even as he fucked her right through her climax. Her back arched off the bed, so high she didn't even know how he managed to keep going. But he did, and her body pulsed again as she kept touching herself.

"One more and you win," she said.

As Jin kept her hips back, pushing deeper and deeper into her, Astrea unraveled immediately. Stars exploded behind her eyelids, and her free hand grabbed Jin's wide shoulders. Warmth settled in her chest as Jin seemed to spill inside her forever. And she would have happily lain there under him forever, basking in that blissful sunshine coating his skin.

He rolled to one side, tugging her toward him and tucking her against his body.

"Four," Astrea whispered. "You win."

A deep chuckle vibrated in her ear. "Tired?"

"Exhausted. Don't think about touching me again tonight."

"I would never." He kissed the back of her head. "That was some good work."

"First night as a husband and you're already making me weak in the knees."

"A good first night?"

"I'd say so."

Jin kissed the top of her head again. "Do you want to lie here for a while?"

Oh, Astrea would've liked that. But she was a mess. "How about you draw a bath?"

"Anything you want."

He kissed her again, then disappeared into the bathroom. And as he returned and picked her up, Astrea didn't protest. She leaned into him as he carried her, and she leaned into him as he settled behind her in the tub.

It was another half hour before they were settled in bed, her head on his chest.

"Are you happy?" he whispered, locking their fingers together.

Astrea looked down at their rings, the silver and gold against his tan skin and against her much paler complexion. "I don't think I've been this happy in a long time."

"Me either."

She peeked up at him. "I love you, Jin."

"And I love you, Az."

CHAPTER 41

After their beautiful ceremony, Astrea and Jin had spent the next day honeymooning—as much as they could with a mission to prepare for and a palace full of people. Kalamian couples typically visited Tornama, the Taipoli Islands, or even the mountains for time to celebrate alone, but they didn't have that luxury. So they'd stayed in bed for half the morning, helped finish up whatever preparation they could, then dined alone and spent more time in bed.

Now, the first hints of sunrise painted the horizon. Astrea slung a dark canvas knapsack over her shoulder. It was hefty, filled with not just her gear but the few other essentials she could pack. For their airship ride down to Thasia, Astrea had opted for a comfortable linen dress, but she also had a few more formal options tucked away in a suitcase. After all, they were supposed to meet with someone from the Tornamian government upon their arrival. Eliana had insisted they all look the part.

Wind tugged at Astrea's skirt. They were just outside the palace compound's walls, dozens of guards and soldiers milling around the large airship waiting to take them south.

"And you'll be safe?" Sarsali asked Balthazar. She patted her husband's cheek. "Never in all our years together did I imagine you going away for something like this."

He kissed her palm. "I'll be back soon, darling. Don't worry."

"Take care of our girls."

The corners of his eyes crinkled. "I will."

Sarsali's gaze flicked to Cressida. "Take care of your father."

"Skies, Ma! We already talked about this."

"I just worry about all of you." Sarsali looked at Saros next. "Don't fixate too hard."

"You worry too much," he replied coolly. "I'll only fixate the right amount."

Sarsali rolled her eyes, then pulled Cressida and Astrea into a quick, tight hug. On the one hand, Astrea was glad Sarsali was staying behind in Talmaris with Noemi. On the other, she would miss her desperately. Part of that decision was because Sarsali would be helpful around the palace, and part of it was that there just wasn't room on the mission. Lucian already felt they were bringing several people too many, and he might've had a point. Twelve of them—plus additional guards for Eliana's security—were flying to Thasia. There, they would leave Eliana and the additional guards, then continue on into Helosia with Rami as the Tornamian delegate for the mission.

They wrapped up their goodbyes, then headed for the airship looming in the clearing. It was a massive thing, far bigger than any airship Astrea had been on. Certainly fit for royalty, as it was Veiko's private ship.

As they stepped inside, Astrea's attention fixed on Jin, who was in deep discussion with Zephyrine and Marko. He excused himself and joined Astrea near the middle of the cabin. She couldn't help but watch the way his rings caught the light as he walked. She wasn't sure she'd ever get tired of that.

"All set?" he asked.

"As ready as we can be."

"Let me show you to your rooms."

Jin herded Astrea, Cressida, Balthazar, and Saros upstairs. The stairs were wide, and the second floor was bright and decorated in cool colors.

A few paintings of Talmaris were bolted to the walls. But even extra space didn't necessarily mean extra comfort; it was an airship, after all. After dropping the others off at their respective rooms, Jin led Astrea to their quarters. It was smaller than she'd hoped, just as cramped as many of their other flights. But it wasn't for all that long; they'd arrive by late the next evening.

"I've already got the rest of our things over there." Jin gestured to the far side of the bed. "Do you need me? I'm going to check on a few things."

That was Jin, always checking on things as the next leg of the mission got underway.

"No, I'm fine."

Leaning down, Jin pressed his lips to hers. Astrea tangled her fingers in his hair, pulling him closer. He groaned against her mouth.

"Is it wrong that I could just stay here doing that all day instead of my job?" he whispered.

"Maybe not wrong but certainly not prudent." Pecking his cheek, Astrea said, "Go."

As Jin went off to perform whatever duties he had, Astrea sat down on the hard bed and sighed. The last couple of days with him had been like a dream, even with final mission preparations scattered among the wedding preparations. Selfishly, she hadn't wanted any of it to end.

She reached up to toy with her necklace but found nothing but empty skin. Right; she hadn't worn any of her jewelry other than her wedding bands. No locket. No opal necklace. No bracelet from Cressida and Eliana. Even the wedding rings didn't seem practical for this trip, but she hadn't been able to bear the thought of not wearing them.

As the ship took off and began its climb high above Talmaris, Astrea unpacked the couple of nice outfits she and Jin had brought for the meeting with the Tornamian president, not wanting to risk them getting wrinkled. She lay down for a bit, but sleep never came. So when Cressida knocked on the door and called her name, Astrea jumped up as fast as she could.

"Hey," Cressida said as soon as Astrea opened the door. "Dad and I were just going to show everyone the plating we made and how it goes into the new armor. You want to come see?"

"Sure," Astrea said, following Cressida out into the hall.

Down in the main cabin, Balthazar stood near the middle of the room, a swath of red armor and dark metal plates set out before him. Lennor and Civan were there, as were Eliana, Nicos, and Saros. Jin, Zephyrine, Adi, and Lucian were nowhere to be seen, while Marko's blond hair was visible up at the helm.

Picking up one of the metal plates, Balthazar held it up for them all to see. It was thin, so much so that it seemed like it could be bent in half. But when he pressed on it, the plate only had a little give.

"We couldn't fully outfit the armor without weighing people down too much," Balthazar said, passing one of the plates to the group. Cressida passed another among them. "So we prioritized the torso, front and back. No shoulders. No arms."

Lennor held one of the sample pieces up, examining it from the side. "I feel like I'll barely be able to move with this thing on."

"It's strong enough to block a blade—including the aetherium ones we made—and small bullets," Cressida said, "but any thicker and, as Dad said, we'd be dealing with too much added weight. With it inserted into the leather, though"—she gestured toward one of the pieces of red armor—"that'll help. Just try not to get hit."

Eliana passed Astrea one of the metal plates. It was somehow both lighter and heavier than she expected—and cold to the touch. Lennor's assessment seemed entirely correct. Astrea had no idea how much something like that would slow her down.

"Ideally, no one's going to even be that close to enemy combatants," Nicos said from the back of the group.

"Ideally," Balthazar agreed. "But better to be prepared just in case."

Astrea stole a glance over at Saros. Orange anxiety vibrated around his entire body. His gaze was glued to the armor on the table.

"It's good work, you two," he said to the Nikaphoroses.

"Thank you, my friend," Balthazar replied with a small smile. "Let me get everyone what they need."

As Balthazar began passing out the metal plates and body armor as needed, Astrea sidled over to Cressida. Her arms were folded tightly over her chest.

"What's wrong?" Astrea whispered.

"I still don't *love* that we had to make more aetherium blades," Cressida said, voice low. She barely motioned to where Eliana and Nicos were chatting with Saros. "We've got enough for Jin's team, Nicos, Eliana, me and Dad, and the Novarians. I didn't think you or Saros would want one."

"I don't really," Astrea said. The thought of carrying something with that kind of power made her nervous, and she didn't think being nervous and handling a weapon at the same time was a very smart combination. Besides, with her souleating, she was able to defend herself well. "I don't think Saros would, either."

No, Astrea certainly didn't think Saros would want one. He became anxious every time he neared aetherium, or at least he had every time she'd seen him around it. She would make sure he was at least armed with a regular weapon, though.

"I suppose I don't have to love it for it to be useful," Cressida said.

"Astrea!" Balthazar called. "Your turn."

Astrea wrapped her arm around Cressida's shoulders and gave her a quick squeeze. "You're helping us all, remember? It's going to be alright."

"Yeah, yeah." With a wry smile, Cressida shrugged her off. "Now go get your things so we can play cards."

Sighing, Astrea went to Balthazar. He passed her the special red armor Adi had made her, the almost-dress. Then he stacked two metal plates on top.

"For you, my dear," he said.

"Thank you for doing all this."

His brown eyes sparkled as he said, "It's no trouble at all. We'll be ready for whatever we find down in the Badlands."

Astrea truly hoped they were ready. But with this team, everyone's experiences, from the Corsycan War to void magic to politics, were surely going to get them through.

The hum of the airship engines covered up the silence of the night. Astrea rolled away from Cressida. The small window near the ceiling offered no light, not even a view of the stars. It had to be well after midnight, and Jin still wasn't back. He was supposed to find her when he was done for the night.

Astrea climbed out of bed as soundlessly as she could, leaving Cressida alone. She barely stirred, so Astrea crept toward the door and opened it on thankfully silent hinges. The ship was quiet, even to her magic. Only a few people seemed to be awake at all.

After checking her and Jin's room and not finding him there, she decided to go downstairs. What could he possibly be doing at this hour?

As Astrea reached the last step, she found not Jin in the cabin but Lucian. He stared out the window on the far side of the space, arms crossed tightly over his chest and barrier pulled in around himself even tighter.

Zephyrine was up at the helm. Was Jin still with Adi? Maybe Marko or Eliana? Trying to plan something? She shook her head.

"Lucian?" she asked, keeping her voice low.

He didn't move as he said, "Yes?"

Lucian hadn't been around much since Ysabel's assassination. Part of that was surely because of his duties, not only to the new grand duke but organizing this mission and trying to keep security tight at the palace with the new diplomats' arrival. Every time she'd seen him, he'd seemed almost too focused. Like nothing else could possibly matter.

"I was just wondering if you'd seen Jin."

"He wanted to speak with Marko once Zephyrine took over for him."

"Oh."

Still staring out the window, Lucian nodded.

"And . . . how are you?" Astrea asked. It seemed like a silly question.

"Fine."

"I'm really sorry about what happened that day," she murmured. "I can't imagine how that feels after knowing and protecting someone for so long."

For a moment, Astrea didn't think he'd answer. He remained rigid. The only sound was those damn engines.

But finally, he rubbed one wrist with the other hand and sighed. "It hasn't been easy."

"I wouldn't expect it to be."

"But it's one of the risks," Lucian said. "One of the risks of being a political leader and another as captain of the guard. Ysabel and Reimo both knew the risks."

"Were you close with the councillor?"

"We'd known each other for nearly a decade."

Another half answer.

"If you're worried about Princess Eliana's safety, don't be. President Sikori's chief of police and security have all gone over their plans with me via phone. The grand duke and I personally spoke with leaders across the continent before we left, and everyone has been increasing security measures with Nazarov's threats hanging over our heads. Their Lightbringers know what to look for."

Lucian may have guessed exactly what some of her anxieties were, but he still wouldn't look her in the eye. Astrea frowned. Even for him, this was not normal.

"And what if it's not void mages he sends to carry out any further attacks?"

"They should still be actively searching for bad actors. Everything will be fine."

His voice was so flat, detached. Like he either didn't believe it or wasn't letting himself feel his emotions after all that had happened. Astrea pressed her lips together. How much did she have a right to say to him? They were colleagues, in a strange sense of the word. He'd never cared about crossing lines, but she did. Pushing someone who wasn't ready rarely yielded good results.

The stairs squeaked. Astrea turned, finding not Jin like she'd hoped but Civan. His hair stuck every which way, like he'd just woken up.

"Sorry . . ." He glanced toward the kitchen. "I just came down for something . . ."

Lucian still didn't move.

"I could use a drink before I go back to bed," Astrea said to Civan. "If you don't mind me joining you."

With a nod, he headed for the kitchen.

When Lucian still made no move, Astrea said good night and followed Civan. She just hoped, whatever complicated things Lucian was feeling, he sorted them out soon. Not just for the sake of the mission but for his own well-being.

Chapter 42

Thasia hadn't changed much since their last late-night arrival, at least not as far as Astrea could tell. This time, their airship landed not in some far-off airfield but one much closer to where the Thasian government sat.

Far in the distance, warm lights lit up the skyline and swallowed a few of the stars. Though the air was less humid than the last time they'd been in the city, a hint of moisture still stuck to Astrea's skin.

Lucian had already left the ship and was now speaking with a slew of Thasian police, all dressed in deep green uniforms. Lavender surprise flickered around two, bright in the dark night. Even still, Lucian turned on his heel and motioned for the rest of them to approach the waiting cars. There was a whole squad of police cars, actually, five total.

"Your Imperial Highnesses," one of the officers said in heavily accented Helosian as Jin and Eliana approached. "Welcome to Thasia."

"Thank you," Eliana said.

"We'll be escorting you to the presidential palace," said the officer. "Please, right this way."

Although Astrea knew they were headed for the safety of the Tornamian president's residence, sliding into the back of the police vehicle was hardly reassuring. Oh, what would Astrea from the beginning of the summer have thought? She'd never have believed any of this.

Astrea ducked her head as she slipped into the car, Jin right behind her and Lucian, of all people, following both of them. She tried to look out the window for where Cressida had gone off to, but Lucian closed the door behind him and asked the driver to go.

The car lurched forward just as Jin asked, "What's with the rush?" He looked out the back windshield. Astrea followed his gaze only to find the rest of the cars following.

"Best to get a move on," Lucian said as he settled onto the seat on Jin's opposite side. It was just one long bench, and Jin was squashed in the middle. "Especially since we're nearing midnight." He leaned forward, switching to Tornamian as he asked the driver, "Will the president be awake?"

"She's awake and ready to receive you, Commander," the man replied. "Her and her spouse both."

Astrea knew very little about Tornamian politics. Unlike the other countries on the continent, Tornama was a republic, and they voted in not just their legislative body but their president, too. The current president was a woman named Mira Vadathe Sikori, who had been elected just the year before. Eliana had attended the swearing in ceremony, as had Kaius. And her spouse, a Fireweaver whose name escaped Astrea, had once played in the mage sports leagues. Astrea only knew that because of gossip she'd heard around the palace back home; none of the nobles could imagine a head of state marrying an athlete. She didn't see what the big deal was.

As the officer drove them through Thasia's winding streets, Astrea settled in next to Jin and rested her head on his shoulder. He snaked his arm around her, pulling her closer. It was comfortable, getting to sit with him like that. She didn't even care that Lucian was next to them. If he had opinions about their marriage, he'd kept them to himself.

"We need to go over our plans again tonight," Lucian murmured as they turned down a wide avenue. Outside, in the light of the passing street lamps, Astrea could make out towering palm trees and lots of green space. "We need to ensure everything's set."

"I know," Jin said.

"I just want to make sure we're on the same page."

"I've been helping plan all of this, Lucian. I'm on the same page."

"Yes, well."

Astrea pressed her lips together. *Leave it to Lucian to be . . . well, Lucian.* Hopefully he wasn't going to continue causing any kind of friction during the trip.

The rest of the drive passed quietly and quickly, taking no more than a half hour. They approached a long driveway marked by tall, wide gates. They swung open, allowing the motorcade to enter the presidential compound.

Through the windshield, Astrea could just make out the presidential residence. It wasn't quite as grand as the palaces she'd seen and lived near, but there was no denying the grandeur. Its facade was white brick, framed by thick columns and decorated with dozens of arched windows. The closer they drove, the more detail Astrea could make out, from the intricate carvings along the windows to the colorful trim and abundant landscaping.

The officer stopped their car a dozen feet away from the portico covering the front double doors. Lucian climbed out, then Jin. He helped Astrea out next, and behind them, everyone was exiting the other vehicles.

"This way, please," the officer said, ushering them up the stairs and toward the double doors.

Two guards flanked each side, all dressed in deep green like the police officer. Their faces were unreadable, their auras calm and energy focused.

Even as Astrea let her senses push out wider and wider, she found no sign of the void.

Inside the presidential palace was beautiful, all deep wood tones, intricate tiles, and color everywhere. It was friendly, welcoming. And ahead, in the middle of the expansive foyer, were three people.

First was a woman in a wheelchair, her curvy build similar to Astrea and Eliana's. Her deep bronze skin shone under the chandelier's light, and her silky black hair hung over her shoulder in one long braid. Her aubergine dress was trimmed with silver and gold stitching.

Next to her was a tall, plump person with the same complexion. Their hair was hidden under a head covering patterned with vines, and their loose linen outfit was even more casual than Veiko's. A hint of gold makeup highlighted their light brown eyes.

And finally, there was Rami Voskara, the most unexpected of all. Astrea had known Lucian was trying to coordinate something with her, but here? In the palace? Astrea had assumed that, if Lucian was successful, they'd meet up near the border. A silly assumption, maybe, but Rami seemed less inclined toward politics than Astrea was.

One of the guards shut the door to the front hall with a thud, making Astrea flinch. Lucian didn't move a muscle as he stared at Rami. Lavender surprise flickered around the woman. Had she not realized Lucian would be there? Or had it simply been a long time since they last saw each other?

Clearing her throat, Rami tucked her hands into the pockets of her dark blue trousers. Paired with her white blouse, she looked so . . . proper. Not like the smuggler Astrea knew her to be.

"Princess Eliana, Prince Varojin," Rami said. "General Kanakos and friends, welcome. For those of you who don't know me, I'm Rami Voskara, former associate of the commander's. May I introduce you to President Mira Vadathe Sikori." She gestured to the woman in the wheelchair. "And her spouse, Presidential Consort Sarya Vadathe Sikori."

"Madam President," Eliana said, stepping forward. "And Presidential Consort. It's so lovely to see both of you again, though I'm sorry it's under these circumstances. You have my deepest condolences for your recent losses."

"Indeed, Princess Eliana," said Mira. "It's been a trying time, but Tornamians are tough. We're pulling through." Her attention turned to Jin. "And it's nice to finally meet you, Prince Varojin. It seems we have much to discuss"—her blue eyes sparkled—"including what appears to be a wedding announcement? I didn't realize one of the Auris siblings was married aside from your eldest brother."

"That's new, Madam President." Jin's hand found the small of Astrea's back. "New within the last week, actually. This is Miss Astrea Sovna, my wife."

My wife. Despite the circumstances of the meeting, Astrea's silly little heart danced.

"Madam President, Presidential Consort," she said, trying to school her features into a polite smile instead of the wide grin stirring just under the surface.

"Congratulations to you both," said Mira. "Well, let's not loiter near the front door when we have things to discuss. Please, follow me."

President Sikori and her spouse led them down a series of wide hallways, showing off the main floor of the presidential palace. It was more of the same elaborate decor, including the thick, ornate rugs Tornama was famous for. Guards were stationed every dozen or so feet.

Eventually, they entered a meeting room with a mahogany table large enough to seat twenty. Maps of Tornama and the rest of the continent lined two of the four walls. On the other were the double doors, and on the final were stained glass windows overlooking the dark gardens.

"Please, have a seat," Mira said as she maneuvered her wheelchair up to the empty spot at the head of the table.

They filled in the various chairs. As soon as Lucian took a seat, Rami sauntered to the other side of the table, sitting almost directly across from him. Neither of them would quite look each other in the eye. Hadn't Marko once told them that Rami would help them because of her connection to Lucian? Had something happened in recent weeks? Astrea frowned.

"Grand Duke Veiko and my ambassador have informed me of what's been happening in Talmaris and Helosia," continued the president, "though I must say, void magic sounds . . . implausible."

"I know it does," Eliana said, "but it is very, very real."

"I've had my doubts," said Mira. "But now, considering those seated around my table tonight . . . two royals, an infamous Helosian general, and head of Grand Duke Veiko's guard . . . this would be quite the elaborate scheme if not true."

Eliana pulled a thick folder out of the bag clutched in her lap, then slid it across the table toward the president. "Grand Duke Veiko asked me to deliver this to you, Madam President. A collection of evidence he's been eager to show you."

Mira leaned forward and took the folder from the table. "Troubling that the late grand duchess did not reveal this to us sooner," she said.

"Grand Duke Veiko sends his apologies; there's a note from him explaining his aunt's intentions," Eliana said. "Frankly, we weren't sure who we could trust or how deep the conspiracy spread. I hope you can understand we were just exercising extreme caution."

"Indeed," the president said. Her thick eyebrows knitted together as she began leafing through the papers. Astrea couldn't see much from her spot, but it seemed to be reports, some of those strange void letters, and maps.

"And you plan to go into Helosia because . . . ?" asked Sarya. Their voice was warm, and it crackled a bit, almost like a welcoming fire. "You personally, I mean, Your Highnesses."

"I won't be going," Eliana said. "But my brother will."

"Yes, Sarya makes a good point." Looking up from the paperwork, Mira frowned. "To go in yourself, Prince Varojin? To put yourself at that kind of risk? Why?"

"I won't put innocent people at risk because of what my father's up to," Jin said, only partially the truth. Councillor Reis had basically given them no choice but to accept the assignment. "Some dissenters have helped supply us with the information they can, and soldiers are defecting at a low but steady rate, but sending a Novarian team in didn't seem fair. And besides, my team and I have firsthand knowledge of the Helosian army."

Mira pressed her full lips together before murmuring, "How noble."

"I'll say." Sarya glanced at their wife. "Don't tell me you've forgotten what Prince Kaius came here claiming."

"What did he want?" Eliana asked.

"He had a similar story to yours." Mira gestured at all the notes spread out before her. "The offer was either an alliance or a warning to stay out of Helosia's way. I wasn't sure what to make of it at the time."

Astrea's lungs tightened. Kaius had tried to sell the same story to the Tornamian president?

"Oh?" Jin asked.

"He came with tales of Novarians arming themselves with dangerous, unfathomable weapons," Mira said. "Yet he offered no proof at all."

"Something about him seemed . . . off," Sarya added, their eyebrows furrowing. "He was agitated the whole time we met with him."

Mira nodded. "Grand Duke Veiko and I may not have had as much time together as would have been ideal, but between what he did share before the attacks and even what you've shown me here . . ." She shrugged. "One would have to be a fool to not see through Kaius's lies."

"Even without reading the reports in depth?" Zephyrine asked.

"Even then," Mira replied.

Relief pulsed around the table. Leaning back in her seat, Astrea let out a harsh breath. Thank the skies President Sikori was a smart woman. She seemed reasonable, at least in the half hour Astrea had known her. And she seemed so . . . sure of herself. Yes. President Sikori was incredibly sure of herself and her decision tonight. The set of her jaw said everything. A major surprise given the skepticism of the crowd back up in Talmaris.

"I'd like to hear more of what you think, Your Highnesses," said the president. "And you, General Kanakos and Commander Astor."

The four of them took turns explaining most of what had happened the last few months, leaving out the bits about the Paragon's prophecy involving Astrea and Jin. They focused instead on the Paragon's end goal and what they thought Emperor Aelius wanted. As her friends spoke, Astrea watched Mira and her spouse carefully. Hints of surprise and anger bubbled up around them, especially at the explanation of aetherium and the new intelligence they had.

"And so, we're hoping that with Rami's testimony," Eliana said, gesturing toward her, "we can sway the delegates in Talmaris into a more formal alliance."

Mira set one hand on the table. "After the attack on Thasia, it's obvious that this Paragon is a threat. And I agree that Emperor Aelius cannot be allowed to have such weapons if they exist," she said. "But war with Helosia? That is a big step."

"Madam President," Lucian said, "if we work together—Tornama, Novaria, the Islands, and perhaps Delia—we have a good chance of stopping both groups."

"Be that as it may, it's not so simple," Mira replied. "I'll need more proof of Emperor Aelius's capabilities to bring to members of parliament. They will want to find the Paragon, but declaring war on Helosia? That's a bigger ask, and one a majority of members must approve."

"Couldn't you declare war on the Paragon, then expand that to Emperor Aelius's regime as appropriate?" Lucian pressed.

Mira held up a hand. "Commander, I appreciate the urgency. I do. But there are more steps to be taken in my government, more people I must convince. Supporting a foreign rebellion? Fighting these shadow mages?" She shook her head. "I'll begin laying the groundwork while you're on your mission, but you must bring me proof."

Just like that, they had the Tornamian president agreeing to join the fight? Well, not *exactly* agreeing to join the fight, Astrea supposed, but it was close.

"Regarding Helosia in particular, I would like to avoid a drawn-out conflict as much as possible," Eliana said. "Perhaps more targeted strikes to take out whatever weapons my father may have already created, plus some way to either get him to abdicate or . . ."

"Or?" Mira prompted, arching one eyebrow.

"Or taking him out of it comes to it." Eliana lifted her chin. "Please do not think of me as a usurper, Madam President, but you must see the writing on the wall. Neither my father nor Kaius can be allowed to rule with the things they're trying to do."

Mira let out a quiet sigh. "I agree. If what you say is true, allowing either one of them to remain in power only presents a threat. Thank you for bringing this matter to my attention."

"Thank you for hearing us out, Madam President," Eliana said. "It's important that the continent knows what we're all up against. It's just not Helosia or Novaria at risk. It's all of us."

President Sikori nodded. "You all can take the train up to Fort Sand-stone first thing in the morning," she said. "From there, my people will provide vehicles for you to take across the border. And for tonight, you will all stay here as our guests."

"Thank you, Madam President," Eliana said. "If it's not me over-stepping, I was planning to stay behind in Thasia while the others forge ahead."

"You are welcome, of course," Mira said. "I have a feeling we'll need time to discuss your potential ascendance to the throne anyway. It may be time for Tornama to ally with the Aurises, should the right one be in charge."

Once President Sikori dismissed them, Rami and a couple of guards escorted their group to a separate wing of the palace. Relief and anxiety twined around Astrea's friends, a mix of mint and orange. She hated the combination, disorienting as it was.

"Here we are," Rami said, gesturing vaguely to several rooms grouped at the end of the ornately decorated hallway. "We'll set out at first light, so get some sleep."

The guards left them first, and just as Rami began to follow, Lucian said, "Rami, wait."

Stopping, she turned toward him. "Yes?"

"We need to talk."

Rolling her eyes, she said to Marko, "You didn't warn me he'd be like this."

"Like what?" Lucian asked harshly. "I asked for your help, and you agreed, yet you show up at the Tornamian presidential palace acting as if you're a member of state? And then you practically ignore me? What is going on?"

"Alright," Marko muttered, putting his arm between them. "Alright, come on, you two." He ushered them into one of the nearby bedrooms.

What Astrea would've given to be a fly on the wall in there. What was Lucian's issue? Rami had been quiet, sure, but she hadn't been hostile.

"We need to talk, too," Nicos said, mostly to Eliana. But then nodded at Jin. "All of us, please."

They followed Nicos into another nearby bedroom, which was hardly big enough for the entire team. Eliana stalked toward the wide canopy bed and asked, "What is it, Nic?"

"I'm going to stay here with you."

Eliana's eyebrows furrowed. "What do you mean? We talked about this. I'll be fine."

The original plan had been for Nicos to join them on the mission, as his formal training in the Badlands and knowledge of the emperor's movements would be useful. Of course, Astrea hadn't felt great about leaving Eliana alone, but that hadn't been her call to make.

"Maybe," Nicos said, "but I can't leave you here alone. It's too dangerous."

"But you—"

"No," Nicos said, the word somehow both soft and hard. "No, El, I can't." He turned to Jin. "You all can go on without me, right? I'm not that crucial of an asset."

Jin scratched his beard and sighed, a tired sound. "*That* crucial? I suppose not, but one man down will make this more difficult."

"Or easier," Nicos argued. "One less person to worry about, one less mouth to feed."

"What's caused the change of heart?" Zephyrine asked. She leaned against the wall near the door, arms folded over her abdomen.

"I trust the rest of you to get this done," Nicos said, turning back to Eliana, "but I can't leave you. Just seeing all the police and guards here reminded me of that. I can't shirk my duties."

"We all have a duty to stop my father," Eliana said.

"And I have a very specific duty to you. To protect you. I can't do that if I'm out there."

Warmth burned through the room, hot like a late summer afternoon, as Eliana gazed up at Nicos. Warring anger and desire, relief and anxiety, swirled around her in an array of colors. "I can't stop you if that's the choice you want to make," she said.

"It's the only responsible choice as far as I'm concerned."

Skies, they stared at each other so intensely . . .

Cressida coughed, making them both jump. "So, we're down a man," she said. "Now what?"

"I'll go over anything I think is relevant with you all tonight," Nicos said. "I'm sorry to make this decision now."

"Don't be sorry." Jin's gaze flicked to Astrea, and her face flushed. "I understand."

"Then let's get started," Zephyrine said. "We've got no time to waste if we want to get any sleep."

Chapter 43

Astrea hadn't been on a train since she was just ten years old, and this was nothing like the one she'd been on all those years ago.

It was worse.

When Saros had moved Astrea from Talmaris to Kalama, they'd only been able to buy tickets for the coach car. It hadn't been awful, exactly, but the seats had lacked any real padding, and they'd had no privacy. It had been a less than pleasant experience for Astrea.

But this military train they were on now? It was loaded up with cargo and typically used to transport soldiers. The car they'd been placed in was cold and utilitarian, all metal. Even sitting next to Jin didn't warm her up like it usually did.

"Skies, how long is this ride going to take?" Cressida muttered. She was seated across from them, in between Lennor and Civan.

"A few hours," Jin said.

"And how long have we already been on the train?"

"You're worse than a child," Jin said with a laugh.

"About an hour and a half, my dear," Saros said to Cressida. He was seated next to Astrea on the left, and Balthazar was next to him. "We'll be there soon."

"I'll just pay my own way for a first-class ticket next time," Cressida mumbled as she shrank down in her seat. "This is the worst."

"Oh, it's not that bad." Lennor smiled at Cressida, but the Metalli continued her sulking.

Adi didn't even look up; his nose was buried in a small novel he'd evidently brought with him. Next to him, Civan kept his attention focused on the ground, like his boots were the most interesting thing in the world.

Lucian, Marko, and Zephyrine were one car ahead, catching Rami up on the entire situation. Rami and Lucian, at least, had seemed to be on better terms that morning when they'd all convened after a short night's sleep. Not friendly, exactly, but more neutral.

With a small sigh, Astrea settled into her bench and leaned against Jin. He wrapped his arm around her shoulders, pulling her closer. There was so much they needed to do. Find out exactly where Emperor Aelius's mining operation was. Figure out how much of it he'd secured already. Slow him down somehow.

And even with Nicos staying behind to keep Eliana safe, Astrea couldn't help but worry about that, too. Would he be able to do so? What if Kaius showed up in Thasia again? Or what if Nazarov did, especially since Astrea wasn't going to meet him in the mountains by his deadline?

None of this felt right or good, but how could it? Did missions like this ever actually feel "right" to anyone? She was tempted to ask Jin, but the audience made her keep her mouth shut.

The door to the next car slid open just as the train's brakes engaged. The low rumble stopped, replaced by a high-pitched screech. Zephyrine stumbled forward half a step with the change in speed.

"What's going on?" Jin asked.

"There's some debris on the tracks," Zephyrine said. "They're going to clear it."

"How long is it going to take?" Adi asked.

"Maybe half an hour before we're up and running again."

Astrea didn't like that at all. "Does this kind of thing happen often? Debris on the tracks?" She wouldn't put it past someone like Kaius or even Nazarov to set something like this up, to somehow be tracking their movements.

"According to the engineers and Rami, this part of the Tornamian forest has some issues with trees falling near the tracks," Zephyrine said. "It should be routine."

Routine. Nothing about Astrea's life was routine anymore.

"Let's check it out, just to be sure," Jin said.

Once the train had completely stopped, Cressida and Balthazar pulled the large door open. Humid air rolled into the car, followed by bright morning sun. Muttering something about "first class" under her breath, Cressida hopped down to the ground.

Balthazar jumped out after her. "Wait for me!"

Astrea hesitated halfway to the door, her senses pushed out wide. There wasn't anyone she could sense beyond those already on the train, and there was certainly no void.

"Stay here," Jin said to Astrea, the twins, and Adi. "I'll be right back."

Was it wise to just leave like that? To just go out there? Astrea just stayed planted to her spot, staring out at the bright green Tornamian tropical forest. The thick canopy made of wide palm fronds offered some shade farther away from the tracks.

Rough frustration scraped Astrea's skin, then boots crunched, and Jin appeared in the door again. "A couple of trees on the tracks," he said, "and some mud. The conductor said there were bad storms this way yesterday. Guess nobody came out to clean the mess up."

"Inconvenient," Adi muttered as he walked back toward where he'd left his book on one of the benches.

Hot anger burned Astrea's skin. She flinched, then cringed as sharp pain lanced her forearm. Either someone was hurt or . . .

"Jin!" Cressida yelled.

He sprinted away, and Astrea scrambled out of the train after him, ignoring Saros's calls for her to stay inside. A hundred feet ahead, earth and metal flew through the air, aided by wind. Light flared, making Astrea squint. No void, though. No void.

But a lot of pain.

Grinding her teeth together, Astrea pushed back against the pain bouncing around in her chest. It centered around her sternum, like when Lucian used souleating on her.

And as the mist and dust settled, Astrea found not just her group but four people dressed in gray, black, and green, all flat on the ground writhing in pain. Lucian's hands were stretched out in front of him.

"What the fuck happened?" Jin asked, his focus fixing on Zephyrine.

"Bandits," she said with a shrug.

On unsteady legs, Astrea approached Cressida and Balthazar. They lingered behind Lucian, Zephyrine, and Marko. Uninjured, as far as she could tell. Cressida flashed a quick smile and thumbs-up.

"Not uncommon lately," Rami said casually as she circled the group to stand next to Lucian. She studied those four on the ground. Something like understanding whispered over Astrea's skin, followed by rough irritation. "Let them go, Lucian."

"They just tried to attack us," he said through gritted teeth.

"I think they've learned their lesson." Her words were tight, almost pained as she stared down her former husband. "Let them go."

Why would Rami want to just let them go? Maybe they were people she knew? After all, Rami's business operations clearly weren't above board, at least not entirely.

With a grunt, Lucian released his hold on them. The pain in Astrea's chest was gone in an instant. The bandits' breaths came in heavy gasps. Nothing about them suggested they might be Paragon or even working for Emperor Aelius; they looked like normal people. They didn't even have weapons on them that Astrea could see.

"Get the conductor," Lucian said to Marko. "We'll take them to Fort Sandstone and let the authorities deal with them."

With an exaggerated roll of her eyes, Rami joined Marko as he went to find the conductor.

Jin shook his head. "What's the matter with the two of you?" he asked Lucian. "Can you two work together or not?"

"We'll be fine," Lucian said. "Rami and I do not see eye to eye on certain issues."

That seemed like the understatement of the century.

"Let's just get this sorted and move on," Lucian said with a sigh. "The commander at Fort Sandstone will be expecting us."

Getting the bandits into custody had been easy enough, and they'd gotten back to the last leg of their journey in practically no time at all. Astrea almost couldn't believe it had worked out, but she wasn't going to complain.

By the time they reached Fort Sandstone, she was sore and stiff from the train's meager accommodations. And they wouldn't be getting a break any time soon. No, they were about to pile into a convoy to head west into Helosia.

Astrea shook out her arms and legs as she waited next to one of the two large trucks idling in the courtyard. They'd been provided by the base's commander, a man named Commander Davan Rakat, who was now speaking with Jin, Lucian, and Zephyrine.

"It's not every day that I get royalty coming through my base," Commander Rakat said to Jin, his voice raspy, almost like he'd smoked blue lotus his whole life. He couldn't have been older than fifty. His light brown skin was dotted with sunspots.

"It's no pleasure of mine to be here, Commander," Jin said, "but I'm grateful to you and the president for helping us."

"She said we're not sending any troops with you." The commander hesitated, gaze darting between Jin, Zephyrine, and Lucian. "It's really just your group going in to try to stop your father?"

"We're just trying to disable part of his war machine right now," Jin said, "while the politicians handle the rest."

Commander Rakat nodded. "Never cared for politics myself. Anything we can do to ensure the mission's success?"

"You've already given us what we need," Jin said, "though if you have anyone who might happen to be nearby—air, land, or sea—have them keep their radios on."

Commander Rakat nodded again. "If we do, I'll be sure to let them know." He shook hands with Jin, then Lucian and Zephyrine. "Safe travels."

Jin pivoted back toward where Astrea loitered with Adi. Everyone else was in the trucks. "Well," he said to them both, "let's go."

Adi circled to the front of the truck and climbed into the passenger's seat. Out of the corner of her eye, Astrea spotted Marko settling behind the wheel. Saros was riding in the front cab of the other truck with Balthazar.

Astrea didn't envy the twins and Saros for being in that truck with Cressida. If Cressida had thought the train was uncomfortable, the trucks were going to be worse, and that meant Cressida was going to complain at least twice before they stopped for the night. Actually, Astrea wasn't sure if they planned to stop or if they would just switch off drivers.

"Az?" Jin asked.

"Hm?" Looking up, she found him already in the truck, extending his hand down to her. "Oh, sorry."

"You're distracted," he said as he helped her up.

Lucian, Zephyrine, and Rami were already inside and seated along the benches on the walls. It wasn't all that different from the truck they'd ridden down to Helosia in. That seemed like it was forever ago.

"Will we be able to make it across the border?" Astrea asked none of them in particular.

"It will be easy enough," Rami said. "The border guards are easy to buy off." As Astrea's eyebrows furrowed, Rami laughed. "Still not used to our ways?"

When could Astrea possibly have gotten used to this? "I just didn't think Helosian border guards would be so easily bought."

"It's how people have been moving in and out of the country for weeks now," Rami said. "Grease the right palms and they look the other way. It's the only way some of the merchants in Thasia have been able to get their goods between the two countries."

"They've locked the borders down that tight?" Lucian asked. "You didn't mention this earlier, Rami."

"Relax, Luce."

Luce? Astrea wished she knew the story behind Rami and Lucian's previous marriage. Marko seemed to know something about it, but he hadn't offered up any more information. Not that it was crucial, but Astrea was dying to know.

They were opposites in every way: Lucian's white skin and pink cheeks, dark blue eyes, and harsh demeanor compared to Rami's brown skin, bright eyes, and subtle edge to her smile. Lucian liked to follow whatever rigid structure he had in his mind while Rami seemed to be willing to change the rules at any moment to make things work. She was involved in smuggling, not just goods but people, and Lucian was . . . well, he was Lucian.

"Relax?" he asked. The truck's engine roared to life, and then the vehicle began to move forward. "Earlier you said we'd be able to squeak by an unguarded section."

"And I now think simply buying passage through is easier," she said.

"You always think buying the solution is easier," Lucian replied.

"Is it not?" Rami arched one eyebrow. "Money solves many problems. You still haven't learned?"

"I think what Lucian's trying to say," Zephyrine said slowly, "is that we risk having the trucks inspected if we try to cross in front of guards. They might find Jin or I, or even Astrea."

Rami waved a hand. "Trust me, they are *not* searching vehicles if the bag of cash is large enough." She patted one of the knapsacks tucked between her feet. "And I have a very large bag of cash."

Just how much money did Rami have in there? And where could she have gotten it all? *Maybe I don't want to know,* Astrea thought.

"Do you plan on giving it all to the guards?" Lucian asked. "What if we need more?"

"We won't need more," Rami said with all the confidence in the world. "Believe me."

Lucian glanced at Jin, who said, "Well, she has a point. There's nothing significant in this part of Helosia, just border towns and whatever military installations my father's still got running. If we stay off the major roadways, we should be fine."

"And what if we need gasoline?" Lucian asked. "More than what Commander Rakat sent us off with?"

"*If* that happens," Rami said, "and *if* we can't find any to steal, then I know a few people in the region."

"Oh, because that gives me full confidence, Rami," Lucian muttered.

Rami held her slender hands up in surrender. "Testy, as always, Luce."

"Must you call me that?"

Astrea definitely envied Cressida and the others now. This was going to be a long drive if Lucian and Rami were going to be at odds the entire time.

"We should be at the border in a couple of hours, and then we'll need to be alert once we cross into Helosia," Zephyrine said. "Let's just try to get some peace and quiet while we can."

Chapter 44

By the time the truck began to slow, Lucian and Rami's bickering had stopped, and the mood had settled into a tenuous calm.

The small window separating them from the front cab slid open, and Adi said, "We're coming up on the border checkpoint. Rami?"

Rami stood and moved closer to the little window, then crouched down. "How long is the queue?"

Outside the front windshield, the sun had begun its descent in the west. Sunset was still a few hours away. A few trucks and cars idled in line in front of them.

"We might be through in ten minutes," Marko said as he stopped their vehicle entirely. "Looks like they're checking papers."

Rami had said they could buy their way through the checkpoint, but Astrea wasn't convinced. Not when their trucks were clearly military. Lucian fidgeted in his seat, the only sign of his hesitation. Nobody else seemed worried. Astrea tapped her fingers against her thigh.

Rami rifled through her bag, then passed a few folded-up sheets of paper through the window. "Here." She pulled out a thick stack of blue-green Tornamian currency and slid them through to Adi. "And this."

"So much?" Adi asked, eyebrows raised.

"Trust me," she said, "they'll probably ask for more."

"And what am I supposed to tell them?" Marko asked.

Paper crinkled as Adi unfolded what Rami had given him. "We're traveling craftspeople?" His eyebrows furrowed. "That's believable?"

"Traveling craftspeople who have very high-paying clients in the countryside," Rami corrected. She slid another stack of paper currency to Adi. "Very well-paid craftspeople who can get them and their crew in the second truck across country lines as needed."

It sounded like a piss-poor excuse to Astrea, but what did she know of smuggling people across international borders? Not a damn thing.

The truck rolled forward, then stopped again.

"Jin?" she whispered. He glanced down at her. "That's actually going to work?"

"Of course it's going to work," Rami said before Jin could reply. "The Helosians aren't being paid shit right now. They'll be eager for the cash."

When Astrea shot Jin a questioning look, he shrugged. "I mean, it's probably going to work."

She huffed. "Probably?"

"Relax, Miss Sovna," Rami said with a smile. The truck inched forward again. Just two more cars in line ahead of them. "You must trust me. I got you into Kalama, didn't I?"

Sure, Rami had gotten them into Kalama—sort of—but that had been a lot more subtle than this.

"Did you ever hear from Magdi again?" Astrea asked.

"Crew's fine." That was all Rami replied before Marko shushed them both.

"Hello, Officer," he said in Helosian as he rolled down his window.

Astrea couldn't see whoever it was he was speaking to, but a feminine voice asked, "Papers?"

Adi passed them to Marko, who surely handed them to the officer. Astrea held her breath.

"What kind of trade are you in?" the Helosian officer asked. Cool surprise whispered over Astrea's skin.

"What *don't* we do?" Adi replied enthusiastically. "Woodwork, metalwork, even interior decorating. I've been known to put together quite the color palette. I'd be happy to give you a discount if you ever need—"

"That's really not necessary," the officer replied.

"You sure?" Adi asked, glancing out the windshield. "Your guardhouse is looking a bit . . ." He gestured vaguely. "Sad. We could spruce it up."

"Not necessary," she repeated. "What business do you have in Helosia?"

"Some of our clients are expecting us," Marko said.

Distrust prickled Astrea's skin. She cleared her throat as quietly as she could, what she hoped would be a signal to Adi.

And he seemed to pick up on it because he said, "Very high-paying clients. And we're running a little late, unfortunately. Blew a tire about twenty miles back. We had to come out here to pick up these tiles. You wouldn't believe them, absolutely beautiful, but the man who makes them—"

"I see," the woman replied curtly. "Tiles for . . . ?"

"We're redoing their entire downstairs and ran out; too many broke in the last shipment."

"Replacing broken tiles," the officer repeated.

"Yup, and if, uh, you wouldn't mind helping us and the rest of our crew in the truck behind us out, we could help you out, too."

That distrust was quickly replaced by a flash of green curiosity that lit up the truck's front cab.

"What exactly are you saying?" the woman asked.

Adi passed Marko one stack of cash. "For us," he said, then took the second stack from Adi. "And for the rest of our crew. We'd really appreciate being able to get back to our jobsite as soon as possible."

"You know how these kinds of people are . . ." Adi trailed off before adding, "Sticklers about time even though we can't make things move any faster for them. They think the world revolves around them just because of their status."

Silence. Silence for one heartbeat, two, three. Astrea's pulse jumped.

"Of course," the officer said. "But I'd suggest you and your crew try to keep your schedule next time. We can't make exceptions like this often."

"We *completely* understand," Adi said. "And we very much appreciate your help today."

Muffled shouts and warm approval came as Marko rolled up his window. Then he pressed the gas, moving them through the border checkpoint with little more incident.

"Adi?" Jin asked.

"They're following," Adi said. "Balthazar and the others, I mean. Guards are waving them through."

Astrea slumped back against her seat. Minty relief pulsed out from Adi, bright and clear in the truck as the coolness coated her tongue.

"See, Miss Sovna?" Rami grinned. "I told you it wouldn't be a problem." She turned to Lucian, then said, "And see? I still have plenty of money."

Lucian shook his head. "I can't believe that worked."

"Adi can be very convincing sometimes," Marko said.

"Oh, so you admit it?" Adi asked. Warm amusement settled on Astrea's skin as pink desire lit up the front of the cab. "After all these months?"

"I'm simply stating the truth," Marko drawled. "Nothing to get so worked up about."

"If you two are done, we need to figure out where we're going next," Lucian said. "Rami?"

"Considering the time, let's head west for a bit, then south," she said.

"West, then south? We're supposed to be heading to the Ring of Fire," Lucian said. "That's more northwest."

"That may be, but we're going to need someplace safe to sleep tonight, and I know just the spot."

"Of course you do."

"Was that not part of why you invited me on this mission?" she asked. "Not just as a representative of Tornama but as a skies damned expert in *my* field?"

"And what is your field, exactly?" he asked. "Aligning yourself with criminal elements?"

Rami chuckled. "Criminal elements. Technically you're breaking multiple laws right now, Luce. Or does it not count because you want to be involved?"

"Never want to see my side, as always," he muttered.

Rami sucked in a breath, ready to reply, when Zephyrine leaned forward on her knees. "Getting through this mission in one piece is more important than whatever strangeness exists between you two," she said, voice firm but kind. "And that's really none of our business unless you want to make it our business. Let's just do what we need to do."

Lucian and Rami both leaned back in their seats, arms crossed over their chests. What exactly had happened between them? Obviously they didn't see eye to eye on the legal ramifications of their actions. Lucian had never had issues pushing Astrea beyond her limits or pushing limits with Grand Duchess Ysabel. So what, was he just fine with breaking the rules, as Rami said, when he *wanted* to be involved? Or had something specific happened to drive the wedge between them?

"Now," Zephyrine said with a nod, "let's go with Rami's plan. If she's got someplace she believes is safe, I'd like to see it. It's certainly better than camping out in the middle of the Helosian forest. Skies only knows where the emperor's got his troops."

Rami guided them deeper into the Helosian countryside for a few hours. They drove directly toward the setting sun. Astrea couldn't see much out of the windshield, just lots of trees and tropical vegetation.

Eventually, they turned south at Rami's instruction. Lucian hadn't said a word in hours. For the best, probably. Nobody had said much of anything, actually, though Astrea could make out murmurs of conversation between Marko and Adi up front.

She spent a lot of the time with her eyes closed, tucked against Jin's side. He kept his arm tight around her shoulders. A few times, she'd found she'd dozed off and that Jin had, too, his head resting on top of hers.

But finally, as darkness blanketed the world outside the truck, Rami said, "Make a left in about a hundred yards."

"Left where? It's just forest," Adi said through that tiny window.

"Just trust me," Rami said. "Left."

"I can barely see a skies damned thing," Marko said.

"Trust me," Rami repeated.

With a grunt, Marko slowly turned the truck left.

"Well, I'll be damned," Adi murmured.

"Told you I was right." Warm satisfaction rolled off Rami in waves. "Go up the drive about five hundred feet and you'll see a tree marked with a red stripe. Go right."

Marko followed those instructions, too. Rami kept directing him, several hundred feet and slow turns at a time.

"Alright, now there should be a gate," she said. "That's the last turn, then we'll be at the right spot."

The truck slowed after a few moments, and Marko asked, "Is the gate supposed to be open?"

"Open?" Rami sat up straighter and leaned forward to look out the windshield. "Shit, now what? Stop here. Turn the truck off."

Unease prickled Astrea's scalp. "There's one person," she said. "Not void. A bit far off."

"House is about five hundred feet from the gate," Rami offered. "You said one?"

"One," Lucian said with a nod. "I feel them, too."

Rami shot him a look, something that said, "I didn't ask you," but she nodded. "I think I know who it is, though he knows better than to keep the gate open. What's wrong with him?"

"How about we go check it out?" Jin said.

"Aye, probably a good idea." Rami reached for the door handles and pushed them open. Humid night air rolled into the truck. "Come along."

Jin turned to Astrea and said, "Stay here with Adi and Marko." His tone left no room for argument, not that Astrea was keen on trying to sneak up on someone late at night.

Zephyrine, Lucian, and Jin all headed outside. Through the open doors, Astrea spotted Saros and Balthazar in the front of their truck, barely discernible in the moonlight and weak headlights of their vehicle. Jin waved them off, then held up one finger, a sign to wait. Then he was gone, disappearing around the side of the truck with the others.

Astrea held her breath, scooting closer to that small window so she could look out the front window. Little was visible, just the shapes of palm fronds. Cicadas buzzed. Her senses pushed out wider and wider. Jin and the others were moving away from her. There was no pain, though. No fear. Just mild confusion and irritation, probably Rami's. Behind Astrea, more confusion.

Fire lit up the night, just a narrow jet of flames shooting into the air. Astrea tensed. Marko tensed. Adi, however, laughed as the fire disappeared.

"What's funny about this?" Marko asked.

"That's Jin's signal. It's fine."

"And that's a subtle signal?" Marko muttered, turning over the engine again. "Can you close the doors, Astrea?"

She scrambled back, yanking them both shut as Adi said, "It's not supposed to be subtle. A makeshift flare, in case we ever got separated back in Corsyca."

The truck rolled forward at a snail's pace, its headlamps barely providing any clear line of sight out in the middle of nowhere. A warm light cast a beam on the ground, a door inside the shadowy structure looming to their left. And there, silhouetted in front, were five people. Jin was easy to pick out, the tallest.

"I guess we're here," Adi said.

Before Astrea could get to the truck's back doors, Jin had them open and had climbed back inside with her. "It's one of Rami's associates," Jin said. "Lucian seems to know him, too."

"Oh, that's going to make for a pleasant night," Astrea muttered.

"It seems there's some . . . history." Jin pressed his lips together. "Hopefully we can just set out at first light."

Together, they gathered up everyone's bags and handed them to Adi and Marko, who were waiting at the back of the vehicle. Then the four of them circled around the truck, where Astrea could more clearly make out Lucian, Rami, and Zephyrine.

And standing with them was a man just slightly taller than Rami. A gold hoop pierced his left eyebrow, and another pierced his right nostril. The beginnings of several tattoos were visible on his neck and disappeared below the collar of his shirt. He had the same sepia skin as Rami, and their hair was the same smooth black.

"Everyone," Rami said as the others exited the second truck, "I'd like you to meet my brother, Zojan."

Chapter 45

Zojan led them into the house, revealing first a narrow sitting room and kitchen combination. Beyond that was a door that led to a small bedroom with four bunks. There was also, according to Zojan, a loft on the second floor with another large bed, plus beds in the basement.

That was going to be a tight fit with thirteen people.

In fact, the energy pressing in around Astrea, so close to her body, immediately set her on edge. But she didn't want to pull her barrier in lest Nazarov pick the worst possible moment to show up.

"How about you all get settled in?" Rami suggested, setting her hand on Zojan's arm. In the cabin's warm, low lights, it was easy to see the resemblance between the siblings, from their complexion and hair to their bright brown eyes. The only difference was that Rami looked to be about five years older. "I need to speak with my brother about this gate situation."

"Sister, you say that as if I don't have a sense about these things," Zojan complained as they headed for the door. "I could just feel you coming."

"What, are you a Lightbringer now?" Rami asked.

The rest of their conversation died off as Zojan closed the cabin door behind him.

Cressida frowned at the tiny sitting room. "I think I'd rather be on that train again."

"It's just for a few hours," Zephyrine said, moving toward the bedroom door at the back of the room. She peeked inside, then shook her head. "Jin, assignments?"

"Me, Adi, Lucian, Lennor, and Civan first," Jin said. "Cress, Saros, Az, Zephyrine, second. Marko and Balthazar, you can get up first thing in the morning with Lucian and Civan again."

"What about Rami?" Lucian asked.

"Second shift," Jin said dryly. "I don't want to listen to you two bickering all night."

"We were not *bickering*," Lucian said with a huff.

"Like I said earlier, we need you focused. If that means you two need to talk it out, fine. Talk it out. If that means you two just stay out of each other's way, that's fine, too. I don't really care," Jin said, though his words lacked any harsh edge.

Lucian huffed again.

"Let's get sorted," Jin said. "It's going to be a long night. Any of us not on watch should sleep either in the basement or upstairs, just in case someone shows up."

Sleeping in a basement was exactly how things had played out at the Whiskey Dream in Kalama, and here Astrea was again, getting ready for barely any rest. She really shouldn't complain though. At least they were safe for the night.

She followed Cressida downstairs. Unlike the Whiskey Dream, which had decently high ceilings and didn't feel too claustrophobic, this space was . . . well, it was exactly the kind of place Astrea hated to see. Dark brick walls. Dark wood floor. Very little light.

She froze halfway down the stairs. Cressida flipped a light switch, and two single light bulbs flickered on. Astrea swallowed hard. There were four cots in the basement. Just four. A couple of storage cabinets. Little else.

"Az?" Cressida asked. Saros and Balthazar were already setting their things up.

"I'll, uhm, be right back."

Astrea hurried back upstairs. Zephyrine and Marko were all climbing the ladder into the loft, and Adi and the twins were disappearing out the front door. And Jin? Well, Astrea nearly ran into him.

"Hey." He steadied her, his hands resting on her shoulders. "I was just coming to make sure you're all settled in down there."

"I can't stay up here?" Astrea asked, voice barely audible.

"What, does Saros snore or something?"

"No, but it's . . ." She suddenly felt silly, like a child. But this was Jin. Jin, her partner, one of her best friends, her *husband*. Still, she couldn't look him right in the eye as she whispered, "It's just dark down there."

"Oh. Oh, I didn't even think about that. Like meteorite?" he asked, brows furrowing.

"No," she said quickly. No, this house didn't have a basement of meteorite, but it may as well have. "I'll be alright."

"Do you want me down there? I can switch the shifts around."

"No, let everyone rest."

"They can rest even if I switch things around."

"I'll be fine."

"Az—"

"I'll be fine," she said again. She had to be fine. She needed to stop being so scared of the dark. She couldn't let that inconvenience anyone or their mission.

Jin pressed his lips together. He obviously didn't believe her, but he said, "Well . . . I'll be outside if you need me."

Astrea took his knapsack from him, then brought it to the basement. Someone had already cut the lights off. Astrea pulled on the tiny thrum of energy under her skin, and starlight danced around her free hand. She set Jin's bag on the ground next to hers, then crawled into the empty cot next to Cressida.

"Everything alright?" Saros asked. He was still sitting up in bed, watching her cautiously, almost as though she was a terrified animal he thought would bolt.

"Fine," she said. "Night."

A chorus of "good nights" came from Saros, Balthazar, and Cressida as Astrea forced her magic back. A few twinkles of stardust faded into the dark basement, and then shadows consumed the space.

Astrea curled up on her cot. She didn't close her eyes, though. No, she watched the edges of the room, and only when she was sure the shadows didn't stretch or shift like in those tunnels did Astrea let her body relax.

"Miss Sovna? Where did you go?"

"Miss Sovna?"

"Everyone needs your help!"

"Astrea?"

"Az?"

Astrea startled. A gentle hand rested on her shoulder, and she found Jin's gaze in the warm glow of his flames.

"It's time to switch," he whispered.

"Where is everyone?" she asked as she sat up. The other three cots were empty.

"I sent them up first." He smiled gently. "I just wanted to check on you. And I'm sorry if you think I'm coddling you, but this stuff doesn't just go away because you want it to."

"I know." She leaned against him, burying her face in the crook of his neck. "I know it doesn't."

He pressed a kiss to the top of her head. "Lucian said everything's been quiet for him, and it's been quiet as far as I can tell, too."

Astrea nodded sleepily against his shoulder. "Okay."

"Okay," he whispered. Wrapping one arm around her, he added, "Are you going to let me go?"

"No." Astrea kissed the side of his neck, then pulled away. "But I guess I have to."

"My offer stands. I'll stay with you."

"Get some sleep." Astrea smiled tightly at him. "You'll need it. I'll come back in a few hours."

Astrea slipped out of bed, then headed for the stairs. Low voices drifted down, growing no less coherent as she ascended. But there, in the low light of the tiny kitchen, were Saros, Balthazar, and Cressida, standing around a coffee pot. Balthazar wasn't supposed to be on their watch; maybe he couldn't sleep?

Wordlessly, Cressida passed Astrea a cup of steaming hot liquid. The earthy smell of coffee met her nose, welcome but maybe not prudent when she still needed to rest for a few hours once Lucian took over the next shift.

Saros and Balthazar were deep in discussion about something, but Astrea headed for the front door. Cressida followed. A roof covered the wide porch, and a couple of chairs looked out over the southern Helosian forest. Cicadas and frogs sang together in a midnight chorus.

Plopping into one of the chairs, Cressida let out a long sigh and sipped her coffee. "Maybe we'll be lucky and this will be one of our last nights spent in cramped basements or on cots meant for children."

"Yeah, maybe." Astrea didn't see that as even a remote possibility, but if it helped Cressida feel better in the middle of the night, she wasn't going to take that away from her best friend. "Have you talked to Len at all?"

"Where the skies is that coming from?"

Astrea shrugged and sat in the second chair. "We haven't really talked about it, and I need something to keep me awake right now." Awake and distracted, surrounded by so much darkness. The trees were little more than shadows against a stygian sky.

"Not that there's much to say there," Cressida said. "I'm just trying to give her space after what happened with Kaius. Just get to know her more."

"Seems like a good choice."

"I do miss sharing a bed, though."

"Does going slow mean you can't have a sleepover? Maybe it would bring her some comfort." Astrea certainly felt better just knowing Jin was around when she was trying to sleep. Knowing she could expect to wake up and find him there if she needed him.

"And then with my parents back . . ."

Astrea took a sip of her coffee. "Ah."

"What?"

"You never did like bringing partners around them."

"That's not true!" Cressida protested.

"It's absolutely true, and I don't know why because they just want you to be happy."

"That's the problem."

"How is *that* a problem?"

"It's like . . ." Cressida waved vaguely at the darkness beyond the porch. "Seeing them with their strong marriage and knowing how long they've been together, I feel like I'm already behind. They were already married at my age."

"So? That doesn't mean you have to be just like them."

"Really? Because ever since they've been back, my dad's been talking about increasing my work at Lodestar once all this is over." Irritation rolled off Cressida in rough rusty waves. "As if I shouldn't get to finally do what I want."

"You've never told me you were that unhappy at Lodestar," Astrea said.

Cressida had been working at her father's engineering firm since she was just sixteen. Astrea had even worked there for a couple of summers as a secretary—she was not cut out to be an engineer—and hadn't found Lodestar Industries a terrible place to work. It was one of the top firms in Kalama, and Balthazar treated his employees very well.

In fact, Cressida was always gushing about whatever new projects she was working on. Helping test new weapons, the prosthetics Lodestar was looking to build not just for the Corsycan War veterans but anyone who might need one, new cars. Cressida loved tinkering and figuring out how to solve mechanical problems.

"I didn't know I *was* until we left," Cressida admitted. "Not like *any* of this is ideal—far from it—but not having to go and be the boss's daughter every day? Not having to live up to those expectations? That's been nice."

"Maybe you should just talk to your parents."

"Right, like they're going to listen. 'Hey Ma, Dad, I don't want to work at the company you've built and been preparing me to take over for a long time.'"

Balthazar and Sarsali Nikaphoros had been nothing but supportive of Astrea and Cressida over the years, at least as far as Astrea knew. They'd always indulged whatever it was Cressida had wanted to learn. Baking classes. Cooking classes. All those years she spent training with a retired mage athlete because she was sure she wanted to enter the leagues someday. Art classes. Had something changed behind closed doors, whenever Astrea wasn't there?

"Do you *know* they'd be upset with you?" Astrea asked.

"Well . . ." Rough hesitation scraped Astrea's skin as Cressida trailed off.

"So you don't?"

"I just know, Az." Cressida let out a harsh sigh before sipping her coffee again. "I know my dad's going to be disappointed if I don't do this. I'm his heir, in a way. The Metalli to continue on the Nikaphoros family legacy in business and beyond."

"Or maybe you're continuing the legacy in a different way," Astrea said. Cressida's eyebrows furrowed. "Doing all this. You don't think that if we're successful, that won't earn you some kind of legacy? Preventing aetherium from falling into the wrong hands would be an incredible feat. Being one of the first Metalli to bring it back after hundreds of years? That's pretty big, too."

"Maybe," Cressida muttered. "I still hate that damn metal, though."

"I know."

"I mean, how are we supposed to prevent anyone from using it ever? Even if we stop the emperor and Paragon now, what about in five years? Ten? A few decades? Someone else might get it!"

Astrea sighed. "People who want to do bad things will always find a way." That thought didn't exactly make her feel any better, because Cressida was right. How might someone use aetherium in the future? "At least we can try to do some good now."

"If you say so."

"You think this isn't good?" Astrea asked.

"I'm just grumpy. Between that and not knowing what to say to my parents, and all this damn travel . . . The worst part is that I still like the work I do there sometimes," Cressida said. "It's just nice to be free from the expectations for once."

Astrea didn't see any choice but for Cressida to come clean to her parents about it. But now also really wasn't the best time, especially because they didn't actually know if they'd be successful. If they'd even stop the emperor. There may not have even been any Lodestar to go back to once this finished.

"I wish you'd told me sooner, Cress," Astrea said. "You know you can always tell me that stuff, right?"

"I know." Her words strained as she lowered her voice even more and said, "You've been through a lot though, Az. I couldn't just put that on you."

"I don't want what I'm going through to mean you suffer in silence."

"Me? Suffer in silence?" Cressida laughed, a warm, genuine sound. "Ellie's been subjected to my complaints, don't worry."

"I'm sure she loved that."

"Yeah, well, what are friends for if not to lend an ear when they can?"

As silence settled over the two of them, met only by nature's nighttime songs, Astrea curled up in her chair. Hopefully Cressida would be able to tell her parents that she wanted a change in Kalama, and hopefully Lodestar and everything else their families had built would be standing by the time this was all done.

CHAPTER 46

She groaned.

"*Astrea!*"

She groaned again, rolling over to press her face against something hard and warm.

"*Astrea?*"

"Az?" Jin asked, just as a more feminine voice upstairs called, "Jin! Astrea!"

"Tired," Astrea whispered, burying her face into Jin's chest. Her whole body ached. Sleeping on the stone-hard cot and trying to share it with Jin had made sleeping nearly impossible. But it had been that or sleeping on the floor, which had seemed worse in the middle of the night.

"I know." He ran his hand down the back of her head, squeezing gently at the base of her neck. "Gotta get up. Time to leave. We can sleep on the way."

Mumbling a few curses his way, Astrea pushed off the cot and grabbed her knapsack off the floor. After a quick detour to the bathroom on the main floor, she was cleaned up and no more awake than she had been, but Jin shoved a coffee cup into her hands. She took it and swallowed a few sips.

"We got some extra fuel and food loaded into the trucks while you were sleeping," Rami said.

"There's another such safe house about a day's drive from here," Zojan said. "There should be more supplies there, but if not, there's a small town—Ragona—about a twenty minute drive from the house. You can restock there. And beyond that, another safehouse much closer to the Ring of Fire."

"Should we be stopping this much?" Lucian asked.

"Ragona is still about a day and a half drive from the edge of the Ring of Fire," Zephyrine said. "There's a tiny village a couple hours from the final safehouse, but Ragona's our last good chance to stock up. We'll set up at the safe house near the Badlands before we head in."

Just two and a half days and they'd be that much closer to Emperor Aelius's aetherium hunt. That much closer to stopping him. Astrea sipped her coffee again, trying to will herself awake. It did no good.

"Come, let's get you back on the road," said Zojan.

"So sorry if this has been an inconvenience," Lucian muttered.

"Like your existence is?" Zojan drawled.

Civan huffed. Astrea shot him a questioning look, but he merely shook his head.

"Be nice, Zojan," Rami warned. Rough irritation scraped Astrea's skin. "And you too, Luce. Zojan's done us a favor."

"Which means he'll want something," Lucian replied. "As always."

"That's how this business works," Zojan said. "Someone goes out on a limb for you, hides you away from *Emperor Aelius Auris*, they get to call in a similarly big favor someday."

"Make sure it's someday far in the future," Lucian said. "Hopefully I'm dead by then."

Jin gritted his teeth, but Zephyrine ushered him out the door. Astrea followed. Outside, only a few rays of sun tinged the horizon, barely visible through the thick tropical foliage.

"I told them to get it together yesterday," he said to Zephyrine. "You were there."

"Obviously there's some bad blood there," she said.

"Lucian assured me he could work with Rami on this mission. And now he's in there antagonizing both her and her brother."

"Let's just get back on the road," Zephyrine said. "If Lucian only has to be around Rami, maybe we can get him to keep his mouth shut."

Jin grunted.

As the others trickled out of the house—Lucian leading the way and Rami taking up the rear—Astrea set her hand on Jin's shoulder. That rough irritation still rolled off Rami, and it was spreading to the rest of the group. Their bodies ached; the more Astrea woke, the more her awareness doubled, tripled. It was going to be a brutal couple of days.

"Maybe Lucian's just grumpy," Astrea murmured to Jin. "If he's feeling everything I'm feeling, he's probably in a sour mood."

"Sour mood or not, we need to get on with the mission," Jin said. "We can't be distracted by their drama."

"Then maybe we should make them talk it out in the car."

"If he snaps like that again, I will." Jin shook his head. "Forcing a forty-year-old man to get his shit together. Just my luck."

Astrea couldn't help but smile a little at that.

Another full day in the truck, sleeping on another stone-hard cot between watch rotations at the next safe house, and still more time on the road had Astrea feeling completely unlike herself. She'd finally started feeling better, a little more like her old self, after all that had happened. And now, it was like she'd been deprived of sleep for days even though she'd been sleeping every chance she got.

But by late that night, they would be reaching the final safe house before they approached the edge of the Ring of Fire. If she could just hold on until then, she would get a longer break from the truck and a little more time to sleep. Maybe there'd even be a real bed. Or a sofa. She'd gladly take a sofa.

Her head was on Jin's shoulder. They'd rotated trucks at one point, mostly to break up Rami and Lucian. Now, they were with Cressida, Saros, and Lucian, while Rami stayed in Adi and Marko's truck.

"So, Commander Lucian . . ." Saros hesitated. "How long have you worked for the grand ducal family?"

Astrea sat up a little straighter. Saros? Initiating small talk? Lavender surprise arced out from Cressida. He was not one to make small talk if it could be avoided.

"For nearly fifteen years, Mister Sovna," Lucian replied.

"You can call me Saros."

"Fifteen years, Saros."

Astrea didn't know Lucian's exact age, but he was somewhere in his early forties, as was Saros. That would've put him close to Jin's age—maybe a little older—when he started working for the Novarian crown.

"I see. I wanted to work for Her Highness once upon a time, actually. To be a Stargazer in her employ. But life had other plans." Saros's gaze flicked to Astrea.

"As it sometimes does," Lucian said. "I was originally in the Novarian military and had a promising career there but ultimately transferred to the palace."

"What made you change course? If you don't mind my asking."

"It's a long story."

Saros gestured to the truck's rear cab. "And we have no place to go."

With a sigh, Lucian said, "After one failed engagement at a young age, I threw myself into my work. I met a woman—Rami—who was stationed at the same joint Novarian-Tornamian base as I was, deep in the southern Antare Mountains. Let's just say that we participated in some missions I gather Varojin would understand based on what I know of his time in the military."

Why was Lucian actually telling them this? Astrea glanced at Cressida, who shrugged almost imperceptibly.

"Rami and I got married soon after a quick romance, but things went south two years in when her brother started calling her more. She started putting in requests for leave far too frequently. Even her commanders were concerned."

"They just let her take that much leave?" Jin asked.

Lucian nodded. "She was always very good at convincing people. I eventually put in a leave request shortly after she left the last time, managing to convince the base commanders to let me go after my wife. I tracked her down and found her helping Zojan out of a very nasty situation he'd gotten himself into. He'd allied with a now-defunct gang in Thasia in a business deal that went wrong."

Maybe that explained Rami's more relaxed attitude when it came to the bandits they'd encountered on the train ride to Fort Sandstone. This connection her brother had to Tornama's more criminal elements . . .

"I helped them out of it, of course, but Zojan also saved my life that day. He promised I could pay him back somehow. I made Rami swear she'd never go back to helping her brother if he returned to that life, one of crime bosses and smugglers and general ne'er-do-wells. She promised."

Astrea could already see where this was going. Obviously Rami hadn't kept that promise, though now it seemed she was at least not working with any crime bosses.

"To make my long story short, Zojan called in his favor one day. Rami all but forced me to go to his aid. We were found out, arrested, and reprimanded by our commanders when we got shipped back to our base," Lucian said with a heavy sigh. "I was discharged for dishonorable conduct. I asked for a divorce that very same day. And two months later, after the divorce was granted, I received a letter summoning me to the palace. Grand Duchess Ysabel had heard of me from a few military officers, and though wary of my discharge, let me explain the situation. My reputation had been solid until that incident. And I guess she saw something worth taking a chance on, because here I am now."

"Rami doesn't seem like she's the type to get caught up with gangsters," Cressida said. "Not that I know her well but, I just don't imagine she'd be trying to help us if she allied with *that* kind of criminal element."

"She never did get that involved," Lucian said. "She was just trying to protect her brother. But she, too, found a new path. Life had other plans for her. Doing what she does now, and apparently with Zojan's help."

"Well, we'd probably be fucked if she wasn't helping us," Cressida said. "Him too."

"Perhaps," Lucian conceded with a long sigh.

"So maybe you need to put your past issues behind you," Jin said. "I'm sorry you got discharged that way, though. I know that must have hurt."

"It was a long time ago, Varojin."

"Doesn't mean it didn't hurt."

Lucian's silence seemed like another concession. After a while, when nobody spoke, he looked at Astrea and Jin and said, "I know you two haven't asked for my advice, but make sure you're honest with each other. Trust each other with your secrets, even family ones. I can't help but think what may have been avoided if Rami had just trusted me with her brother's issues in the first place. All three of us may have led different lives."

Did Lucian regret the divorce from Rami? Maybe not exactly, since there was so much bad blood between them, but did he regret what could have been? What they didn't have? Astrea frowned.

As silence reigned again, Saros tilted his head at Jin and Astrea, almost as if to say, "See? It wasn't that hard to make him talk." How he managed it, Astrea had no idea. Lucian never seemed to want to talk about himself.

The ride turned bumpy, then the truck swerved. Cressida and Saros swore. Jin kept Astrea pulled tight against him, bracing them both.

"Balthazar?" Lucian shouted.

"Think our tire went out!" Balthazar called back.

The truck stopped. Astrea's breathing turned shallow, and her pulse thundered through her entire body.

Cressida muttered something about "skies damned trucks" before unlocking the back doors and hopping to the ground. Outside, the landscape had changed from tropical forest to a much sparser landscape. The sun was high above them, beating down on the trucks with white hot intensity.

Astrea shaded her eyes as she followed Cressida outside. There was no void around, nor was there anyone else. They were alone.

Another string of curses left Cressida. She stood near the front left tire, near the driver's side. Balthazar hopped out from behind the steering wheel, rusty annoyance spiking high above his head as he also took in the damage.

"What happened?" Jin asked.

"Beats me. There wasn't anything in the road that should've caused it," Balthazar said.

The second truck had backed up and was now stopped a dozen feet away. Everyone was leaving that vehicle, too. Rami wandered over first.

"Can you fix it?" Jin asked Cressida.

"I *could* fix it if we weren't in the middle of fucking nowhere." Cressida threw her hands over her head. "I haven't seen any spares lying around."

"There are sometimes spares hidden under the floors in these trucks," Rami said. "We can check."

"And I don't suppose the commander or your brother would've packed us up some tire plugs and rubber cement?" Cressida asked Rami.

"Doubtful," she replied. "Give us a few minutes to check."

The others scattered, going to empty the trucks of their contents to check under the floors for spares. It seemed like a strange place to Astrea, but she wasn't exactly an expert when it came to these things.

Scrubbing at her face, Cressida let out a loud groan. "Fuck. Skies damn it, I just wanted to make it to the next stopping point."

"Anything?" Jin called to Adi.

"No!"

Cressida cursed again.

"There's nothing you can do, Cress?" Jin asked.

"No. Not without *something*. Where's the closest town?"

"Far," Zephyrine said, strolling up to them. "Too far."

"So . . . what now?" Astrea asked. "We all try to fit into one truck?"

"Wait!" Rami called. "We've got one! But it's small."

"Oh, good," Cressida muttered. "That's going to make this so wonderful."

With some effort, Balthazar and Jin got the spare tire pulled out of the truck and rolled over to where Cressida stood. She crossed her arms over her chest and shook her head. The replacement tire was, indeed, quite a bit smaller than the original.

"It'll work," she said, "but not well. We'll need to go a bit slower than we have been."

"But we can make it to the next safe house on it?" Jin asked.

"We can make it," Balthazar said.

"Then I guess we'd better get to work," Cressida said. "And nobody better complain. It's not going to be a fun ride."

Chapter 47

Cressida had warned them not to complain, and Astrea had managed to not utter a negative word during the slow, bumpy ride the rest of the day. But skies, she hated trucks.

Hated trucks, hated missions, hated everything.

The increasingly warm weather made the vehicles sweltering inside. And though Astrea had been spared riding in the truck with the too-small replacement tire, every bump in the road, combined with heat, had only resulted in Astrea growing nauseated. She would kill for a cold shower and real bed.

But as Balthazar finally pulled the truck up to the final safe house, Astrea was fairly certain she would get neither of those things. *Maybe* the cold shower if the stars had any luck to spare for her. It was just as small as the other two locations. At least it was empty.

"Fuck me," Astrea muttered as she jumped out of the back of the truck and into the humid but cooler night air. She'd never been so grateful for solid ground. Solid, unmoving, non-bumpy ground.

"We're alone," Lucian said to Jin as they both exited the vehicle. "No one here but us."

Jin shouldered both his and Astrea's knapsacks as he headed for the building. "Either way, let's not linger."

Sucking in one more deep breath, Astrea followed Jin and Lucian, leaving the others to unload themselves and stretch their aches away. The house was unlocked—still strange to Astrea, but the second safe house had been that way, too—and Jin led them inside.

It was much like the first two houses, basically a cabin in the middle of nowhere. Rustic, sure, but small, too. Small kitchen, small sitting room, two small bedrooms, a small bathroom. Even on watch rotations, the house was barely big enough for half the team.

As Astrea peeked into the bathroom, her shoulders sagged. A shower. She'd take a quick one, just five minutes, once everyone was settled inside and they'd figured out next steps.

Back in the kitchen, Jin, Lucian, and Zephyrine had spread a map of the region out on the narrow kitchen table. Everyone else was filing into the house one by one, their fatigue pressing heavily—painfully—into Astrea's bones. Gritting her teeth, she moved to stand next to Jin.

"We're right around here," Zephyrine said, pointing to a spot southeast of the Ring of Fire, the volcanic chain at the southern edge of the Badlands. "And if we follow this road"—her narrow finger traced a curving road northwest, into the Badlands—"we can begin our search."

"We don't know exactly where we're going?" Saros asked, squeezing past Cressida and Adi to join them near the table in the kitchen. Astrea stepped aside so he could look at the map.

"There are no bases out here that I know of," Zephyrine said, and Jin and Adi echoed her. "Anjou's contacts said it was somewhere near the border of the Ring of Fire, in the eastern half. They weren't exactly sure of where."

Zephyrine again traced the map with her fingertip. The volcanic region bordering the Badlands was expansive; even narrowing it down to the border of "the eastern half" would prove too much for them to search easily.

"Where were you searching for the ore for my father?" Jin asked Balthazar and Saros.

"Here," said Balthazar, tapping a spot east of Fort Blackrock.

"And here." Saros pointed to a spot farther north. "There, too." His pointer finger moved due south. "Maps in his office were marked up with potential locations all over the Badlands. Nothing I saw near the Ring of Fire, though."

"So," Lucian said, "we start scouting, see what we can find or if you can sense anything, Saros. It's a lot of ground to cover, but the emperor can't hide a large operation *that* easily."

"What if we break into Blackrock?" Adi asked. "He's likely funneling people through there on their way south. See if those commanders have any proof of his plans. Something."

"If we do that, we're going to need to tread very carefully," Jin said. "I'm sure my father will have warned his base commanders to be on the lookout for most of us."

"I can go," Marko said as he came up behind Adi. "Rami and I can go. They wouldn't know us."

Astrea pressed her lips together. It didn't seem like a good idea, sending just the two of them that far off course.

"How long would it take us to get to Blackrock?" Lucian asked.

"By car? A couple more days," Zephyrine said. "And we need two trucks if we're going to do this. Even if we just start scouting, we need two in good working order, not what we have now."

"And how are we going to get a better replacement?" Saros asked.

"We steal one," Zephyrine said. "Troops move through on the main roads all the time. We'll stage ours as broken down, flag them down for help, and ambush them."

Unease prickled Astrea's skin. It didn't feel right, ambushing random Helosians, even if they *were* the emperor's soldiers. What were the odds they even knew what Emperor Aelius was doing? Knew what was truly at stake?

"First thing in the morning, we get to work on that," Jin said to Zephyrine. "I'd rather not do that in the middle of the night."

The general nodded. "First light."

"Alright." Jin scratched at his beard. "Rest up, clean up. I'll figure out the watch rotation."

One by one, the team took showers while Astrea helped Cressida and Balthazar rummage through the safe house's cupboards. There wasn't much, but as Zojan had promised, there was a small canister of extra gasoline, and there was a bit of food. Mostly dried, cured meat and crackers, things to store easily. He'd sent them off with a box of that, too, the other morning.

It wasn't much, but at least they had that and running water. As people finished up in the bathroom, they returned to the kitchen to grab their measly dinner. The cycle continued on until finally, it was Astrea's turn to shower, the last one except for Lucian and Jin.

She closed the bathroom door behind her, groaning quietly as she took in the actual shower. She'd been too relieved before to see just how small it really was. It was barely large enough for her to turn around in.

Still, she turned the water on and wiggled out of her clothes. The water was freezing, shocking her awake. Her teeth chattered. But finally, the nausea was clearing her system. Food, a shower, and pulling her senses in for just a few minutes helped.

Just a couple more days, and they'd be where they needed to be. Just a couple more days. *Maybe we can even steal an airship to go back to Thasia,* she thought ruefully. Probably a terrible idea. But a girl could dream. She'd never take an airship for granted again.

She really didn't want to go back out to the group, nor did she want to sleep in a terribly dark room or stand watch out in the oppressive darkness of the forest. *Just do your job, Az.* With a resolute sigh, Astrea shut the water off and let her barrier loosen. Cold swept over her, prickling her skin and chilling her to her core.

"Jin!" she shouted, aggressively wiping the water off her body with the rough towel someone had left out for her. "Jin! Lucian!"

Not here. Not now.

Why now?

Scrambling out of the shower, Astrea started yanking her clothes on. Her heart beat wildly as more void mages popped into her awareness, six if she was counting right. Maybe more.

How could she have been so irresponsible? How selfish of her to shut herself off from the world, even for just a few minutes.

"Jin!" she yelled again, then tugged her under-armor dress over her head. She'd foolishly left her gear with her knapsack in the other room.

The bathroom door swung open just enough for Jin to get inside. His jaw was tight. "I know," he said before Astrea could utter a word. "Lucian's got eyes on them."

"Is it him?" Astrea asked.

"No."

If it wasn't Victor Nazarov, then who was it? Caliban? Her confused expression must have said everything, because Jin added, "Theo's back."

"Your Theo?"

"Unfortunately."

"Is Nazarov coming?"

"I don't know."

"I felt six jump in for sure," Astrea said as they left the bathroom. She tugged on her boots as quickly as she could manage. "How many?"

"Eight total, including Theo." As Astrea straightened, Jin put a hand on her shoulder and said, "They claim they only want to talk to us, Az. They said it's crucial they speak with us, especially you."

For just a moment, Astrea let her eyes close. She didn't want to know what this was. She didn't. She just wanted them to leave her alone.

But that obviously wasn't going to happen.

Squaring her shoulders, Astrea headed for the front door. Jin was just half a step behind her.

Outside, the rest of their group had surrounded Theo and the void mages. Saros had summoned a brilliant light, letting it hang over the trespassers. Clouds darkened the sky, and far in the distance, south near the ocean, lightning flashed.

"Astrea," Theo Kadis called, "I'm so sorry if we caught you at a bad time." He sounded . . . genuine.

He looked every bit the same as he had the last time she'd seen him. The gray-brown curls, his glasses, the friendliness that seemed to always permeate the air around him. Cold pulsed out from the six void mages behind him, the feeling hitting Astrea in slow, steady beats. The short woman standing next to Theo was no void mage, open for Astrea to read. She radiated a dizzying mix of anxiety and excitement. All of them dressed in black, but no masks.

No masks?

"What do you want?" Astrea folded her arms across her chest.

"To speak with you, urgently," Theo said. "We need your help."

A strangled laugh escaped Astrea before she could stop it. "You need *my* help?" she asked. "Why would I help you?"

"You are the moon," said the woman next to Theo. That voice . . .

"Ninette?" Astrea whispered.

The woman smiled. Astrea had never seen her face before; she was an average woman, with pale white skin, round cheeks, and a small nose.

"Yes, Astrea," Ninette said. "And the truth has been revealed. That you are not just our moon but our new One."

Chills took over Astrea's body, and she shuddered.

"Victor has finally told us the truth," said Theo. "That you were The One's niece, that Valen was your father."

"It is our tradition that our leaders are Dreamwalkers, not Souleaters," said Ninette. "But you are the moon, and you are his last blood on this earth, and we need you now. We've been trying to find you."

Astrea took half a step back, bumping into Jin. She searched the circle for Saros, finding his concerned gaze.

Valen.

That was her father? The One's brother?

"No," Astrea said.

"Please, Astrea, just listen—" said Theo.

"She said no." Jin's voice was cold.

"But Victor has lost his mind," Theo said. "I always knew his methods were unorthodox, even when we started working together at the winter solstice, but with The One's death and Tovan's death, something in him has changed. I fear the worst."

"I already told you I'd never help you," Astrea said. "I don't care if he's lost his mind. Our values don't align." An understatement, but the truth nonetheless.

"Please." Ninette's voice strained. "We do not want Advocate Nazarov as our leader, but he has convinced some that his way is the true path. It is not. We need your help. We do not want what he wants, and with the moon as our One, we can get away from him."

Astrea finally unfolded her arms, trying to stand taller as she stared down not just Ninette but Theo. She desperately wanted to lean into Jin, grab his hand, something, but she forced herself to remain still.

"Oh, my." Ninette gasped. Lavender surprise and teal approval twined around her, bright under Saros's summoned spotlight. "Oh, my, please tell me, have the sun and moon united as one?"

The same colors filtered around Theo for half a heartbeat.

"We are not this sun and moon," Jin said coldly.

"They have," Ninette said, ignoring him. She turned over her shoulder to the void mages. "They have united, look at their hands! The sun and moon are one!"

As soon as the void mages moved, trying to get a better look, the earth rumbled. Dirt and rock swelled up, tightening around their legs and all the way up to their waists. Balthazar's extended hands balled into fists.

"What reasoning could you possibly have for this except as some kind of ill-plotted trick?" asked Jin, attention fixed on Theo. "Telling me that Nazarov's gone too far isn't good enough, nor is Astrea's apparent heritage."

Theo pushed his shoulders back and lifted his chin. "Those things are both true, but you're right, there is more than that." When Jin gestured for him to continue, he said, "Victor knows there is a schism within our ranks. He's begun talking about finding a way to legitimize his rule." Theo glanced at Astrea. "Through whatever means necessary."

"Meaning?" Lucian snapped.

"If he must kill Miss Sovna, he's prepared to do so," Theo said. With another heavy sigh, he said, "Or continue Tytas Ramkas's bloodline."

Surprise, confusion, anger—they all bled into the night, a nauseating mix of colors and pain in Astrea's bones. Her throat constricted.

Continue Tytas Ramkas's bloodline.

"And I must warn you both, he is more interested in the second if it means bringing peace within the Paragon," Theo finished.

"But we do not want to separate the sun and moon," Ninette said quickly. "We will never support him!" Murmurs of agreement filtered out from the void mages behind her.

Astrea's stomach turned violently. She spun on her heel and retched all over the ground behind her, gagging as her meager dinner left her and all that remained was bile. Jin was beside her in a second, holding her braid back.

Was Nazarov's plan to capture her again and force her to bear a child? Was that why he'd demanded to meet her in the mountains? Was that what he'd meant about them having plans to discuss? That she was touched by the void?

If what Ninette said was true, Astrea bearing him a child didn't seem like that would fix anything. But maybe it was only a small fraction of them not keen on following Nazarov. Maybe he thought it would fix enough.

"Az?" Jin whispered.

When she peeked up at him, all Astrea could see was the steel pain and orange fear twining around his limbs and obscuring those beautiful eyes.

Chest heaving, she wiped her mouth with the back of her hand, then forced herself to turn back around to look at Theo. It took all of her willpower to look him in the eye and not focus on the colors dancing around the team.

"Why should I believe you?" Astrea hated the way her voice trembled. "All Nazarov's ever tried is to bend me to his will, and you seemed keen on helping him do just that not long ago."

"I would never lie to you about this," Theo said. "I believe that balance must be restored, yes. And I know all of you can see that"—he briefly looked over each shoulder at the team—"otherwise you would not be trekking through Helosia to try to stop Emperor Aelius."

"What could you possibly know about that?" Jin asked.

"I know you know of the power the meteorite has by now," Theo said. "It's the only thing that makes sense. Victor knows, too. He wants that metal just as much as the emperor."

Jin crossed his arms. "And you don't?"

"As I said, I believe balance must be restored," Theo said. "But what Victor wants to do is . . . what he's *now* proposing is just as bad as every other empire on this continent. He's no better than your father, and he is not what the Paragon or the world needs. His recent bombings and his plans for Astrea are proof enough."

"Give us something more," Jin said, "and maybe I'll start to believe you."

Tapping Theo's shoulder, Ninette pushed up on her toes and whispered something in his ear. He squinted, then nodded.

"You're here to look for the meteorite," Theo said. "I will tell you where we know the emperor is working."

"In the Ring of Fire," said Zephyrine. "We already know."

"We've been trying to monitor Aelius's movements," Theo said. "Now, I'm going to reach into my pocket. It's for a map. Nothing more."

When Jin nodded, Theo slowly reached into his jacket pocket. Paper crinkled, and he pulled out a folded-up square. He offered it up to Jin, but Zephyrine stepped forward and snatched it. She unfolded the map, then brought it over to Jin. He frowned.

Astrea couldn't bring herself to look. She kept her focus trained on Ninette, on those void mages. This could all just be a trick. She knew that. She knew that, and even though her heart was in knots and her stomach was threatening to rebel again, she held firm.

"If this checks out," Jin finally said, "we'll consider opening talks to some kind of agreement with you, Theo."

"Oh, come now, Jin—"

"That's my only offer. I suggest you take it."

Theo peered down at Ninette, and she nodded vigorously.

"Alright," he said. "Consider what we've told you. Go see this operation for yourselves. We'll be in touch."

One by one, the void mages jumped away in puffs of shadow. One grabbed onto Ninette, the other onto Theo, and then they, too, were gone.

Gone. Every single one of them.

Leaving Astrea, Jin, and the rest of the team in stunned silence. Saros's light waned.

Setting a hand on Astrea's shoulder, Jin whispered, "Az—"

She ran back into the house, barely making it to the bathroom in time as what little remained in her stomach forced its way up her throat.

Continue Tytas Ramkas's bloodline.

She could never let that happen.

Chapter 48

Astrea didn't know how long she spent on the hard bathroom floor, dry heaving over the toilet. Cressida rubbed big, smooth circles on her back. Outside, Jin periodically barked orders. Part of Astrea wanted him in there with her, too, but the other was glad he was taking charge and figuring out what to do.

She sure couldn't.

Continue Tytas Ramkas's bloodline. Theo's words ran circles in her mind, spiraling into oblivion and dragging Astrea down with them. She needed to get control back, not let those words haunt her.

Had Nazarov known all along that Astrea was The One's niece? Had that been his plan after first trying to kill The One? Keep Astrea in that house and in some sick, twisted move to establish power, make her birth some kind of heir? Something to legitimize him as the next leader among those more faithful to The One's vision and heritage?

What if that had been The One's plan, too? He'd threatened to break her down, to transform her into someone who would help the Paragon. What if he'd intended all along to mold her into some kind of successor of his, perhaps even force her to continue the bloodline, too? Maybe elevate someone in the Paragon's ranks by having them be the father?

Her stomach turned and tumbled again, but there was nothing left. All Astrea did was cough and rest her head against the cold porcelain toilet. A few tears rolled down her cheeks.

"Az?" Cressida asked. In all the years they'd been friends, Astrea had never heard Cressida's voice be so quiet.

"I'm sorry." Sitting up straight, Astrea wiped at her tears. "I'm sorry. We have things to do. Does Jin need help?"

"Hey." Cressida tugged on Astrea's hand as she tried to stand, pulling her back down. "He doesn't need help right now. Let the military folks deal with the military things. What's going on with you?"

"That was why he wanted me to go to the mountains to meet him," Astrea whispered. "What if that was what he was planning to do the whole time, Cress? What if he always knew? And that was his plan?"

Rough hesitation scraped Astrea's skin, but words began tumbling out of her mouth and didn't stop.

"What if he always knew I was Tytas Ramkas's descendant and that Jin was a Sunreaper? He knew Jin and I were together. He knew. What if he was going to . . . and tell Jin, set him off on some kind of . . ."

"Hey." Cressida pulled Astrea into a tight hug. "Hey, I get it, okay? I get it. But that didn't—" She swallowed hard. "That didn't happen. Right?"

Black dots swirled in Astrea's vision. "I don't know. There's so much I can't remember. I never even thought . . ."

Cressida squeezed her tighter. "Theo said Nazarov has *begun* talking about those options, right? So I think we can assume he didn't know any of this until recently."

"Why is this happening?" Astrea buried her face in Cressida's neck. "Why is this happening to me?"

"I don't know." Cressida stroked Astrea's hair. "I'm sorry, Az. I don't know. I wish I could make it all stop."

"And all I can think about is how it affects me."

Cressida pulled back then, anger jabbing Astrea's arms once, twice. "Look at me, Az." Astrea forced herself to look up into her best friend's eyes, that vibrant jade, as she continued, "I love you, but you're being far too hard on yourself. It *does* affect other people, but *you're* the target. I can't even begin to imagine what this feels like. Be a little selfish. Focus on you."

The bathroom door creaked open, then Jin poked his head inside. "Az? Cress?"

"Did you get everyone organized?" Cressida asked him.

"All set," Jin said. "Lucian's going to stand watch all night just in case Theo or any of the Paragon try to come back. Marko too. Asked if you could make them some coffee, Cress."

Cressida disentangled herself from Astrea and slipped out the door past Jin. He took her place, closing the door and sitting on the floor with Astrea. There was even less space with him in there, and had she had the heart, she would've laughed at how silly he looked trying to sit there with her, all long limbs and nowhere to go. But he didn't even seem bothered; he just pulled her into his lap, holding her close.

"I'm fine," she whispered.

"You're a terrible liar," he said, still crushing her to him. "Please don't pretend you're fine. I'm not. I feel terrible right now."

"Really?" Astrea sensed nothing from him, just that heavy, desperate wall.

"Would you believe me if I said I considered asking Theo to take me to Nazarov tonight just so I could kill him?"

"Yes."

"If he comes anywhere near you ever again, it will be the last time." Jin pushed her off his chest, tilting her chin up to force her to look at him. "It will be the *last* time. He will not kill you, he will not take you, he will not touch you. Do you understand?"

Astrea barely nodded.

"I've made sure every single person out there knows that, too. Victor Nazarov is kill on sight. No hesitation. I don't care who does it as long as someone takes him out."

Astrea barely nodded again.

"I mean it, Az."

"I know."

And she did. She knew that as long as Jin had air left in his lungs, he would do everything in his power to stop Nazarov.

"Do you think Theo was being truthful?" she asked.

He nodded. "At least about that. Obviously Theo misled me for a long time, but everyone has their limits."

"Ninette, that woman he was with, was the one who watched me while they had me. I don't think that's a line she would cross, murder and—"

"I don't think so either." Holding her face in his hands, Jin wiped a few stray tears away with his thumbs. "As soon as we're done with things down here, we're finding Nazarov and taking him down. Let the other powers deal with my father."

Leaning in, Astrea pressed her lips to his. Gentle, chaste. But Jin's slow, burning kiss pulled her in and didn't let her go.

"I love you, Az," he whispered, leaning his forehead against hers. "I'm going to keep you safe."

"And I love you. So much."

"I know." With a smile, Jin kissed her again, then said, "Lucian wants to start planning to scout out this apparent excavation site."

"Then let's go."

With Jin's help, Astrea finally got up off the bathroom floor. She smoothed her braid, then the front of her dress, and followed him into the kitchen. Lucian, Zephyrine, Saros, Marko, and Adi were all there.

What, had Jin sent the twins and Rami out to stand watch first? What about Balthazar? Cressida?

Saros tried to catch Astrea's eye as she joined the others around the kitchen table. But she couldn't bring herself to face him, not after what they'd just heard. He still didn't know anything about what had happened months ago. He had no idea what Nazarov had already done.

"If we leave first thing in the morning, we should be able to get to this location early afternoon tomorrow," Zephyrine said, drawing an invisible line between their safe house and the spot Theo had marked on the map he'd provided. "If what Theo says is true, then by the time we get back here tomorrow night, we can start to figure out next steps."

"I should go with you," Saros said. "To help you determine if it's truly aetherium or something else. As should Balthazar."

"As should a Lightbringer," Lucian said. "Astrea?"

Embarrassment swept through Astrea like an uncontrolled wave, almost disorienting. To admit this out loud, and to Lucian—to Saros—of all people . . .

"I don't think I should go," she said. "Not until I get my head on straight. I can't guarantee that will be by the morning."

"A wise choice," he said. "You'll be alright here?"

"Yes." Astrea wasn't sure she could focus on a mission to Emperor Aelius's supposed camp, but she could at least keep an eye on things at the safe house.

"Then I'll go," Lucian said. "But I'll need some rest tonight. I had planned—"

"I can do it," Astrea said. "You sleep tonight."

"If you take the first watch, I'll get up a couple hours before sunrise," Lucian offered. "I'll make sure everyone's up before we leave."

"Then it's settled," Zephyrine said. "Lucian, Saros, Balthazar, and I will go."

"Just you four?" Adi asked.

"Best to keep the party small," the general replied. "And maybe you can figure out how to get us a new tire on the second truck."

"Oh, boy." Adi's sarcasm was palpable, thick in the air.

"Let's all just get some rest," Lucian said. "Astrea, wake me two hours before sunrise."

After a quick dismissal, Astrea headed out onto the front porch with Jin. Bugs and frogs croaked in discord with each other, a cacophony that grated on Astrea's fried nerves. She sat down on the front steps, pulling her knees up to her chest.

There was no void here, not anymore. No void mages surrounded by their team. No Theo Kadis or Ninette standing there, just a dozen steps from where Astrea now sat.

Draping his arm around Astrea's shoulders, Jin pulled her into his side. He pressed a kiss to the top of her head. He didn't say anything. There wasn't anything to say. Not now, anyway. She might want to talk more about it later, but just sitting there with him for the time being was nice.

Lennor's occasional quiet chatter met Astrea's ears, but she couldn't see the Tempest. She peered around, out into the darkness, but still saw nothing.

"They're on the roof," Jin said.

"Oh."

"It's a good vantage point."

"Sure."

None of the others had come out of the house, but Astrea figured Jin had put them on a different watch shift. They sat like that for a while, Astrea staring up at the stars any time they appeared between breaks in the clouds. Thunder rumbled far in the distance.

A tangle of heavy anxiety pulsed in the air, then a throat cleared behind them. "Varojin, may I speak with Astrea?" Saros asked.

Jin glanced down at Astrea, and she nodded. He headed back into the house, leaving them alone. As Saros walked across the creaky porch, Astrea turned back to look out at the darkness. He sat on Astrea's other side from where Jin had been.

"That was unexpected tonight," Saros said.

"Yes."

Void mages showing up didn't come as much of a surprise to Astrea anymore. But Theo's apparent split from Nazarov was a surprise. Ninette's appearance. Somehow getting tracked down here, all the way across the continent from where Astrea thought the Paragon still were. How had they done so? The voices in her dreams, the ones asking for help . . . had that been them? Tracking her? Trying to find her, as Ninette had said?

Would she ever be able to outrun the void mages? Live away from them, without any of them following her?

Even if Jin was right, that they would get Nazarov and put an end to him, that still left them with a very obvious, major problem: the Paragon who believed Astrea was their new leader.

People who believed that as a descendant of Tytas Ramkas, she was some kind of Paragonian royalty. That continuing the bloodline was important to bring on the next generation of leadership.

They have united, look at their hands! The sun and moon are one! Ninette's words flashed through Astrea's mind unbidden. That nausea returned, bubbling up Astrea's throat and choking her.

Yes, being forced into that role by Nazarov would be unimaginable torture.

But knowing these people believed Astrea and Jin were some kind of prophesized pair . . .

What did that mean about their future together?

Astrea and Jin had never talked definitively about someday having a family, just that they both shared the hope they would take that step. That day seemed impossibly far away with all the threats they faced. And even if it weren't for those threats, Astrea still wouldn't want to take those steps for years. That was why they were so careful now, ensuring that Jin had his mavustro herbs every day, that he always had plenty of supply on hand.

But could they have a family, knowing these people were out there? What if they never stopped all of the Paragon? If Astrea and Jin ever had a child, would they also become a target? The next One, as Ninette kept saying?

Astrea's breath hitched.

Being put in this position, elevated to this strange pedestal without ever being asked . . . All she'd ever done was keep her head down, try to be a good friend and good person. But because of old history and vendettas, long-dead rulers and the sins of her long-lost father, the Paragon were not only stealing her present but her future, too.

It scared her, yes, but it also infuriated her. It was not fair. It was not right. And worst of all, she still never seemed to truly feel safe anymore.

But when had she ever? That wasn't fair, either.

"When we were in the Islands, I asked you if you were alright," Saros said quietly. "I know you're not alright, my dear." He reached for both of her hands. "What happened? How did you know that woman?"

Fresh tears pricked Astrea's eyes.

A part of Astrea just wanted to lean into her uncle's once-familiar hug and cry, tell him all that had happened. But as she even thought about speaking those words, her chest and throat tightened to the point she couldn't breathe.

She couldn't tell him. She just couldn't.

And she couldn't tell him here, now, with so many people around. All these people, most of whom knew just part of the story.

Nobody really knew. Nobody knew the worst of it.

How could they? How could they know the pain she felt when Nazarov, Solana, and Tovan had shown up in her cell?

How could they know the terror she'd endured in those tunnels when she'd thought Nazarov and Tovan were going to take her back to her prison?

How could they know the bone-deep betrayal and sadness she'd felt, thinking everyone had abandoned her?

How could any of them know?

Jin was the only one who knew even a fraction of any of that. And even then, there was so much she hadn't been able to tell him. He'd gotten bits and pieces of it out of her, usually in the middle of the night, whispered between tears and nightmares.

Astrea buried her face in her trembling hands as her tears spilled hot and fast down her cheeks. She sucked in one shaky breath, then another, willing herself to calm. Lennor and Civan were just above them on the roof. Everyone else must have been inside. And if she let loose the deep wail building in her chest, they would all know.

They would know she still couldn't talk about it, still held onto those feelings, still hadn't really moved on.

And they had a mission to complete. Not just the scouting in the morning but a mission that could mean the difference between thousands of deaths and . . . not.

Astrea had to hold it together. She had to hold it together, just for a little while longer.

When they'd stopped the emperor from getting his hands on the aetherium, she would let herself break. She would tell Saros. She would tell Saros, Balthazar, and Sarsali. Maybe not the details but at least the general story. She wanted and needed their support.

Saros set his hand on her shoulder. "Astrea?"

Sniffling, Astrea lowered her hands and clasped them together in her lap. "We've had multiple encounters with the void mages," she said quietly. "Some more violent than others. That woman, Ninette, is one of the quieter Paragon members. She truly believes I am the moon in their prophecy, almost in a reverent way."

"I see."

"It's just a lot. Seeing her again, this news Theo had . . . I don't even know what to believe, what's real or what's a trick."

"Particularly disturbing news on all counts," Saros murmured. "Varojin has assured me that Nazarov won't get near you."

Astrea swallowed hard. Nazarov had already gotten near her so many times. The Whiskey Dream. Emperor Aelius's dinner party. Capturing her. The night club in Talmaris. The airship attack near Irvina.

She wasn't sure she could survive him again.

"The team will do what needs to be done to stop him and the emperor," Astrea said, her voice thick with false belief. She hated lying to Saros, but he couldn't become any more distracted than the night's events would already make him. "It's just hard to hear, that's all. I'll be fine tomorrow."

Saros squeezed her shoulder. "Promise me you'll get some rest while we're gone?"

"I promise."

"Good. I'll go get Varojin." Saros squeezed her shoulder again, then stood and crossed the creaky porch.

"Uncle?" Astrea said over her shoulder.

"Yes, my dear?"

"Could you ask him to bring some coffee out with him?"

Saros smiled. "Of course. Anything else?"

"No, thank you."

As Saros disappeared into the house, Astrea turned back to the thick darkness. *Someday*, Astrea promised herself. Someday she would find the strength to tell Saros and the rest of her family. Someday she would let go of her anger and pain and fear. Someday, when she was ready and able.

Even if the day before had been a mess, Astrea was grateful for two things: fewer people pressing in against her senses and a decently comfortable bed to share with Jin.

She still didn't feel very good at all after what Theo had revealed the night before, nor did she love the thought of Saros and Balthazar trying to confirm Theo's intel about Emperor Aelius, but things didn't seem *as* bad in the light of the new day.

"Alright, team," Adi said, slamming his hands flat against the kitchen table, "we have work to do today."

Jin arched an eyebrow. He sat next to Astrea at the table, nursing a coffee. "Lay low and wait for the others to get back?"

"No, fix up the second truck." Adi rolled his eyes. "Honestly, I expected *you* to be more on top of this."

"It's been a long night, Adi."

Astrea hadn't gotten all that much sleep, maybe a couple hours in total. And though Jin hadn't said it, she'd felt him awake most of the night, too, even when their watch shift was over. Had felt him holding onto her a little tighter than usual.

They hadn't talked about Theo's claims any more. And maybe they didn't need to right that second. They could set aside some time to talk once they actually wrapped things up in Helosia.

"Well, maybe a little physical labor will help wake you up," Adi said. "Where's Cress?"

"Here," came Cressida's sleepy response. She strolled down the short hallway that led to one of two bedrooms in the small house. "Can't a girl at least have a cup of coffee before she gets assigned work?"

"Rami and Marko are already outside looking at it," Adi said. "Let's get to it."

"How do *you* have so much energy, Adi?" Astrea asked. "It's not like you got much more sleep than the rest of us."

"He's always like this when there's a task in front of him." Jin stood, stretching his arms out wide with a groan. "Learned to stay focused in the field very quickly."

"Damn right I did." Adi scooped his coffee cup off the nearby kitchen counter, then headed for the front door.

Pushing her shoulders back, Astrea followed him out of the house. Lucian and the others had taken not just the truck with four good tires but also most of the extra supplies with them. They'd be gone well into the night, which left the rest of them plenty of time to figure out how to fix the second truck.

Marko and Rami circled the vehicle, arguing in Novarian as they pointed to the small spare tire and the forest beyond them. At the sight of the rest of them, though, they stopped bickering.

Cressida wandered toward the truck, her posture rigid. Orange spiked around her, bright against the early morning sky. The previous night's clouds had cleared, and now, morning birds sang their songs. Coffee clutched in one hand, Cressida extended the other in front of her, muscles and fingers relaxed.

"Well?" Adi asked Marko, passing him his mug.

Marko took a healthy drink, then said, "I think the original suggestion Zephyrine had to stage a breakdown is probably our best bet. There's really no other alternative, unless we want to try to drive back to the last town we saw—if we can even call it that—and see if we can get it replaced."

On their way to the safe house after losing one of their tires, they'd passed the tiniest of towns, just a few buildings. Everything had been closed, and nobody had wanted to risk stopping at that point. Zephyrine had said it was small, but it was *barely* a village.

"The last town was nearly two hours away with a *good* set of tires," Adi said.

"Exactly." Marko took another sip of coffee.

Cressida lowered her hand. "Truck's structure is fine if you do want to drive. Just won't be a comfortable or efficient ride."

Rusty annoyance flowed through the group, accompanied by the heavy fog of exhaustion Astrea couldn't shake. Whether it was more hers or her friends', she wasn't entirely sure, and it didn't matter anyway.

"Won't some kind of ambush just send up red flags in the area?" Astrea asked. "What if we rob the wrong person and they're expected somewhere, or manage to go tell someone? It seems to me it's going to create more problems than it solves."

"We need gas, too," Marko said.

"Do we have enough to get far at all?" Jin asked.

"Far enough to get back to that town, but that's it," Marko said. "I imagine Lucian will be using most of the extra fuel we had on his journey today."

"We're fucked either way, then," Jin said. "We have to go to town."

"Pretty much, unless whomever we rob happens to have extra fuel," Marko said.

Rami shrugged. "They might, driving through these parts."

Astrea's head hurt. She pinched the bridge of her nose, rubbing at her tired eyes. "So, what, we all go to town?"

"You and I can't," Jin said. "Cress can't. If my father had Wanted posters of you two up in Kalama, there's no way he hasn't spread those across the empire."

"And Kaius may have put out arrest warrants for Civan and Lennor by now," Adi said. Yellow worry sparked around him. "Me too, I guess."

"So, what, Rami and I go alone?" Marko asked.

"Can you handle it alone?" Jin asked.

"Of course we can handle it," Rami said. "Just what do you take me for, Your Imperial Highness? An amateur?"

"No disrespect meant, Rami," Jin said with a tight smile. "But I don't know your background very well, and I don't like the idea of the team being so split up."

"The way I see it, there's not much of a choice," Rami said. "We try one of our plans. If it fails, we try the other."

"Skies, I hate this," Jin muttered. His tight, desperate wall from the night before was gone, replaced by rough frustration and cool understanding. "Fine. Marko and Rami, you two go back to the last town we saw. If you need supplies before then, do what you have to do, but be discreet."

"That won't be a problem." Rami flicked her braid over her shoulder and headed toward the house. "Just let me get the money."

"You sure you're good with this, Marko?" Jin asked as the front door slammed behind the smuggler.

Marko shrugged. "As Rami said, we don't have a choice."

"I know."

"We'll make it work." He smiled tightly, first at Adi, then at Astrea. "Just take care while we're gone, yeah?"

Marko passed his empty coffee cup to Adi just as Rami returned, her knapsack slung over her shoulder. Adi gave Marko's forearm a small squeeze.

"We'll be back by nightfall," Rami called as she circled the truck. "And if we're not, well, don't send my ex-husband after me. Marko and I will find our way back."

"Good luck," Adi whispered.

"Thanks," Marko said. "I suppose we'll be needing it."

Marko climbed into the driver's seat. After a few moments, the engine roared to life. And then they were off, rumbling down the hidden drive and disappearing around the corner of the thick forest.

All day, Astrea tried to both distract herself and focus. Distract herself by focusing. Anything to stop Theo's words from running circles in her mind.

After all, there was nothing to be done about it in the meantime. She hadn't told Saros about all she'd been through because she wanted him to be focused on the mission. And she needed to be focused, too.

There wasn't all that much for them to do while they waited for everyone else to return. At Jin's insistence, they took naps in turns, just a couple of hours each. That had helped Astrea feel a bit better, more like she was grounded in the world around her. And it had allowed her to sleep off the worst side effects of healing a headache Cressida had.

Sitting out in the hot southern Helosian sun all day hadn't done anything to help Astrea's mood, so she'd spent much of the day indoors, where it was at least cooler. And it didn't change how far her awareness spread; the house was too small to make much of a difference. Nobody could approach without her knowing.

After rationing out some dinner, they gathered in the kitchen and sitting room, all six of them. It was too much on Astrea's senses in such close quarters, the warring anxiety and calm, worry and suspicion. She breathed in deep and held it for a few seconds before letting it out slowly.

"You know," Cressida said around a mouthful of dried meat, "if I'd known this was our future, I would've made sure to fill up on all my favorites before we left Kalama. I miss the fried ravioli at Ravintola, Az." She chugged water from a canteen, then said, "I mean, skies."

"What's Ravintola?" Lennor asked.

The twins had both been quiet all day, so unlike how Lennor, at least, used to be at the old base in Novaria. Civan's stillness was more in line with his usual demeanor.

He snapped a small square of chocolate off from the bar in front of him. He must've brought it from Talmaris, but Astrea had no idea how it had survived the heat.

"Obviously it's a restaurant," he said to his sister. He caught Astrea's eye, then broke off another square of chocolate and silently offered it to her. She took it, and popped it in her mouth, letting the sweet treat melt on her tongue.

Lennor rolled her eyes. "*Obviously.*"

"It's this little place near my parents' house in Kalama," Cressida said. "It's been there for decades. Really good cocktails. And fried ravioli. And espresso. Oh, and this mango sorbet they sometimes make in the summer."

"Now you're just making the rest of us hungry," Adi said with a laugh.

"You went there a lot?" Lennor asked.

"Az and I used to go pretty often, yeah." Cressida grinned at Astrea and Jin. "I caught those two on a date there before we left Kalama."

"What?" Adi asked. "Really?"

"It wasn't a date," Astrea said.

"I do not trust your judgment at all," Cressida replied. "Jin?"

"Maybe not one in the traditional sense . . ." Jin smiled down at Astrea, that soft, secret smile. "We did go for a drink. After nearly kissing for the first time."

"Yes, but we were there to discuss all this void nonsense, and then you invited Cress to sit with us when she showed up," Astrea said. "I don't think inviting a friend into the evening still qualifies it as a date."

"*Still* qualifies it?" Lennor asked.

"Yeah, Az, sounds like Jin and Cress are right," Adi said with a grin.

"Whatever." Astrea rested her elbows on the table and slumped forward. The weight of Adi's amusement pressed down on her, not the worst feeling but overwhelming in that moment.

"Well, this Ravintola sounds good," Lennor said. "I'd like to go."

"I'll take you someday," Cressida said without missing a beat. Her aura immediately lit up with magenta embarrassment, the heat washing over Astrea a second later.

Lennor smiled shyly, then nudged Cressida's shoulder with her own. "I'd like that."

"Do they have regular ravioli?" Civan asked. "Fried sounds odd."

"Yeah, they do," Cressida said with a smile.

Their chatter continued on like that, mostly between Lennor, Cressida, and Adi. Jin chimed in occasionally, especially when the conversation focused on Kalama's restaurant scene again.

Eventually, Astrea felt her eyelids growing heavier. *Not a chance, Az,* she silently scolded herself. She'd promised Lucian she would watch over things here. *Do your job.* Pushing out of her seat, Astrea went to the small pour-over coffee maker sitting on the counter.

"Do any of you want—" A chorus of yeses cut her off, so Astrea got to work preparing a large pot. Based on the remaining beans, it seemed they'd likely only have enough for one more pot, maybe two, after she made this one. Not ideal, but they'd survive.

As the coffee percolated, Astrea leaned against the counter and crossed her arms over her abdomen. Adi said something that made everyone else laugh. Peach amusement flared in the air. Astrea tried not to wince. It wasn't even a bad feeling, but her nerves were on fire. It was all too much.

A soft hand on her shoulder made Astrea look up, where she found Jin.

"I'm fine," she whispered. "Tired."

"I know." He frowned. He and Civan were the only ones in the room Astrea couldn't read. Jin's hand settled between her shoulder blades, then tilted his head toward the nearly ready coffee. "Let's take ours outside."

Jin prepared two cups for them—just coffee, no sugar or cream to add—and picked them up. "Az and I are going outside," he said. "Help yourselves."

"Terrible service," Cressida joked. "You won't be getting much gratuity with the bill."

"Getting tired of our wonderful company?" Adi called as Jin headed for the front door.

Jin turned over his shoulder. "Very much so!"

More of that amusement settled against Astrea's skin, warm and bright, as she followed Jin. He gestured for her to sit, but she paced a little ways away from the house, grateful for the distance from everyone's energy. Her shoulders sagged. Jin followed her and passed her one of the coffee cups. The ceramic was scalding.

"It's just a lot," she said before he could ask her anything. "Feeling everything. Not being able to let go of it for a little while. It reminds me of—" Well, it reminded her of all the years of her life when she'd had very little control over her lightbringing. "It's a lot."

"The good news is that we should just need you to do this for a few more days," Jin said. "Maybe you and Lucian can take turns after tonight, give both of yourselves a reprieve from it all."

"Yeah, maybe."

Astrea hated the thought of closing herself off at all, especially after what had just happened with Theo's reappearance. Sure, she'd been trying to give herself a break so she could stay sharp, and sure, she wouldn't have been able to do anything differently with the news Theo had shared if she'd been open the whole time, but it just felt . . . wrong.

The stillness at the edges of her senses shifted, subtle at first but then exploding with anxiety and a throbbing pain in the side of her head, her arm, her shoulder.

"I think Rami and Marko are back," Astrea said. "And someone's hurt."

"Adi!" Jin called. "Len—"

Everyone else was quick to come out of the house, arriving just as a familiar truck—no longer lopsided—pulled around the bend. Rami was driving. Astrea couldn't see Marko, though she felt him. Or, she *thought* it was Marko.

Rami parked the truck just steps away from the house and turned the engine off. She hopped down to the ground with a grunt, hurriedly explaining something about "a change in plans."

"Where is he?" Astrea asked Rami. She really didn't care what had happened. Marko was hurt. Pain pounded in the back of Astrea's head, her shoulder, her arm, all just slightly off beat with her heart.

"In back."

Shoving her coffee into Jin's hands, Astrea sprinted around to the back of the truck. Adi was already there, ripping the doors open as white terror sparked around him.

"I'm fine," Marko groaned as Astrea hauled herself into the vehicle. He was sprawled out on the floor, barely moving and eyes closed.

"You are not." Adi settled on his other side. "Skies, Marko . . ."

Astrea tugged on her magic, lighting up the back of the truck and creating strange shadows. She placed her hands on his bloodied forearm first, where a nasty gash was still oozing blood. "What happened?"

"We went to town like we said we would," Rami said, calmer this time.

Astrea pushed her light into Marko's arm first, gritting her teeth as ghost healing and pain warred on her own skin. He groaned.

"Everything was fine at first. Got what we needed. Stopped on our way back for a quick break, only about an hour away from here, but these Helosian soldiers stopped, too."

Astrea moved her blood-covered palms up to Marko's shoulder. He groaned again as Astrea pressed her hands down, her light obscured by her flesh. The pain in her body doubled, dying off again as her healing took hold.

"Did you hit your head?" she asked him.

"Right on the back, against the corner of this stupid fucking truck."

Adi helped Astrea roll Marko over. Sure enough, his blond hair was matted by blood, but as Astrea separated his tresses, she found the wound wasn't too deep. Setting her hands on either side of the gash, Astrea tugged on her light again. Her head lolled forward as pain stabbed the base of her neck. She truly hated head wounds.

"Where are the Helosians now?" Jin asked Rami.

"Dead in a ditch."

"Did you kill them?"

"Not on purpose. They asked us a few questions, we stuck with the tradespeople lie, showed them our papers, told them we'd gotten a bit off track and were trying to get back on the road. They demanded payment to let us go, which I gladly gave, and they told us to be on our way and left."

"Then how did they end up dead?" Jin asked.

Slumping forward, Astrea pulled her hands away from Marko's head. "You'll be sore for a couple hours, but it looked worse than it was," she told him.

"They came back just a few minutes later," Rami continued. "Picked a fight, decided we hadn't paid them enough."

"And you didn't just pay them more?" Adi asked.

"We're basically out of money at this point," Rami said. "What little I did offer them wasn't what they wanted. They attacked, we fought them off, and Marko hit his head as one of them went down. With them distracted, we managed to take off. They pursued, lost control of their car, and went off the road, down a ravine."

"Shit," Cressida muttered.

That white terror still pulsed brightly—painfully—around Adi.

Marko rolled onto his back again and reached for Adi's hand, then placed it onto his chest. "Feel that?" he asked, keeping their hands locked right over his heart.

"Yes," Adi whispered.

"It's going to take a lot more than a couple of pissy Helosians to kill me."

Adi hovered above Marko for one second, two. The white terror dimmed. Then Adi leaned down, pressing his mouth to Marko's in a delicate kiss.

"Oh," Astrea whispered, leaning back to try to give them more room.

"Just so you know, you'll have one very pissy Helosian to deal with if you ever scare me like that again," Adi said as he pulled away. "One *very* pissy Helosian."

Marko smirked. "Noted."

"Maybe we should give Marko some space?" Jin said. "Or he should go wash that blood off?"

"Just take it easy for a couple hours," Astrea said as Adi helped him sit up. "Sit inside for a bit. Have something to eat."

As Marko started to protest, Adi said, "Nope, you're listening to Az. Come on. Let's get you inside."

Once Adi had taken Marko back into the house, Jin shook his head and turned back to Rami. "You're certain those Helosians are dead?"

"I'm certain. I checked."

"And you weren't followed?"

"Not as far as I could tell. We never saw anyone else on the roads, just those two."

Glancing toward the house, Jin shook his head. "Alright. Let's just lay low until the others return. And please, for the love of all that is good, nobody else get hurt tonight."

Chapter 50

The night was calm, and the house had finally cooled off after the warm day. Astrea closed the bedroom door behind her as she stepped into the hall.

It had taken much convincing, but Adi and Astrea had finally gotten Marko to lie down for the night despite the fact that it was after midnight. Adi was staying with him for a few hours, then would get up to help keep watch.

Astrea padded down the hall as silently as she could. The twins were sleeping, too, as was Cressida. Just Jin and Rami were awake now. As she rounded the corner into the sitting room, she found them chatting quietly.

"How's Marko?" Jin asked, scooting over on the threadbare loveseat to make room for her. It looked like it had once been pink, but it was hard to be sure. Red, maybe?

"Finally asleep." Astrea dropped down next to him and sighed. "He's not in pain anymore, but I'd prefer he doesn't tap in for watch tonight if we don't need him. Let him get some rest."

"Fine by me," Jin said.

Rami sat across from them on an equally shabby chair. The fabric still held hints of the vibrant green it once was. "You going to make it until Lucian gets back?" she asked.

"I'll make it." At least, Astrea hoped she would; fatigue pulled at the edges of her mind. Jin slid his arm around her shoulders. "Do you think Ellie and Nicos have made any progress with President Sikori?"

Rami's eyebrows furrowed. "I doubt Mira can convince her parliament without some proof beyond my word, but maybe they've been able to start greasing the wheel."

"You seemed friendly with President Sikori when we were there," Jin said. "Friendly enough, at least."

"I donated to her campaign."

"I'm a bit surprised she'd take money from a smuggler, no offense."

Rami laughed. "None taken. We go back years. I knew her from my military days."

"Lucian mentioned that was where you two met?"

A hint of bitterness coated Rami's words as she said, "Where we met and where we parted ways." She sighed. "I didn't think seeing him again would be so hard. Truth be told, I missed him, even if I can't stand him sometimes."

"He can be a bit hard to get along with."

"Now there's an understatement," Rami replied as she leaned back in her seat, peach amusement spiking high above her head.

"Has he always been that way?"

"He used to be more curious about the world. Things began changing not long after we got married."

"Changed how?"

"Prying into my business, Auris?" Rami asked, no edge to her voice.

"Marko doesn't care to explain much about the commander, and I could really use some insight," Jin said. "He and I haven't seen eye to eye on much these last months, and it's frustrating."

"Lucian lives by his own set of rules and principles," Rami said. "Some in line with the majority, some not. He thinks he knows best. Thinks he's right. Annoys him when you do something a different way than he would and still succeed."

"Yet you've still been helping us and him."

She chuckled. "I've always had a soft spot for him, even after what happened."

"With your brother? He mentioned a bit about that."

"The way he weaponizes emotions . . ." Rami shook her head. "He did that to me once. I don't think he meant to, but that didn't matter. Everything just spiraled out of control from there, and, well"—she gestured vaguely—"here we are now. Never could quite find our footing again. What happened with my brother just added fuel to that fire."

Lucian hadn't meant to turn Rami's emotions against her? Astrea couldn't imagine the commander ever losing control of his magic—of himself—like that. Almost everything he did seemed so deliberate.

"That's terrible," Jin said.

Rami shrugged. "Like I said, I don't think he meant to. We were young, in a very heated argument about some different principles, and things got messy. I wasn't on my best behavior that night either and did some things I regret. I forgave him a long time ago."

Leaning her head on Jin's shoulder, Astrea let her eyes drift closed. Was Lucian this exhausted, too, after keeping watch for the scouting party? She'd built up so much stamina that a few low-grade injuries and leaving her barrier open all day shouldn't have made her feel this bad. Maybe it was just the endless travel and lack of sleep catching up to her.

Or the knowledge that Nazarov had very specific plans that involved her in a way far worse than she ever could've imagined.

The world pulsed against her exposed skin. A whisper of worry danced over her cheeks and forearms. Heavy fatigue pressed into her bones, pushing her deeper into the sofa cushion. Rami and Jin's words hovered above her, like she could hear them but not. Energy buzzed just under Astrea's skin. Jin's strong, comforting arm was still wrapped around her.

And there. A ripple, a change, fluttered across Astrea's skin and into her muscles.

"Someone's coming," she said. The world swam as she started to move.

"Who?" Rami asked.

"Not void."

"It could be the others." Jin untangled himself from Astrea and helped her stand. "Let's go see."

Outside, the moon was barely visible through the thickening clouds. It smelled like rain, and the strong wind cleared away some of the humidity. It was nice, actually. The closer those new balls of energy got—four in total—the more Astrea's shoulders relaxed.

"I think it's them," she said.

Headlamps turned the corner of the dark road leading away from the house. A sparkle of starlight popped next to the driver's seat.

"That's Lucian," Rami said. She'd taken her long hair down from its dual braids at some point, and the wind played with the ends. "That's our old signal."

As the truck rumbled closer and rolled to a stop, Astrea felt no pain or injury, just more exhaustion. They waited as the others unloaded themselves from the truck. Balthazar, Saros, Zephyrine, and Lucian moved slowly, as if they'd been running all day.

"No one followed us," were the first words out of Lucian's mouth. "But we found exactly what Theo Kadis said would be there . . . well, perhaps more."

"What do you mean more?" Jin asked.

Lucian tilted his head toward the house. "Let's sit."

As they all shuffled into the house, Balthazar squeezed past to go into the kitchen. He poured glasses of water for them all, which Saros and Zephyrine greedily drank. Saros got up to fill his cup again as Lucian settled into a seat at the kitchen table.

"The site was a couple miles away from where Theo marked it on the map," Lucian said, "but he was right. Emperor Aelius is excavating something there."

"Not *something*." Saros set his empty glass on the counter. "Aetherium. I could feel it."

"How much?" Jin asked. "You said it's more than what Theo claimed was there?"

"A lot of it," Saros said.

"But it's more than just the amount of ore," Zephyrine said. "It's the size of the operation, Jin."

"Meaning?"

"It's more than just a few mages and soldiers to guard them. It's a whole fucking operation," she said, moving her hands to suggest something enormous. "An entire camp, with some permanent structures. Nothing like this was ever hinted at to the council this summer. Even Anjou's network didn't suggest *this*."

"Nor did the emperor have us go to this site," Balthazar said, gesturing to Saros.

"Do we know how long they've been operating?" Rami asked.

"Not a clue, but the tents didn't look very worn or dirty, so I'd say not terribly long." Zephyrine shrugged. "A few weeks, maybe a little over a month?"

"Still gives them a big head start," Jin said. "What would you say, a few hundred soldiers?"

"Maybe not quite that many," Zephyrine said. "Maybe two hundred, plus the excavation teams. I'd just been expecting far less if the emperor's trying to keep it quiet."

"Maybe he's not trying to keep it quiet anymore," Rami said.

Astrea drummed her fingers on the worn tabletop. Would Emperor Aelius tell all those people what it was that he was working toward? She didn't think so.

"Regardless, we can't just let him continue on," Jin said. "We need to try to slow them down until we can move a bigger operation in."

"If there are that many of them and so few of us," Balthazar said slowly, "what are we supposed to do?"

"I have an idea." Lucian looked pointedly at Jin. "Sunreaper."

Jin's jaw tightened. "Excuse me?"

"You can control it, can you not?" Lucian asked. "This massive power you have over fire?"

"Barely," Jin said. "It requires a great deal of effort on my part. It drains me the way Astrea's souleating drains her when she takes on too much energy."

"That doesn't exactly sound safe or ideal," Saros said quietly.

"Would blowing up as much of the aetherium as I can at least buy as some time? Slow my father down?" Jin asked.

"That wouldn't necessarily destroy it or make it unusable," Balthazar said. "Not to mention whatever shrapnel that kind of explosion would create. Would you be able to protect yourself from that?"

"What if you, Cressida, and Adi bury it deep, deep underground?" he asked Balthazar. "Would that at least slow my father down?"

"Honestly? Probably not much."

"Damn."

"Wouldn't going in now just put us at risk?" Saros asked. "Having Varojin considerably weakened doesn't seem wise. How would we escape?"

"We still need proof of what Emperor Aelius is up to for my government," Rami said. "Unless you want this whole escapade to be pointless."

"No," Jin said quickly. "No, I don't want it to be pointless. We need something to bring back, even if we can't deal a heavy blow to my father's efforts now. Maybe we just get that proof back to Thasia as quickly as we can, then mobilize the joint armies."

As silence settled over the small kitchen, Astrea rubbed her tired eyes. Just how were they supposed to get past that many Helosians and steal some kind of proof? Maybe this had been pointless from the start. Maybe they should've found a different way to convince the Tornamians or brought more people along. A small army . . .

"Just how big do these explosions get, Varojin?" Lucian asked.

Jin's eyes narrowed. "What are you really asking me?"

"How many could you take out with such power?"

"I will not do that."

"This is war, Varojin."

"I know. I've done it before," he said, voice low and hard, "and I will not do it again if I don't have to."

"Our mission would be much easier if we could wipe out half the camp or more through your efforts alone."

Sucking in a heavy breath, Jin ran a hand through his hair. "You've just asked me to commit mass murder, Lucian."

"This is war," the commander said again, sharper this time. "*You* are a weapon. How is this any different than when your country drops bombs on its targets in Corsyca?"

Astrea stiffened, and around the table, it was like nobody dared move a muscle. Lucian and Jin stared each other down.

"It's very different when you're one man and cause that much destruction with your own magic," Jin said. "A lot of those soldiers in that camp? Probably not there of their own free will. Same with the excavators. Probably forced there like my father forced Saros and Balthazar to get involved."

"So?" Lucian asked. "Civilians—and soldiers, quite frankly—across the continent need us to put an end to this now. If taking out a few innocent people—"

"A few? You're talking about possibly taking out hundreds."

"They are but a few when looking at the total population."

There he was. The cold Commander Lucian. The ruthless Commander Lucian, the one who crossed lines that couldn't be uncrossed.

Asking Jin to do that . . . to take out so many people . . . It was inhumane on all counts.

"Lucian," Rami said, voice low, "do not ask this of Varojin. Do not do something that neither you nor he can come back from."

"As if you have a problem with crossing lines, Rami?"

"Are you really comparing my bribes and deceit to *that*?" she snapped. "Skies, you'd think after all these years, you might've learned the difference."

"The Paragon already dealt a bad blow to Novaria—to the continent," Lucian said. "We cannot let your father do the same. *We* must deal the bad blow first this time."

Jin sighed heavily.

"If you don't like that plan," Lucian said with a huff, "perhaps we work in a few more of our skills. Balthazar and Cressida turn aetherium against the Helosians. You do your explosion. Astrea and I take control of anyone left over."

When he put it like that, it sounded even worse. So callous. And messy. That wasn't a real plan. He was suggesting a massacre, nothing more. And maybe that was part of the reality of war, but it didn't sit right with Astrea.

"Even if we could manage to do all that," Zephyrine said slowly, "I don't know that it's wise to just go in, guns blazing so to speak. To drain not just Varojin but you and Astrea, Commander? And surely the effort you ask of the Nikaphoroses won't exactly be easy on their energy."

"Then what do you suggest, General?" Lucian asked.

"Our original thought was to disguise ourselves as Helosians working at the site and sneak in that way."

Scoffing, Lucian crossed his arms over his chest. "You think it's better to try to sneak around a camp of people who will surely recognize Varojin? And you?"

"I'm suggesting we go in around a shift change, after we disguise ourselves. Slip in, get our proof, see what we can do to slow down the aetherium mining, and get out. Then we take our proof back to Thasia, and hopefully get a joint Novarian-Tornamian fleet of airships here to attack from above."

"So that will only take, what, another week by the time we get back over the border?" Lucian asked. "And more time to coordinate the armies?"

"Sometimes going the slower route is the more responsible way. A more targeted strike, a more organized effort, might get us the necessary results."

"Fine." Lucian's displeasure prickled Astrea's skin.

"Then we will set out just after the eighth morning bell," Zephyrine said. "And I'd recommend we all get as much sleep as we can. It's going to be a long few days until we're back in Thasia."

Chapter 51

Red was not Astrea's color.

In fact, it didn't suit any of them.

But they were there, dressed in their Helosian red, parked deep within the forest that bordered the Ring of Fire. Evening storm clouds gathered at the horizon, a low rumble of thunder promising the potential of rain. Beyond that, hidden behind those dark clouds, was the brilliant sunset, deep gold and blood red.

"Does everyone know the plan?" Lucian asked.

They'd gone over it that morning and again on the drive, but apparently twice was not enough for the commander.

"Adi, Zephyrine, Astrea, you're in charge of finding whatever paperwork or documentation you can to prove what the emperor is up to," Lucian said.

What had been the point in his asking if he was just going to reiterate the plan anyway? Astrea fidgeted with the end of her braid.

"Rami, you will watch the base from afar. If there seems to be some kind of commotion or other issue, you will create a distraction out here."

Rami nodded. "Of course."

"The rest of us will do whatever we can to sabotage the emperor's efforts. We meet back here in two hours. Understood?"

"Understood," they all echoed.

Astrea watched Jin from where she sat on the edge of the back of one of the trucks. She didn't know why Jin—or Zephyrine—wasn't the one in charge. He stood just behind Lucian, an intimidating sight dressed in the faux Helosian uniform. He, Adi, and Zephyrine had assured Astrea that what they had was as close to authentic as they could get, that nobody would look twice at them.

She stared down at her own "Helosian" uniform, the red battle dress Adi had made her. With the added plating, it was heavier than she liked. And it didn't quite look right, not mixed in with everyone else. Adi had told her that, if anyone asked why her uniform wasn't up to regulation, she could tell them she'd received special permissions from the quartermaster at Fort Avalon. She wasn't so sure that'd convince anyone, but maybe nobody would pay her much mind anyway.

"We leave in five," Lucian said, turning away from Astrea and walking toward the other truck. "Be ready."

As the others broke off to talk among their respective groups, Saros approached where Astrea sat. His smile, though gentle, was a bit awkward.

"Are you ready?" she asked him. He had one of the most important jobs of the night, helping guide the rest of them toward that strange, void-like metal.

"Not exactly what I'm trained for, my dear, but I'm certain I can get the job done," Saros said. "And you?"

She gave him a tight-lipped smile. "Same."

"It's certainly not where I imagined us at the start of this year," Saros said.

Astrea shrugged. Some days, her reality was barely fathomable. The Paragon, void magic, Nazarov, basically living in Novaria again. Being married to Jin. It was all a surprise, though at least there was that one good thing.

Jin approached them both, looking so wrong in that Helosian red. "Saros," he said, "may Az and I have a moment?"

Saros glanced between the two of them, the corners of his mouth quirking up. "Take all the time you need."

Jin watched Saros leave and, once satisfied, nudged Astrea's closed legs open with his knee, then stepped closer. Her whole body heated.

"Listen to Zephyrine and Adi." He took her face in his hands, stroking her right cheek with his thumb. "Don't stray from Zephyrine's side for a second. Trust her and her instincts. She got me through the Delian War in one piece."

"I feel like I should get her some kind of thank-you gift for that."

Jin smirked. "Probably."

"You'll be safe, too?" Astrea gazed up into those beautiful eyes of his, taking in the orange anxiety and soft pink love twining around him.

"You don't even have to ask me that. Trust yourself tonight. Remember everything Adi and I taught you."

"Not what Lucian taught me?"

"Smart-ass." He leaned down, kissing her gently. As he pulled away, he whispered, "You are the most important thing in the world to me, Astrea Sovna. I need you to be in one piece at the end of this. Promise me."

"I promise," she whispered, an uncomfortable knot tying itself around her heart.

"Good." He kissed her a second time. "I love you."

"I love you, too."

Taking her hand, Jin helped Astrea to the ground. As she twined her fingers with his, the cool metal of his wedding band brushed her skin. She'd asked him that morning if it was safe to keep them on, and he'd said yes, that plenty of soldiers kept on their wedding bands. Not only that, but he'd said he was never taking his off if he could help it. So she'd worn hers, too, a small piece of him to take with her.

The group reconvened around Jin and Astrea, a thread of orange winding its way between their bodies, contagious almost. The only ones not obviously impacted by the anxiety were Lucian, Zephyrine, Marko, and Civan.

"Alright," Jin said. "Two hours. In and out. Whatever we accomplish, we accomplish, and we'll figure out the rest when we get back to Thasia. Understood?"

Echoes of agreement bounced around the team.

"Then let's move out," Jin said.

Untangling her fingers from Jin's should've been simple, just one quick movement. But it was one of the hardest things she'd ever had to do. Her hand was like lead, and his didn't seem to be moving, either.

But finally, Jin's grip loosened. He smiled down at her and whispered, "See you soon." He nudged her toward Zephyrine.

Even as Zephyrine ushered Adi and Astrea away from the others, Astrea couldn't help but look over her shoulder. The whole team was watching them leave. An especially tight knot of anxiety wound its way around Jin, but even as the distance between them grew, his familiar sunshine warmth stayed glued to her skin.

She waved at him, and he waved back.

Then Astrea faced forward again, squared her shoulders, and headed deeper into the darkening forest.

Trekking through the humid, semitropical forest with a rainstorm fast approaching just made Astrea's head hurt.

Thunder rumbled behind them. The scarce wildlife they'd seen had disappeared entirely. They'd been walking in silence for the last twenty minutes, heading for an entrance away from the one the others would use.

"Is this really going to work?" Astrea asked. They were supposed to tunnel underneath the base with Adi's earthmoving and get into the camp that way. "Won't they feel us coming?"

"Not with the shift change," Zephyrine replied casually.

"As if it's that simple?"

"I've been doing this for many years, Astrea." Zephyrine flipped her long white braid over her shoulder. "We must make our entrance as seamless as possible. No taking out guards. No abducting them and tying them up in the forest. Everything must seem to be in order."

Astrea wasn't so sure it would work, but Zephyrine *was* the expert. She'd probably completed many missions like this before. Astrea had to trust her, like Jin had said.

As they walked on, the storm clouds moved closer, obscuring the last remnants of the sunset. Zephyrine's fingers twitched occasionally, and Astrea couldn't help but wonder if the general's magic wasn't having some influence over the weather.

It was only after another fifteen minutes and walking past a few too many large spiders for Astrea's comfort that Zephyrine stopped. There was no sign of anyone else in the forest; as far as Astrea's senses stretched, there was no one. Nothing. And the spot didn't look like anything significant. To the north, through the thinning forest, Astrea could just barely make out the distant tops of tall, dark peaks—the southern edge of the Ring of Fire.

"Right here," Zephyrine said, "if you would, Adi."

Adi cracked his knuckles, clapped his hands together, and pulled them out wide as if flinging double doors open. The earth in front of him trembled slightly, then opened. With a stomp of his left foot, earthen stairs ascended from the dark tunnel below.

"Go," Adi said, shooing them inside. "Before this rain starts."

A few droplets splashed on Astrea's cheeks, so she hurried down the stairs after Zephyrine. A tiny star burst to life over Astrea's palm, illuminating the darkness drenching the space. Their shadowed silhouettes danced across the dirt walls.

"It's due west from here," Zephyrine said as Adi joined them underground, then closed the hole again.

Adi took the lead at the front of the line, punching out occasionally to push the earth away and build their tunnel. Even with Astrea's starlight, the shadows lurking at the edges of the tunnel taunted her. She pushed her anxiety into that tiny star until it was sufficiently bright. On and on they walked, until finally, Zephyrine instructed Adi to start heading northeast.

Astrea hoped that Jin and the others were doing fine, presumably in a tunnel of their own. With Cressida and Balthazar there, it would only make sense for them to arrive in such a way. How nice it would've been to have a portable radio to stay in contact with them.

After a few more minutes, Zephyrine said, "Alright, stop here."

Nothing in their position seemed different. Behind them was just that oppressive darkness, and ahead was just more dense earth.

But there.

Energy, flickering in and out of Astrea's awareness.

"I think there's ore above us," she said. "Or they're using the metal in some way? I can feel them . . . and then not . . . and then they return."

"Maybe they're carrying it around and it's creating blocks?" Adi suggested.

"Maybe," Astrea said. It was hard to focus on it and track it with so much energy swirling around above her. Confusion, irritation, fatigue, amusement, even hunger. "They seem like a mess up there."

"Perfect timing, then." Zephyrine looked down at the narrow watch on her wrist; Astrea hadn't noticed it before, but its gold face shone in the light. "Careful as we go up. And do let us know if we need to stop, Astrea. Focus on anything suspicious."

With a heavy sigh and even heavier tangle of anxiety winding around Adi's limbs, he created an earthen ramp and began leading them up toward the surface. They went inch by inch, slowly, until Adi held his hand up for them to pause. The earth right above his head barely cracked open. He pressed his face to the hole, then backed away.

"Zephyrine?" he asked.

They switched spots, and after a moment, Zephyrine nodded. "Take us up here."

The energy swirling above the surface had only increased the closer they got, and as Adi pulled open the earth and ushered them all up, it became clearer why. A voice over a loudspeaker was calling shift assignments and giving orders for dining tent rotations. Rain had begun to fall in heavy drops. They were sandwiched between two walls, one stone and one wood, shadowed by the growing darkness and weather.

"Stay close," Zephyrine whispered, pulling a red hood up over her hair. The rain swirling around them made Astrea wish she had one. Adi didn't seem to have the option, either.

They followed Zephyrine between the two buildings, then out into the busy camp. All around them, Helosians hurried about, most focused on wherever their next destination was. Row after row of tents spread out in front of them, all of them flying the red, white, and gold Helosian flag.

The soldiers around them wore red in varying shades, some of them pulling up hoods much like the one Zephyrine had. They continued on that way, heads down to avoid the attention of the dozens of soldiers milling about. Zephyrine led them through the throng, and when she bumped into one tall, broad man, Astrea's pulse tripled. She was sure they were going to get caught, but the man only grunted and continued on.

"This way," Zephyrine murmured over her shoulder.

Just where was the general taking them? The rows of tents to their right eventually gave way to a few more buildings, all of which were made of wood and fairly small. One was larger than the rest, and smoke rose from a chimney at its rear. That was where Zephyrine was headed.

How, exactly, were they going to get in? Astrea's blood roared in her ears as Zephyrine simply walked up to the building. She didn't ask Astrea anything, but also, as far as Astrea knew, Zephyrine, Jin, Adi, and the rest of their teams used to go out without Lightbringers, that the Helosians kept Lightbringers secluded for their healing talents.

Zephyrine opened the door and ushered them inside. Stepping into the narrow corridor, Astrea tried to parse through the energy around her. There were just two in this building despite several closed doors lining the hall.

"Straight," Zephyrine whispered from behind. "Last door at the end."

Astrea pulled the edges of her energy closer and closer to herself until all she could feel were not just her allies but those two in the building. Both were to her left, not straight ahead. She trudged on, and eventually Zephyrine slipped past to take the lead again.

They passed a door on their left, and it swung open. A surprised gasp escaped one of the two women in the doorway.

"Sorry, we didn't see—" one started.

"Back to work!" Zephyrine called with such authority that even Astrea stood a little taller. "Or I'll report the both of you for fraternizing!"

"But we weren't—"

"You dare question leadership?" Zephyrine barked, making white fear swirl around the two soldiers. "Go, now! Before I write you up! And don't let me see you around here again!"

The women scurried off and out of the building, no questions asked. With them gone, Zephyrine knelt near the closed door in front of her. She pulled two thin pieces of metal from within her armor and slid them into the lock. A few soft clicks later and Zephyrine had the door open.

"How did you know this would be here?" Adi whispered as they entered what appeared to be an office.

A narrow desk sat in the middle of the tiny room, and two chairs had been placed in front of it. The desk lamp was still on, casting a warm glow, and a small fire burned in the nearby hearth.

"Helosian camps are usually set up the same way," she said. "Easier to build but a bad idea if our schematics are ever stolen or too many get mapped. I've warned the emperor about this multiple times, and here we are."

At least he's too arrogant to listen, Astrea thought. She let her senses spread back out far and wide, almost to a disorienting distance. The world pressed in around her again, painful. But she sensed no void, no suspicion, no mistrust. Just a whole lot of the same as before.

"Look for anything about this excavation," Zephyrine said. "Should be the camp commander's office. Some kind of formal documentation, maybe a proclamation or something of the sort."

While Zephyrine went to the desk, Astrea headed for a small credenza tucked on the opposite wall. Everything was stacked up neatly, from the books to rolled-up maps to a few envelopes with torn tops. Carefully, Astrea picked up the pile of envelopes and opened the first. It didn't seem important, just a list of supplies needing to be restocked. The second was a personal letter from someone, talking about a family farm. The third made Astrea pause, though.

It was from Emperor Aelius's office. The gold phoenix seal and thick paper were enough to tell her that. With trembling hands, Astrea unfolded the letter.

Commander Masalis,

His Imperial Highness Emperor Aelius Auris would like to thank you for your dedication to the empire. All your work will be for the betterment of Helosia's future and military.

Kindly note that an additional five thousand lire has been deposited into your bank account.

You are also invited to dine with Emperor Aelius Auris at the Palace of a Thousand Suns when you return to Kalama after the project's completion.

His Imperial Highness requests that you find a way to speed up the mining process in the meantime. It is of the utmost importance.

Best,
Edouard, Secretary

Commander *Masalis*?

"Is Nicos's mother still in the military?" Astrea asked quietly.

"What?" Zephyrine asked.

"I have a letter here addressing 'Commander Masalis,'" Astrea said. "His father died a few years back, but I don't know if his mother still serves."

"Bring it with us," Zephyrine said.

It wasn't exactly a smoking gun, but Astrea tucked the letter into the deep pocket of her skirt. Nicos's mother? Could she really be running the camp? Or maybe he had a cousin or relative in the army that Astrea didn't know about? She hated the thought of him finding out about this either way.

"I have something," Zephyrine said, holding up several sheets of paper. "About the research the emperor wants done on the aetherium. It's on his letterhead and signed by him personally."

Cold fear pierced the air. Astrea pivoted, finding Adi holding an open ledger in his hands.

"He's testing the aetherium here," Adi said. "Bullets, knives . . . he wants to build bombs with it, if I'm adding up the materials correctly."

"He's testing it here?" Zephyrine asked. "How?"

"He's using it against his own people," Adi whispered.

Astrea hurried over to where he stood. Sure enough, documented carefully on the pages, were test dates, the type of weaponry, and the results it inflicted. They'd been testing the metal under various conditions, probably trying to recreate what the Paragon had discovered, that a Sunreaper and powerful Metalli were needed.

How could Emperor Aelius do that? Test such weapons on his own people? Astrea's stomach threatened to revolt.

"Tear a few pages out," Zephyrine said. "We need to go; we've got less than an hour before Lucian will be expecting us back."

With a sigh, Adi ripped a handful of pages out of the ledger, then folded them up and shoved them under his shirt and armor.

Skies, Astrea hoped it would be enough. If that couldn't convince the other countries of Emperor Aelius's intentions, what could?

Chapter 52

Leaving the base commander's office proved easier than anticipated. They were out without another word, and those two women from before hadn't returned. Zephyrine even had time to relock the door using those long metal lockpicks. Good, at least, to cover their tracks, though the few seconds it took just set Astrea's nerves alight.

With that settled, Zephyrine adjusted her hood and led them back out into the chaos of the camp. Things had only gotten worse in the time they'd been inside. Lightning flashed through the sky, startling several of the nearby soldiers.

"Skies damn," one of them muttered as Astrea slipped past, Adi right behind her. "That's the third thunderstorm in three days."

"Well, what'd you expect?" someone else said. "There're always thunderstorms down here."

Adi nudged Astrea between her shoulder blades, pushing her toward Zephyrine. She hurried onward, almost losing the general in the sea of red hoods. But at least she was tall, easier to pick out even with the wind and rain beginning to blind Astrea.

How could Zephyrine possibly know where they were going?

And why were so many soldiers still outside with the storm?

A bell sounded over the camp's intercom, then a tinny voice called out something about five minutes before everyone needed to be back at their stations.

Which meant they had five more minutes to take advantage of this chaos and disappear back underground.

Astrea grew dizzy, the energy of the camp threatening to overwhelm her. Annoyance, frustration, someone's debilitating headache—rust red, tree bark scraping her skin, pulsing in her head. She focused on Adi's hand still pressed to her back, like he was afraid of losing her in the crowd.

Zephyrine turned right, dipping past a burly man growling about the working conditions. Astrea followed. Zephyrine pivoted left, and Astrea followed again.

Rain and wind swirled around them, soaking Astrea's hair, her armor, right through her skin and to her very core. Tiny ice pellets stung her face—hail? They turned again, then again, winding a serpentine path through the soldiers complaining about the storm. They turned one more time, near a building. It looked like the building they'd tunneled in near—

Zephyrine stopped dead in her tracks, right before slamming into a tall, red-haired woman. Two guards flanked her, a watery umbrella over their heads keeping the rain away.

"Well," said the woman, her voice deeper than Astrea expected. Her pale skin was dotted with freckles. "This is not what I expected today, but it's so nice to finally meet you, General Kanakos."

"I'm sorry, Commander, but you have me mistaken—"

"Mistaken?" The woman laughed. "There is no mistaking you, the infamous General Kanakos. And who do we have with you today?"

Panic, panic, panic. It pulsed against Astrea's every sense, overwhelming her vision and chilling her to the point of goose bumps.

"Cat got your tongue, General?" the woman mocked.

Astrea took half a step back into Adi, who clutched her arm tightly. A warning, maybe? She could barely see past the wind and rain now.

"Four behind us," Adi whispered, so close to Astrea's ear she could feel his breath. "Don't move."

She swallowed hard.

"Nice of you to finally show your face in the country again," the woman—Nicos's mother, Astrea assumed, based on her hair and that letter—drawled. "But breaking into my camp?" She tsked. "I thought this day was ruined, what with the storm, but perhaps things are looking up after all." She snapped her fingers. "Take them to my office."

Zephyrine didn't move a muscle. Adi didn't move a muscle. Not when the guards stepped forward, not when they began tying rope around their wrists, and not when dark cloth bags were placed over their heads.

Astrea squeezed her eyes shut, trying to block out the darkness of the hood. Panic swirled within her and around her, pulsing in time with her heart and what she thought might be Adi's heart, too. But Zephyrine was calm.

Calm.

They'd been caught, just like that, and the general was calm.

Astrea just hoped she had a plan.

Leaving her senses open while being dragged through the storm blindfolded was disorienting. Astrea kept trying to feel for Jin and the others, but it was fruitless. There was no way to find them in a camp that large, let alone surrounded by so much energy.

The rain stopped as someone shoved Astrea forward. The muddy ground turned to wooden floors. A guard half dragged her through the building, until finally, another door clicked open.

Chair legs scraped across the floor. Her breath caught in her throat. The darkness. The rough rope binding her hands together. She tensed, expecting a needle to sink into her skin at any moment.

But it never came.

Someone shoved her to the ground. She dropped onto her bum, then someone let out a harsh breath as they dropped next to her. Adi, maybe? He nudged her shoulder, as if to say he was there.

"Keep their hoods on," came the base commander's voice. "Leave us."

Footsteps, then the door closed.

"Now," she said, "just what am I going to do with you, General?"

"Commander Masalis—that's your name, right?" came Zephyrine's calm, airy voice. "Do you even know what you've gotten mixed up in?"

"Do I know what I've gotten mixed up in?" She laughed, a haughty sound. "Do you know what *you've* gotten mixed up in, General?"

"Commander Masalis—" Zephyrine started.

"Emperor Aelius warned me that you all might not stay out of this," said the commander. "Especially Princess Eliana and Prince Varojin. Brats, both of them. Tell me, General, where is my son if he's so dedicated to their cause?"

So she *was* Nicos's mother. Astrea swallowed hard.

"He has more important things to worry about at the moment."

"I always told him not to get mixed up with the Aurises."

"As if you're not?" Zephyrine replied.

Instead of answering, the commander said, "Tell me, is Varojin here?"

"Neither Varojin nor Eliana are here," Zephyrine said. "Surely you and the emperor know it's too risky to bring such high-value targets into a war zone."

"High-value targets." Commander Masalis punctuated each word. "Traitors, you mean."

"Some might consider you the traitor."

"*Me*?"

Was pushing this woman really the right idea? Astrea pulled against the rope binding her hands together. Could she grab onto the commander's energy without seeing the colors? It was there, annoyance scraping over her skin, leaving invisible scratches down her cheeks and arms.

She might be able to do it, but was it wise?

Probably not.

Astrea nudged Adi's shoulder. He nudged her back. What did that mean?

"You know," Commander Masalis began as she walked away from where Astrea sat, "I would've expected more loyalty out of someone who's done so much for Helosia, General."

"Done for the people, not for the emperor," Zephyrine said.

"Done for the people." She chuckled. Papers scraped against wood, making Astrea cringe. "Well, if that's what you must tell yourself, General. We'll see what Emperor Aelius thinks about that."

"What do you mean?" Zephyrine asked. "I'm fairly certain I know what he thinks."

"I *mean*," Commander Masalis drawled, "that you picked the perfect day to sneak into my camp. Emperor Aelius and Prince Kaius are en route. They should be arriving shortly."

Zephyrine may as well have sucked all the air out of the room with her Tempest magic. Astrea's pulse roared in her ears, making it almost impossible to hear the commander's next words.

"Imagine His Imperial Majesty's delight when he learns I've caught not one but three traitors snooping around here."

When they remained quiet, the only sound their breathing and the heavy pitter-patter of rain, the commander chuckled.

"Nothing to say to me now, General?" she asked.

"Fuck you."

"That's not very nice."

"Nor are you."

Astrea could hardly believe this woman was Nicos's mother. She was so unlike him, so brusque, brutal. Rude. Nicos had never talked about his family much, but she hadn't gotten the idea that their politics would be so vastly different.

"Where did things go so wrong for you, General?"

"I hardly think wanting to prevent the emperor's use of aetherium is wrong."

"Haven't your years of service taught you anything about loyalty? Duty? But I suppose you wouldn't know anything about that, would you? Serving the traitorous princess."

"Is she a traitor when she wants peace?" Zephyrine asked.

"Does she truly have Helosia's best interests at heart?"

Astrea pulled at her wrist bindings again. Her breath was humid against the cloth over her head. She was suffocating. She needed out. They needed to find a way to warn Jin and the others.

The commander sucked in a breath as if to speak, but the door opened with a small squeak. "What do you want?" she snapped as uncertainty whispered over Astrea's limbs.

"Commander," said a small, quiet voice, "you're wanted at the rear gate."

"Why?"

"Another vagrant," the soldier said. "She won't go away. She's acting erratically. We didn't know what to do."

"Must I do everything around here?" The commander let out a dramatic sigh. "Fine. You stay out in the hall, and don't let anyone into my office until I return."

Two sets of footsteps retreated, as did their wildly bouncing energy. Astrea slumped against Adi's shoulder.

"Well, fuck me," he muttered.

"Hopefully the vagrant is actually Rami." A force of wind gusted near Zephyrine. The general grunted, then coughed. It sounded like she was walking around. "Skies. Hold on."

"Zephyrine?" Adi asked, voice low.

"I'm looking for something sharp."

"In my boot," Adi said.

Zephyrine passed Astrea. Fabric rustled. The pair spoke in broken sentences. An echo of pain flared in Astrea's wrists and forearms, then Zephyrine grunted again.

"There," the general said. "Hold on."

She took their hoods off first. Astrea blinked against the light, trying to slow her breathing as fresh air entered her lungs. They were in the same office as before. Zephyrine still had rope tied around each wrist, but she'd cut through the middle, just as she was now cutting through Adi's bindings. She cut through Astrea's next.

As soon as Adi pushed to his feet, he hauled Astrea up to hers, too. "We gotta go," he whispered. "Move quietly."

As if that needed to be said.

"There's just the one outside the door," Astrea said, voice low. Her heart beat erratically as she pulled the remaining rope from her wrists.

Adi and Zephyrine crept closer to the door. As Adi slowly turned the handle, Zephyrine's hands raised up. Confusion danced across Astrea's skin, rough and heavy. She turned away just as the door opened and wind swept into the hallway beyond. A sickening crack echoed through the silent room, followed by just the quickest flash of pain.

Dead.

That soldier was dead.

"Come on," Adi said over his shoulder.

"We go fast," Zephyrine said as she led the way down the familiar hall. Astrea kept her eyes trained on Adi ahead of her, not the soldier with the neck crooked at an unnatural angle. "Back to our meeting point. Understood?"

"Understood," Astrea whispered as they hurried back out into the raging storm.

Chapter 53

Outside was as chaotic as before, only now, soldiers were shouting about an airship's imminent arrival. Through the rain-filled sky, Astrea couldn't see any sign of the emperor's ship, but surely he would be arriving all too soon.

Zephyrine led them through the crowds, who seemed oblivious to the fact there were traitors in their midst. Nicos's mother hadn't exactly been subtle about dragging them to her office. Maybe nobody would pay them any mind with their attention focused on Emperor Aelius's arrival. Or maybe nobody recognized them among the crowd.

Adi reached back, taking Astrea's hand in his. She held onto him, a lifeline, as anger, excitement, concern, and fear pulsed brightly in the air around them. She was going to drown.

They slipped among the Helosian soldiers, unnoticed in the crowd urgently pushing toward the center of the camp. Zephyrine pitched right, breaking off from the group and heading toward the side of one building. Adi pulled Astrea that way just as Zephyrine disappeared into the shadows. Cold wind and rain battered Astrea's body. She shivered violently.

"What about Rami?" Adi asked.

"She assured me she could handle herself," Zephyrine said, stopping and wiping rain from her face. "I trust her."

Lightning flashed blue across the dark sky. Thunder boomed an instant later, rocking the ground. Water and wind continued their torrential dance. It was like they were in the middle of a hurricane.

A crackling screech echoed through the alley between the buildings, making Astrea's ears ring. Then a tinny voice, barely audible above the storm, said, "All soldiers, make your way to the front gate to greet your emperor and heir apparent. I repeat, all soldiers, make your way to the front gate to greet your emperor and heir apparent."

"Shit," Zephyrine muttered. "Anyone around, Astrea?"

"Plenty," she whispered. Energy pushed into Astrea's body from every angle—some people unreadable, others curious, angry, excited, and everything in between.

"We'll just have to take the risk with everyone distracted." Zephyrine continued forward, mud squelching under her boots.

Adi and Astrea started after her. They rounded the corner of the building, slipping into the dark, empty space between the camp's outer wall and a few tents. The ghostly glow of lights flickered inside, but there were no shadows, no people. Empty.

"I repeat, all soldiers make your way to the front gate!" called the same voice over the radio. Glancing up, Astrea found the speaker mounted to the tent's tall pole. "Now!"

"Let's go, Adi," Zephyrine said.

A dark, muddy hole opened up just in front of Adi's feet. Zephyrine started to push Astrea that way when white lit up the sky in the distance.

No lightning.

Panic.

Pure panic, electric and cold against her skin.

Panic, panic, panic.

No . . .

"Jin and the others are in trouble," Astrea said, tugging against Zephyrine's hold. When the general started to question her, Astrea gestured to the sky and said, "Panic, brighter than the lightning. No soldiers would be panicking like that right now."

No, Jin and the others had been caught.

Or worse.

"They were supposed to have been gone by now, headed back toward camp," Zephyrine muttered. "Why was he still here?"

The earth closed again, and Adi started back toward the buildings.

"Skies damn it." Dropping Astrea's arm, Zephyrine lunged forward and grabbed Adi, yanking him back.

"We can't just leave them," Astrea said, focusing on the sky. The panic never returned, but there had been so much of it . . .

"We're not leaving them. We just need to get a plan together first." Zephyrine surveyed the walls towering around them, then whispered another curse. "We go up. Try to get eyes on the camp."

"And do what?" Adi asked.

"Something."

"Oh, *great* plan."

"Just follow my lead." Zephyrine sprinted toward the two-story wooden building a few dozen yards ahead of them. Astrea and Adi took off after her. At the base of the structure, Zephyrine tilted her head back and shielded her eyes from the rain. She shook her head, then said, "Adi, you're going to have to take us up. Subtle as you can."

Gripping Adi's arm, Astrea braced herself. The sodden ground under their feet trembled slightly, then again. It separated from the rest of the earth with a wet sucking sound. Up and up they went, just a few heartbeats before Zephyrine shoved Astrea onto the slick, slightly slanted roof.

Astrea braced herself, barely avoiding falling onto her ass. She sucked in a sharp breath as more panic surged high into the sky. "Something's really wrong," she whispered.

"Stay here," Zephyrine said. Crouching, the general inched toward the middle of the roof. She settled just below the peak and stared out above the camp.

"Well?" Adi asked.

"Hard to see with the rain, but they're congregating below," Zephyrine said. "Airship just landed outside the gate."

"Any sign of the team?"

"No."

"Well, fuck."

The rain slowed slightly. Astrea wiped droplets from her lashes just as heat singed her cheeks. She didn't dare move. She just might slip and fall. "Someone's angry."

"Commander Masalis, it looks like," Zephyrine said. "She's moving off with a group of several soldiers . . . oh, I think that's the emperor."

Cold prickled her skin, that familiar, empty feeling.

"I think he has his void guard with him, Caliban," Astrea said. "If they have Jin, they'll bring him to his father. We've got to stop this."

Oh, she could only imagine the fate that awaited Jin at his father's hands. The fate that awaited not just him but Cressida, Saros, Balthazar. Lucian and Marko, foreign operatives. Lennor and Civan, deserters.

"Masalis is moving away," Zephyrine said, moving back down to the edge of the roof. "Let's get down there. We won't be able to do anything from up here. Astrea, stay close to us. If we have to split up, stay with Adi. Is that understood?"

Astrea nodded vigorously.

"Heads down," Zephyrine said. "Engage only on my mark."

She nodded again.

Zephyrine jumped from the edge of the roof, a gust of wind easing her fall. Adi nudged Astrea forward next, and with a final gulp of air, she jumped. It was far easier than jumping out of an airship, and her boots were on the ground in just a heartbeat. Adi landed next to her with a thud.

With the camp's roads mostly empty, Zephyrine stuck close to the tents, buildings, and trucks left out, abandoned as everyone went to the meeting spot. It wasn't far from the building they'd just been on top of, maybe a few hundred feet. The crowd was a sea of red amid the rain.

There had to be at least two hundred soldiers, maybe more. They whispered among themselves, questions about why the emperor had arrived and when the storm would end.

Astrea's breathing turned shallow. They were right there, at the edge of a group of Helosian soldiers. Officers. Caliban somewhere up ahead, and the emperor and Prince Kaius, too. She could barely breathe.

As Zephyrine settled into a spot at the back of the crowd, Adi nudged Astrea just in front of him. His tall, wide frame blocked her from view of anyone who might approach from behind.

"Listen up!" someone yelled from the front of the crowd. "Your emperor approaches! Quiet!"

Astrea stiffened.

Adi leaned down and whispered, "You see Jin anywhere?"

No, Astrea couldn't see Jin anywhere. They were all blending in too well, impossible to pick out. Maybe the commander wasn't going to bring them up here after all. Maybe she'd lock them away, save them for the emperor to deal with privately.

Panic and pain filtered into Astrea's senses, far off, distant.

It moved closer.

Panic and pain and *pride*.

Turning, she pushed up on her toes and whispered to Adi, "I think they're coming."

"Make way!" Commander Masalis shouted above the murmuring crowd. "Make way! I must bring these traitors to your emperor!"

Shock exploded around Astrea, slamming into her so hard she actually stumbled. Adi caught her.

Every fiber of Astrea's being screamed at her to pull her barrier back, to shut herself off from the swell of energy. The energy and that cold made for a disorienting mix. But she could not close herself off. Not with Caliban right there, somewhere nearby.

Satisfaction swept over Astrea's skin, heavy and warm. Then a familiar voice called out, "Well, brother, your boldness has finally caught up with you. I didn't expect you to be stupid enough to break into this camp."

Kaius.

Astrea pushed up on her toes again, trying to gain a better view above the crowd. The ground underneath her feet shook just a little, pushing her up higher.

There.

A stone overhang, almost like a makeshift pavilion, sat at the front of the group.

Emperor Aelius and Prince Kaius. Both dressed in Auris red uniforms, obviously tailored to perfection, cut from the finest cloth trimmed with gold thread, and decorated with badges neither of them had probably earned. Snowy-haired Caliban, standing a few steps behind the royals.

And . . .

A group of eight, also dressed in red, with hands bound in front of their torsos and brown cloth bags over their heads.

Her family.

White terror and orange anxiety threaded among them, making it hard for Astrea to tell who it started and ended with.

Her chest squeezed painfully. Adi's hand settled on her shoulder, like he knew exactly what she was thinking. That they could not let Emperor Aelius have any of them.

The rain slowed.

"On their knees," Emperor Aelius barked at one of the guards escorting their team.

The guards circled the group, and as they did, the emotion seemed to blink out, then back. Out and back as the guards circled her family.

"I think they're armed with aetherium," Astrea whispered to Adi.

It made sense. Of course it made sense. They were not only mining the material here but having some successful weapons tests. At least Lucian and Saros surely knew the guards had aetherium. They would have warned the others.

The mission was still important. They still had to get this information back to Veiko and Eliana. The mission had simply expanded. Rescue their family, then get the information out of the country.

Astrea's heart thudded in her ears. How were they going to manage any of that?

When she stole a glance over her other shoulder, Astrea found that Zephyrine was gone. Where could the general have disappeared to? The rain had slowed, but the wind was picking up again.

"She'll be back," Adi murmured.

"Take those ridiculous hoods off them," Emperor Aelius commanded. "I want to see these traitors."

The aetherium-armed guards stood in a line behind Astrea's family and yanked their hoods off one by one. Caliban sneered.

Rage burned across Jin's face as he glowered at his father.

"Varojin," Emperor Aelius said.

Jin lifted his chin, silent.

Eyes narrowing, Aelius turned to face the crowd and called out over the rumbling thunder, "Loyal soldiers! I thank you for your dedication and patience. I know you expected me to arrive today with good weather and exciting news about our efforts, but instead, the skies have opened up and exposed my wayward, traitorous son."

Murmurs and shock rippled through the crowd. Astrea tried to keep her gaze focused on the soldiers—not Jin, not her family. Competing white panic, rusty annoyance, and orange fear spiked high in the air. Disbelief scraped Astrea's skin painfully, aggressively.

How many of these soldiers had been told that Eliana and Varojin had left Kalama for their own safety? Had word not spread here after the battle up north? Did they not know where Eliana really was?

"And not just my traitorous son," the emperor continued. "One of my former generals, a trusted advisor whom I let into my palace. My own Stargazer, working against me. And now they bring Novarians onto our soil and attempt to sabotage our plans to make Helosia greater than it's ever been."

Whispers erupted from the crowd, but when Emperor Aelius lifted his hand, they silenced.

"I know. Surely you are confused considering you all thought Prince Varojin and Princess Eliana fled the capital for their own safety," he said. "I must admit, I have lied to you, but it was in an attempt to quell their rebellious attitudes and avoid exactly what is playing out now."

Despite herself, Astrea almost rolled her eyes.

"For you see, my son has corrupted your once-loyal princess," the emperor said.

Anger surged through the crowd in waves of red. Astrea swallowed hard. Emperor Aelius was going to pin this all on Jin? Did he think he could still somehow force Eliana back into the fold? Or was it because too many people loved her to place any blame on her?

"She always looked up to Varojin despite him being a bastard." Aelius glared down at Jin. "Despite him being one of the greatest mistakes of my life. I can only still be thankful that my wife forgave my indiscretions, and I can only be shocked and angry that after all I did to give him a good life, he has turned on me."

Emperor Aelius turned out to the crowd again. "Loyalty is one of the greatest gifts a country can give its leader," he called. "Something the Auris dynasty has graciously received from the Helosian people since the Great Wars. You have trusted us since the reign of the Sun King, the first Auris leader in this great nation."

He glared at Jin again. "And yet some have forsaken this tradition. Some have never shown true honor or loyalty, including this young man kneeling before you now. You welcomed him with open arms as part of your royal family, and he has turned his back on this country."

Jin's jaw muscle flexed, like he was working hard to keep his mouth shut.

Emperor Aelius motioned to where Jin knelt. "And he has even followed in my footsteps, I am ashamed to say. He's gone and bedded a Novarian whore. My Stargazer's niece, whom I welcomed into my palace as a child. Who has lied to me and this country about who she really is. A Lightbringer who dodged the draft and kept her talents to herself when so many people were in need."

Astrea balked. *Novarian whore?*

Rage flashed bright and hot around Jin, searing Astrea's skin. That same anger was mirrored around Kaius but, she suspected, for entirely different reasons.

"We did not come here today for a trial," Emperor Aelius said. "Trials are for loyal citizens who deserve a fair chance to explain their actions. Trials are not for traitors and rebels. But I am a fair and just ruler, and it would not sit right with me executing my own son without giving him a chance to explain himself."

Executing my own son. The words ran circles in Astrea's mind as Adi's panic exploded behind her. But Jin was calm. Steady. All that rage seemed to bleed away from him.

Aelius motioned to Kaius, who took a step forward to be shoulder to shoulder with his father.

"First charge: abandoning his military post," Kaius called over the crowd. "Second charge: espionage and attempting to steal Helosian military secrets. Third: illegal crossing of the border. Four . . ."

Kaius prattled on with more so-called charges, many of which sounded the same to Astrea. She scanned the crowd, trying to judge how many people might be on their side. The growing disbelief and discontent, the growing worry, suggested to her that some, at least, might support Jin. And if not support, they could at least feel there was something wrong with the whole spectacle.

"So conclude the charges," Kaius called. "Father."

"Sixteen counts," Emperor Aelius mused as he scowled down at Jin. "Well, son? Do you have anything to say for yourself?"

Jin pushed to his feet. "Sixteen counts," he echoed. "Sixteen counts, many of which I'll admit to."

Astrea held back a gasp. What was he doing?

"But for good reason. You're nothing but a warmongering dictator out for blood," Jin said. Shock spiked high above the crowd. "That's all you've ever been. All the Auris family has ever been. Expanding borders and power at the expense of everyday people, people you force to serve and die on your behalf. Is that loyalty?" he asked. "Is it loyalty when their only options are to serve your orders or go to prison?"

Hands still bound before him, Jin motioned stiffly toward the crowd. "My father speaks of honor, and yet I wonder if he's told you what you're really doing here in this camp." Whispers escaped the crowd. "I wonder if he's told you that man right there"—he tilted his head toward Caliban—"is actually a void mage, that there is a sixth branch of magic, that the ore you're mining here is not just for new weaponry but weaponry connected to the void. That it will bring untold destruction."

Shock, disbelief, anger, fear, understanding. It all pulsed against Astrea's being, calling to her. Her magic wanted to reach out, grab hold of all those colors and the energy charging the air. Her skin prickled.

"You all know I have served in not just one but two of my father's wars," Jin said. "I did so because I had no choice. He gave me no choice. Just as he never gave you, your parents, your children any choices. Serve or face the consequences. But that's loyalty and honor, right?"

Jin scoffed. "He speaks of respect, yet he calls my wife a whore." Shock rippled through the crowd again, electric. Rage burned around Kaius as Jin continued, "He speaks of duty and sacrifice, but what was the last thing he gave up for the betterment of Helosia? He isn't even paying your salaries on time or in full!"

Anger sparked in the crowd, a swirl of red. Astrea watched it spread, mingling most strongly among those whose auras revealed their fear, too.

"He sends you all to Corsyca with little training, few supplies, and a promise that *this*, somehow, is for the good of the empire," Jin called out to the soldiers. "That is not the future either my sister or I want for this country. For you. We want you to have a say, and we want you to be able to live without fearing death on the battlefield. If it is a crime to fight for that, and if it is a crime to try to stop him from unleashing untold power on this continent, then yes, I'm guilty. And I would always rather be guilty than have any more innocent Helosian blood on my hands. Because that is what this Auris dynasty is built on: the lives of innocents. That will not change until my father is gone."

"Traitor!" someone shouted from a few rows ahead of Astrea.

"He's right!" someone else yelled. "Prince Varojin is right!"

Boots shifted on the hard dirt. Astrea's scalp prickled. Aelius and Kaius's attention was focused on the crowd. Caliban moved, his eyes narrowing as he stared out into the storm.

The hairs on Astrea's arms stood.

No.

That cold void swept in, making her shiver violently.

Around the edges of the crowd, shadows rose from the ground. Masked figures clad in black took shape in a tight circle, some of them jumping with green-clad Zaikudi fighters in tow.

"Shit," Adi whispered, so low Astrea was sure only she could hear. He grabbed her hand, tucking her even farther from view of anyone who might have popped up behind them.

Darkness swirled a dozen feet in front of where Emperor Aelius stood, and a familiar form took shape. Victor Nazarov emerged from the shadows, slow clapping as he walked toward the emperor. Shock and disbelief exploded from the crowd.

"What a lovely speech, princeling," Nazarov said to Jin. "Beautiful, really. *So* moving."

Out around the crowd, more Paragon appeared. One by one, they jumped into the camp, until there had to be at least four dozen, if not more—not to mention the Zaikudi. Astrea couldn't keep count.

"Lord Nazarov," the emperor growled. "Who do you think you are, besides being another traitor, of course? Showing your face here after you escaped my custody is bold."

"Traitor?" Nazarov chuckled. "I'm no traitor. *You* are the traitor. Your son and I don't agree on much, but he's right. You're a warmongering despot out for blood. Your family should have been stopped centuries ago."

"Just who do you think you are, Lord Nazarov?" Kaius snapped.

"Lord Nazarov?" His toothy smile turned vicious. "No. I'm Victor Nazarov, king of the Paragon, and our existence shall no longer remain a secret."

Chapter 54

"King of the Paragon?" Kaius said with a laugh. "How adorable."

"Adorable." Nazarov strode toward the crowd of soldiers, his expression hard. "Is this adorable?" Shadows stretched toward him as lightning crackled high above. He disappeared, swallowed by darkness, only to reappear twenty feet deeper into the crowd. "Or how about this?" he yelled over the storm.

Shadows exploded over the crowd, blocking out the next flash of lightning. They spread over the Helosian soldiers, bright white panic rising into the darkness. And then the screaming began.

"Get him!" Emperor Aelius shouted.

Nazarov reappeared just inches from the emperor and Kaius, grabbing the fronts of their uniforms and dragging them away through the void with him. Caliban disappeared a moment later. The aetherium-carrying guards ran off into the crowd, no doubt in search of their emperor.

Jin strained against his bindings, fire bursting to life between his palms. As the crowd began turning on the void mages and Zaikudi, Adi shoved Astrea forward. She sprinted ahead, Adi's hand still clutched in hers. They zipped past green-clad Zaikudi and red-clad Helosians duking it out, ducking to avoid fire and water blasting through the air.

A dozen feet separated them.

"Az!" Cressida called.

Jin's bindings went up in smoke just as they reached the group. Adi shoved Astrea toward Jin with one hand, pulling out his dagger with the other.

"Anyone else have weapons?" Adi asked.

"Confiscated them," Jin said. "Keep watch, Az."

Adi moved on to Cressida next, cutting the rope around her wrists, as Jin summoned fire over his pointed finger and began burning Lennor's away. They worked in tandem, freeing the team one by one. Around them, chaos reigned, a cacophony of thunder and fire, rain and wind, color and pain and cold. They'd been all but abandoned by the Helosians, forgotten.

"Where's Zephyrine?" Jin asked.

"She left," Adi said. "Up to something, I'm sure."

"Then let's go," Jin said, nudging Astrea forward. He grabbed Astrea's hand. "Come on!" he yelled to the team. "Now!"

He took off at breakneck speed, dragging Astrea along with him. She forced her legs to go faster, carrying her through the rain and deeper into the camp. Risking a glance over her shoulder, Astrea found the others in tight formation behind them. Panic and worry circled around them, bright against the dark storm and void fire scouring the Helosian crowd.

Where was Jin taking them? Couldn't they try going underground again, disappear from Nazarov and the emperor's sight?

They zipped past several tents and buildings, and through the rain, in the distance, red rose high above the camp's tall fence.

An airship.

Bodies surrounding it.

Flashes of white and black hair inside.

Jin wanted to steal his father's airship, and Rami and Zephyrine seemed to already be working on it.

Lightning crackled through the air, but it wasn't the storm. It skittered past Astrea, blue bolts of electricity. Like Eliana's.

"Get to that airship!" Jin ordered as he skidded to a stop. "Adi, Marko, with me. Cress, Len—"

Cold lashed out at Astrea's skin in spiky tendrils. Pivoting, she threw her arms out in front of her. Kaius was just a few dozen feet behind the group, Caliban not far behind. His attention was trained on Astrea, Kaius's on Jin.

Ice coated her fingers and arms as she reached for his veil, that void that surrounded Caliban. Her teeth clenched so hard she thought they might break. But there, underneath. Hate and anger, determination and rage. She held them tight with one hand, and with the other, reached for Kaius's colors. Red anger and steel pain, green focus. Hers.

She yanked hard on them both. The men stumbled, falling to their hands and knees on the muddy ground. The lightning crackling around Kaius's fingers died, and his rage spiked.

Jin shouted orders again, but Astrea couldn't make them out as thunder boomed. Kaius and Caliban both strained against her hold. Astrea's fists clenched tighter, so tight she thought she might make her own flesh bleed. More energy moved in behind them, threads of color weaving together with the magic filtering through the armies.

"Let Kaius go." Lucian's voice next to Astrea made her flinch. "I'll take him."

"Ready?" Her voice trembled.

"Do it, now."

Astrea dropped the burning rope of color that arced out from Prince Kaius, replacing it with the icy cold of Caliban. With a roar, Kaius shoved to his feet. In the next moment, he fell again. Ghostly pain pinged in Astrea's sternum. Kaius roared again, visibly straining under Lucian's control.

Earth rumbled up, encasing both Kaius and Caliban's bodies. Astrea didn't dare let her hold on Caliban go, though. Not even when Lucian let Kaius free, nor when Jin said something to Astrea about letting go.

She could not.

Caliban would attack. Hate pulsed brightly under his veil, hot and determined.

"Making your wife do the dirty work for you?" Kaius spat at Jin. He struggled against his earthen prison as he added, "Coward."

Astrea's arms shook as Caliban strained against her hold. His energy surged against hers, barreling into her like a tidal wave. Her knees and elbows locked.

"Oh, she's having trouble," Kaius cooed. "No match for Caliban this time, Miss Sovna? Or do I call you sister now?"

Astrea's eyes shut. Hot rage exploded around her. She shrank back. New heat burned her flesh, the echo of pain as it ripped through her muscles. Kaius let out an enraged, frustrated scream.

"We've got incoming," Lucian said to Astrea.

She forced her eyes open again. Kaius strained against his earthen prison, and beyond him, beyond Caliban's shadowy veil, was more. Vines of darkness rippled through the air, then disappeared, only to come back again, closer and closer.

"We need to move," Lucian said.

Astrea couldn't let Caliban go. She just couldn't. Not until everyone else was to the ship, but the sounds of fighting came from behind her, too. And Jin was gone.

Caliban shouted. His energy slammed into her again, forcing her back another step. He wrenched control from her, forcing her back, back, back. Astrea cried out. As darkness writhed up Caliban's features, shimmering starlight burst to life in front of her. Turning, she found both Lucian and Saros holding the solid wall.

"Go!" Lucian yelled. "Go, Astrea! Get to that ship!"

Beyond that wall, not only was Kaius struggling against the earth, but Caliban had jumped free from his. And behind him?

Lightning and dark fire. Emperor Aelius and Nazarov, fighting. Drawing closer.

"Az, come on." Jin grabbed Astrea's hand, returned from wherever he'd gone. "We're breaking through the line. Gotta get to that ship."

Astrea hesitated. She couldn't leave Lucian and Saros.

"We'll be right behind you!" Saros yelled over his shoulder.

Beyond their wall, Nazarov was leading the emperor closer and closer, jumping in and out of this plane, a taunting dance. Hundreds of feet away still, separated by that wall of light, but it was like his eyes found hers.

Hello, Miss Sovna, he whispered in her head. Then he disappeared in swirls of shadow, making red rage spike high around Aelius. *I'm so glad you're here. We have much to discuss about our future.*

Astrea ran.

A few hundred yards separated them from the edge of camp and that ship. Up ahead, amid the swirling rain, Cressida and Balthazar fought back to back, ripping guns and weapons from the hands of soldiers with little more than flicks of their wrists.

Just a little farther.

Cold spiked all around Astrea, like someone had just shoved her into a frozen lake. Shadow swirled ahead of her and Jin, to their sides. So much shadow, dozens of mages. But as their darkness cleared, it wasn't masked faces but open ones, all staring worriedly at Astrea and Jin.

And with them, Theo. He pushed his glasses up, his curls already flattened by the rain. "Do you see now?" he asked. "Do you see that Victor has lost his mind?"

Astrea looked over her shoulder again. Saros and Lucian, running toward her and trying to fight off Caliban and Kaius. Nazarov jumping closer and closer, emperor in tow.

One thing. Theo wanted one thing.

"If you really think I'm your queen, that Jin is your king," she said hurriedly, "then prove it, Theo. Help us escape, and we'll discuss some kind of alliance when we're back to safety."

A terrible decision, she was sure. A promise Astrea knew she couldn't keep and a price she would pay later. But if it meant getting out of here, if it meant distracting Nazarov and the emperor, it was worth it.

"Do that for me," she screamed above the next crash of thunder, "and we'll talk to you!"

"So The One commands!" Theo shouted to the void mages. "Fight for her!"

The mages disappeared one by one, taking Theo with them. And then they appeared again, blinking back into Astrea's awareness. They surrounded not just Kaius but Caliban, a wall three rows deep as Nazarov and the emperor moved closer still. Pain flared in Astrea's torso and back as Nazarov got a hit on Aelius. Lightning and fire burst from his fist in a combination of blue and red.

With the void mages standing between them, Saros and Lucian sprinted ahead, toward Astrea and Jin. Adi and Marko joined them. Astrea's head swam; she couldn't focus, not with so much cold piercing the very center of her being.

Jin's grip on Astrea tightened. She pushed her legs faster.

One shot rang out through the night, then another. Pain ripped through Astrea so sharp and fast she didn't know if it was hers or someone else.

Up ahead, Cressida tumbled to the ground. Thunder swallowed Astrea's cry.

Another piercing shot.

Jin stumbled. His hand fell from hers, then his knees hit the ground.

Hot and cold fire burned in Astrea's veins. That wrong, wrong fire. The one she'd first felt so long ago in Kalama, when that woman died behind the museum.

Astrea screamed. She fell to her knees and rolled Jin over. Shadows snaked up his hands, disappearing under his armor.

"No!" she screamed again.

Pain, pain, pain. It twisted Astrea's heart and tore it in two, pulsing through her so fast she thought she would explode. She was going to vomit.

"Jin!" she cried, searching his body for the bullet hole. "Adi, help! Lucian!" She tore her eyes away from Jin for a moment, only to find Adi sprawled out on the ground. Panic surged around Lucian and Marko.

No.

No, no, no.

She looked at Jin's face again, finding his eyes locked on hers. Those beautiful eyes, gold flecked with amber and shadow.

"It's okay," he rasped. White terror. Silver acceptance. Deep blue regret. Pink love. So many colors danced around him, a torrent despite the shadows crawling up his neck.

"No," Astrea cried. "No."

"Yes." Somehow, Jin's hand found hers. "It's okay. Find Zephyrine."

"No!"

She had to try. But where did she start? This was exactly where she had failed the very first time, how that woman had died behind the museum in Kalama. And based on the way Jin's loose hold on her hand weakened, how the pain flared hotter and colder in her chest, he didn't have long. Adi wouldn't, either.

Astrea pushed to her knees, then moved to straddle Jin's waist. His lids fluttered closed. His breathing turned shallow.

White light danced over Astrea's hands. She laid them on either side of his shoulder, where black blood oozed out. Her magic sped forward, eager to work as the pain in Astrea's body doubled, tripled, quadrupled. Even so, her light barely seemed to creep forward. It gained just an inch when she needed so much more. She pushed and pushed, and still, her magic barely seeped into Jin's body.

He couldn't die. He couldn't.

She didn't care what aetherium did. Didn't care, didn't care. She'd fix this. She had to.

"Astrea!" Saros shouted.

She focused on the rapid rise and fall of Jin's chest. Her light pushed forward, inch by inch, as she tried to think of everything good she could. As she tried desperately to ignore the all-consuming pain and the way shadows crept into the edges of her vision.

The way Jin had made her a nightlight. How he always found a way to hold her as they slept. That sunshine warmth. His laugh, his secret smile.

Her magic pushed forward.

"Astrea!" Saros shouted again.

Panic slammed into her just as a strong hand grabbed her braid and yanked her back. She tumbled backward, her light dying.

"Don't you dare think about it, Miss Sovna," Kaius hissed. "He deserves to die, traitor that he is."

"No!" she screamed, trying to scramble upright. She had to heal Jin. She had to heal Jin, then get to Cressida and Adi, and—

Kaius dropped her braid. A loud "oof" followed, then ghost pain slammed into Astrea's shoulder.

"Heal him!" Saros shouted.

A sickening crack came from behind her, pain echoing in her jaw. Astrea knelt at Jin's side, hands back on his sternum as she pulled and pushed on her light. The shadows eating at his skin seemed to recede, dance forward, then back, then back again. She was doing it. She was healing him.

"Yes," she whispered. "Yes, come on, Jin." Her light glowed brighter, a beacon among the shadows still swirling in the air. Nearby, more light sprang up.

"Astrea!" Saros shouted again. "Astrea!"

Why was he trying to distract her? Why was—

Bile crept up Astrea's throat as cold fire lanced her from behind, penetrating deep into her chest and belly. She screamed; she couldn't take it. She was going to burn away.

Was this it, then? The end?

But as she tore one blood-covered hand off Jin's shoulder and tried to find whatever it was that struck her, she found nothing.

Nothing...

She turned. There Saros was, sprawled out behind her. A dagger stuck out of his abdomen. Shadows snaked up his arms and face. Blood splashed out of his mouth with every cough.

Astrea's heart twisted and twisted into a painful knot. One hand still rested on Jin's rapidly rising and falling chest. She couldn't—

How was she supposed to—

A cold, familiar pair of eyes looked into Astrea's. Gold. That cruel, cruel gold that belonged to Kaius. He pushed up on his hands and knees, uniform covered in scorch marks. Saros's doing, no doubt.

Saros coughed, smile faltering.

Jin shuddered under her hand.

"Uncle," Astrea whispered.

"It's alright, my dear." His hand gripped the knife in his belly, then yanked it out. Pain flared hot and new in her abdomen. "Look away."

"What are you—"

"Look away," Saros said again. With a trembling hand, Saros brought the knife toward his throat.

"No!" she shrieked.

Astrea slammed her other hand onto Saros's arm, clamping tight around it as she pulled on her light again. Her body strained as she gripped them both. And her light . . .

It wasn't doing enough. It wouldn't *go*. Like it was stuck, held at bay by the void magic these weapons held.

"Save him." Saros choked out the words. "Look away."

Tears streamed down Astrea's cheeks. She couldn't let Saros—

Jin shuddered again. The shadows crawled an inch up his tan skin, regaining lost ground. The more she tried to split her healing . . .

"Heal him," Saros said again.

She wasn't strong enough. Wasn't strong enough to save Jin. Wasn't strong enough to let Saros go. Her hands trembled.

"Look away, Astrea. Look away."

She couldn't save them both.

Squeezing her eyes shut, Astrea let go of Saros's arm. She turned back toward Jin. Placing both hands on his shoulder, Astrea held her breath and pulled on all the pain swirling in the air. The pain and fear and panic and rage.

And all the pain behind her, that hot and cold . . . Sharp pain sliced across her throat. She choked as fire and ice clawed their way up from her lungs.

And then it stopped.

It was gone.

Saros.

Saros was gone.

Tears leaked down Astrea's cheeks.

Saros was gone. Saros was gone. Saros was gone.

Jin's pulse slowed under Astrea's palms, sticky with his blood.

Heal him. Save him.

She pulled and pulled and pulled on her magic, begging it to come forth. Balance. She needed balance to the pain, something good. Everything good.

She could not lose him. Astrea would not lose him. She could not fail. Not when she'd just failed Saros. She couldn't fail Jin, too.

More hot tears poured down Astrea's cheeks. Light built around her hands, so blindingly bright she could barely see. Fear and pain arced out somewhere nearby, orange and steel and white.

What was good?

When Jin remembered her favorite café after being gone for eight years. When he'd protected her secret. When he'd taken care of her burns on Solstice Night when she couldn't heal herself. All the time they spent in the gardens as children.

How he used to try to make Astrea laugh during lessons with Saros despite that it would get him in trouble. Whenever he checked in to make sure she'd remembered to eat. The way he held her every night.

How Saros used to hold her tight when she was little and missed her mother. Whenever he'd looked on with subtle pride when she practiced her magic in that old observatory tower. How he'd introduced her to cinnamon pancakes and encouraged her love for studying and reading. His advice to her and Jin on their wedding day, how he only ever wanted her to live a safe, good life.

Something exploded in Astrea's veins, so bright and hot that she nearly collapsed on top of Jin. But she kept her hands in place, eyes closed against the brightness.

Around her, shouting. Someone—Marko—calling her name, trying to pull her away.

No. The mirror healing was there, she could feel it. That bright, hot pinging in her chest.

"Get away!" Astrea shrieked, shrugging him off. "Get away!"

Please, Astrea begged her magic as she grabbed everything she could feel—terror, love, pain, acceptance, confusion. All of it was hers for the taking. *Please, please, please.*

Her hands burned. Her body burned. She could burn away for all she cared if it meant Jin wouldn't die.

Please, please, please.

Jin's breath shuddered again.

She burned brighter, hotter. Everything. Anything. She would give it all to not lose him again.

She would tear the shadows out of Jin, and then she was going to make Kaius pay. She was going to make all of them pay for this—Kaius, the emperor, Nazarov, the Paragon. For everything they'd done. Everything they'd stolen from her.

She burned hotter still, magic building under her skin. It hurt. Her body screamed.

Yes. This was what she wanted.

Terror and joy and love and confusion and pain and everything from the last few months spun around Astrea, whirling and building in her mind's eye. Her magic could take it. Her magic could have it all. Jin could have it all if it just meant he would live.

Astrea sobbed. Magic burned through her veins, tearing her up from the inside out. The ground under them shook as her light grew brighter and brighter until—

It stopped.

She felt nothing. No rain. No heat. No pain. Not even Jin's shuddering breaths.

As her light died, Astrea collapsed on top of him, sobs racking her body before darkness finally took hold.

Chapter 55

Warmth drifted around Astrea. Sunshine spread over her skin as she stared up at the clouds high above. She smiled and let her eyes close.

It was nice. She could lie there like that forever and just—

"When is she going to wake up, Commander?"

"I don't know, Your Imperial Highness."

"What do you mean you don't know? Are you a healer or not?"

"These things—"

"Take time, I know. Bullshit."

Astrea's eyelids seemed to be glued shut. Her entire body was heavy, like Adi had earthmoved a ton of rocks onto her.

Something soft cradled her. A bed, maybe? There was no more rain or wind or muddy earth.

"Hey!" Eliana sounded surprised. Astrea still couldn't open her eyes. "Hey, Az, it's alright . . . do you know where you are?"

Tears burned Astrea's throat. "Where's Jin?" she asked. "Where's Saros? What happened?"

"Az, you really need to—"

"No, where's Jin? Where is he?" she asked again. "Where's Jin? Where is he?"

She couldn't breathe. Her eyes cracked open just enough to see the blue sadness coating Eliana's body.

"Where's Jin?" she whispered. "Where, Ellie?"

A frown tugged at Eliana's mouth. "Az, it's—"

"Let her be, Eliana," came Lucian's command. He nudged Eliana out of the way and tipped a vial to Astrea's lips. "Go to sleep, Astrea. It'll be alright."

No, Astrea couldn't go to sleep. She didn't want to go to sleep. She had to fix . . .

"Jin?" Astrea called. "Saros?"

The darkness didn't answer.

"Jin?" she called again. His name echoed around her. "Saros?"

Still, silence.

Silence, silence, silence. It didn't matter how many times she screamed their names. No response came.

"Who gave you the authority to continuously drug her?" a familiar voice asked.

Astrea tried to move, but she couldn't. She couldn't—

"It's for her own safety. She's unstable."

"She's *grieving*, not unstable."

"She cannot recover if she does not rest, and she will not rest whenever we do allow her to wake."

"If you don't stop, Commander, I'll force you to. Do you understand?"

Skies, Astrea was tired. The simple effort of being conscious made her body ache. She tried to open her eyes wider, but they fluttered shut against her will. Even breathing took incredible effort.

Something crackled. Fire? Yes, fire. The faint smell of burning wood permeated the air. It was nice. Cozy. Warm. Where was she?

Something heavy rested in her lap. Someone was holding her hand. Lifting her free hand, Astrea reached out. Her fingers brushed against soft hair, then hard muscle. Even that simple movement took too much breath and energy.

That heavy something—someone—shifted. A low groan followed, then a sweet, gentle warmth slid over Astrea's skin.

Sunshine.

"Az," Jin whispered.

No . . . it couldn't be Jin. He'd died. Astrea hadn't been able to save him or Saros. She'd felt it.

Maybe this was some cruel dream. Maybe the void had taken her and Jin both. Maybe that would be the most merciful thing.

Tears spilled down Astrea's cheeks.

"Hey." Jin brushed some of the tears away, his skin warm and familiar. "Hey, you're alright. You're safe."

A sob broke from Astrea's chest, a nasty, ugly sound. She choked on the next breath she managed to suck in.

"Hey." The bed dipped as that heavy weight passed over her, then settled next to her. Jin took Astrea in his arms. "Hey. It's alright. You're alright."

No, this wasn't a dream. This wasn't the void. This was a warm room, a soft bed. Jin's skin on hers, her heart beating wildly in her chest.

She was very much alive.

Astrea couldn't even move. She was too bone-deep tired, like her limbs weighed a thousand pounds. She just lay there, sobbing, as Jin curled around her, his warring pain and sunshine weighing her down even more.

"I couldn't save him," she wailed. "I couldn't save him, and he—and so he—"

"It's alright, it's okay," Jin whispered. "It's alright. Breathe, Az."

Her cries drowned out whatever it was Jin was trying to tell her. She barely registered the image in front of her. Golden eyes, looping chestnut curls, tired tawny skin, scruffy beard. No trace of shadows.

No shadows.

Jin was alive.

No shadows.

She cried harder, trying to bury the image of Saros being consumed by those shadows. The image of him pulling that weapon out of his gut and bringing it to his neck. That ghost pain slicing her throat as he took his own life. It crossed her skin again and again and again.

"Lucian!" Jin shouted. "Lucian!" But then he pulled Astrea closer. "I'm sorry, Az. I'm sorry."

The bedroom door slammed open. Astrea clung to Jin even as someone put a vial to her lips and made her drink something. She clung to him even as that darkness took hold again, and all she could think about was that Jin was *alive*.

Astrea's head pounded in an unsteady beat. Her eyes barely opened, then shut.

"You've had her sedated for days, Lucian."

"I already told you that she is not well. She hasn't recovered."

"She is *my* wife. *My* family. *I* get to make this decision. If you have no medical reason to keep her under, then we need to let her wake up."

"You tried that this morning, and it didn't go very well. It will hurt her."

"It's going to hurt her no matter how long we keep her under. Is her body stable?"

"It's stable." Pause. "She will be weak, though. I've never seen anything like that."

"Then we will care for her, but please, no more drugs. Not unless she truly needs them."

A heavy sigh. "Very well."

Footsteps. Heavy footsteps, two pairs. One retreated and one moved closer.

"Hey," Jin whispered, his gentle smile greeting her as Astrea forced her eyes open again.

White terror, icy shock, and lavender surprise exploded around him, quickly taken over by minty relief that cooled Astrea's burning skin.

"You're awake," he said.

When she tried to speak but found she couldn't, Jin disappeared. Astrea let her heavy, swollen lids close. He returned with a glass of water, bringing it to her lips. Astrea hated that she needed help, but she was too tired to even move her arm. She drank.

"Do you want more?" Jin asked as she pulled away.

"No." She cleared her throat, but it still felt like sandpaper.

"Do you need anything? Lucian just left."

"Just sit," Astrea whispered.

Jin watched her for a moment. "You're sure?"

"Please." Astrea didn't want to see Lucian or Eliana. She didn't want to see the Nikaphoroses. She didn't want to see anyone.

Jin pulled a chair close to the bed, then sat and took Astrea's hand in his. "How do you feel?"

"Everything hurts. I'm tired."

"What do you remember?"

"I thought you died." That hot and cold fire, the ghostly knife against her throat, the terror in Jin's eyes, the way his blood had felt on her hands . . . "I thought I didn't save you."

"Hey." Reaching up, Jin smoothed hair away from Astrea's forehead and face. "Hey, you did, alright. I'm alive."

Saros wasn't.

"How long has it been?" she whispered.

"Four days."

"Where are we?"

"Thasia."

"How'd we get back?"

"Theo and his void mages helped," Jin said. "Or at least, that's what Lucian told me."

"How's Adi?"

"Recovering."

"Was he shot with—"

Jin shook his head. "Not aetherium, no. Different bullet."

"How are the others?"

"Alive but not well. Cress needed surgery, but she'll be alright. She . . ." He shook his head again. "She was hit with aetherium, but I promise she'll be just fine. You should talk to her when you're up for it."

What did that mean? Cressida was hit with aetherium but was alive? Had Lucian saved her?

Astrea sucked in a shaky breath, trying to focus on the feeling of Jin's hand wrapped around hers instead of everything else her mind wanted to show her. She would check on Cressida later.

"Nazarov and your father?" she asked.

"I don't know. No one is sure, but Lucian said that whatever you did out there . . . it didn't just save me. It caused a lot of damage."

She remembered someone trying to pull her off Jin, the way she screamed and let even more magic course through her veins. Had she pushed all that energy out again, like when she was under that house?

"Did we . . ." The question stuck to the tip of her tongue. "Did they bring Saros back, too?"

Jin pressed his lips together. "They did."

At least she could give him a proper send-off even if she hadn't been able to save him. At least she could say goodbye.

"How do you feel?" he asked. "Physically, I mean."

"Like a dozen streetcars ran over me."

Jin kissed the top of her head. "Do you want Lucian to come check on you?"

"No." She wiped at the tears building on her lash line. "No, I think I just want to sleep."

"Then sleep." He kissed the top of her head again. "I'll be right here when you wake up."

And so Astrea burrowed into the blankets and begged the darkness to take her again. Anything would be better than feeling that hole in her heart.

Sharp pain on her throat. Fire in her veins.

"Look away, Astrea. Look away."

Silver eyes. Shadows. So much red.

"Look away, look away, look away."

Cold sweat coated Astrea's skin. She clawed at her night shirt, at the base of her throat. All she could feel was that void fire, that knife, the way her veins—Saros's veins, Jin's veins—burned with ice.

"Az?" Jin's sleepy voice called out to her. His arms curled around her, tugging her against his bare chest. "Az, hey."

"I felt him do it." Clinging to him, Astrea buried her face in the crook of his neck.

"Felt him do what?"

"He took his own life." A knot tied itself around Astrea's heart and yanked hard. She couldn't breathe. "I felt it. I felt it. He told me to look away, but I still felt—"

Jin shushed her gently as the tears came, like he knew there was nothing he could say. Because there wasn't. Nothing could make this better.

"I can't stop feeling it. It won't stop."

Astrea hiccuped, choking on the air she gulped in. She couldn't breathe. She coughed, a loud, barking sound. Tears and snot leaked down her face. She couldn't—

How could Saros do that to her?

How could he do that to her when he knew she would feel it?

How could she have given up so easily?

"He...he didn't...he wouldn't..." She barely choked out the words between her cries. "I f-failed him ... after all these years ..."

Pushing her away from his chest, Jin cupped Astrea's face in his hands. "Listen to me, okay?"

She nodded and swallowed her next sob.

"You did not fail him."

"But I—"

"You did not fail him."

"But ... but I'm a ... a healer ..."

"You did not fail him." Jin wiped away some of her tears, little good it did. In the low, warm light of the fire, his irises seemed to glow molten gold. "You made him so proud, Az. He was hit with aetherium. There was no coming back from that."

"But I saved . . . I saved *you* . . ."

Save him. Look away.

"Yes, but look at what it cost you."

"I just feel sick."

"Az . . ."

The way Jin trailed off made Astrea look at him again. His eyebrows furrowed, and he gently pressed her fingers to his skin, just underneath his right shoulder and his clavicle. There. A knotted scar, and spiraling out from it were faded shadows. Her eyes burned.

Aetherium had left its mark, forever, on Jin.

"Lucian and the Thasian healers who've been treating you weren't sure how long it would take you to recover," he said. "They felt the pain of the aetherium in your body for days, like it was clinging to you."

"What?" She blinked slowly. That . . . didn't make sense. It was supposed to be ghost pain, diminish when the healing was complete.

"I don't know. It took me two days to wake up. That's what Lucian told me. I don't think he'd lie about that."

"You were asleep for that long?"

Jin nodded. "Lucian felt it in my body, too, but it went away more quickly."

She pressed her fingers against that scar again, but Jin didn't react. "Why?" she asked.

"He doesn't know. I still don't feel quite right. All I know is he said it took substantial effort to keep us both stable, to keep us from going into shock. He's still stunned that you managed to save me at all."

If it had taken Astrea that much to heal Jin, if it had left her completely useless for days . . .

She truly could not have healed them both.

She couldn't have. Healing Jin had left her unconscious for days. And she couldn't save Saros while she was out of it like that.

Could another healer have saved him, though? Had he been too quick to sacrifice himself?

She would never know.

Chapter 56

Numb. That was all Astrea felt.

It didn't matter what was going on around her. It didn't matter how many times Lucian stopped by to check on her. It didn't matter when Eliana and Adi came to visit her. Lennor and Civan visited, too. Marko. Balthazar hadn't come by yet, only because Cressida was still recovering after her surgery. She was alive, at least.

Alive, but she'd lost her left hand. Lucian had explained it a couple of times to Astrea, that Cressida had been hit in the wrist with an aetherium bullet. She'd ripped it out of her own body with her magic, before the aetherium's poisonous magic could spread too far. But it had seriously damaged her hand to the point that it couldn't be healed. Not just from the aetherium but the physical trauma. Magic couldn't fix everything.

Even Jin's sunshine didn't help. A comfort to know he was there, yes, but it didn't ease the pain settling deep in Astrea's bones. It didn't stop her mind from replaying those few moments over and over and over again.

"Well," Lucian said, pulling his hand away from where it rested between Astrea's shoulders, "I feel nothing other than your fatigue. Nothing that needs healing."

She sat on a narrow chair in the room she'd been sharing with Jin. He stood just a couple feet away in front of the fireplace, arms crossed over his chest.

He looked about as good as she felt. Dark circles under his eyes. Scruffy and unkempt beard. The slight paleness to his skin. She couldn't tell where her exhaustion ended and his began.

"Alright, thank you," Astrea said to Lucian.

"And how are you feeling, Varojin?" the commander asked.

"Fine."

Lucian pressed his lips together, obviously not believing Jin. "Take another day to rest," he said. "Your sister has a meeting with President Sikori tomorrow. She would like to hear from you about what happened."

"Sikori doesn't already know?" Jin asked.

"We've told her what we can, but obviously there are some things we cannot explain." Lucian glanced down at Astrea. "If you're open to speaking with her."

"Whatever I need to do." Astrea's words felt hollow, wrong. Just like the rest of her. "If it convinces her government to side with us, I'll tell her whatever she wants to hear."

"Yes, well . . ." Lucian nodded. "As I said, rest today. The mission will continue tomorrow."

Always with another skies damned mission.

Astrea slumped back in her chair. The room was comfortable, set somewhere deep within the Tornamian president's residence. All around her, Astrea could sense people. Guards, most likely. Soldiers.

"Az?" Jin asked.

"I'd like to see him."

"Who?"

"Saros."

"Az . . ." Cold pain swept over Astrea's skin. "Are you sure that's a good idea?"

"I need to see him."

"I—"

"Please." The word was harsher, more desperate, than Astrea meant for it to be. But she had to see Saros. She had to see those shadows again, reassure herself there was nothing more that could have been done.

Jin was silent for so long that Astrea wasn't sure he'd respond. And he didn't.

"I can take you to see him," Lucian said quietly. "If that is what you want."

"It is."

As they stepped out into the hallway beyond their bedroom, Astrea barely took in the furnishings or layout. She barely saw the Tornamian guards and security details wandering the building. All she could focus on was the deep, aching thump of her heart in her chest as she and Jin followed Lucian through the building.

They walked for what seemed like forever. Down corridors, through ornate foyers, and finally, down another set of stairs. The walls changed from beautiful wood and wallpaper to pragmatic brick, all furnishings gone. The air chilled.

Jin's hand found the small of Astrea's back as they neared a door at the end of another hallway. The single-bulb lights overhead buzzed.

Lucian pushed the heavy door open. More cold air prickled Astrea's skin.

The room was mostly bare except for a handful of boxes, rows of shelves on the far wall, and a few empty tables. Empty except for one, covered in a thick white sheet.

She couldn't breathe.

"Az?" Jin asked when she didn't move from near the door. "We can go back up—"

"No." She had to see this.

Lucian walked to the sheet-draped table at the far end of the room. Astrea followed, Jin right behind her.

"Can I see him?" she asked Lucian, voice barely above a whisper. "Please?"

Lucian watched her carefully, like he was trying to gauge what her reaction might be. Jin rubbed slow circles between her shoulder blades as the commander lifted the sheet from Saros's face and down to his shoulders, still covered by that red Helosian uniform.

His eyes were closed. If it weren't for the dark shadows etched into his skin, it might almost seem like he was asleep.

But he wasn't.

His skin was unnaturally pale, and his hair was all wrong, like it had lost some of its nearly black pigment.

An angry red gash cut through the middle of his throat. The memory of that ghostly pain flickered on Astrea's skin.

This was wrong, all wrong. So, so wrong.

It wasn't supposed to be like this. This mission wasn't supposed to have failed so badly.

It was not simply that she'd lost her uncle.

No, Astrea grieved, not just for the time when he was alive but the future they would never have. The future she would never have with him nor her mother.

They would not see her become the Lightbringer everyone believed she could be. They would never meet her children or witness the life Astrea would someday build for herself.

The last of her blood family, gone. Forever.

She grieved not just for the future she'd lost but the past she couldn't fix. All the days and months she'd spent angry with Saros, all the time they'd lost because they'd both been too stubborn to come around. All the stories and family history she'd never asked him for and that he'd now never tell.

Astrea's shoulders shook. She buried her face in her hands, unable to look at him a second longer.

This couldn't be happening. He couldn't be gone.

Jin wrapped his arms around Astrea. She buried her face in his chest as the first sob escaped her. It bounced around the empty room, taunting her.

"Why did he—" She couldn't finish the question out loud.

Why did he step in front of Kaius's blade? Why did he leave her with so many questions? And why was she angry with him at all when he'd undoubtedly saved her life? Saved Jin's life, in a way.

"I know, Az," Jin whispered into her hair. "I know. I'm so, so sorry. I'm sorry."

This wasn't supposed to be happening. *She* had been destined to die. Not him.

Astrea forced her eyes open, blinking back against the tsunami of tears. The red Helosian uniform Saros still wore nearly blinded her.

Yes. She had been destined to die, not Saros.

"He knew," Astrea said, voice cracking.

"What?" Jin brushed away some of her tears with his thumbs. "What did he know?"

"This. It was his vision that he had fourteen years ago." As gray confusion swirled around Jin, Astrea said, "He saw me dying on the Helosian battlefield. It . . . it must have been his vision. He always said anyone could change the future . . . I just didn't think . . ."

"Hey." Jin pulled her close again. "Hey. Come on. Let's get out of here. You don't need to be here right now."

"I can't go back to that room." She'd been trapped there for days. "I can't . . . I can't be *here*—"

"Go to the gardens," Lucian said, covering Saros with the sheet again. "Get some fresh air. I'll send Marko out."

Astrea didn't want to see Marko. She didn't want to see anyone. But going outside sounded better than staying in. If she stayed inside—anywhere near that table, Saros's body—a second longer, she might be sick.

As much as she wanted to take in the beauty that was the Tornamian presidential palace and gardens, Astrea couldn't. Her eyes registered what she saw, but her mind didn't retain it. If someone had asked her how she ended up on a bench with Jin near a bubbling fountain deep within the gardens, she couldn't have told them. She didn't even know how long they'd been sitting there.

Astrea wiped at her tears, little good it did her. They wouldn't stop. Hadn't stopped since seeing Saros.

It was a bright, sunny afternoon. All wrong.

A few ducks swam in the bottom tier of the large fountain. It was some sculpture that was vaguely familiar, a woman with many long braids and a crown. Had she seen that somewhere before? Astrea begged her mind to focus on it, to figure it out. Maybe in a painting back at one of Kalama's museums . . . they housed many pieces of Tornamian art. Was she some ancient ruler?

Gravel crunched behind them as two wary sets of energy drew closer. Lucian had said he was just sending Marko.

"There you are. We've been looking all over for you two."

"Hey, Adi," Jin said quietly.

"You missed lunch," Adi said as he sat on the edge of the bench next to Astrea. "You hungry?"

"No," Astrea whispered. The food Jin had been forcing her to nibble on the last few days may as well have been ash in her mouth for all that Astrea had tasted. The thought of eating just made her stomach turn. "Thanks though."

More footsteps, then Marko said, "The commander wanted me to tell you both that he's got Lightbringers patrolling the gardens."

"No news on Nazarov?" Astrea heard herself ask.

Marko shrugged. "No."

"Maybe he and the emperor destroyed themselves," Adi said.

Astrea doubted it had played out that way. Nothing ever seemed to go in their favor, especially not when it came to Victor Nazarov. She plucked at the wrinkles in her dress.

A fortnight. Just a fortnight before, she and Jin had gotten married. How had so much changed in a fortnight?

"I need to see Cress," Astrea said, mostly to Jin. "Where is she?"

"She hasn't let any of us go see her except Ellie," Adi said.

"Where is she?" Astrea repeated. Saros may have been gone, but Astrea still had to see the rest of her family. She had to. "Take me to her."

With a hesitant sigh, Adi led Astrea and Jin back inside. They went down hallways, up staircases, until finally, they arrived at a closed door. It was in a different hallway than Astrea's room had been; she could tell only because the wallpaper was blue instead of green.

"She really doesn't want to see anyone," Adi whispered.

Astrea knocked anyway. Footsteps shuffled inside, and a whisper of surprise danced over Astrea's skin just before the door cracked open. One jade iris peeked out.

"Az?" came Cressida's voice, raspy like she hadn't had enough to drink.

"Can I come in?" Astrea whispered. "Please."

Cressida glanced behind Astrea, to where Jin, Marko, and Adi all stood. She huffed. "You and Jin can come in. Everyone else, out."

Rough disappointment scraped over Astrea's skin. She pushed it away, instead focusing on squeezing through Cressida's barely cracked door. Jin shut it behind him with a soft click.

Cressida's bronze skin lacked its usual glow. She wore loose pajamas, and her hair was twisted up in a colorful head wrap. And her left arm was up in a white sling, obscuring her injury. Blue sadness and steel pain wrapped around her willowy figure. Her eyes were bloodshot, like she'd either been crying or not sleeping. Maybe both.

Aetherium was supposed to kill. Be practically impossible to heal.

And yet Astrea had healed Jin. Cressida had stopped the magic from getting that far into her system. Two impossible feats.

"I'd ask how you are, but it seems pointless," Astrea said.

Crossing the short distance between them, Cressida pulled Astrea into a tight embrace. She kept her body away from Cressida's recovering arm but still held onto her, a lifeline as the world threatened to drown them both.

"Lucian's keeping the pain dulled with tonics," Cressida said as she pulled away. "He won't leave me alone."

"I'm not surprised." And that explained why Astrea felt no echo of pain in her body. "How's your dad?"

"Not good. He's really torn up about all of this. Wouldn't even let Ma come down." Her gaze flicked toward Jin, who hadn't moved the whole time. "You look like shit."

He gave a halfhearted chuckle. "Good to see you too, Cress."

With her right hand, Cressida dragged Astrea over toward the bed. They sat, and Astrea took Cressida's hand in hers. She traced Cressida's aura with her eyes, chasing the blue, mint, steel, crimson. Cressida had been hit with aetherium, and she would have a long road ahead, but she was alive. Astrea forced herself to breathe.

"You look like shit too, Az." Cressida squeezed her hand. "What's going on? Why do you look like you saw a ghost?"

"He knew, Cress," Astrea whispered.

Her eyebrows furrowed. "What?"

Astrea swallowed past the lump in her throat. "Saros knew. His vision . . . his vision of me when we first moved to Kalama. Me on the battlefield, dressed in a Helosian uniform, dying as I tried to heal someone. He put himself between me and Kaius's blade. He knew."

"Fucking skies," Cressida muttered. "Fuck, Az, I'm so sorry."

"What am I going to tell your parents?" Astrea asked. "How could he do that?"

"Because he loved you," Jin said gently as he joined them. His hand settled on her shoulder, then slid to the back of her neck. It was heavy, warm. Comforting. "He didn't want you to get hurt."

"Saros was a lot of things, Az," Cressida said, "but I never, ever doubted how much he loved you. Even when he was an ass."

Astrea choked out a laugh as fresh tears spilled down her cheeks. "I know."

Saros had sacrificed everything for her over the years. No, he hadn't always made the right choices. He'd been beyond stubborn. Secretive. But he had also done his best. He'd tried so hard to give her a good life and keep her safe. Flaws and all, Saros had loved her more than anything in the world. And she would give anything to have him back so that they could keep trying to fix this together.

"I want to take him back to Irvina," Astrea said. "When we were there together, he said it felt like going home. I want to take him home. To his home."

"Whatever you want," Jin said. "We'll make it happen."

Astrea nodded. She wanted to get Saros home as soon as possible, but this mission was too important. If she was going to take down Kaius, Emperor Aelius, and Nazarov, she was going to need all the help she could get. And if that meant waiting around Thasia for a few more days to speak to the president, it would be worth it.

Cressida and Jin couldn't have suffered for nothing, and Saros couldn't have died in vain. He just couldn't have.

One way or another, Astrea was going to finish this.

CHAPTER 57

Another day of sleep had helped ease some of Astrea's fatigue, but her body still protested every movement. She'd checked herself over with her own magic, but nothing was wrong with her body. Nothing that her magic could find, anyway.

And now, she had to go sit through some skies forsaken meeting with politicians.

But this was it. Part of their mission. Where they'd failed in every other way, they still had this opportunity.

Eliana ran a brush through Astrea's hair, loosening the curls she'd put in with the hot iron. Astrea hadn't wanted to do anything other than take a shower and put on a somewhat presentable outfit, but Eliana had shown up an hour before and made Astrea sit down. She'd even sent Jin away to check on Cressida—who wasn't feeling up to the meeting—and to help Zephyrine prepare.

"There." Eliana set the brush down on the narrow desk they were using as a makeshift vanity. She'd even brought a small mirror with her and set it up on the table. "All done."

"Thanks." Astrea tucked her hair behind her ears. "Just let me get changed."

Grabbing her dress from the back of the chair, Astrea headed for the bathroom. The dress was light green, not a color she would've chosen for herself but what the president's staff had provided. It was fine, surprisingly casual given the meeting was between Eliana, President Sikori, and a Delian ambassador. Astrea wiggled into the loose linen garment, fixed her hair, then rejoined her friend.

"You don't have to do this, you know," Eliana said as she packed up the small makeup bag on the vanity.

"Yes, I do." Astrea sucked in a shallow breath. "I have to. This is the only part of the mission that didn't fail, Ellie. I have to see it through."

"We can—"

"Can what?" Astrea asked, the words sharper than she meant. "Skies, I'm sorry, just . . . I have to. I'm the one who healed Jin. I'm the one who somehow . . . stopped the aetherium. I'm the one who saw what Kaius did to Sar—" She swallowed hard. "I have to. My testimony might mean something."

Astrea's testimony would be especially important given Cressida wouldn't be there to provide hers. Lucian was planning to speak to what happened and how Cressida had managed to save herself, and hopefully, paired with Astrea's version of events, it would be enough. The papers they'd stolen from the base that detailed the weapons testing and mining efforts had been damaged by the storm, not entirely useless but not the full picture, either.

Blue sadness wavered around Eliana. "I know you're right. I just don't want you to *have* to do this. It's not fair."

None of this was fair. Nothing had been fair for a long time, not for Astrea and not for many other people.

"What time are we supposed to meet them?" Astrea asked.

"Ten or so minutes. . . We should go now."

As they headed out into the hall, Astrea was greeted by the sight of armed guards, all in dark green uniforms. The guards at Ysabel's palace were all mages and hardly carried weapons, so seeing them with knives strapped to their bodies and large guns slung over their shoulders was as foreign as the president's home.

Nicos fell in step behind them as Eliana steered Astrea down the hall and toward a wide set of stairs. Astrea hadn't seen much of him since they'd returned from the mission, though apparently he hadn't taken the news about his mother siding with the emperor very well. Even now, hidden behind his barrier, Astrea could almost sense the desperation and anger he no doubt felt.

At the next junction, another heavily armed guard met them and joined Nicos as their escort. Though not as grand as the Novarian palace, the Tornamian president's home was beautiful and bright. Astrea might've admired it if the situation were different.

Inside the meeting room, Jin was talking with Adi, Marko, and Lucian. Zephyrine and Rami were speaking with the president's spouse, Sarya. Astrea didn't see President Sikori or the Delian ambassador anywhere. The large oval table could seat a dozen, but all the chairs sat empty.

"Hey," Jin said as Astrea joined him. "We should get started soon."

For a few minutes, Adi and Marko tried to fill the heavy air with small talk. Adi spoke of how glad he was to get to try authentic Tornamian food. Marko said he was looking forward to being home, and Lucian agreed with him.

Astrea wrapped her arm around Jin's waist, leaning into him. He tugged her closer to his body, like he couldn't stand the thought of having any space between them.

"I'll have someone bring in some tea for you all," Sarya called out. "Let me go see where my wife is. Please, make yourselves comfortable."

They all took seats around the table; Astrea was sandwiched between Jin and Adi. When tea was brought in, Astrea accepted it and focused on the way steam curled from the porcelain cup in front of her.

Another member of the president's staff set out three-tier trays of pastries and sandwiches. Astrea didn't have an appetite, but she still took one of the little guava tarts. It wasn't as good as the ones Cressida made, but Astrea managed to eat a few bites.

"Good, everyone's seated and ready to go, I see," called President Sikori as she wheeled into the room. She maneuvered her wheelchair up to the empty spot at the head of the table as the Delian ambassador took his seat. "Let's get started, shall we? I do apologize for the delay."

"I hope everything's alright," Eliana said.

"You know how those days go. Just can't stick to the schedule," the president said. Her gaze shifted to where Jin and Astrea sat. "I'm glad to see you two up and moving around. I'm eager to hear your version of the story."

"I'm afraid my version won't paint a full picture, Madam President," Jin said. "There's a lot I didn't witness."

"Of course," the president said. "I'd still like to hear whatever it is you have to say. Your wife's version, too."

Jin went first, detailing more information about the aetherium deposits Astrea hadn't known. Saros, Cressida, and Balthazar had guided them to the metal, only to find the mine went deep into the earth. It had been a huge operation, and part of why Jin and the others had been delayed was because they'd been trying to find any way they could to sabotage things. They hadn't found anything.

And then it was Astrea's turn. She explained what she could about what happened in the camp commander's office, at which point Adi and Zephyrine added additional details. All that was left was the horrible, horrible tale of how the mission had gone wrong.

Astrea explained in fits and starts what happened, somehow managing not to cry as she told them about the fight with Kaius, how Jin got shot, how Saros took Kaius's dagger to save her.

"Miss Sovna," said the Delian ambassador, "it's my understanding that this aetherium ore has properties from the void, that it cannot be healed. Or that was how it was explained to me by Her Imperial Highness."

"Obviously it can be healed, Ambassador," Eliana said. "She healed my brother after he was struck by it, and our other friend is still alive."

"At great cost, Ambassador," Astrea said. "That was days ago. I still don't feel up to my normal strength."

"Perhaps it wasn't the healing but the . . . what did you say happened, Commander Lucian?" asked the ambassador.

"I'm fairly certain it was the healing, Ambassador," Lucian said. "Miss Sovna let forth a wave of healing so strong it knocked out a lot of fighters."

"How can healing do that?" the ambassador asked.

Lucian shrugged. "Raw power? I've never been able to generate so much. Miss Sovna is a very strong mage. If not for that, I think Prince Varojin would have died."

Astrea's lungs tightened painfully. Under the table, she gripped Jin's hand in hers. How was he so calm when those words just left Lucian's mouth?

And if that was true, if that much healing power was needed to reverse the effects of aetherium . . . Well, the implications were terrible. Besides, hadn't Nazarov stabbed The One with aetherium in that house back in Talmaris? It seemed that way at the time. So how had he survived? Could the power of several weaker healers be enough to save someone, or did the Paragon have elite healers at their disposal? Astrea shook her head. She'd never know for certain—at least, she wouldn't know today—and getting stuck on it didn't seem useful.

"It sounds like nothing short of a miracle that Miss Sovna was the one to heal Prince Varojin, then," the ambassador replied, blue eyes fixed on her. "You don't know what's become of this Paragonian leader or Emperor Aelius?"

"No," Lucian said. "After Astrea's energy surge, another group of void mages—these ones loyal to her and Varojin—helped us transport out. We wouldn't have gotten away if not for them."

Goose bumps prickled Astrea's skin. Jin had mentioned that, too, but hearing it from Lucian was different. Theo and his followers had kept their word, helped them escape.

"And where are these other void mages now?" President Sikori asked.

"That, I could not tell you," Lucian said. "Once we got close to the Tornamian border in the stolen airship, they said they would be in touch, then jumped from the ship."

"Jumped?" the ambassador asked.

"That is when the void mages seem to transport instantaneously," Zephyrine cut in. "We still don't know how to prevent them from doing so."

President Sikori took a sip of her tea, then sighed. "As far as we know, either the Paragon or Helosians—or both—have access to all that aetherium. Everything that's already been gathered."

"It would seem so, Madam President," Zephyrine said.

"Do they know we're here, in Thasia?" Lucian asked.

"I cannot say," President Sikori replied, "though I would be shocked if they hadn't guessed we were somewhat aiding your efforts. The Zaikudi are refusing to cooperate with us. It seems they've fully aligned themselves with the Paragon."

"So what now?" the Delian ambassador asked. "If a single aetherium bullet can take down a man Prince Varojin's size, it's imperative we stop both Emperor Aelius and this Victor Nazarov from controlling any more aetherium than they already do. How do we destroy it?"

"It's hard to say," Lucian replied. "We could try damaging it beyond usability, but we don't even know if that's possible. And there's so much of it at that camp . . ."

"What if we dropped a bomb on it?" asked the ambassador. "Would that work?"

"I don't know," Lucian said.

"Would these other void mages, the ones loyal to you two"—the president motioned to Jin and Astrea—"be able to tell us that?"

Jin let out a long sigh. "Honestly? I don't know. Part of me doesn't even trust Theo's being honest about abandoning whatever plans Nazarov has, even if he did help us escape."

"They helped us," Astrea said. "I truly think they've abandoned Nazarov's cause." It was as she'd thought days ago, that there were some lines Theo and the others just wouldn't cross.

"Then we should talk to this Theo," said President Sikori. "If he can help, I would like to know what he has to say."

"I'll talk to him," Astrea said before she could change her mind. "Next time he reaches out to me, I'll try to find out what he knows." When the president began to protest, Astrea said, "Madam President, I have no way of contacting him right now. We will just have to wait." And Astrea didn't think they'd make her wait very long, not if Nazarov and the emperor were both still on the loose.

"Very well," said President Sikori before turning to Eliana and the Delian ambassador. "I would feel best if we formalized our intent to work together before you return to Talmaris. A majority of parliament has agreed. It seems the only way we have a chance of stopping Emperor Aelius and the Paragon is by pooling our resources and knowledge."

"And stop them we must," said the ambassador.

Astrea leaned back in her chair and closed her eyes. At least part of their mission had been a success.

CHAPTER 58

Just because politicians agreed to work together didn't mean things went quickly. It had taken two more days for the Tornamians and Delians to draw up an agreement that Eliana and Veiko were willing to sign, and it would be sent to the Taipoli as well. It hadn't been easy, not with all necessary parties scattered across the continent.

In that time, it had been agreed that after the Helosian soldiers had witnessed the Paragon's attack, it was time to fully expose the truth around void magic. The truth was going to get out as soon as those soldiers started sending letters and making calls; Emperor Aelius couldn't silence them all. All it would take was one person to slip up and expose the truth.

So, the Tornamians and Novarians were going to coordinate two efforts. First, they would begin air strikes on Helosian targets in the Badlands, where Emperor Aelius's excavation efforts continued. Next, they would drop information pamphlets from small airships, spreading them over towns and bases around the Badlands. The pamphlets would explain what had happened near the Ring of Fire and urge them to find the truth. Both governments were going to warn their citizens of what was to come.

Astrea wasn't sure that would do much of anything, but if they could get even part of the Helosian military to turn on Emperor Aelius, or if they could help civilians stay educated and safe, it would be worth the effort.

But now, she had something more important to focus on. It was time for her to say goodbye to Saros.

They'd gotten to Irvina earlier that morning to most everything taken care of. Grand Duke Veiko wouldn't be in attendance, but Mariya the Stargazer was there. A few folks from town had helped set up everything.

Now, Astrea stared out at the lake she'd grown up near. The setting sun cast the water in orange and gold, and high, high above, the first few stars had started to awaken.

There, at the edge of the lake, was a funeral pyre. A body—Saros's body—sat atop it, covered in a black sheet.

She'd been there before, fourteen years prior. She'd been just ten years old then, and her mother had been the one lying under a swath of black fabric.

Astrea didn't even have it in her to cry. She had barely stopped crying since Saros had died. In fact, the last week had been mostly a blur, almost like none of it was real.

But it was very real.

The autumn breeze rolling in off the water made Astrea shiver. That orange horizon was quickly giving way to deep blue and black.

"Hey," Cressida said as she came up next to Astrea. She looked a little better, a little more like her old self. She'd traded her white sling for a black one, to coordinate with her dark blue dress. "We don't have to do this, you know, if you're not ready."

Astrea would never be ready. She could not do this. She could not, but she had to. Saros deserved that much.

"I'm fine."

"You're not."

"No, I'm not." Astrea couldn't bring herself to look over at Cressida. "I'm not."

Saros was gone. After fighting so hard to find answers, to reunite with him, he was gone. Taken from Astrea, from Sarsali, Balthazar, and Cressida.

Crossing the beach, Jin joined them and said, "We're ready."

Astrea took Jin's outstretched hand, then took Cressida's on the other side. And together, the three of them moved closer to the water. Adi and Marko were there. Sarsali and Balthazar. Eliana and Nicos. Mariya. Lucian and Zephyrine. Lennor and Civan. Even Vernie had joined.

"It is with a heavy heart that we're here today," Eliana said. "I don't even know what to say, honestly."

"You don't have to say anything, Ellie," Astrea said. "It's alright. Saros never was one for speeches."

"He may not have been one for speeches," Balthazar said, "but I'm going to give him one anyway." He smiled. "Saros, you and I always had a strange friendship, certainly not the pair people would expect. But we had fun, you and I, in our own way. A friendship that started simply because your sister and my wife were friends, but I'm grateful every day that I knew both you and Roxana, and it brings me comfort to know the two of you are reunited."

Astrea sucked in a shaky breath.

"Saros's passing will always hurt," Sarsali said, voice wavering. "He was family. He was always dedicated to doing his best and protecting those he loved, until the very end."

Astrea's eyes closed.

"For all the times I wanted to shake some sense into Saros, he was a good man," Cressida said. "And I'm grateful every day that he brought Astrea to Kalama. My sister."

Eliana and Nicos both shared an anecdote about Saros, as did Zephyrine. Even Mariya said a few words. Around the circle they went like that until they got back to the Nikaphoroses.

To Astrea.

"I don't think my uncle ever planned on being a parent." Wiping her tears, Astrea stared at the unlit pyre, shadowed by the darkening sky. "For those of you who truly knew Saros, I'm sure you know why. But he was just twenty-six when he became my guardian . . . when my mother died. His whole life changed in an instant, and he never complained."

Astrea's voice trembled as she said, "And I'm sorry he didn't get to chase whatever it was he really wanted in life. But I'll always be grateful that he chose me and that he raised me. I wouldn't have survived all these years without him."

I'm sorry, she thought. *I'm sorry, Uncle. I'm sorry, Mom.* Some small part of her hoped the stories and old beliefs were true, that Saros and her mother really would be reunited among the stars. That they might be up there somewhere, away from all this and not so alone.

"Saros," Jin said quietly, "months ago, you pulled me aside and asked me to protect Astrea. Just weeks ago, you asked me to take care of her. And I'll make that promise to you again. I will always protect her and take care of her. You can rest easy, Saros Sovna."

Fresh tears spilled down Astrea's cheeks. Her breath caught in her throat. She swallowed the building sob.

Zephyrine picked up two unlit torches from the sand. And when she brought one to Astrea, Astrea shook her head.

"I can't," she whispered.

She could not. It was too hard, saying goodbye to him. She couldn't do it.

"Do you want me to?" Jin asked.

"Please."

With Astrea's permission, Jin, Eliana, and Nicos stood in a line behind the pyre. And on Jin's mark, they summoned their flames and took aim.

With Balthazar, Sarsali, and Cressida's arms wrapped around her, Astrea watched the fire and smoke climb higher into the sky as she said her silent, final goodbyes to her uncle.

They stayed on that beach for hours, not leaving until the pyre had burnt itself out and Saros's ashes could be returned to the earth. The Nikaphoroses had taken over that part, following Astrea's guidance on where to bury what little remained of him. They went to the base of a large tree, the same one where Saros and Astrea had buried her mother's ashes fourteen years earlier. They'd carved a small S and A into the trunk all those years ago, and she'd managed to remember where it was and find it in the middle of the night.

It was only now, in the last hour before sunrise, that they were returning to Fort Silverpine.

The numbness that had taken over Astrea's body the last week had settled back in her bones, making her immune even to the cold night air.

"We'll plan to fly back to Talmaris in the next hour," Eliana was saying as they stepped out of the truck they'd been riding in. "I know that's not much time to rest, but there's much we need to do."

"Sure, Ellie," Jin said quietly.

"I'm sorry to force us to get back on track," Eliana said gently. "I don't want to disrespect Saros or what you're going through, Az—"

Astrea shook her head. "It's not disrespectful. It needs to be done. I need something to focus on, anyway." Anything to keep her afloat and distracted from the heaviness in her heart. Maybe being away from Irvina for a while would be a good thing. She could visit Saros and her mother again, after they stopped Emperor Aelius and Victor Nazarov.

"Let's take a walk," Jin said to Astrea. "We'll meet you at the airship in half an hour, Ellie."

"Just don't wander too far," Eliana said.

"We won't."

Jin took Astrea's hand in his, then tugged her away from the line of trucks and the waiting airship. As they walked, two tight balls of sadness followed. Astrea peeked over her shoulder to find Adi and Marko following at a distance.

"Thank you," Astrea whispered to Jin. "Thank you for—"

"Of course." His thumb drew circles over the back of her hand. "I meant what I said, too. I'll keep my promise to him."

If she'd had any tears left, Astrea would've cried. But she was all tapped out. All she could do was exhale a shallow breath.

They couldn't get far in the fort without running into more people, but Jin managed to steer them clear of most of the soldiers. They were making a loop around the large courtyard.

"How are you?" Astrea asked Jin. "I feel like I've barely checked in with you."

"It hurts to see you hurting this bad, but physically, I actually feel alright."

"No lingering effects from the aetherium?"

"A little tired, but nothing else as far as I can tell."

Astrea hadn't been able to find anything wrong with him during several magical exams, either. It seemed that whatever issues the aetherium had caused were truly gone. She'd managed to heal it all somehow.

"You almost died," she whispered.

"I almost died on Ilesouria, too," he said wryly. "Haven't gotten me yet."

"Are you really making a joke about this?"

Jin stopped and pulled her around so she faced him. "Hey." He gripped her hands tighter. "I almost died, yes, but I'm still here, Az. I'm alright, I promise. A bit shaken up but fine."

Faint colors danced around him: mint green relief, steel pain, deep blue regret, pink love. But no physical pain touched her body, and none of his emotions overwhelmed her. He was telling the truth.

"I love you," he whispered, taking her face in his hands. "I love you so, so much. It's going to take a lot more than what Kaius did to take me away from you, understand?"

"Yes."

"Good." He leaned down and pressed a gentle kiss to her mouth.

"And I love you, too."

He kissed her again, barely letting her say the words.

A throat cleared nearby. Jin pressed his forehead against Astrea's. "Yeah, Marko?" he asked.

A Novarian soldier loitered near Marko and Adi a dozen feet away, arms crossed behind their back.

"There's apparently something we need to see at the front gate," Marko said. "Urgently."

The soldier sent to get them headed for the opposite side of the courtyard, weaving past trucks and the airship they were to take back to Talmaris. Astrea could barely track them in the early morning twilight or among the growing confusion and alarm spreading through the ranks.

"Something's wrong," Astrea whispered to Jin.

He gripped her hand tighter as they continued for the gate. As they circled around the airship, Astrea saw a group of Novarians forming a loose ring around someone. What, had Theo shown up but nobody got the message he was, for now, on their side?

Lucian broke through the crowd, his lips pressed into a thin line. "There you are."

"What's going on?" Jin asked.

"I . . . I think it's best you see for yourselves," the commander said as he stepped to the side.

A man stood at the center of the circle. He wasn't much taller than Marko or Cressida. His black hair was cut short, and his skin was pale. And even in the low morning light, Astrea could make out his light blue eyes, so light they were almost white.

His voice was calm and steady as he said, "My name is Valen Ramkas."

Astrea's knees weakened.

"And I'm here because I've been told a young woman is looking for me," Valen said. "I'm here to see Astrea Sovna."

Jin tried to hold her back, but Astrea took a step forward, shouldering past Lucian. "That's me," she barely whispered. "I'm Astrea Sovna. I think I'm your daughter."

To be continued

BOOKS BY H.E. BAUMAN

Forged by Flames: A Darkened Skies Prequel

Under Darkened Skies: Darkened Skies Book One

Into Whispering Shadows: Darkened Skies Book Two

Amid Twisted Chaos: Darkened Skies Book Three

Beyond Veiled Destinies: Darkened Skies Book Four

Coming in 2024:
Toward Dawning Light: Darkened Skies Book Five

ACKNOWLEDGMENTS

Writing this story and seeing readers connect with Astrea and her friends has been nothing short of an incredible and humbling experience.

To Kayla, Laura, and Michelle, as always, thank you for helping me smooth out the story, and I'm sorry for making you cry!

To Jeanine, thank you for all the hours you put in to help me get these books polished.

To my street team, thank you all for your ongoing support of the series. I couldn't do it without you.

To my husband, family, and friends, I know this series has taken a lot of my time, from late nights to early mornings and weekend work. Thank you for all your support and understanding as I keep working on these books and chasing my dreams.

And finally, to all my readers, thank you for loving these books. Thank you for talking about them, sharing them, and messaging me. You make all of the aforementioned long hours worth it.

About the Author

H.E. Bauman is a fantasy author fascinated with all things magical. After spending her childhood writing stories, she went on to receive her bachelor's in English and has continued writing ever since. When she's not reading or writing, she enjoys playing tennis, immersing herself in video games, and spending time with her family.

If you want to get in touch, visit H.E.'s website or follow her on social media.